# WHERE WILD THINGS GROW

## BRIAR VALLEY #2

## J ROSE

WILTED ROSE PUBLISHING LTD

# DEDICATION

*For all the single parents, fighting for a better future for their children. No matter the cost of starting over, again and again.
I think you're pretty fucking awesome.*

# TRIGGER WARNING

Where Wild Things Grow is a small town, reverse harem romance, so the main character will have multiple love interests that she will not have to choose between.

This book is dark in places and contains scenes that may be triggering for some readers. This includes human trafficking, forced marriage, domestic abuse, sexual assault, PTSD, bereavement, self-harm and unplanned pregnancy.

If you are triggered by any of this content, please do not read this book.

# J ROSE SHARED UNIVERSE

All of J Rose's contemporary dark romance books are set in the same shared universe. From the walls of Blackwood Institute, to Sabre Security's HQ, and the small town of Briar Valley, all of the characters inhabit the same world and feature in Easter egg cameos in each other's books.

You can read these books in any order, dipping in and out of different series and stories, but here is the recommended order for the full effect of the shared universe and the ties between the books.

For more information: www.jroseauthor.com/readingorder

*"We plant the seeds beneath the bruise. It hurts like hell, but then we bloom."*

- Kristin Kory

# PROLOGUE

IF I COME HOME – SUZI QUATRO
& KT TUNSTALL

## WILLOW

ROLLING OVER in the warm sheets covering me, I let loose a contented sigh. The heat from three familiar bodies sandwiches me in until I'm bathed in comfort and reassurance.

*Home.*

*Safe.*

*Protected.*

I can feel Killian's heartbeat pounding through his burnished skin that's pushed up against my chest. Zach lazily strokes my hip from behind while Micah kisses his way up my exposed leg.

Between the three of them, the grip of sleep releases me, and I feel the furnace between my thighs roar to life. I'm on fire. Tingling. Aching. Begging for the relief of their touch.

"You boys sure know how to wake a girl up," I groan.

Killian's lips brush my earlobe. "You're ours, baby."

"And we'd do anything to protect you," Zach adds.

Micah's mouth reaches my pubic bone. "Anything."

With my eyes still shut, I smile at their antics. "I love you three so much it scares me. I'm terrified that I'll lose you all."

"You'll never lose us," Killian growls.

"But I can't let Mr Sanchez hurt you," I reason. "I have to keep you safe from him. He'll use you against me."

"Nothing can tear us apart, angel. We're a family and not even you can change that now. Come home and let us prove it to you."

"Home?" I repeat, feeling more awake.

Killian's voice deepens into an angry rasp. "Come home. Stop running. We need you."

Loud, insistent knocking causes my heart to suddenly explode in my chest. I shoot upright in a tangle of sweaty sheets on the cramped, queen-sized bed and wrestle my eyelids open.

Nothing.

Empty.

Alone.

The tears well up in my eyes like they do every morning when I realise the bed next to me is empty. Nothing but my loneliness and regret surround me as another day of torture begins.

It was all a dream.

I'm not home.

I'm still lost.

The sound of knocking comes again, mirroring the beat of my heart. When the door to my bedroom slams open, Arianna bursts in with a scowl on her face, still dressed in pyjamas.

She doesn't smile much anymore. It kills me inside, more with each passing day, to see her fade back into the scared little girl I birthed alone seven long years ago.

"The door, Mummy. Someone's here. It's too early."

Reaching under my pillow, I grab the switchblade that I keep stashed in case of emergencies. Arianna's eyes grow wide with fear. I motion for her to hide under the bed, safely out of sight.

"Mummy?" she whines.

"It's okay, baby. Keep nice and quiet for me now."

"I'm scared."

"You're okay, sweetie."

Once she's hidden, I hold the switchblade tight and pad into the dreary kitchen at the centre of our cheap, dated apartment. The knocking on the front door is constant.

I'm barely dressed in panties and a loose t-shirt, my now-short, raven hair barely brushing my shoulders. The warm, golden tan that I developed in Briar Valley has been replaced with pale, ghost-like skin.

With the switchblade in my hand, I leave the safety chain on the door and open it an inch, peering out into the crisp winter air.

"Seriously?"

A familiar face waits for me, framed by long black locks and a forced smile. Her bangs cover the twisted scar marring her face, but her moss-coloured eyes haven't changed.

"Let me in," Katie pleads. "It's cold out here."

"You're early by several hours. We agreed you'd never do that. Arianna is hiding under the bed!"

"I know, darling. I'm sorry, but we need to talk. Inside."

Sighing heavily, I shut the door then slide off the chain before reopening it on her weary face. Katie lets herself in then slots the deadbolt back on behind her.

Taking in my disgruntled state, she raises an eyebrow at the switchblade still held ready and waiting in the air. I set it down on the kitchen counter and force air into my lungs.

"Planning to stab me, huh?"

I glare at her. "I thought you were here to kill me."

"Not today." Sadness coats her words. "Get dressed while I put the kettle on."

"Did something happen?" A vice clamps around my

hammering heart. "I haven't spoken to Lola since last week. Did you hear something? Are the guys okay?"

"I'm not here to talk about Briar Valley." Katie collapses in a chair at the dining table. "Go sort Arianna out. You don't want her to hear this."

Blinking rapidly, I force myself to move, unable to form words. My mouth has turned into the Sahara Desert, my legs trembling beneath me as I return to the darkened bedroom.

Plastering on a fake smile for Arianna's sake, I crouch down to peer at her underneath the bed. She's curled up in the farthest corner, hugging the butterfly sculpture that Micah gifted her to her chest.

"Is it safe to come out?" she whimpers.

"Yeah, Ari. It's safe."

"I'm still scared." Her eyes are squeezed shut with tears spilling over her cheeks. "I don't think I want to come out yet."

My heart twinges at the palpable fear in her voice. This is no life for a little kid. In many ways, it's worse than when we lived in the mansion. I've torn the only home she ever knew away from her.

We're so isolated out here and stuck in this crappy apartment twenty-four hours a day, too scared to even set foot outside for fear of being recognised at any given moment.

It's a nightmare that feels like it will never end, stretching on endlessly, agonisingly, into the bleak unknown. For as long as Mr Sanchez breathes, we will never be safe. Not here. Not anywhere.

"You can stay under there if it makes you feel better." I stretch out my hand. "Or you can take Mummy's hand and sleep in a big girl's bed. How does that sound?"

"Will you sleep with me?" Her eyes peek open.

"I need to talk to Katie for a moment about some stuff. I'll come cuddle with you after, if you want?"

Her eyes narrow in defiance. "I want to cuddle now."

"We can watch the new Frozen movie again later," I try to sweeten the deal. "I'll even let you break open the emergency ice cream. How's that for a deal?"

Arianna manages to nod. "Okay. Katie's here?"

"Yeah, she's here. I'll come wake you up when it's time for breakfast."

Settling Arianna into my vacated bed, I tuck the covers up to her chin. Her blonde hair has grown so long now, it's spilling down to her lower back. She blinks up at me with jewel-like, bottomless blue eyes.

"I like your bed, Mummy. It's nice and big."

"That's because I have a bigger body than you, Ari. Keep eating your greens, and you'll grow up to be big and strong too."

"How big?" she demands sassily.

"Taller than the tower that Rapunzel was trapped in."

Arianna's sadness swims back to the forefront as her eyes glisten with tears again. "We're in a tower too."

I drop a kiss on her forehead. "I know, baby. It isn't forever though, I promise."

"I want to go home."

The sorrow in her voice is like a knife in the heart.

"We can go home soon, and you'll see your friends again."

"You said that last month," she deadpans. "And the one before."

Arianna sucks her thumb into her mouth, rolling over and giving me her back before I can muster up another crappy excuse to appease her. It takes everything in me not to break down.

I stare for a moment, completely gutted by her words and letting the moisture leak down my cheeks. I'm the world's worst parent. She's suffering along with me, and I can't fix this shit.

Pulling on my discarded sweats from the floor, I flee before she can hear me sob. I'm too ashamed to even attempt to console her. There's nothing I can say to make this any better.

Back in the kitchen, Katie has filled two chipped mugs with fresh coffee and sat back down. She lights a cigarette with shaking hands, slowly inhaling before letting the smoke out.

I take the seat opposite her, pulling a steaming mug into my hands. Not even the hit of strong coffee can alleviate the cloud of exhaustion that has infected us for the five months we've spent hidden.

"Since when did you start smoking inside?" I ask tiredly.

"Sorry." She quickly puts it out. "Long night. We had two new families arrive at the centre. I had to get them temporarily set up in a hotel until an apartment becomes available."

Believe it or not, Katie was the one who saved our asses when we fled. She has connections in local councils across the country due to her work resettling families for the government.

She managed to get us in this crummy apartment when we were hopping from one cheap hotel to another, desperate to stay off the radar.

In a weird way, she stepped up when I needed her the most, and I had no one else in the world to turn to. For the first time in my whole life, I had a mother there to save me.

"Katie," I prompt, my grip on the mug tightening. "The news?"

Staring into the depths of her pitch-black coffee, her mouth is pinched tight with tension. My leg begins to bounce underneath the table, expelling the nervous energy eating away at me.

"Since you've dropped off the radar, Dimitri Sanchez has been playing the sympathy card—claiming you had a nervous breakdown and left with Arianna."

"I already know this," I snap.

"He's used your disappearance to his advantage through a

slick PR campaign that's removed any and all suspicion from him."

"The news has been full of his face for months," I spit out. "He's been releasing those stupid statements, playing the doting father and husband."

Katie nods. "His campaign to discredit you has been very well-coordinated. The entire world is convinced that you ran away with Arianna and are endangering her life."

Tears prickle my eyes. It hurts to be accused of deliberately harming my daughter, even when it's far from the truth. The world doesn't hear that. Mr Sanchez is the only voice they care about.

"But we're still safe, right? He hasn't had a location on me since Briar Valley. He doesn't know about you either."

"Sanchez hasn't found you, Willow. This location is still secure and safely off-grid for the time being. That's not why I'm here."

"Then why are you here?"

She rakes a hand through her hair. "I know you don't want to talk to him, but Ethan Tarkington has been in touch again."

*Shit.* Ryder's boyfriend. I've dodged his phone calls and emails for months now, unwilling to assist in his company's investigation.

"What does he want?"

"He works for Sabre Security, who has been investigating a global, multi-million pound human trafficking ring for the last twelve months."

"He mentioned it to me when we were in Briar Valley. That has nothing to do with us or Mr Sanchez, though."

"Willow," Katie whispers bleakly. "Dimitri Sanchez has been named as a person of interest in their case along with several other men. Sabre is asking for victims to come forward."

Her voice is drowned out by the loud ringing in my ears.

Ticking. Buzzing. Screaming. Ten long years of tears, pain and anguish drown out everything else as her words sink in.

"A human trafficking ring," I repeat, my mouth feeling like cotton wool. "I don't understand."

"You told me what he did to you, sweetheart. That's textbook human trafficking. You may not be the only person he's hurt."

I stare deep into her worried eyes. Nothing is computing. What he did to me was beyond the realms of evil, but the thought that there could be others like me out there is unhinging my sanity.

"He's a suspect?" I say in a robotic voice.

She nods. "It's early days, but I've seen the file. It's definitely him. From what Ethan has told me, there are many players involved. He's one of the big ones."

A hissed breath escapes my clenched teeth before I drop my mug. It shatters against the worn kitchen floor, spilling coffee and sharp ceramic shards across the room.

"Willow." Katie recoils.

"N-No!"

"Just breathe for me and think this through. Ethan needs your help to bring Dimitri Sanchez down."

"I c-can't do that... He's too powerful. He has friends everywhere, and I won't risk Arianna falling back into his hands."

"Every second that he's allowed to continue living freely poses a risk to you both and other potential victims. He has to be stopped."

I'm under no illusions. I know what he's capable of, and if the world knew how many people he'd hurt, Mr Sanchez would be locked away for the rest of his life.

That doesn't mean I'm strong enough to do anything about it. Going public would mean facing the demons I fled from when I left Mexico and confronting my past head-on.

"I can't do anything to stop him," I repeat shakily.

"We have the chance to prove that you were trafficked and abused by him." She clutches my hand tight. "We could take him down, Willow. Do you understand what I'm saying to you?"

I slowly nod, feeling the tiniest flicker of hope for the first time in five long, agonising months of emotional hell. This is what I've been waiting for all along.

"I could go home to Briar Valley."

# CHAPTER 1
# WILLOW

RIDICULOUS THOUGHTS – THE
CRANBERRIES

TUCKING my short black hair into a worn baseball cap, I slide a big pair of sunglasses on then check my reflection in the rearview mirror. I'm well-disguised.

The pale blue sweater I'm wearing is loose, hiding my slimmed-down body. Eating isn't something I manage much of these days. I'd probably starve if Arianna didn't need to be fed.

Once a week, I brave the trip to the local supermarket, leaving Arianna safely behind. I have no choice but to leave her alone. It's a risk, but so is breathing while Mr Sanchez still roams free.

Shaking out my hands, I switch off the car engine then recheck the handful of notes that Katie passed over yesterday in an envelope. It's enough to get us through this week.

"Just go inside," I whisper under my breath. "He isn't here. Walk in there, and do what you need to do."

Sliding my hand in my pocket, I finger the sharp switchblade. Mr Sanchez has proven that he can still reach me, even here in England, far from the darkness of his mansion.

Nowhere is safe for us.

Not anymore.

The news stories about our disappearance are relentless as he continues his savage campaign to discredit me by any means necessary.

I'm the evil, unstable mother who kidnapped her daughter and left the golden boy of the real estate business high and dry. The entire world hates my guts, and they don't even know me.

Grabbing a shopping trolley, I keep my chin tucked down and walk into the supermarket as casually as possible. My grip on the trolley is white-knuckled.

The security guard spares me a glance, frowning ever so slightly, but he soon turns his attention to the next shopper. I blow out a heavy breath, repeating my inner-mantra.

*Breathe, Willow.*

*In and out.*

*Get it done.*

I keep my baseball cap and sunglasses in place even inside the supermarket, offering me some sense of protection. I'd rather look like a lunatic than risk being spotted.

By halfway through the weekly shop, my palms are slick with nervous sweat, and I'm itching to run at full speed as far away from this place as possible.

Every person who walks past causes me to freeze, then I have to mentally dig myself back out of a hole of panic to keep walking.

When the cheap burner phone in my pocket vibrates, I let out a shuddered breath before answering the phone call. She's never a second late for our scheduled calls.

"Hey, Grams."

"Willow." Lola sighs in relief. "It's so good to hear your voice."

"It's the same voice you spoke to last week and the week before." I grab a bottle of juice. "How is everything? Are you okay?"

"We're all fine," she answers vaguely.

"What's happening in Briar Valley?"

"The first snow fall came a few days ago. Albie is outside gritting the road as we speak. You should have seen the kids, all screaming and running around."

I smile to myself. "Sounds lovely."

"It was. How's the weather there?"

"It's cold here, but no snow. Arianna keeps waiting with her nose pressed against the window. She's determined to see it for the first time, but I don't think we're far enough into the countryside."

Lola sniffles, and I know she's started to cry. She rarely gets through one of our scheduled chats without shedding tears. The last five months have taken a heavy toll on us all.

Tucking the phone against my shoulder, I reach over an older gentleman to grab some fresh bread, stacking it on top of the canned goods that I also picked up.

"I'm sorry," Lola says. "It's just… we miss you both so much. It isn't the same here without you. The town feels so empty."

"You spent two decades without me," I remind her. "I know it's hard. This isn't easy for us either, but you know that I have no other choice. It wasn't safe to stay."

"I know… it just doesn't make it any easier. It's been months, Willow. Surely it's safe for you to come home now?"

"He's still on the news every single night appealing for information," I grit out. "That isn't safe, and you know it. Not while the world believes the lies he's spent months spouting."

Lola clears her throat. "Perhaps one day it will be safe again. I wish we knew when that day will come, though."

Agony lances across my chest as I battle to remain strong for her sake. My tears are only allowed to make an appearance when I'm alone. I have to be a mum first—strong and unwavering.

"How are…?" I hesitate, swallowing hard. "The guys?"

"They're alive, poppet."

"That bad?"

"I won't lie to you and pretend like everything is fine when it isn't. They're hanging by a thread, much like I'm sure you are."

The backs of my eyes burn, and I clamp my hands into fists until my nails dig into my palms. I have to keep my anguish at bay. I can't afford to fall apart here. It isn't safe.

"Micah crashed Killian's truck last week," Lola reveals. "He knocked over a lamppost."

"He crashed the truck? What was he even doing driving it?"

"He was drunk," Lola admits.

My heart seizes, freezing into a lump of solid ice, impenetrable and alone on a mountain of misery. I'm stranded in a barren wasteland, without them to hold me close.

"Micah's drinking again?" I ask in a low, broken voice.

"Forget I said anything."

"Grams—"

"How is Arianna? Do you need anything?"

"Don't do that. I need to know. How bad is it?"

Heading towards the checkout counter, I freeze when someone stops in front of me. I make myself take a breath when panic grips my throat. It's just another shopper. They don't even spare me a glance.

"He's hurting, Willow."

A bubble of anxiety lodges itself in my throat. "What about Killian and Zach? Aren't they helping him?"

"They have their own feelings about your departure to contend with, sweetheart."

"I see."

If not even Zach is capable of staging an intervention for Micah right now, things are worse than I'd feared. I've broken them all.

"I wish I could tell you something better, but the fact is, the longer you're away… the more it breaks them. I'm starting to think they've given up hope of ever seeing you again."

Leaning against the cart, I cover my mouth with my spare hand, grateful for the sunglasses covering my streaming eyes. Not even my public surroundings can hold the tears back now.

"Willow? You still there?"

"I'm here," I choke out.

"I didn't mean to upset you. Let's talk about something else. Do you need more money? I want to help you."

"Katie… Um, she gave us some cash. We're fine. I don't need your help."

"Please," Lola begs. "You don't have to do this on your own."

I let out a strangled laugh. "I am on my own. Just like I always have been."

"You're not. Maybe it's time to come home. These news stories, it's all bullshit. He can't hurt you, and you can't keep running forever. You have to face this monster sometime."

"I can't do that."

"This plan is doing more harm than good now."

"It isn't safe. I can't come back until it is."

"This investigation could take years," Lola argues. "What are you going to do? Hide until it's all over?"

Composing myself, I resume pushing the trolley with one hand. "Katie told you, then. So much for privacy."

"Ethan wants to help you, poppet. He's a good man. The entire team at Sabre Security is very capable. They can help."

"I wasn't trafficked, Lola," I whisper in a fierce voice. "He was my husband and an abusive asshole."

"You're in denial. You have to face this."

"Denial? Seriously? Give me a break."

"Come home," Lola demands. "It's been five months. Dimitri Sanchez has slinked back to his shady corner of the globe and long since stopped checking if you've come back to Briar Valley."

"That doesn't mean he won't check again at any moment and threaten you all to get to me. I can't let that happen, Grams."

"Please... Just come home."

I swallow the scream attempting to claw up my throat. "I'm sorry, but I can't stop running until he's dead or behind bars. I'm not discussing this anymore."

"Willow, wait—"

Hanging up the call and switching off the phone with numb hands, I feel like the floor is caving in beneath me. Those damned words have echoed in my brain since Katie's visit.

Human trafficking.

Lola's right... I'm burying my head in the sand and feeding myself a pack of lies to scrape together whatever shallow comfort I can find. It isn't working, but I'm out of options here.

Checking out on autopilot, I stuff groceries into bags at random. My mind is too busy yelling and going into self-destruct mode.

*It's not safe.*

*You have to run.*

*Arianna's at risk.*

The cashier gives me an odd look when I smack my fist into my forehead and whimper under my breath. I barely manage to hand over a stack of cash, my hands are shaking so badly.

All I can think about is getting back inside the safety of the old, beaten-up car outside that Katie lent us. After randomly throwing bags in the boot, I climb into the driver's seat and slam all the locks on.

Only then do I let myself crumble completely, slumped over the steering wheel as my lungs wheeze and struggle for air. My vision is fuzzy from a lack of oxygen as a panic attack seizes me.

In my mind, a deep, grumpy voice takes over. Previously, Mr Sanchez taunted me, but now another man haunts my darkest moments. His absence delivers the worst pain imaginable.

Picturing Killian's familiar, fire-lit eyes, his mouth curved down in a scowl, I imagine him whispering to me.

*Just breathe, princess.*

*In and out.*

*I've got you.*

"I miss you so fucking much," I cry, my cheeks stinging with tears. "I never should've left. I hate myself for hurting you all."

Searching for the lump of cool steel still resting in my coat pocket, I clutch the switchblade in my trembling hand, choking on endless sobs.

In these moments… Micah always comes to me too. Staring into my eyes with those forest-coloured orbs of pure intelligence, he offers me a tiny smile, just like he did when he found me bleeding all those months ago in the bathtub.

*You don't need to hurt yourself anymore.*

*You're not alone.*

"I'm alone, and I deserve to be."

*You made a promise.*

*Please don't do this to yourself.*

"This is all I have left, Mi."

Blocking out his imaginary voice, I flick out the blade and roll up the sleeve of my sweater. New, shiny scars mark my skin. Anxiety is a fucking bitch, and I'm a slave to it now more than ever.

This is the only thing that gives me the strength to plaster a smile on in front of Arianna and be the best parent I can be despite all this carnage.

Even though every time I cut myself to cope, I feel like I'm failing Arianna and failing myself too. It's the single source of control I have left as we freefall through our destroyed lives.

Dragging the blade across my arm, I release a long breath, tasting the relief of oxygen at last. Warm blood runs down to my elbow, and I quickly grab a pack of tissues from my handbag.

We're not living, stuck here in limbo. I'm existing for Arianna yet failing her all at once. What if Lola's right? Is this the worst mistake of my entire life? Have I doomed us all?

Shaking my head, I wipe my eyes then roll my sweater down to hide the fresh cuts. I have to go home. One foot in front of the other. That's how I survived before, and it's how I'll do it again.

Finding that awful, empty space that kept me going for ten long years, I'll continue to float there, inches from drowning, until someone comes along and pulls me out again.

## CHAPTER 2
# ZACH

IT'S ALL FADING TO BLACK –
XXXTENTACION & BLINK-182

PARKING RYDER'S truck outside the bar, I kill the engine and study the hordes of people packed inside through the steamed-up glass. Saturday night is in full swing with all the locals gathering inside and spilling out onto the snow-covered pavement.

The thump of shitty karaoke makes me wince from here. Some inebriated moron is killing cats in there with that awful screech. Checking my phone, I scan Trevor's text again.

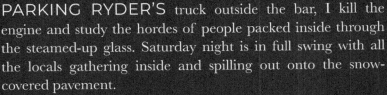

Trevor: You need to take Micah home before I kick his ass out onto the street. He's already punched someone and broken a table.

"Great," I mutter to myself.

Turning up my coat collar, I hop out then slam the door a little harder than necessary. My twin is being a self-destructive dickhead at the moment, and I'm so over it.

Wrestling my way through the sweaty, leering crowd inside, I manage to get to the bar. Trevor's eyes connect with mine from behind the counter, an annoyed scowl plastered on his face.

"Took you long enough to get here."

"I'm here now." I cross my arms. "Where is he?"

"Bathroom, last I checked. This is the third time this week." He fills up a pint then passes it to an awaiting customer. "I'm not his babysitter, Zach. It needs to stop."

"You think I don't know that?"

"He's in here all the damn time, drinking himself into an early grave and pissing everyone off. Next time, I'll toss him out."

"Calm down. I got the message."

Grabbing Lola's credit card from my pocket, I slide it across the bar. Trevor eagerly takes it then rings up the outstanding tab.

"Give yourself a generous tip as well. I'll go scrape Micah's drunk ass off the bathroom floor."

Trevor slides the card back. "Good luck, kid."

Picking my way to the back of the crowded room, I slip into the men's bathroom. Immediately, the bitter stench of vomit, spilled beer and cigarettes assails me.

*Jesus fuck.*

This is really not how I planned on spending my Saturday night. Truthfully, I'd like to be at the bottom of a bottle too, but I have to save my stupid twin from himself instead.

"Micah!" I shout angrily. "Where the fuck are you?"

Groaning comes from the farthest stall. I duck down to peer underneath the door after finding a familiar pair of paint-splattered Chucks peeking out.

He's passed out on the filthy floor, curled up in a tight, semi-conscious ball next to the toilet bowl. Charming. It's one of the worst states I've found him in of late.

"For fuck's sake." I gingerly nudge his limp foot. "Micah. Wake up. It's time to go home."

"Piss off," he whispers.

"No can do."

Managing to wrestle his eyes open for a second, he takes

one drunken look at me and groans. His eyes screw shut again.

"Just be glad it's me picking you up and not Killian," I reason. "He would take you to a quiet corner and shoot you between the eyes with the mood he's in."

Taking a coin from my wallet, I use it to pick the lock on the stall door. Micah hasn't moved an inch. I doubt he's capable of even walking right now, judging by his liquor-fuelled scent.

Ducking inside, I slide my hands underneath his gangly arms then drag him up to rest against the wall. He's lost a lot of weight recently, given his entirely liquid diet.

He promptly slumps against me, unable to hold himself up. His head drops on my shoulder, and I can feel the pain that's still radiating through him. He hasn't drowned it out yet.

"How much have you had to drink?" I demand.

"Leave... alone... Z-Zach."

"That's not going to happen. You can sleep it off on the way back, but you've got to answer to Lola this time. She's mad at you for pulling this shit again."

"I'm allowed... drink if... want to," he slurs.

"You'll be off to rehab in no time if you keep this shit up. Hold onto me, little brother. I've got you."

"Three m-minutes younger."

"Yeah, yeah. I know."

With his arm wrapped around my neck, I drag him out of the bathroom, his head limply lolling forward. Trevor waits outside to help lift Micah so we're sharing his weight between us.

He's a decent guy. Most people in his position would just call the police and have Micah thrown in the drunk tank for being such a disruptive mess, night after night. He calls me instead.

"Thanks, Trev. I appreciate your discretion."

"Get out of my bar, the pair of you. Go on, beat it."

With a final nod of thanks, I wrestle Micah all the way outside and back to Ryder's borrowed truck. It's like trying to fit an octopus into the front seat as he starts to drunkenly fight me.

"Get the fuck off me," he growls.

"Stop it, for God's sake!"

I try to pin his wrists, but when he clocks me in the face with a strong punch, I lose patience. Spitting blood, I slam him against the side of the truck, knocking the air from his lungs.

"Micah! You're a mess. Don't start with me."

"I said let go!"

"No!" I shout back. "You're my brother and my responsibility."

When he tries to punch me again, I duck the blow and slam him even harder against the truck for a second time.

"Get your stupid ass inside before I knock you out. I'm not afraid to do it either. Don't test me, Mi."

Just when I think he's going to relent and climb in, Micah's face hardens. He lunges forward, slamming his forehead against mine hard enough to send me stumbling backwards.

Using the distraction to attempt to run back to Trevor's bar, he stumbles in the direction we just came from. I spit more blood on the ground and grab his dirty denim jacket before he can get far.

"Stop it!"

Using momentum, I throw him to the pavement, and he lands with a hiss of pain, staring up at me with hazy green eyes.

"Did you just headbutt me?" I yell, gaining the attention of several nearby people. "Jesus Christ. I don't even recognise you anymore. Who the hell are you?"

Rather than answer, he lays there pathetically, rubbing his bruised tailbone. One of the customers from outside the bar walks over to us with a sympathetic expression.

"You need a hand with this one?"

"Thanks, man."

"No problem. Looks like he's a handful."

"To say the least," I scoff.

Between us, we get Micah strapped into the truck's passenger seat, then I slam the door in his stupid face. The guy returns to his friends, leaving me to catch my breath.

This is a fucking shit-show.

Micah has been on a downward spiral for months. He managed to hide it at first, but as Christmas approaches, the last few weeks in particular have been pretty messy.

There's only one person who can save him from himself, but unluckily for us, she's disappeared off the face of planet Earth. When Willow left, she took all of our hope with her.

Nothing was left behind but three empty husks of the men we used to be, with none of us functioning or able to get through the day. By saving herself and her child, she ruined us all.

I wish I blamed her.

I wish I hated her.

I can't do either.

Back behind the wheel, I find Micah's passed out again, leaving me in blissful peace. The drive back to Briar Valley passes in silence with only the quiet chatter of the radio in the background.

Getting back up the mountain road in the icy, snowy conditions is a nightmare, even with the treads that Ryder fitted on the wheels last week when the first snowfall hit.

After several near misses and sliding back down an icy patch of rock, I have to call it quits. We're going to get into a nasty accident if I keep pressing on in the steadily falling snow.

"Fucking perfect."

Micah's silence answers me.

Peeling off my coat, I drape it over him then tuck it

around his body to keep him warm. I can see my breath in the truck with the engine off, but at least he won't get hypothermia while asleep.

It's a long, miserable night in the freezing cold. Snow settles on the windscreen, and I shiver in the driver's seat, my hands frozen into two lumps of ice. Micah stirs as dawn breaks.

"Oh God," he grunts.

"I hope your head is killing you."

Shifting in his seat, he looks over at me. "Shit. You're shaking."

"I'm cold. We got stranded in the snow."

"Well… double shit."

When he notices my coat piled on top of him to keep him warm, Micah's eyes duck in shame. I wordlessly accept it back and slip it on to warm myself up again.

"What happened?"

"You were drunk," I huff out. "And acting like a cunt again. Thanks for the punch too."

His gaze sweeps over my face where I know at least one dark bruise has formed. My face aches from the punches and headbutt. He's lucky I didn't leave him in the snow to die.

"Fuck, Zach. I'm so sorry."

"Are you? If you were really sorry, we wouldn't be having this conversation at all. I told you to stop drinking after the accident."

"I can't—"

"If you're about to give me some bullshit excuse, spare me," I interrupt. "You made promises then broke them all over again. Now you can apologise to Grams instead."

Lips sealed, he can't even nod. His entire posture is carved with palpable self-hatred. As much as I want to punish him for being a selfish jerk, it hurts to see him in so much pain.

"Where is she?" Micah whispers.

"I don't know, Mi. Not here."

"It's been months. She should've come home by now."

I swallow the lump gathering in my throat. "Willow is never going to come home. Haven't you realised that by now?"

"Don't fucking say that, man."

"It's the truth, whether you want to hear it or not."

The winter sun begins to crest on the horizon, highlighted by impending storm clouds as the next dumping of snow prepares to arrive. We have to move fast to avoid it.

"Buckle up," I order shortly.

Wrestling with his belt, Micah doesn't bother arguing with me again. He's torturing himself by holding out for Willow to return. Giving up that pointless hope will make this easier for all of us.

Sweeping the snow from the window screen, we gingerly take off and continue up the mountain. The snow has settled into a slippery ice rink, so I drive at a snail's pace to remain in control.

It's another hour before we make it into town safely and in one piece. Frigid sunlight sparkles on the compacted snow, and the daylight reveals an awaiting welcoming committee.

Killian sits on Lola's porch, his head in his hands. The sight of him causes my heart to stutter in fear. I quickly park up the truck, narrowly dodging a dangerous bank of snow.

"Kill!" I shout after climbing out.

His head doesn't lift.

Leaving Micah to struggle out of the truck alone, I sink through huge snow drifts and manage to clamber up Lola's porch steps. Still, Killian doesn't respond to my shouts of his name.

"Kill? What happened?"

When he does look up, the sheer intensity of grief burning in his eyes steals my breath. He's been crying. Unshakeable, terrifying Killian, unaffected by the whole world, has sobbed his eyes out.

"What is it?" I repeat.

All he can do is shake his head.

With the fear of God settling in my heart, I abandon him and run inside the cabin. It's deathly quiet. The usually crackling fireplace is empty.

No freshly baked cookies or brewed coffee scents linger in the air. Something's wrong. Lola is always up at the crack of dawn, baking and setting about her town duties for the day.

And Killian hasn't been awake before midday for months, let alone stepped outside to brace the real world. Just seeing him sitting there was a shock to the system.

Following the faint murmur of voices upstairs, I come across the next obstacle on the staircase. It's Ryder. He's staring at the phone clutched in his hands, the screen displaying an unknown number.

"Ry? What the fuck is going on?"

His gaze crashes into me. "Zach. You're too late."

"Too late for what?"

I watch his Adam's apple bob. Ryder's eyes are bloodshot and swollen too. He stands up then leads me down the hallway where he clasps my arm tight.

"It's Lola. Something happened last night."

My throat constricts. "Is she okay?"

Ryder shakes his head. "We think she had a heart attack. It all happened so fast."

Trying to push past him to burst into Lola's bedroom, he holds me back, keeping me pinned against his chest. His voice is an agonised rasp.

"She's gone, Zach. I'm sorry."

*No.*

*This can't be happening.*

*Not Grams.*

"This is some kind of sick joke." I shove him backwards. "Where is she? What do you mean she's gone?"

"Zach," he placates.

"No!"

Pushing past him, I reach her bedroom then race inside. The awaiting scene tramples on the remains of my heart. Albie is crouched next to the bed, holding Lola's limp hand.

On the left, Doc is talking in low whispers with Rachel and Miranda. Everyone looks wrung-out and pale. Exhausted. Tear-streaked. I look between them before facing Lola's body.

"Grams?" I croak.

Albie looks over to me. "Zach. She's... gone."

"No. This isn't real."

Approaching the bed, I fall to my knees as they fail to hold up my weight any longer. The moment I touch Lola's papery, pale skin, I feel just how cold she is. Waxy. She's already left us.

Reality sets in then. Cruel and painful. I'm staring at her dead body, bereft of the warmth that encapsulates every inch of Briar Valley. That light has vanished from sight.

"No," I croak. "Grams... No."

It doesn't bring her back. No amount of sobbing or screaming at an uncaring God will make her eyes lift. I snatch her hand and let my head crash into the bed, hiding my tears from sight.

Dead.

Dead.

*Fucking dead!*

I remember the moment when I realised my father had passed on. The emergency services removed him from the bathroom beneath a white sheet, leaving a shell-shocked, younger Micah behind.

I'm staring at the same emptiness. Hollowed out and left to rot. With a scream tearing at my aching throat, I shout endlessly, begging Lola's eyes to reopen. Just once. Even a flutter.

There's nothing. Not a single twitch. A breath. A whisper of life. She's dead and gone. I didn't even get to say goodbye.

I saw her a matter of hours ago. She gave me her credit card last night and told me to bail Micah out again. I vowed to bring him over the second we got back so she could give him a talking to.

"Zach," Albie says in a strangled voice. "I'm sorry, son."

"When?" I squeeze out.

"Only a couple of hours ago."

"I wasn't here."

"You couldn't have known." Ryder hovers behind me. "Everything happened so fast. You know she's had high blood pressure for years."

"I doubt recent stress helped matters," Doc comments. "Lola's health had been suffering for a while now, but she didn't want to worry anyone."

Hearing that she's been battling with her health alone triples my pain. Lola's there for everyone, yet she couldn't even tell us she wasn't well. That hurts more than anything.

"Did... Did anyone try to revive her?"

The look in Albie's eyes is haunted. "I tried. It was too late. She was gone before I even had a chance to fight back."

The bubble of vomit in my throat is searing hot and almost spews out. I feel sick to my stomach. While I scooped Micah off the bar's floor and worried about him... Grams was dying.

"That son of a bitch," I snarl.

Albie startles. "Huh?"

"I was out there saving Micah's stupid fucking ass while Lola took her last breath. She needed me. I wasn't here."

"Zach," he attempts. "Don't think like that."

"I wasn't here!"

Before he can stop me, I abandon Lola's bedside vigil and thump back downstairs. Snow is swirling in the early morning air as I launch myself outside to find my worthless twin.

He's slumped against the tailgate of the truck, peering into the thick, dense snow clouds high above us. Killian still hasn't moved, staring through his silent, never-ending tears.

"You!" I shout.

Micah stirs, his still-hazy eyes sliding over to me. "What?"

"This is your fucking fault!"

Marching up to him, I grab his denim jacket and let my fist sail straight into his face. Micah doubles over, clutching his now red-stained nose.

"What the hell, Zach?"

"I was out dealing with your shit last night and Lola was alone. She died alone because of you."

The colour drains from his face.

"D-Died?"

I jab a thumb over my shoulder. "Go and see for yourself. Lola's dead. She had a heart attack last night."

Staying to watch the realisation dawn on his face isn't an option. I can't keep it together for a second longer. Climbing back into the truck, I slam the door to keep everyone else out.

This is going to break us all.

We need Willow.

We need our family back.

# CHAPTER 3
# WILLOW

## HELL – OLIVVER THE KID

DIPPING the sponge back into the bucket of soapy water, I wring it out then resume scrubbing the sparkling kitchen floors for the third time this week.

They're spotless and permanently smell of bleach, but I can't lay in that bed for a moment longer, staring at the ceiling. My hands crack and bleed as I keep scouring at a vicious pace.

Still, the thoughts roll through my mind like tumultuous waves, one after another, never once relenting. I didn't sleep a wink last night. I was too tormented to relax.

*Human trafficking ring.*

*International investigation.*

*Prime suspect.*

Katie sent over the information that Ethan's company provided to her. I read it over a bottle of wine, drinking half before passing out at the kitchen table for a mere half an hour of rest.

The words *Anaconda Team* are watermarked all over the papers. I barely know Ethan, but Ryder loves and trusts him implicitly. That tells me enough. He's the real deal and a good person.

This is happening.

It's real.

The more I turn it over in my mind like an awful, disgusting pancake, the more sense it makes. I was a minor— vulnerable and clueless. He paid for me and took me overseas against my will.

How many other girls did I see getting beaten, raped and tortured in that house? How many lives were taken in front of me? They all blur into one now.

The sound of Arianna watching a movie on the laptop Katie let us borrow crackles from the other room, startling me out of my daze. She screamed at me when I tried to turn it off.

*Scrub.*

*Scrub.*

*Scrub.*

If only I could cleanse my soul the same way I'm washing the living daylights out of these spotless floors. I want to cut the memories from my skin and bleed myself dry of his poison.

*They need your help, Willow.*

*Scrub.*

*Testify against him.*

*Scrub.*

*Free yourself.*

*Scrub.*

When the pain in my hands becomes too much to bear, I sit back on my haunches and toss the ragged sponge aside. The folder of information on the table is screaming at me.

There're pages of evidence inside, all classified yet given to me in an attempt to sway my decision. Mr Sanchez is one person in a pool of suspects, all being investigated for human trafficking.

He's the real deal. The devil. The head of the snake that's

rotting from the head and awaiting a single match to burn its carcass. I hold that power in the palms of my hands now.

"Mummy? The phone!"

Startled out of my thoughts, I heave myself off the floor and snag my phone from the bedroom table where it's ringing. Lola's name is flashing on the screen, but it's outside of our usual schedule.

My stomach flips as I suck in a panicked breath. Shaking myself out of it, I return to the kitchen for privacy then press the phone to my ear.

"Lola? Everything okay?"

There's a long stretch of silence, punctuated by an odd rustling sound like someone's walking on the end of the line. I hold a hand over my pumping heart, beginning to freak out.

"Lola?"

The distant sound of gulping ends the silence, followed by a wet, strangled kind of sob that tugs at my trembling heartstrings.

"Hello?" I repeat shakily.

"Baby."

The kitchen floor is damp beneath my knees as I feel my legs sag. One word in that roughened, aged-whiskey voice of his and the last five months melt away like no time has passed.

"Killian."

He breathes heavily down the line. "Hey."

"It's really you."

Clearing my throat, I let my eyes slide shut, picturing those fire-lit eyes that first greeted me so many months ago.

"Why are you calling me?" I ask in a whisper. "Why now? Killian?"

It takes me a moment to realise that he isn't answering me because… he's crying. Quiet, soul-destroying sobs, betrayed only by the odd sharp intake of breath and tiny whimpers.

Big, scary, impenetrable Killian is sobbing down the line,

and I have zero clue what to do. Terror is wrapped around my throat.

"You never should have left," he chokes out.

I feel my own cheeks grow wet. "I know, Kill. I'm so fucking sorry. It was my only option. I didn't know what else to do."

"Willow... she... Lola..."

He trails off, and the sound of the phone clattering against the floor causes me to shout down the line, desperately calling Killian's name even as I hear footsteps thumping away.

Arianna sticks her head out of the bedroom, her eyes widening when she finds me losing my mind on the kitchen floor.

"Mummy?"

"It's okay, sweetie." I wave her away.

"Is it Giant?"

"Ari, go! Watch your movie."

She reluctantly disappears. "Fine."

I pull the phone away from my ear to check and find it's still connected. There's a faint shuffle and some far-off whispers before someone else comes on the line.

"Willow? It's Ryder. You still there?"

"I'm here," I reply quickly. "Shit, Ryder. It's good to hear your voice."

"You too, doll. Look... something's happened. We need you to come home."

"What? Is it Micah? Did he get hurt?"

Ryder sighs, muttering something to another person before returning. "No, it's not Micah."

"Then who?"

He hesitates before speaking in a much firmer voice.

"Just pack your bags, and get in the car. You're needed."

"You know I can't do that, Ryder. I left for a reason."

"Your family needs you," he says curtly. "Fuck that

scumbag Sanchez, and fuck this plan. It's time to come home."

"Ry—"

"We can't do this without you!" he snaps. "There's so much to sort out, and the funeral… shit…"

My blood freezes in my veins. I curl my hand into a fist then bite down on it as anxiety floods every inch of my body and leaves me freezing cold. I must've misheard him.

"What funeral?"

Ryder curses. "I didn't want to tell you like this."

"What fucking funeral?"

"I'm sorry, Willow. It's Lola. She had a heart attack… and she's gone."

Folding over to hug my midsection, I stay silent for several long seconds. His words echo on an endless loop, on and on without ever sinking in.

This can't be real.

I just found her. She isn't gone. Not like this. Not now. He has to be mistaken. The sound of Killian's devastating crying comes back to me, and I realise why he was so distraught.

"Willow? Are you still there?" Ryder asks weakly.

"When?" I bite out.

"Last night. Doc tried to revive her, but it was too late. I'm so sorry. I don't know what to say to you to make this better."

"What's h-happening now?"

"Everyone's a mess, and we're still figuring things out. You have to come, Willow. The guys need you more than ever."

I try to silence my own desperate tears. Knowing that Arianna is mere metres away, completely oblivious, gives me the sense to break down quietly, at least.

Ryder stays on the line until I can form words again between my ragged breaths and the steady stream of piping-hot tears. It takes a few minutes to scrape myself together.

"I'm coming home," I finally say. "Give me twenty-four hours."

"Where are you? I'll come and get you."

"I can't... I can't say. Not over the phone, it isn't safe. Don't worry about me, I can find my way back to Briar Valley."

"Are you sure?"

"Just... tell the guys... crap," I curse myself. "I have no idea. Tell them I'm going to make this right."

"We'll be here waiting for you."

We whisper our goodbyes. I'm left staring down at the phone, my ears ringing too loud for me to even think. I spoke to Lola only a handful of days ago.

In the bleak nothingness of our exile, she's been the one constant. The voice at the end of the phone. A tangible, real reminder of the family still waiting for us out there.

I'll never speak to her again.

I'll never get to say goodbye.

It's too late now.

"Mummy?" Arianna peeks her head out past the bedroom door again. "Was that Giant? Is he coming to get us?"

Gulping hard, I find my way back to my feet then bundle Arianna's small body into my arms. We curl up together in my bed with her spooned against me.

My face buries in her long, blonde ringlets. I can feel her heart hammering as she realises I'm crying and begins to panic.

"Are we going on an adventure?" she whispers fearfully. "I don't want to run anymore. I'm tired of running. I want to go home."

"It's okay, Ari." I stroke her hair. "We're going to go home now. Back to Briar Valley. We don't have to stay here any longer."

She turns over to face me. "Really? We're going?"

I nod, biting my lip. "All I ever wanted was for you to be safe, baby. That's it. I'm sorry for putting you through all this."

Arianna strokes the tears from my cheek. "I know, Mummy."

"It still isn't safe, but… there's something we've got to do. I need you to be a brave girl for me again, okay?"

Arianna offers me a devastating grin. "Always. You taught me how to be brave."

"I think you did that all on your own, Ari. I had nothing to do with it."

Curling up in my arms, she snuggles into me like she used to do when she was a baby. I breathe deeply, inhaling the scent of her strawberry shampoo, trying to ground myself in the familiarity.

Arianna gives me the strength to keep going. She always has. I'm going to need that strength now. We all are. Once she falls asleep, I dial Katie's number and slip outside to answer.

"Willow?"

"Katie. Did you hear the news?"

There's a pause.

"Albie called half an hour ago. Who told you?"

"Killian called, and I spoke to Ryder. We have to go back to Briar Valley. I'm going to pack up and leave tonight."

"I'll come to help," she offers.

"No, we're fine. Can I take the car?"

"Of course, sweetheart. We'll be there in a couple of days, I just need to wrap up some business in the city. Will you be okay?"

I rub a hand over my sternum, searing with grief. "I don't know the answer to that question right now."

She sniffles, and I breathe deeply, trying to stop my tears from joining hers. I'm holding them back with a razor-thin slice of control. Not here. Not now. I can't let it out yet because I won't survive if I do.

"I'll see you in Briar Valley."

Hanging up the phone call, I slump against the wall and hang my head. The waves begin. Building. Cresting. Crashing over me. Pain comes thick and fast until it feels like I can't breathe.

The buzz of the phone in my hand drags me back for a second, an unknown number flashing. The only person in my contacts is Lola, so I know one of the guys is reaching out.

Unknown Number: Please hurry.

Squeezing the phone, tears drip down my cheeks. The thought of seeing the three shattered pieces of my heart again is equal parts exhilarating and terrifying.

It's time to return to Briar Valley.

Time… to go home.

## CHAPTER 4
# WILLOW
HEAVY METAL – DIVELINER

"ARE YOU SAFE?" Katie asks through the hands-free.

Stuffing notes back into my purse, I shove it back in my handbag. We stopped again after driving for hours to refuel and get more coffee for the road. I'm barely able to keep my eyes open.

"We took the long route to avoid the main roads. No issues so far. I left the apartment keys under the plant pot for you."

"Good. Be careful."

"We will."

"Willow?"

I indicate to pull away from the petrol station where we just refilled our tank. "Yeah?"

"If you ever need to come back to the apartment... it's yours, alright? I know things haven't been ideal, but I'll always be here if you need me. I mean it."

"Thank you, Katie. For everything."

"I really wish you'd call me Mum."

"Yeah, I know," I reply lamely.

Katie sniffs, presumably stifling her own tears. I don't offer any comfort. I'm too numb, and frankly, I'm all cried out.

There's nothing left in me to feel any kind of emotion right now.

I'm running on zero sleep and crappy petrol station coffee in order to get us home as fast as possible. The last twenty-four hours have been a blur of tears, packing and grief.

It took all day to get everything ready for the journey while figuring out the quickest route back up north. I planned it methodically, avoiding all main roads and cameras.

"Let me know when you arrive," she requests.

"I will."

Disconnecting the call, I feel like an asshole for treating her like shit. Our relationship is still new territory for me. She's proved herself in the last few months, but my trust is flimsy.

"I don't like her," Arianna comments, her feet propped up on the messy dashboard. "She's annoying and moans too much."

"That's your grandma, Ari."

"No, Lola is my grandma."

I blink to clear my vision. I've tried my best to explain things, but getting a seven-year-old to understand death is tricky. Even when Pedro died, she still believed that he was out there somewhere.

"Lola's your great-grandma." I keep my eyes on the snowy road. "But she's in heaven now, remember? She won't be there when we get back, baby. I'm sorry."

"I know, but I can still visit her in heaven. Right?"

"Sure, baby. In your dreams, you'll still see her."

"Like Pedro."

"Like Pedro," I confirm. "Go to sleep, Ari. We've still got three hours to go. Shut your eyes."

Grabbing my coat, I use my spare hand to drape it over her, letting her snuggle up in the seat. The radio is tinny in the background as I keep driving through the night.

The farther north we get, the thicker the snow falls. As

dawn rises, we approach the mountain summit that leads into Briar Valley. Mount Helena is as majestic as I remember.

Arianna stirs in her sleep but doesn't wake up, too busy sucking on her thumb. With a final breath for courage, I pull onto the rocky terrain and begin the steep ascent.

Within minutes, we've spun out of control and are stuck on a huge patch of ice. This is ridiculous. Eyes burning, I rest my forehead on the steering wheel and take a breath.

All I can see is Lola—her bright, friendly smile and wizened face. Her scent is in my nose. Freshly baked cookies and all things homey, transferred through her warm embrace.

I loved the way she always pinched my cheeks before saying hello. Our pep talks around the dining table were one of my weekly highlights after we resolved our differences.

"Dammit," I hiss, scrubbing my cheeks. "Get it together."

Grabbing my phone, I send a message to the one number I have saved then wait for whoever is sitting on the other end to come and rescue us. It won't be long, I'm sure.

Turning up the heater, I point the vent in Arianna's direction then hug myself, staring at the minutes counting down on the dashboard clock.

Within half an hour, the glow of headlights finds us. Ryder's bright-red truck pulls up a short distance away, but someone else steps out into the rising blizzard.

Inching through the heavy snowfall, a pair of short, muscled legs approaches the car. Glancing at Arianna, I decide to climb out and do this reunion without waking her.

I'm freezing in just a long, thick sweater and tight yoga pants as I slam the door shut and turn to face our rescuer. Dull green eyes meet mine through the white-laced air.

"Zach," I whimper.

His overgrown, nut-coloured brown hair is windswept and long overdue for a trim. The enthusiastic smile that usually curves his soft, boyish features is nowhere to be found.

His light has dulled.

Vanished. Gone.

"Willow?" Zach stares right at me.

I shuffle my feet while being battered by the wind and snow. "Hi."

Before I can react, he rushes at me in a blur of movement. I'm suddenly crushed against his firm chest. Two strong arms wrap around me like steel bands, and the pressure feels amazing.

I fist my hands in his hoodie, breathing in his familiar, fruity scent. It's haunted my dreams for months. I can almost hear the wild beat of his heart tearing free from his chest.

"Willow," he repeats like he can't believe it.

"It's me." I breathe him in.

"You're here."

Holding me at arm's length, he stares at me, his emerald eyes blown wide with disbelief. There are heavy bags marking his exhaustion, and he seems colder, more serious somehow.

I half expect him to crack a joke, but he slams his lips on mine instead with raw, primal need. I kiss him back, unable to resist. His fingertips stroke along my face as his tongue tangles with mine.

All I can feel is him. His touch. His taste. The sweet, playful, shining light inside of Zachariah that made me fall so irrevocably in love with him even when I didn't want to. It's still in there, beneath the grief.

When we break apart, our foreheads rest together in the chaos of the snowstorm as he lets out a bitter laugh.

"I've spent months imagining what I'd do when I saw you again," he admits in a low whisper. "How much I'd scream and shout at you, or tell you to never set foot in our fucking lives again. Even had a whole speech rehearsed."

I brush my nose against his. "You can yell at me. I deserve it. I've hurt you all, and nothing will ever excuse that."

His hand grasps my jaw to trap me in place. "I'm sure you've hurt yourself more than anyone else. Come on, we have to go before we get trapped out here. We can scream at each other later."

"I'll hold you to that," I murmur.

"I doubt I'll be the only one. Where's the kid?"

"In the car. I'll get our stuff."

Between us, we get everything unloaded and transferred into Ryder's truck. After Zach extricates Arianna from the front seat, he tucks my coat tighter around her and presses a kiss to her forehead.

"Hey, trouble. I missed you."

I have to look away when he brushes a loose strand of hair behind her ear, staring at her sleeping face with the same heartbreaking look of disbelief. It severs my heartstrings to watch.

I did that.

His pain is because of me.

"Zach—"

"It's fine," he interrupts. "I just missed her, that's all."

"She missed you too."

He nods. "Let's move."

All loaded up, I slide into the passenger seat of Ryder's truck, fixing my gaze out of the window as Zach climbs in after tucking Arianna into the back. She hasn't stirred once.

He manoeuvres the truck onto the icy road, relief loosening my shoulders when the tyre treads keep it from spinning out of control like we did. We make it halfway up Mount Helena before he speaks again.

"Where've you been all this time?"

I shrug listlessly. "Here and there. Katie relocated us to an apartment complex in Southampton for displaced families."

"Southampton?"

"We've been hiding out there for the past few months. It's hardly been a five-star holiday. More like witness protection."

He scoffs. "Hasn't been a walk in the park for us either."

I pick at a loose thread in my sweater. "You can hate me

all you want, I'll take it. But I came back for Lola, not us. That's the truth."

"How thoughtful," he snarks. "I'm not going to fight with you. Not now. Let's get through this and figure our crap out later."

"Fair enough." My throat locks up, making it difficult to swallow. "How is everyone? The town?"

"In a state of shock. Albie is a wreck. He was with her when it happened. Doc doesn't think she suffered or was in any pain, though."

"Should I be grateful for that?" I ask honestly.

Zach shrugs. "I have no clue. Maybe we should be."

"It's something, right?"

"All I know is the place is a mess already. We don't know how to function without her. She was the whole reason Briar Valley exists."

Reaching over on instinct, I take his free hand and curl our fingers together. Zach spares me a glance before refocusing on the road, his Adam's apple bobbing like crazy.

"She would want the town to live on." I blink away my tears. "It's more than just one person. The family is what makes Briar Valley a home."

"Our family is broken. Has been since you left."

"Zach—"

"Forget it."

I let my hand fall away from his and watch the snow build outside. The sun has risen now, lighting the path ahead as we begin to descend into the woodland surrounding the town.

"How's Micah?"

"Don't ask," Zach growls.

*Okay, then.*

The awkward silence stretches on until the trees clear to reveal the beginning of cobbled streets. I'm slick all over with anxious sweat, and my hands tremble in my lap.

The idea of facing everyone makes me want to curl up in

a corner and hide away from prying eyes. Zach's eyes briefly dart towards me, assessing my knees knocking together.

"Your hair's different," he observes.

"I had to cut it."

"Looks nice."

"Thanks. What happens now?"

"Do you want to get some rest before… everything?"

I nod quickly. "That would be good. I've been awake for over thirty hours."

"Jesus, Willow. How are you not dead on your feet?"

"Every time I shut my eyes, I dreamed of you three," I admit. "Sometimes it's less painful to stay awake until the point of exhaustion than face that every night."

Zach flexes his grip on the steering wheel. "The bed felt so fucking empty without you in it. Our entire lives did."

My chest aches. "It hurt me too, Zach."

"I know, babe. I'm just struggling to understand why we've wasted so much time apart. Life is too damn short."

There it is again—the all-consuming pit of pain when I remember that I'm not coming home and walking into my grandmother's arms. Life really is too short.

She would want us to embrace even the tiniest shreds of happiness, however fragile they may seem in the midst of so much grief. We have to live. For Lola. For her memory.

Zach drives straight through the deserted town. Nobody is braving the weather, remaining safely inside, granting us some privacy. Snow is falling thick and fast.

We haven't seen a single soul when we reach the guys' cabin, nestled amongst white-capped trees and shrubs atop the rugged hill overlooking the valley. It looks magical, coated in December snow.

I deliberately ignore our old home across the road. Just thinking about all that we left behind makes my heart hurt more than it already does. Zach turns off the engine and sighs.

"Micah will be passed out in his workshop. He's on lockdown after his recent behaviour."

"Drinking?"

Zach nods. "Daily."

"Jesus. For how long?"

"A couple of months now."

Unable to dive into that, I force an even breath. "What about Killian?"

"I think he's still with Albie in Lola's cabin." He scrapes his hands down his unshaven face. "You should have a few hours of privacy before all hell breaks loose."

We fall back into awkward silence until I break it.

"Will you shout at me if I say I'm sorry again?"

"Most likely." He blows out a leaden breath.

"Then I won't." I unbuckle my belt. "I'll take Arianna inside."

Before I can climb out, Zach grabs me by the wrist. I fight to conceal my reaction to the bite of pain as his fingers grasp the fresh cuts beneath my sweater that I really don't want him to know about.

The look on his face is scary enough as he looks right through me. Past all the bullshit and lies. My attempt at displaying a strong face. He sees deep into the pits of my tormented heart and understands.

"Willow… I'm so fucking angry at you right now, but I'm also glad that you're home," he finally says. "And I love you."

I manage a tight nod. "I love you."

"Maybe that's enough for now. Lola wouldn't want us to fight about this." He shakes his head. "She'd just want me to be relieved."

Tugging my wrist, he pulls me closer until his lips are within reach. We kiss again, but slower this time. Tenderly. Filling the empty spaces in one another that we each left behind.

There's a burning ache deep inside of me. Far deeper than

I could even attempt to reach myself. In Zach's presence, it reignites, burning in slow, lazy embers until my whole body is alight.

"Zach," I whine into his lips.

"I know, princess. Let's get the kid inside. We're going to freeze to death out here otherwise."

Grabbing our bags, I let Zach tuck Arianna into his chest to protect her from the snow. We race through the flurries and escape inside the cabin where the guys' familiar scents slap me in the face.

It smells like pine trees and bonfires. Oil paint and whiskey. Roast dinners and home. All my favourite things, bottled into one essence, pure and inarguably *them*.

"Jesus Christ."

Zach glances around the huge mess. "Yeah. May've let things slip a little bit."

The cabin is the same, but it's covered in layers of clutter, discarded clothes and unwashed dishes. Killian always kept things clean and semi-tidy. This is a complete disaster zone.

I notice they don't even have a Christmas tree up. We didn't either. The big day is only a couple of weeks away, yet I had no plans to celebrate beyond a cheap dinner with Arianna.

"Your room isn't made up," Zach says over his shoulder. "I'll put this one in my room for now. Make yourself at home."

Dropping our bags, I bounce on the balls of my feet. It feels wrong to just invite myself back into their space like nothing has changed. I'm frozen in the entrance and unable to move.

That's where Zach finds me when he returns a few minutes later. His eyes scrape over me, incisive and searching, seeing far more than I'd like him to. Our sadness whispers to each other.

"I should get some sleep," I croak. "Before later on."

"You should." Zach clears his raspy throat. "Unless…"

Trailing off, the need written across his face is so obvious, he may as well be screaming out for my arms around him. I feel the same, but I still can't close the distance between us.

"Babe," he hums. "Please… I need to hold you. I just need to feel you in my arms one more time to know you're real."

My feet move of their own accord. We meet somewhere in the middle, the messy cabin falling away as the softness of Zach's t-shirt meets my nose. God, I've missed his smell.

"Fuck." He rhythmically strokes my hair. "Fuck!"

"I'm right here, Zach."

"You don't feel real."

Unpeeling myself from his arms, I take his unshaved face into my hands and force his eyes to meet mine. The round, youthful angles are covered in stubble, framing his hollow eyes.

"I'm real," I whisper fiercely. "I know this has been the hardest time of our lives, but I'm here now. I'm in your arms."

"Why did you leave us?"

I brush my nose against his. "Ari. It's all for her."

"We could've kept you safe."

"No, Zach. You can't. No one can. We won't be safe until this is all over and Mr Sanchez is gone."

His lashes lift, casting shadows over dimpled skin. "Gone?"

"I don't want to talk about him right now. I just want to feel you. Hold you. Touch you."

Lips pecking mine, I can feel his smile. "I can do that."

Zach's hands move to cup my hips and hold me flush against him. I wind my arms around his neck and lose myself to his kiss, bold and insistent, demanding for me to stay at his side forever.

When his hand moves to hook my leg up on his hip, I begin to shift, needing more friction between us. I can already feel the press of his hardness against my core, and it's driving me insane with need.

When his tongue pushes past my lips to tangle with mine, I can't help moaning into his mouth. Our tongues duel, both fighting a losing battle. He wants the only thing I can't give him.

Forever.

A kept promise.

Our future.

Until we're safe and the monster hunting us has been shackled in the depths of hell, I can't give any of them what they deserve. And that's exactly why I had no choice but to run.

"The others," I gasp. "What if they come in?"

Zach moves to grip my ass. "I don't give a shit. Let them watch."

Lifting me so I'm hooked around his waist, he walks me over to the huge, L-shaped sofa in front of the open fireplace and deposits me on it. I let him quickly peel off my yoga pants.

Wrapping a hand around my ankle, he plants a gentle kiss there then begins to trail his lips upwards. Higher. Higher still. Kissing, nipping and licking a burning path to my inner thigh.

"So fucking gorgeous," he grunts.

Kissing my left hip, his mouth traces the seam of my plain white panties. I know I'm soaked through already. I haven't been touched since I slept with Micah on that mountain top.

"Tell me to stop, babe."

"No," I moan as he kisses on top of my mound. "Please… Zach. I need to feel your lips on me."

Hooking his fingers beneath the elastic, he torturously peels my panties off, inch by slow inch. Bare from the waist down, Zach wastes no time burying his face between my open thighs.

When his mouth latches onto my pussy, I grab handfuls of his long hair and cry out. His lips move like a ravenous machine, his tongue delving into my core and parting my folds.

Thumb swiping over my nub and beginning to circle, I moan again, slamming a hand over my mouth to prevent myself from waking Arianna up. His touch feels incredible.

"You're so wet for me," Zach marvels as he flicks my clit. "Did this sweet little pussy miss me?"

Swiping his finger through the flow of moisture, he thrusts it into my slit in one fast pump. I'm already on the cusp of falling apart, the fast thrust of his fingers driving me to the edge.

"Oh God, Zach!"

"That's it, babe. Say my goddamn name. Don't you dare forget it ever again."

Giving me a moment to catch my breath as I lay tangled in a gasping mess, he quickly unbuckles his belt and shoves his jeans down. His moments are clumsy, he's rushing so fast.

Grabbing his arm, I yank him back down so his body covers mine then wrap my legs around his waist. My hand pushes his boxers down to find the hardened steel of his length.

"Willow—"

"I need you inside of me," I groan pathetically. "Right now."

With fire burning bright in his irises, he lines himself up and doesn't give me the benefit of a warning. The sudden pump of his hips feeds his cock deep inside my entrance.

I bite down on his shoulder to silence the moan of pure bliss. My teeth leave a swollen welt, the sight bringing me pleasure. We're marking each other tonight.

"Hold on," Zach warns.

Keeping a tight grip on his neck, I let him pound into me at a relentless, bruising pace that betrays his still white-hot anger. Each thrust is its own individual punishment for leaving.

Over and over, his cock worships me in the most brutal way possible. When he pulls out and quickly flips me over, all I can do is grip the sofa cushions and let him raise my ass high.

Zach re-enters me at an even deeper angle now that I'm bent over at his mercy. The smack of his hand on my butt cheek sends tingles down my spine like hungry fire ants.

"Fuck you for leaving," he hisses while spanking me again. "And fuck you for thinking we could ever survive without you."

"I won't apologise again," I gasp back. "I had to keep her safe."

Slamming into me again, Zach's voice is a guttural bark. "That's our damn job too, and you know it."

"I'm... her mother. I had to—"

His next thrust cuts me off and all I can garble out is a strangled cry for more. This isn't the sweet, dirty Zach that I remember. He's fucking me even more brutally than his cousin once did.

His fingertips feel like they're bruising my hips, but I don't care. I'm thankful that I was able to keep my sweater on, at least. I don't want any of them to see my arms.

Guided to the edge of a plummeting drop, I stare over the cliff and prepare to be shoved. Zach's reaching his own release. I can feel it in the increasingly rough slam of his hips on my rear.

Just when I'm about to fall apart in the most spectacular fashion, the pressure of his dick inside me vanishes. It's cruelly ripped away as he pulls out and takes a huge step back.

"What?" I scream. "Zach!"

A hand wrapped around his shaft, he pumps it one last time and groans through his release. Come shoots all over my ass until I'm covered in his seed and still hanging on the edge of an orgasm.

I scream and rave. Shout and curse. I'm dripping wet and sticky from his release, but Zach remains at a distance, catching his breath. I realise that he isn't going to let me come tonight.

"That's for leaving," he grunts.

Semi-dressed, he turns and vanishes deeper into the cabin before I can utter a single word of frustration. I'm left alone—coated in come and on the verge of a complete meltdown.

"Fuck you, Zach!" I shout in anger.

There's no response.

This is my punishment.

# CHAPTER 5
# KILLIAN
SILENT LOVE – JAMES BAY

HEAVING ALBIE'S unconscious body into his room, I dump him on the bed. He can't sleep in Lola's bed after she died there. Even if it's empty and available. The undertakers took her body to Highbridge a few hours ago.

Ryder was no help either. He passed out with his head on the dining table after single-handedly polishing off a bottle of rum. I can handle my liquor, but the world is spinning even for me.

We spent the whole day making a list of what needs to be done. Funeral arrangements, property deeds, complicated legal matters that always seem ridiculous when your loved one is dead.

But life is a cruel motherfucking bitch, and this isn't my first rodeo. I had to grow up fast and take over when my folks died too. I'm always the one to pick up the broken pieces.

"Where's Lola?" Albie mumbles drunkenly.

"Sleep it off, Al. You'll feel better in the morning."

"Lo," he whines.

"She isn't here. Sleep."

With a grumble, he passes the hell out again. I leave him

to wallow alone and stumble back into the living room in their cabin. Ryder hasn't moved an inch on the table.

Grabbing a cushion from the sofa, I prop it underneath his head then throw a blanket over his shoulders to make him a little more comfortable. We're all going to have sore heads tomorrow.

It's dark outside, but the heavy dousing of snow somehow manages to brighten the world into a weird, twilight state. When I was a kid, I used to get so excited to watch the first snow fall.

It always made me think of fresh starts and so many endless opportunities in the blank, powdery canvas that would settle over town. Tonight is no different.

Months of pain and torment have all come down to this. While inebriated, Ryder let it slip that Willow was on her way home. I told him that I'll believe that when I see it, already steeling myself against the disappointment.

Perhaps this is our fresh start. A second chance. Or maybe I'm a stupid old fool, destined to get my heart crushed. Crunching through the snow, I'm nearly home when I freeze on the spot.

There are footsteps imprinted in the snow around my parked truck. I follow without thinking, the roar of my heartbeat in my ears the only sound that I can hear.

The footsteps lead across the cobblestone road towards the lake behind Willow's still-dark cabin, cloaked in frozen icicles and crisp, cold darkness.

But there's something else.

A person.

Sitting cross-legged at the lake's frozen edge, a figure stares out into the nothingness. I can just make out the curl of dark, raven hair beneath a baseball cap, far shorter than I remember.

A thick lump gathers in my throat as I draw to a halt several metres away. She's shivering beneath the knitted blanket wrapped around her shoulders and familiar, curved body.

"Willow?" I say like a prayer.

Shoulders trembling, her head turns to spare me a brief, tear-logged glance. Our gazes collide, amber on hazel, despair on grief. Love on irretrievable loss.

"Kill," she sobs.

I'm stuck between running for my life and gathering the bundle of bones into my arms. It's her. My light. My love. The breaker and fixer of my long-dead heart.

"Willow," I repeat.

"Please... I can't do this right now. I want to be alone."

"You haven't seen me for months, and that's all you have to say? You don't want to see me?"

Her head drops, hands moving to cover her face as she turns back towards the lake. "I never got to say goodbye."

The pain in her voice crushes my heart. Tentatively approaching her, I ease myself down next to her in the snow. Neither of us touch, keeping a safe distance.

I manage a quick look at her pale face, lit by the blanket of white all around us. Crystalline flakes of snow pepper the surface of the lake and blanket our surroundings in silence.

"Lola loved you," I reply simply. "And she knew that you loved her. That's all that matters."

"I just wish I could've told her," Willow whimpers. "Last time we spoke, I hung up on her. I was so tired of the same old argument."

"What argument?"

"I was tired of running. Tired of fighting her. All I wanted was to shut my eyes and wake up here, surrounded by my family."

Anger shoots through me. "You never should have left."

"You think I don't know that?"

I shrug, the alcohol in my veins loosening my tongue. "I

think you didn't care enough to stay. We didn't matter enough."

Willow suddenly stands up, looming over me on shaking legs. She rips the cap from her head, letting her shorn black hair tumble down to her shoulders.

Her furious eyes strip me down to the core with a mere look. Pain. Anguish. Indecision. Grief. Hope. Despair. It's all there in myriad, confusing shades of hazel-tinged chaos.

"If that's what you believe, then you're not the person I thought you were," she utters. "I left to keep my daughter safe, not to spite you or your ego."

"Baby—"

"Don't *baby* me, Kill. I was in love with you. I still fucking am. I've spent every day dreaming of when I could come home."

"So why didn't you?" I ask pointedly.

Rather than answering me, she turns and storms off, away from the lake and her cabin. I hesitate for only a second before chasing after her like a dog following a dangled bone.

"Wait!"

When I grab her arm, she yanks it free from my grasp, her teeth gritted against an angry hiss. I've kicked the hornet's nest now.

"Do not grab me," Willow warns.

I let my hand drop. "Look, I'm sorry. I'm drunk and stupid and... I'm so fucked up. I don't work without you, princess."

"I can't be what you want me to be. I have to protect Arianna. That's why I stayed away. Not to punish you or to be a bitch, but because it wasn't safe to be here."

Inching closer to her, I reach out, driven by desperation alone. She stares at me with such pain, but she still refuses to budge. I close the final distance between us and tug her into my arms instead.

Fuck asking for permission.

She collapses against me in a weightless puddle of exhaustion. Crushing her into my barrel chest, the rage I've felt since she left dissipates into sheer relief.

"I've got you," I whisper into her hair. "You don't have to walk alone anymore. I'm here, baby."

"You're not," she replies.

"Let me be the judge of that. I swear to whatever God is out there, I'm never letting you go again. Even if you want me to."

"I don't want you to."

"Good, because that is not happening. We deal with this as a family from here forward."

"You'd take me back? After everything?" she scoffs.

I brush my lips against her temple, my throat locked up tight. "I never let you go. Not once."

"Me neither, Kill."

Releasing her, I glower at the dark circles beneath her eyes. The unmitigated exhaustion reflected back physically pains me. She looks dead on her feet and barely functioning.

"When was the last time you slept?"

Peeling herself away from me, she takes my hand. "I don't know. We arrived early this morning after travelling through the night."

"Why didn't you sleep?"

"I couldn't rest, knowing you were out there, hurting all alone. Arianna's gone back to bed inside."

"Come to bed, then," I plead shamelessly. "Just let me hold you for tonight. Everything else can wait."

Willow bites her lip and nods. "Okay."

Hand in hand, we walk back up the garden, leaving the empty cabin and all its memories alone. I hold the front door open for her to enter the warmth.

"After you."

She flashes me a brief smile. "Thanks."

Stepping into the dark kitchen, I shake snow from my long

mane of dirty blonde hair. The light in Micah's workshop is glowing from the bottom of the garden, but I don't bother to disturb him.

Willow's been through enough for one day without discovering how much of a mess he's become in her absence. I'm sure Zach's only given her a PG-rated version of that disastrous tale.

"I should check on Ari."

"Where is she?"

Willow walks down the hallway. "In Zach's bed, I think."

After pausing to check on Arianna, fast asleep in Zach's arms in his bedroom, Willow lets herself into my room at the end of the hall. I hesitate, taking a peep in at the little monster myself.

*Fuck.*

An invisible weight lifts off my chest at the sight of the tiny, blonde-haired lump curled up under the bedsheets with my snoring cousin. I've missed that fucking kid and her sharp tongue.

Seeing her asleep and so innocent looking, the impenetrable wall of ice around my heart begins to crack. Only a couple of millimetres, but enough to let a shred of warmth in.

Willow did what she thought was necessary to keep Arianna safe. If I were in her position, I doubt I would have done any differently. I just wish she'd trusted us to protect them both.

The anger is still there. Simmering. Cooking away on a rolling boil, ready to explode. But not tonight. Right now, I'm grateful. She's back and alive. That's enough for me.

"Killian?" Willow sighs.

"Coming."

When I reach my darkened bedroom, I stop dead in the doorway. Willow has removed her wet, snow-stained sweater, and she's slowly peeling her tight yoga pants over her hips.

"Stop staring," she snaps.

"Can't help it, princess."

Studying the scrap of panties left on her body and the swell of her bare breasts, I nearly lose sight of what we're doing here in the first place.

She needs to trust me again. I can't be a caveman, no matter how much I want to bury myself in her right now, bad blood be damned. My primal self wants to devour her whole.

Pulling off my own t-shirt and ditching my jeans, I slowly approach and gather her tiny body into my arms. She's lost so much weight. Even I can tell in the darkness of the room.

"You haven't been eating?" I trace her ribcage.

"Not now, Kill. Please just hold me."

Easily lifting her, I crawl into the unmade bed, draping her across my bare chest. Willow burrows closer, slotting into my side like we were made for each other, lock and key.

"I missed this so much," she murmurs.

"Yeah," I croak. "Me too."

"You have no idea how many times I dreamed that I was right here with you."

"I have a pretty good idea."

Staring up at the ceiling, I clear my thick throat and prepare to lay it all on the line just as footsteps move through the cabin and the light from a phone flashes into the room.

"Willow?" Zach whisper-shouts.

"In here," she responds without moving. "I'm with Killian."

He stares in at us with sheer longing. "Arianna's asleep. Mind if I join you guys?"

"After your stunt earlier?" Willow drones.

Zach remains silent. I don't bother to ask. He's far angrier than he'll ever let on after months of dealing with Micah's self-destruction. I'm sure he gave her a hard time.

"Fine." Willow breaks the silence. "Come in."

I roll my eyes, shifting Willow over so there's space behind her for Zach to slide into my bed. Luckily, it's big enough for all three of us.

"Come on, kid. Before I change my mind."

"You won't break my legs if I climb in?" Zach asks with a low chuckle.

"If you start snoring, then no promises. Keep your fucking mouth shut for once, and we won't have an issue."

Zach rips his t-shirt over his head. "That's a risk I'm willing to take."

Once he's stepped out of his jeans, he approaches the bed, easing in and trapping Willow between us. She recoils, seeming reluctant to let him cuddle her at first, but eventually gives in.

"I'm sorry for earlier," Zach mumbles.

"Guess I deserved it."

"No. You didn't."

"What did you do?" I ask tiredly.

Zach keeps his mouth shut. Not even Willow is willing to tell me what happened. Fluffing my pillow, I reposition myself into a comfier place on the bed.

"Whatever. Don't tell me."

The silent minutes tick by, broken only by the featherlight patter of heavy snow falling outside my window. My eyes are too heavy to hold open, as much as I want to cherish Willow's warmth.

"Can somebody pinch me?" Zach whispers into the darkness. "I'm not entirely convinced this is real."

Willow jabs him in the ribs with her elbow. "Real enough for you? Some of us are trying to sleep here."

"Noted," Zach groans in pain.

"Shut up, the pair of you." I press a kiss against Willow's soft neck. "I'm drunk and tired. Talk in the morning."

"Killian's drunk?"

"Apparently," Willow surmises.

"I always wondered what that would look like."

"Zach," I warn again. "Zip it, loudmouth."

Falling silent, Willow lets out a contented sigh between us. Just feeling her in my arms again, stroking her soft skin, inhaling her familiar, sweet scent… Fuck me.

It almost makes the last five months of pain, anger and regret worth it. *Almost.* But nothing can ever bring that time back to us, and I have no guarantee that she won't do it all over again.

The only thing that will keep her here, safe in my arms, is if I bring her that asshole's head on a stake. Then she'll finally be free to live the life she's always wanted.

Challenge accepted.

I'll cut it off myself.

## CHAPTER 6
# WILLOW
### RIBS – LORDE

SEARCHING THROUGH THE FRIDGE, I start pulling out ingredients at random. Tomatoes. Eggs. Sausages. Even some slightly questionable looking spinach to go in the omelette too.

The guys are still asleep. Neither stirred as I snuck out of bed, unable to lay there for a second longer. I managed a few hours before I woke up in a dog pile of muscles and limbs.

My heart was pounding from another stress-induced nightmare. Mr Sanchez was there, as he always is, ready to lash out at me with his ice-cold blue eyes and razor sharp tongue.

*I know where you are, Mrs Sanchez.*

*I'm coming for you and that little brat.*

*You will be mine again.*

Startling, I realise an egg has hit the floor, smashing after falling from my trembling hands. *Shit.* I make myself take a breath to force the nightmarish whispers aside.

Half an hour later, I've ruined my first three attempts at the omelette, burned my hand on the stove, and dropped a mug of coffee on myself in between the madness.

With a growl, my back meets the cabinet, and I let myself

sink to the cabin floor to bury my face in my hands. I'm so tired. Not just physically, but on a bone-deep, irreparable level.

I thought I'd feel better the moment I set foot back in Briar Valley, but it's like all the shit that's built up in the past few months has followed me here.

Letting my fingers glide underneath Killian's stolen flannel shirt I threw on to cover up my arms, I let out a deep breath while stroking the healing cuts across my wrist.

I'm itching to take my switchblade from my suitcase and cut again, over and over, until this nervous energy leaves my body, and I can finally get some rest.

"Are you going to sit on the floor and cry all day?"

Opening my eyes, I find Killian staring down at me with his arms folded across his bare, chiselled chest. My throat immediately seizes up at the sight of so much burnished muscle.

He's wearing only a pair of dark-green sweatpants, hanging low on his defined hips. His hair is still a long, tangled bush of dirty-blonde strands around the strong, defined angles of his face and jaw.

"Well?" He cocks a brow.

Wiping the tears from my cheeks, I try to plaster a smile on my face but fail to summon it. Killian's featured in my dreams for months, but seeing him in front of me still makes my body hum.

"Breakfast is a disaster."

"So I can see," he quips back. "Were you trying to decorate the kitchen with food?"

"I'm trying to cook, and it's all going wrong!"

He crouches down beside me. "Christ, Willow. Did you sleep at all?"

"I don't need to sleep," I snap, ignoring his outstretched hand. "What I need is to get my shit together and figure out what needs to be done. I have no idea where to even start, planning a funeral."

"It's all done. You don't have to worry."

"Wait, what?"

Killian stares at me. "I took care of it all."

"What are you talking about?"

"The funeral home is sorting the arrangements. They're gonna call me back today. Lola's lawyer will be here in a few weeks to go through her affairs."

My mouth clicks open then shut again. "You... sorted it all?"

"This isn't my first family death." Killian scrapes a hand over his sculpted beard. "I figured you would be overwhelmed with it all, so I took care of it."

"I can't believe you've done everything. I thought I'd have to do it all as her last living relative."

"Why are you so shocked?"

"You know why."

Expression softening, he helps me to stand back up, his hand grasping mine tightly. His skin is rough and calloused against mine.

"Because I'm still in love with you. I've loved you since the day we met, for fuck's sake. That's why I wanted to help. Besides, she was my grandmother as well."

"I love you too," I admit. "It killed me to leave."

"Good," he snarls.

My eyebrows draw together. "Why is that good?"

"Because you almost killed my family with this stupid fucking decision, Willow. You need to know how much it hurt us."

"I do!"

"You did this to us. No one else. You can't blame Dimitri Sanchez for your own decisions, even if he was the cause of them. You could've chosen to stay instead."

"And let him take Arianna?" I almost shout.

"He wouldn't have gotten remotely close. We dealt with him once and all the other times his cronies came back again, looking for you. You didn't give us a chance to keep you safe."

I try to push him away, but he grips the edges of the kitchen counter, preventing me from being able to escape. I'm caught against his lines of god-like, carved muscle.

"You took off and broke my damn heart. Zach's been a wreck. Don't even get me started on Micah. That's on you, princess."

Tears burn in my eyes. "Kill, stop."

"I won't stop. Not until you understand and swear that you'll never leave us again. No matter how scary life gets."

"I can't promise that!"

His jaw tightens into a hard, cruel line. "Then you might as well go now."

Moisture spills over and leaks down my cheeks. He wants me to hurt. Killian needs to see my pain for himself to know if we have a future worth fighting for or not.

"You want to know the truth?"

He waits, silent and demanding.

With a flicker of courage, I throw off the oversized flannel shirt that covers my arms, revealing healing cuts and new scars from our time apart. The remaining colour in his still-tanned face drains away.

"There's your truth," I lash out. "You want to know if I regretted my actions? Every goddamn day. But I had no choice."

A single finger trailing its way down from my wrist, Killian traces the violent slash of a healed cut. It's pink and tight, contrasting with the still-raw wounds from a few days ago.

"What the fuck is this?" he demands in a flat, terrifying voice that pricks the hairs up on my skin. "Who did this to you?"

"I did it to myself, Kill."

"Yourself?" he grinds out.

"Yes."

Yanking my arm away, I throw the flannel shirt back on to cover up the vulnerable parts of myself. I didn't want to show him, but I need him to understand. I didn't run for my own pleasure.

Zach was right. For all the awful pain they've suffered, I have endured it along with them—every last stab in the heart with the time that we were kept apart.

"Willow. Please talk to me."

"There's nothing else to say."

"You can't just show me that and walk away. Tell me what to do." His voice shifts to a desperate rasp. "I want to fix this."

"You can hate me if you want, but hate me for the right reasons. I didn't deliberately hurt your family. I was protecting mine."

His mouth hanging open on a response, the patter of light, child-sized feet halts his next words. The door to the kitchen opens, and Arianna appears, rumpled and dazed in her bunny pyjamas.

"Mummy?" she yawns.

"Morning, baby."

The moment her eyes open properly, she spots Killian. Her sleepiness vanishes, replaced by excitement. She whoops and launches herself straight at him.

"Giant! Giant!"

Killian easily catches her. "Hey, peanut."

Lifted into his huge, tree trunk arms, he swings her around the kitchen in a circle. Her squealing cuts through my brain, but I don't mind. It's the happiest I've heard her in months.

"I can't believe you're here!" she screams.

"I didn't go anywhere." Killian spoons her against his chest and strokes her messy bedhead. "Missed you, peanut."

"I missed you more, Giant. Did you get smaller?"

He suppresses a laugh. "I don't think so. You're just getting bigger."

"I must be growing!" she declares triumphantly.

"Alright, Ari. Let the poor man breathe."

Placed back on her feet, Arianna circles her arms around his legs and refuses to let go. I shove them both out of the kitchen so I can clean up and continue with breakfast.

Killian's still watching me closely, our argument hanging in the tension in the air, as he sits down with Arianna on his knee.

"What have you been up to?" he asks conversationally.

Arianna pouts. "Nothing. I missed my friends and school."

"Well, now you can go back to school. Can't you?"

"I can?" she gasps.

Cracking a fresh carton full of eggs into a bowl, I bite my lip. She doesn't need to know this may just be a quick visit for the funeral. In fact, none of them need to know that yet.

"Did you hear that, Mummy?"

"I did," I hum back.

"I can see Johan again. And Aalia, Rachel... Miranda too! I'm so happy to be home."

The look on Killian's face is so smug. I narrow my eyes at him. He can act innocent all he wants, I know what his game plan is here. Emotional warfare. He's going to play dirty.

"Did you miss Briar Valley?" Killian asks innocently.

"So much," she gushes.

"And do you want to stay here now that you're back?"

Arianna's smile freezes. "We aren't going to stay? Mummy?"

"I... don't know, Ari."

Spotting the signs of a meltdown a mile off, I quickly wipe off my hands and give all of my attention to her. Arianna's eyes fill with tears.

"But we just got back! I'm not leaving!"

"Ari, things are complicated—"

"No!" she screams.

Killian looks surprised at her outburst of anger and

quickly backtracks. "Peanut, don't worry. We'll figure it all out."

But Arianna's already fallen into one of her now-regular tantrums as her face turns bright-pink, and tears begin to streak down her cheeks in thick rivers.

"I don't want to live in the apartment anymore," she cries hysterically. "I hate feeling scared all of the time."

"Good job, Kill." I cast him a glare.

He scrubs a hand over his face, his smug smirk no longer in sight. Things have changed while we've been gone, the uncertainty taking a heavy toll on Arianna's behaviour. It isn't her fault.

I approach her slowly with raised hands. "Calm down, Ari. We're home. You're safe."

"I'm not leaving!"

"We're going to stay for a while, baby. I have to sort out Grams's things, and you're going to see all of your friends again."

Peering up at me through her lashes, she looks on the verge of calming down before her tears intensify, and her wails ricochet off the walls around us. I kneel down and pull her into my lap.

"Shh, baby. I've got you."

"What the hell is this?" Killian demands.

"This is your fault!" I yell at him.

"I wasn't trying to upset her."

"But you did with your stupid little games."

He falls silent as I attempt to calm Arianna down. She's hiccupping and clinging to the lapels of my flannel shirt when Zach makes a bleary-eyed appearance in the kitchen.

"What happened?" he asks.

"Your cousin happened."

Killian huffs. "It's my fault."

Crouching down next to me in his plaid pyjama bottoms

and t-shirt, Zach peels Arianna from my lap and boosts her into the air.

"Hey, monkey. Why the tears?"

Her chest shakes with hiccups. "I d-d-don't want to leave."

Bouncing her on his hip like she's a little toddler again, he dances around the kitchen and goofs off until Arianna is smiling. Her tears are quickly replaced by laughter.

"Zach! Lemme down!"

"Not until we turn that frown upside down," he singsongs. "Let's finish off this breakfast together, shall we? I'm sure I can burn it much better than your mama can."

"Okay," she submits.

"You're in charge then, Ari."

"I am?" She peers up at him with eager eyes.

Zach waggles his eyebrows. "I'm not gonna be the adult here. Now, where do you want me, chef?"

"I want eggs!"

"Then eggs it is."

He takes Arianna into the kitchen to begin whisking eggs, and I glance at Killian's weirdly anxious face. His emotions are at the forefront as he watches Zach entertain my daughter.

I lower my voice. "Ever use my daughter to emotionally manipulate me again and we're going to have a serious fucking problem. I am not kidding around."

With his head hanging in shame, I breeze past him and step outside to clear my head. It's freezing cold, the snow now stopped and settled in thick, white tides of powder.

It's a winter wonderland and the perfect setting for the approaching festive season, but I doubt we'll be here to see it. Mr Sanchez can find us here. We're not safe.

But for the life of me, I can't find the strength inside myself to leave again. The pain I felt last time has already expanded overtime, and I'm being crushed beneath its weight right now.

There's a loud crashing sound from the bottom of the

garden where Micah's cabin lies. Lights are glowing from inside. I can't avoid him forever, even if part of me wants to.

Approaching the cabin and knocking on the door, I wait to be let inside. The crashing continues, and no one comes to open up. I have to heave open the lump of hewed wood myself.

"Mi? You in here?"

*Bang.*

*Crash.*

*Shatter.*

"Micah!"

There's chaos inside—unadulterated, destructive chaos. His studio has been trashed, from ripped canvases to smashed sculptures. Tools have been thrown and windows smashed.

"Oh my God."

Collapsing amidst the madness on a bean bag surrounded by empty beer cans, Micah is semi-conscious. There's a half-empty bottle of vodka still clutched in his paint-stained hand.

The sight of him causes my heart to squeeze.

"Mi?"

His caramel-brown hair is pointing up in all directions, his features mirroring his identical twin brother's soft, rounded face, despite his pierced button nose and slightly darker eyes.

"You again," he slurs.

"Me… again?"

"You always haunt my dreams, angel."

"Oh, Mi. I'm not a dream."

His glazed-over emerald eyes meet mine. "Of course, you are. The others told me to let go and forget you, but I just can't do it."

Heart splintering, I pick my way through the rubble and shards of glass. Micah continues to loll on the beanbag as I finally reach him and crouch down next to it.

"What have you done to yourself?" I whisper, swiping unruly hair aside.

As my fingertips brush his skin, his eyes flutter shut in a brief look of ecstasy. It takes him a moment to realise that the hand touching him is real and not a dream.

"Willow," he breathes.

"I'm here, Mi. I'm real."

"Not… real."

Burying my fingers in his hair that's slick with grease, obviously unwashed, I press the lumps and bumps of his skull. My hand travels around to grasp his chin to make him look at me.

"Come back," I plead. "We need you. I need you. I'm sorry for leaving and making you do this to yourself to cope."

Tentatively reaching out, his hand strokes over my short, curling hair, verifying the inky black strands are indeed real. With his test satisfied, a streak of soberness enters his gaze.

"Holy fuck. You're here."

"I'm here," I repeat.

Looking a lot more awake, his eyes shine with unshed tears that cause thorny spikes to slice into my throat. He still won't move to embrace me as I desperately want him to.

"Why did you leave me?" he croaks.

*Fuck. His voice.*

"I'm so sorry," I choke out.

"My head… You left me alone in it."

Uncaring of whether he wants me to or not, I throw my arms around Micah's slimmed-down body and hold him close. He curls up against my chest like a tiny baby in need of love.

"I'm here… I'm here," I reassure.

Each time I repeat the words that he needs to hear, I circle his back in slow, comforting strokes. The smell of beer and liquor clings to him like a second skin, along with the stench of cigarettes.

This is the worst I've ever seen him. I've only heard rumours about the darkest depths of his worst depressive episodes, when the drinking escalates, and he stops taking care of himself.

"How long has this episode lasted?" I ask gently. "You don't look like you've showered or slept in weeks."

"Fine," he mumbles.

"You're not, Mi."

His head lifts, and two devastating eyes scour my face. "I can't believe... you're here. It's really you. Am I that drunk?"

"This is real. I'm home for Lola's funeral. We came as soon as we heard about what happened."

At the mention of her death, he pulls away from me. Micah staggers to his feet and takes a swig from the vodka bottle still tucked into his hands.

"She died while I was out drinking," he bites out. "I d-didn't get a chance to say goodbye. Neither did Z-Zach."

"We didn't either, Mi."

"But that wasn't your fault. This was m-mine."

Taking a seat at the chair in front of his crafting area that's miraculously still standing, Micah's head hits the table with a thump. A second later, his snoring begins.

I stare at him for several astonished seconds, unsure of exactly what I've just witnessed. He's passed out. Stone cold asleep.

I did this.

Me.

It's all my fault.

Grabbing his denim jacket from the hook on the wall, I carefully drape it over his shoulders so he's at least warm. There's a fire crackling in the corner of the room, and I add some more logs too.

He needs a shower, hot meal and proper sleep in a warm bed, but that can be tomorrow's task. I'm here now. I will fix what I've broken and look after him in his own personal darkness.

Back inside the cabin, Killian is washing up mixing bowls

and utensils while Arianna eats her omelette on the sofa with Zach. I'm too emotionally exhausted to make her move and sit at the table.

"Micah's drunk," I say quietly.

Killian doesn't even look up from his task. "No doubt."

"You don't have a problem with that?"

He slams a wooden spoon down a little harder than necessary. "I have several problems with it. But it isn't something I can fix."

Abandoning the washing up, he mumbles about needing a shower and leaves the kitchen. I'm left standing in the mess of breakfast with my mouth hanging open.

I don't recognise the people I've come home to. The men I remember aren't here and a terrified part of me is worried they'll never return, just like the old Willow won't either.

Maybe, we're all too broken.

And this cannot be fixed.

# CHAPTER 7
# WILLOW

HOW DO I SAY GOODBYE – DEAN
LEWIS

WITHIN THE WEEK, the time to say goodbye to Lola has rolled around, and she's ready to take her final resting place next to my grandfather, Pops.

Finishing off Arianna's braided hair with a glossy black bow that Killian appeared with, I gently pat her shoulder. She's wearing a simple, black skater dress and shiny new brogues.

"You're done, baby."

Her bottom lip wobbles. "Thanks, Mummy."

"What's wrong?"

"I don't want to say goodbye to Grams."

Turning her around, I pull her into a tight cuddle. "This isn't goodbye, Ari. You'll see her again one day. I promise you."

Her icy blue eyes shine with tears. "Swear it?"

"Swear it." I cross a finger over my heart. "Now go and find Killian and Zach. I have to help Micah for a moment."

Once she's gone, I leave the spare room we've slept in for the last few days and move to Micah's bedroom across the hall. I haven't found the courage to return to our abandoned cabin yet.

We've barely stepped outside, only to reunite with Ryder and Albie yesterday. Everyone else has kindly stayed away to give us the space we needed to adjust and rest after our journey home.

Letting myself into Micah's room, I find the curtains drawn and a lump beneath the covers. I heard him come in late last night after ignoring me for the last few days he's spent in his studio.

My plain black shift dress bunches around my thighs as I kneel on his bed and shake him as gently as possible to wake him up.

"Come on, Micah. You need to get showered. The funeral begins in an hour."

"Not going," he groans.

"You sure as hell are."

Refusing to let him wallow, I peel back the covers then pull on his ankle until he's forced to sit up. My breathing halts. Even with the weight he's lost, his body is carved in lean, muscular lines.

And he's naked.

Completely. Freaking. Naked.

"Where are your pyjamas?" I squeak.

He cracks a yawn. "Don't sleep in them."

Squeezing my eyes shut to offer him a semblance of privacy, I keep tugging on his ankle. "Shower. Now."

"Don't like what you see?"

"I didn't say that."

He eventually agrees to shower after a lot of hungover complaining. When he unsteadily stands up, I'm forced to open my eyes and balance him as we stumble into his en suite bathroom.

"How on earth did it come to this?" he asks groggily.

Leaning him against the bathroom sink, I bypass the bathtub that's full of our shared memories and flick on his small shower in the corner.

"I don't know."

I can feel his eyes on me, hot and searing. His gaze burns me down to the bone and leaves me feeling shaken.

"You look different. When did you cut your hair?"

"Shortly after I left Briar Valley." I check the water's temperature then step back. "Alright, get in. Clean yourself up."

Micah hesitates. "Can you stay?"

Trapped by uncertainty, I nod. "Sure."

"Thanks."

He sneaks past me and climbs into the warm spray, his shoulders curved over like he bears the weight of the whole world on his back. Even showering is a monumental task.

Clicking the door shut, I lean against the wall and let Micah wash in silence. He takes regular pauses to rest on the tiles, exhausted by even the smallest of tasks, obviously feeling like shit.

I get it.

Depression is a killer.

I've been in that dark place myself, where everything is too much and what should be the simplest of tasks, like brushing your teeth or eating, feels like climbing Mount Everest instead.

Flicking the water off, he opens the door, and I hand him a towel from the rack. The tiniest smile blooms on his face at the simple gesture.

"You don't need to do this."

"Would you have showered if I didn't?" I challenge.

"Well, no."

"Then I'll stand here and make you shower every single day until you're able to do it alone. I'm not going anywhere."

"For now," he says sadly.

Unable to argue with him, I head for his wardrobe to look for something suitable to wear, the pad of his wet feet following me. His wardrobe is full of t-shirts and ratty pairs of jeans that won't work.

Micah taps a zipped dress bag. "I wore this to my Aunt and Uncle's funeral. It should still fit."

I'm too afraid to unzip the bag for fear of the grief and sadness that may wash out of it in a tidal wave if I do. Instead, I grab a fresh black t-shirt and a pair of semi-tidy jeans.

"Here. You don't need to be fancy."

Leaving him to get dressed in peace, I find the other two sitting with Arianna in the living room. Killian's wearing his usual flannel shirt and jeans, though he's cleaned up his beard and picked a pair without holes.

Zach is the only one wearing all black with a long-sleeved dress shirt tucked into his tight black jeans. He's trimmed his hair and also shaved for the occasion, lightening his shadow-lined face.

"Micah's just coming."

"Did you get him to shower?" Zach frowns.

"He's showered and getting dressed."

He whistles under his breath. "Neither of us have managed that."

"I didn't exactly ask nicely."

Killian snorts in amusement. "Nice work."

We wait until Micah makes an appearance—pale-faced and contrite—but actually resembling a human being. His twin and cousin both stare at him like he's an alien.

"Shit," Zach curses. "He's alive."

Micah flips him the bird. "Fuck off."

"Little ears!" I scold them.

Laughing to herself in Killian's lap, Arianna is thoroughly enjoying their antics. She missed having them all around to fill the silence.

We filter out of the cabin to join Albie and Ryder outside in the snow. The moment Ryder sees me, I'm pulled into his engine grease-scented embrace for a cuddle.

"You holding up okay?"

"Yeah," I reply flatly.

"You don't need to pretend around me, sweetheart. We're going to get through today as a family. All of us."

His headful of dark ringlets tickle my face as he pulls back to pin me with his warm blue eyes and reassuring smile that match his handsome looks. I've missed my friend so much.

"Promise," he adds.

"Thanks, Ry."

Passing me off to Albie, the silver-haired grump pulls me into another hug. His clear eyes are already covered in a sheen of tears. I've never seen him in a suit before. He looks strange.

"I'm so sorry, Al."

"Me too, kid. Never thought I'd see this day come."

"None of us did."

Interrupting our moment, Arianna is squealing at the top of her lungs as she jumps through the fresh tides of snow that fell last night. Killian stops me before I can shush her shouting.

"She's letting her hair down," he explains simply.

I reluctantly back off. "Alright."

Lord knows, she hasn't had the opportunity to do that of late. Not while cooped up in the cramped space of our old apartment, watching the rain hit against the windows.

We begin the slippery walk into town together. Snow covers everything from the branches of pine and fir trees to the slick, cobbled stones that carve the winding path beneath our feet.

I'd forgotten just how beautiful Briar Valley is. Mount Helena hangs high above us in sharp, jagged points that boast an even heavier dousing of snow, while white-dusted shrubs and trees cloak us in a sarcophagus.

Zach catches up to me and takes my hand in his. "You ready for this? The whole town is gonna be there."

"Not really, but I don't have a choice."

"You don't have to stay for long. Just get the service out of the way, and show your face."

"I can't bail on my own grandmother's funeral."

His fingers clench mine. "You do whatever you need to get through this in one piece. Fuck everyone else and what they need from you. That isn't our priority."

I stop in the snow. "What is your priority, Zach?"

Letting the others pass us, he tilts my chin up and exposes my lips to him. Our mouths meet—hesitantly, tender and exploratory, fuelled by the uncertainty our separation has doomed us with.

"You," he murmurs into my mouth. "It's always been you, Willow."

A tingle runs down my spine. "Does this mean you've forgiven me for leaving?"

"It means that I'm tired of hating you, and I want my family back. We've already lost enough. Today, more than ever, we need each other."

"I need you too," I blurt.

He kisses me again, harder this time. "You've got me, babe. I never stopped loving you. It would take the end of this damn world for that to happen, and even then I'd follow you into the beyond."

Somehow, I smile. "Ditto."

"Then we're on the same page."

Curling into his side, I let him guide me down the steep slopes that descend into the town centre. Familiar faces begin to appear around us, staring at me with varying degrees of shock.

"Willow," Harold bellows while walking into town with his wife, Marilyn. "You're back."

I manage a weak wave. "I'm here."

To my surprise, he captures me in a hug when we rejoin the others. His silvery whiskers tickle my face before he releases me, and Marilyn smacks a wet kiss on my cheek.

"We missed you around here," she explains with a tight smile. "Especially this one."

Harold harrumphs at her comment. "Scared the hell out of me, Willow. Where'd you go?"

"Around," I answer vaguely.

"You back for good?"

Before I can come up with some half-assed answer to get him off my back, the scream of another familiar voice interrupts our reunion.

In the town square, Aalia is standing next to Johan and a tall, dark-haired man with two children. She takes one look at me approaching and freaks out.

"Willow!" she yells.

Aalia races towards me as fast as her skidding snow boots beneath an ankle-length, beaded dress will allow. We collide somewhere in the middle in a sobbing, happy tangle.

"Hi, Aalia."

"I can't believe it's you," she weeps.

I stroke her long brown hair, the coarse strands framing olive-toned skin, deep, almond-shaped eyes and pillowy lips. She's stunning and looks spotless, even with two kids to look after.

Looking over her shoulder, I realise that the man standing with her is holding baby Amie on his hip. It's Walker, the gentleman Katie introduced at my party, with his kids.

We join him in the town square where the guys exchange handshakes with him. Walker nods to me, passing a much-bigger Amie back to Aalia before she starts to cry.

"Willow, right?"

I tentatively shake his hand too. "You remembered."

"Hard to forget that party, it ended pretty spectacularly." His gaze saddens. "Your grams made a hell of a scene with Katie, if I'm remembering correctly."

"She sure did."

"Sorry for your loss."

"Thanks."

Aalia touches my arm. "We mean it, Willow. I know this can't be easy for you. We're here if you need anything."

"I appreciate that."

Arianna has bundled Johan in a hug. The pair are clearly glad to see each other. Aalia kisses her next while Zach fawns over Amie, pulling ridiculous expressions to satisfy her almost one-year-old mind.

We pass countless friendly faces and smiles as we head into Lola's cabin to meet the others. Albie trails at the back of our group, requiring Killian to strong-arm him back inside.

In the living room, Doc, Miranda and Rachel are clustered around the lit, open fireplace, awaiting our arrival. They all give me kisses and hugs, whispering their gratitude that I've returned.

Katie has also made an appearance with her fiancé, Don. She moves to embrace me first. I hug her back to the surprise of the entire room watching us interact.

"You good?" she murmurs.

"Bearing up," I force out.

"I'm here if you need to talk, darling."

"Thank you, Katie."

There's a dull ache behind my eyes already. Plastering on a smile and pretending like I won't run again at the drop of a hat is getting challenging. Worse still, I know from Killian's grimace that he sees through my act.

"Willow," Ryder calls from the doorway. "You remember my boyfriend, Ethan."

*Ah, shit.*

After filtering into the house and brushing snow from his dark blue suit and grey pea coat, Ethan offers me what he must think is an easy smile, but I can see the tension behind it.

"Nice to see you again, Willow."

I swallow the lump in my throat. "You too."

"I've been trying to get in tou—"

"Are we ready to go now?" I interrupt.

Ethan's mouth snaps shut, and understanding filters into his gaze. I offer him the subtlest shake of my head to warn him off from attempting to broach that topic. Not in front of the guys.

"She's in the kitchen," Doc answers. "If you want to say a private goodbye first."

"S-Sure." I glance at Arianna. "Can you guys watch her please?"

Zach nods, an arm wrapped around her shoulders. "We'll wait here."

Before I can escape, Killian steps into the path of the doorway. I'm forced to look up into his bonfire eyes.

"Need me to come with you?" he growls.

"I'll be fine, Kill."

His eyes move lower to my covered up arms. "Sure about that?"

A hot blush creeps across my neck. "Yes."

"Fine. But I'll be right outside."

It feels like an eternity before he eventually moves aside so I can pass him and Ethan by. The burning, hot weight of his gaze follows me all the way into the kitchen where I click the door shut.

My breath seizes.

The coffin has been placed on the kitchen table where nearly a whole year ago, I woke up, penniless and afraid in an unknown place. That was the day I met Lola and discovered the family I always had.

She welcomed me into town with open arms and did absolutely everything in her power to look after me. Even when I pushed her away out of pain and spite, she refused to budge.

I'll never get to thank her for that.

She deserved to know how much she was loved.

Thankfully, the coffin is closed. I take a seat in one of the kitchen chairs and rest a hand atop the smooth mahogany lid, inscribed with her name and the word *Grams*. That's when the tears come flooding back.

"I'm so sorry," I gasp in pain.

The coffin is silent.

"I wasn't here to say goodbye. You begged me to come home, and all I did was ignore you. I'll never be able to forgive myself for that."

Still, she cannot answer me. That sweet, lilting voice, simultaneously filled with the gentlest brand of love and her own personal sense of supreme authority, will never speak to me again.

My hand strokes the coffin's lid. "I need to say thank you for everything you did for me and Arianna. I didn't know what it felt like to be loved or have a real family until I met you."

In my head, I can see her. Twinkle-eyed and acid-tongued. She tuts at me for apologising and pulls me into her cookie-scented embrace for a cuddle that will never be replicated.

"Thank you." I sniff, wiping my tears aside. "Thanks for saving my life and for giving my little girl a home. Thank you for giving us safety and security when we needed it most. Thank you... for being my Grams."

Standing up, I press a kiss on the inscribed metal plaque that's attached to the coffin then force myself to walk away from the woman who saved my life in the absolute darkest of times.

It's the hardest goodbye.

Lola is gone forever.

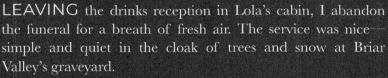

# CHAPTER 8
# WILLOW

I STILL LOVE YOU – BISHOP
BRIGGS

LEAVING the drinks reception in Lola's cabin, I abandon the funeral for a breath of fresh air. The service was nice—simple and quiet in the cloak of trees and snow at Briar Valley's graveyard.

Lola's final resting place is beneath a huge cherry blossom tree that will bloom in the spring in a field of wildflowers that will scent the air when summer returns. Pops lies next to her in his grave.

Outside the cabin, I crunch down the wide porch steps then make a beeline around the back of the cabin to find the quiet vegetable patch where I can have a moment's peace.

I don't expect to find someone already there—his head tilted downwards as he rapidly taps out a text message on his phone.

"Willow." Ethan startles, a cigarette clasped in his other hand.

"Oh… I'm sorry." My feet quickly backtrack. "I… should get back inside."

"No, wait. Please just let me have five minutes of your time."

Stuck between a rock and a hard place, I have no choice

but to grit out a breath and join him. He offers me a cigarette which I politely decline, the acrid smoke curling in the freezing cold air.

"I'm so sorry about your Grams," he sympathises. "She was a good woman."

"She really was."

"You came back to Briar Valley fast."

I spare him a look. "I didn't have much of a choice."

"I know that Katie passed along our information to you. My team is working night and day to bring this human trafficking ring down."

"I wasn't trafficked, Ethan."

"Listen, love." His voice is filled with infinite patience. "We all know what that bastard did to you. Continuing to live in denial is helping nobody, including yourself."

Mouth snapping shut, I sigh through my nostrils. He's right. Out there somewhere, Mr Sanchez still has the freedom to beat, bruise and kill whomever he pleases. I'm allowing that to happen.

If someone else had been able to wield the power to free me, I would've begged for them to save us. For Arianna. For a single second of peace from the pain and abuse. Now I'm allowing others to endure the same thing.

"I want to help," I say in a tiny voice. "But I'm so fucking scared. You don't know him like I do."

"I've spent the past twelve months investigating that son of a bitch and his associates across the globe," he replies grimly. "I know enough to confidently say he'll rot behind bars for the rest of his life."

My laugh is bitter. "He has power and influence in places you can't even begin to imagine. Prison wouldn't hold someone like him. Trust me."

Crushing the cigarette in the snow, Ethan rests a hand on my shoulder. "Trust us, Willow. Sabre Security is the real deal. Give us a chance to prove ourselves to you."

I look up into his hopeful gaze. "How?"

"Talk to us. Tell us your story, and let us help you. All we want is justice for every last person this trafficking ring has hurt. There're a lot of people out there waiting for that."

Caught in a trap of indecision, my heart feels like it's going to explode out of my ribcage and tear itself into a million anxious pieces. The thought of another Arianna being stuck in a mansion seals the deal for me.

"I'll do it."

Ethan clasps my shoulder. "You will?"

"On the condition that your company offers me and Arianna protection," I decide. "We want round-the-clock surveillance until this is all over and Mr Sanchez is behind bars."

"We can do that. I'll need you to come down to London to testify, though."

"Okay."

"I'll let you know a date to come down," he rushes out excitedly. "Want to tell the guys about this, or should I?"

"I guess it should be me."

"You're doing the right thing, Willow. We're going to catch this motherfucker, and you'll finally be able to put this all behind you."

I rest a hand on top of his. "I really hope so."

With another smile, Ethan leaves me to have a moment of privacy. It doesn't last long. The crunch of footsteps approaching soon ends my solitude, and I know who it is without having to look.

The combined warmth of Killian and Zach sandwiches me in. I press my face into Zach's dress shirt and feel Killian's hands move to hold my hips as he nuzzles the back of my head.

With their strength around me, I let my brave face fall aside. I don't need to pretend in front of them that everything is even remotely okay when it feels like my entire world is ending.

"What was that all about?" Killian rumbles.

"Mr Sanchez," I whisper into Zach's chest. "He's being investigated by Ethan's company, and I've agreed to testify to help bring him down."

Zach pushes my shoulders back so he can see my face. "You're kidding? Why didn't we know about this sooner?"

"I heard a couple of weeks ago from Katie. I wasn't planning to do it until now."

Killian squeezes my hips with his two paws. "Why not?"

"Because he's a powerful son a bitch with the money and influence to wipe Briar Valley off the map. You don't mess with someone like that. Not when they know exactly where you are."

His nose teases the slope of my neck as he inhales my scent. Feeling the brief touch of his lips on my skin has my pulse racing, even as the funeral continues in the cabin behind us.

Killian's been a tough nut to crack ever since I returned home several days ago. His anger still bubbles to the surface when I least expect it. But he's trying hard to be fair and hold it at bay.

"Can we get out of here?" Zach complains. "The kid's playing with Johan and the others inside. Everyone else is going to head home soon too."

"I'll go and get Ari," I offer.

"No." Killian traps me to stop my movements. "Aalia will watch them for a bit. We need to talk first."

"About what?"

"Not here. Let's go home."

He pins me against his hard, muscled side and marches me out of the vegetable patch. Zach follows, and we ascend the steep, snowy slope back up to their shared cabin.

Once inside, Killian flicks on lights and locates a bottle of amber-coloured liquid from the cupboard. He sets us up with three glasses then sits down at the breakfast bar.

"This time nine months ago, we sat in this very spot," he begins thoughtfully. "We asked you to stay in Briar Valley, where we could keep you safe. And you agreed."

I linger in the kitchen, afraid to move any closer. "I did."

Zach remains at my back, his breath stirring my curls. "We're asking you the same thing again now. You need to stay now that the funeral's over. This is your home."

"I don't have a home," I answer sadly.

Killian knocks back a mouthful of liquor. "Now that's not true, is it?"

Pushing me forwards with a hand on my lower back, Zach moves me closer to his cousin until I'm again caught between them. But this time, I'm looking up at Killian's impassive expression.

The strong curvatures and razor-sharp angles of his face all could slice deep into my skin and rip me apart, limb from limb. I wouldn't even mind right now. I'm turning into putty beneath his intense gaze.

"Is it?" he demands.

"I... don't know, Kill."

"Yeah. You do."

Grasping my legs, he lifts me up and encourages my legs to wrap around his broad waist. My body can't help reacting on instinct, trained by mere touch alone to react to his strength and domination.

"We can't do this right now," I gasp.

"Right now is exactly when we should be doing this," he counters. "We need to feel alive and appreciate what we've got, baby, because it's fucking special. That has to be protected."

I close my legs around his waist. "I think what we have is special too."

"Good."

Then his mouth is on mine, hot and demanding, as his hands cup my butt. Zach's hard chest meets my back again, and his two hands land on my hips to hold me against his cousin's hardening cock.

Zach's lips graze against the shell of my ear. "That's more like it. My left hand just ain't cutting it anymore."

"Charming." I pepper kisses down Killian's beard-covered neck. "So there haven't been... you know, any other women?"

Abruptly, Killian freezes, his tone turning hard and angry. "Are you kidding me with that shit? You really think we would do that to you?"

"Well, I don't know."

Zach's fingers painfully dig into my hips. "There's been no one. You really think any other woman would match up to you?"

Trailing a hand down Killian's chest, I unfasten his jeans and slip a hand inside his boxers to cup his cock. His eyes darken as I find his length and stroke teasingly.

"Nobody?" I double-check.

He leans in to bite my lip hard enough to draw blood. "Hell no, baby. I couldn't stop thinking about you, even when I hated the living daylights out of you for leaving."

"Seconded," Zach hums in a playful voice.

"Should we take this to the bedroom?"

Killian smirks. "Why? I quite like the idea of seeing you naked and begging in my kitchen."

His hands disappear, leaving me to slide down his body. Killian spins me around so I'm facing Zach again before reaching beneath my dress to rip my panties down in one swift move.

I'm left bare and wet beneath the dress, my pussy contracting with the waves of need that blur my vision. My brief, interrupted session with Zach the other day has done nothing to sate my desires.

"Is our girl wet for us?" Zach wonders.

Killian's hand sneaks between my legs to find my dripping core. "Soaked as always."

Mouth capturing mine, I gasp into Zach's lips as his cousin's fingers slide through my folds, gathering moisture before pushing inside me. His thumb swipes over my clit, causing me to moan.

"So wet and tight," Killian murmurs.

Zach breaks the kiss. "I want a taste."

"Wait your fucking turn, kid. She's mine right now."

"Spoilsport," he mutters.

Spinning me back around before dropping to his knees in front of me, Killian lifts the hem of my dress to expose my bare cunt to him.

His lips graze over my heat, tongue flicking across my sensitive bundle of nerves. I cover my mouth with my hand to silence my moaning.

Each touch feels like the first time I've ever been pleasured by a man. It's been so long, my body is working on overdrive, with every sense dialled to ten.

Killian pushes his finger back inside me, securing his mouth to my clit at the same time. I whimper, the sound filling the cabin as Zach prises my hand away from my mouth.

"Let me hear you," he growls. "I want to know how much you love my cousin eating your pretty little cunt out."

"Fuck," I moan as Killian adds a second finger.

He's stretching me wide, using his digits to work me into a frenzy of need. Zach's erection rubs into my ass while he softly kisses my neck and shoulder. I need to feel them. Touch them. Taste them.

"Please. I'm ready."

"Not yet," Zach purrs. "You have to wait."

"I want you to fuck me, Zachariah."

"Do you now?"

He slaps my backside hard enough to sting. My ass cheek tingles, but it only adds to the cresting wave of pleasure that's on the horizon, rapidly moving closer. It's going to swallow me whole.

"Come all over Killian's face," Zach whispers into my ear. "Then we'll fuck you raw, baby girl."

Tweaking my clit again, Killian moves his fingers even faster. In and out. Circling, swirling, curling deep inside of me to reach that tender spot that forces me to explode.

"Now," he commands.

I cry out as my release hits, spreading come across his face that's still buried between my thighs. He thrusts his thick fingers into me until I have nothing left to give.

Coming up for air, there's stickiness scored across his mouth and lips. He licks up every last drop, making sure not to waste a single bit. The sight of him cleaning his lips makes me wet all over again.

"Is it my turn yet?" Zach whines, still standing behind me.

"Not yet, kid." Killian's eyes blaze with carnal fire as he looks up at me. "Ready for me, princess?"

"Yes," I breathe.

He sits back on his haunches, pulling his massive, bulging cock out of his jeans. "Come and ride me then, baby."

Too excited to think of anything but filling myself with him, I slide free from Zach's grip and position myself in Killian's lap. Zach takes the opportunity to sink down to the floor, pouting in disappointment.

"I'll just watch then," he complains.

I glance over my shoulder at him. "Be with you soon, Zachariah."

"Fucking better be."

"Eyes on me," Killian snaps, regaining my attention.

Holding the base of his dick, he feeds the long, hard length deep into my entrance. The moment he's inside of me, I throw my head back and mewl in ecstasy.

"Fuck," he hisses. "That's it, beautiful. Ride my cock."

I lift myself then slam back down on him with the fuel of

desperation behind me. Killian's dick sheathes even deeper inside my cunt, and the pressure is almost unbearable, I feel so exquisitely full.

With each thrust of his hips rising to meet my movements, we collide in a spectacular fashion, both battling for ownership of the other. I want to brand myself back into the meaty flesh of his heart.

An insecure part of me couldn't help but wonder if there had been anyone else. I wouldn't have blamed them if there was. I was gone for a long time. But an even bigger part of me is satisfied that there wasn't.

They're mine.

All. Fucking. Mine.

Breathing hard, I look back over my shoulder at Zach. He's freed his cock and strokes it, his eyes locked on us fucking mere metres away. When I wink at him, his eyes sparkle with devilish promise.

"Hurry up," he mouths.

Spanking my ass, Killian forces me to look back at him. He ruts into me with fast, frenzied strokes, battering his possession into my soul with the same ferocity that I'm reclaiming his. We're back. Alive. This is where we belong —together.

Without warning, Killian roars through an orgasm, and I feel the hot spurt of his come filling me up. The sensation causes me to fall apart again, stronger this time, crying out my own incandescent relief.

Warmth spreads between us, and the feeling is so exquisite. I'm full of him, coated and claimed. Killian hides his face in my chest as he battles to catch his breath.

"Shit." He swipes his forehead with the back of his arm. "I wasn't expecting to finish so fast."

I kiss the top of his dark-blonde hair. "It's okay. I came too."

"What about me?" a voice drones. "I've waited very patiently."

Standing behind us, Zach's naked from the waist down now and fisting his proud length. I watch as he pumps his cock, the heat burning bright in his emerald eyes.

"Princess," he rasps. "I need you too."

I take his offered hand and clamber off Killian's lap. Zach seizes the zip on the back of my dress then quickly shoves it down. Thankfully, he's too preoccupied with removing my bra to notice my arms.

With the bra discarded, his mouth secures to the hardened point of my left nipple. His teeth graze against the peak, causing desire to flood my veins again. I want him inside of me too.

"Table," Zach grunts.

Walking me backwards, my tailbone connects with the solid lump of wood. I hop up and let him shift me backwards so he can settle between my legs and return his mouth to my chest.

Killian sits on the floor, watching us both as Zach presses up against the slick heat of my entrance. I'm even wetter after my first two orgasms and still dripping with Killian's seed, but Zach doesn't seem to mind.

"I love seeing you soaked in my family's come." He flashes me a wolfish grin.

"Zach," I groan.

"Don't worry, princess. I'm gonna make you feel good."

"Please. Now."

Suddenly, he surges inside of me, burying himself deep and letting out a guttural sound. The table shakes each time he pushes back into my cunt, slam after slam, pump after pump.

His strokes set my soul on fire and leave me to burn into handfuls of ashes. I can't breathe. Think. Feel. Exist. All that I am is contingent on him, and him alone, for these breathless moments.

"So fucking perfect," he praises while hammering into me.

I grip the edges of the table and hold on for dear life. The salt and pepper shakers go flying and smash against the floor, but no one pays any attention. Not even Killian who watches us fuck with interest.

We cause chaos as we slap against each other in a heat-fuelled tangle. Zach moves to clasp my throat. I was hoping he'd pull out his signature move.

There's no other man in the world I'd allow to hold such power over me again, but when Zach does it, I don't mind surrendering to him. In return, he gives me the safety of knowing he'll allow me to breathe again.

His nails dig into my neck as he roughly fucks me into the table, causing pain to slice through me. I relish in it—every satisfying drop of agony that makes me feel alive for the first time in months.

"I couldn't breathe when you left us behind," Zach says gruffly. "You made me feel like this, beautiful girl. Like I was slowly dying with no way out of the darkness."

His grip intensifies. I don't tap out. Not yet. I need to be punished. To feel the pain that I inflicted upon them. To hurt. To suffer. To be reborn in ashes and rise again into the person I previously became here.

"I fucking loved you with everything I had to give," he adds. "And you threw my heart away like it meant nothing to you. How can I forgive that?"

Hand loosening enough for me to answer, I choke out a response. "You can't."

Zach shakes his head. "You're wrong. I fucking can, and I fucking will."

When he releases my neck, the rush of oxygen into my lungs is excruciating. Pain bursts in my chest and my vision swims from the sheer intensity of relief that the end of his torture brings. I could cry.

I'm being forgiven.

Reborn.

Reclaimed.

Slamming his lips against mine, Zach swallows my scream of pleasure as he climaxes at the same time. Our bodies press together in a slick ocean of sweat, blending us into one unidentifiable person.

He pours himself into me, and I'm filled with his hot come. I can feel it spilling over my thighs as he lifts his head to look up at me.

"Jesus Christ."

"You okay?" I laugh breathlessly.

"That wasn't what I had planned on doing today."

"Are you complaining?"

"Not in the slightest."

Killian grabs a sheet of kitchen tissue and tosses it over Zach's shoulder. He looks sheepish as he moves it between my thighs after pulling out, cleaning up the mess he's made all over my legs.

My mind is a puddle of numbness. No other thoughts dare to creep in. All I care about is the treacle-like warmth pumping through my veins, bringing molten happiness and satisfaction.

"Willow?" Zach asks uncertainly.

"Hmm," I reply back.

"We meant what we said before. You have to stay. There's no other option on the table anymore."

My pleasure fades as I reopen my eyes to look at them both. They're wearing identical expressions of desperate, borderline obsessive hope. I fear for my life if I utter anything other than *yes* right now.

"What if he comes for us?" I vocalise my fears.

"Let the bastard fucking try," Killian growls darkly. "I'd

enjoy seeing him face to face. Though he won't have much of a face left by the time I'm done."

"Kill," I gasp.

"Exactly."

Fighting the urge to faceplant, I push Zach's shoulder to make space for my feet to land back on the floor. After cleaning myself up, I ditch the tissue in the rubbish bin and face them both with defeat.

"It's not like I want to run."

"Then stay," Zach demands.

Killian bobs his head in agreement. "Forever."

Between the weight of their combined gazes and the pressure that's reaching a breaking point, I have no choice but to nod. It takes all of my courage to summon that one gesture.

"Fine. But we're moving back into our cabin."

I'm almost knocked off my feet by the pair rugby-tackling me. Sandwiched between them, there's no space to breathe, let alone change my mind. Our fates have been sealed.

We're home.

For good.

# CHAPTER 9
# MICAH
## GONE – NF & JULIA MICHAELS

CHRISTMAS IS NEVER a happy time for me.

It's when my grief hits the hardest.

This year is no different. I wake up to the steady fall of snow the week after Lola's funeral. Things have been quiet around here. The town feels lifeless and empty without her in it.

Working on my latest project—a full-sized watercolour print of St David's Pointe in all its rugged beauty—I ignore the creak of the door opening.

Willow has taken to walking in rather than knocking when I've ignored her. She's determined to pull me out of the depression that's drowning me and has made it her mission to force me to eat.

"Mi?"

*Shit. Zach.*

Ignoring him, I focus on the snow-capped peaks and white-dusted fir trees that line the mountain pass on my canvas. I had planned to gift this to Lola for Christmas. She loved the mountains so much.

Now I'm going to finish this piece of art and destroy it. Just like every other sculpture and painting I've created since her death and left in ruins around me. None of them are good enough anymore.

"Micah. You need to come inside."

"Go away," I say absently.

"Not a chance." Zach stops next to me. "It's Christmas Day, and Willow's struggling enough without Lola here. Get your ass inside before I kick it."

Pain bites into my chest. Fuck. Of course, she's finding today difficult. Lola's barely been dead for two weeks, and already we're all expected to move on with our lives. It's unfair.

"She doesn't need me in there, making everyone even more miserable."

"For fuck's sake," he grumbles. "You're really starting to piss me off, little brother."

"Still just three fucking minutes."

"And you have exactly three seconds to get inside before I lose my shit. Your family needs you. Willow needs you. Stop being such a selfish prick."

My hand stilling against the canvas, I let the brush drop. Shame floods my cheeks. It's easier to hide out in here rather than face the concern that still blooms in their eyes at the sight of me.

Things have been rough.

My recent depressive episodes have taken everything out of me, especially since Lola's death. Today is the first day I've made it to sit at my easel, rather than wallowing or drinking.

"Mi," he urges. "Please. I'm begging you."

I feel my resolve crack. "Alright."

"You'll come inside?"

"If you promise to get the hell off my case already."

"Pinkie swear," he vows.

Putting my tools down, I wipe my paint-slick hands off on a rag and follow Zach out of the cabin. Each step adds to the pressure on my chest. I can't believe I'm letting him talk me into this.

I've never celebrated Christmas. Not even last year when Lola cooked a huge family dinner for us all in her cabin and invited the whole town for carol singing.

I always hide in my studio until it's all over and the memories of my father slink back into their badly sealed box. It's easier that way. Simpler. Safer. I don't bother anyone else with my grief.

The moment Zach opens the cabin door, warmth hits me in the face. The fire has been lit, and Killian is bent over the oven, basting a huge turkey surrounded by roughly cut roast potatoes.

"Jesus," I curse.

Killian glances at me. "Well, I'll be damned. Look who decided to show his face."

He's wearing a flowery apron over his red flannel shirt and blue jeans. Willow's trying hard not to laugh as she watches him cook with a glass of red wine in hand.

Her head immediately turns on a swivel to face me, and she smiles broadly with a look of relief that steals my breath. Fuck. I've missed that stunning, ear to ear smile so much.

"Micah," she breathes.

I offer an awkward wave. "Hi."

"You joining us to eat?" Killian asks.

"He is," Zach answers for me.

Giving me a hard shove, I fall farther into the room. It smells amazing in here. Killian is far better in the kitchen when under Willow's supervision than left alone to his own devices.

"Micah!" Arianna shouts.

In the living room, she's curled up in front of the fireplace with… a fucking puppy. The ball of midnight-black fur is asleep in her arms as she strokes its little belly and ears.

"Who got her a puppy?"

Zach chuckles. "Who do you think?"

We all turn to face Killian, the tips of his ears slowly turning bright-red. "What?"

"A puppy? For real?"

"She needs something to protect her."

"But... a puppy?" I repeat.

"Yes! It's a damn puppy!"

He glowers at us all until we're forced to look away before he whips us with a wooden spoon. It wouldn't be the first time. That stony-faced asshole is a complete softie for Arianna.

"Her name is Demon," Arianna states matter-of-factly.

"Demon?"

"Yes." Her smile is wan. "Because nobody will hurt us if we have a demon by our side. Right?"

"Right, baby." Willow ruffles her hair.

Zach snorts. "Just another normal day in Briar Valley, right?"

Snagging a beer, I quickly put it down again when I catch the look on Willow's face. Her momentary happiness has vanished, and she looks gutted at the thought of me drinking alcohol in front of her.

Instead, I approach her and offer a hand for her to take. She hesitantly puts hers into mine, and I curl our fingers together to pull her closer. My lips brush against her mouth in a tentative whisper.

"Merry Christmas, angel."

It takes a moment for her to kiss me back, her hand lifting to bury in my messy crop of hair. "Happy Christmas, Mi."

"Eww!" Arianna squeals. "Stop kissing my mummy."

"Sorry, squirt."

Pecking Willow's mouth again, I leave her and attack the little monkey instead. She screams and wriggles as I tickle her ribs relentlessly, disturbing the cute ball of fur in her lap.

The puppy is an adorable little thing—she looks like a tiny black Labrador Retriever. Her tongue is lurid pink against her pitch-black fur as she attacks me in a storm of teeth and tongue.

"Alright!" I shout. "Ari, call your attack dog off."

"Here, Demon." She claps her hands together.

The dog finally relents and returns to her owner's lap for more cuddles. I'm left covered in hair and slobber, much to Zach's amusement.

"Well played," he mouths.

I glower at him. "Could've helped."

"I didn't tell you to go to war with a puppy."

Killian steps into the room in his flowery apron. "Grub's up."

I'm not sure I can remove the image of him in an apron from my brain without the assistance of industrial-strength bleach. But Arianna and Willow are clearly loving it based on their bright, happy grins.

Having them here feels weirdly good. I was dreading coming inside and had no intention of eating with them, but with their presence here, the cabin doesn't feel so empty anymore.

Arianna rises to wash her hands, stopping in front of me to grab my wrist. "Come with me, Micah."

I'm dragged over to the kitchen sink to wash my hands, her strength surprising for a tiny seven-year-old. She squirts soap onto my paint-splattered skin then traps my hands between hers to lather them up.

"You're always dirty," she scolds.

"Sorry, kiddo."

"Where have you been? I wanted to practice my finger-painting with you, but Mummy told me to leave you alone."

I swallow the lump in my throat. "I'm sorry. I've been feeling poorly."

"Poorly?" She frowns up at me. "I think you mean sad. I don't know why. You need to be happy, Mi."

Drying off my hands, I boost her up into a hug then settle

her on my hip. "I'll help you with finger-painting tonight. Is that a deal?"

Arianna grins at me. "Deal!"

"Alright then, monkey."

Carrying Arianna over to the table, I sit her down next to Willow. Ryder appears through the front door a moment later, a Christmas hat covering his curls.

He spots me and does a dramatic double take that makes me roll my eyes. Here we go. He's already prepping some stupid remark.

"Holy fuck. He's alive."

"Language," I snap.

Willow jabs a finger at him. "Micah's right. Language."

Scolded, Ryder spreads his hands in surrender and takes a seat at the table. "You rejoining the land of the living, Mi?"

"For now."

"Aren't we blessed."

"You should be."

"Shut up, you rowdy lot." Killian stands over the table with the turkey in hand. "Time to play happy fuckin' families."

"Kill!" Willow shrills in exasperation. "How many times do I have to tell you guys off for your language?"

With a smirk on his face, he places the turkey down on the table amongst veggies, pigs in blankets, cauliflower cheese and a giant jug of gravy that could wash all of Briar Valley away.

"Happy Birthday, Jesus," he declares triumphantly. "Everyone dig in."

Zach doesn't have to be told twice. He's already shovelling a pile of potatoes on his plate as Killian carves up the bird. There's a ridiculous amount of food on the table.

Ryder watches Killian carve with sadness in his eyes, and I know he's thinking of Lola. Her Sunday night roast dinners are a staple of the town's history and part of what makes us one big rowdy family.

"Wait," Ryder blurts.

Everyone freezes.

"We should… you know, raise a toast. To Lola."

Placing the carving knife down, Killian's expression turns solemn. "Yeah. We should."

Everyone lifts their drinks as I pour myself a glass of water from the jug on the table. Willow's gaze shines with appreciation.

"To Lola," Ryder toasts, his beer raised. "Grams, hope you're having a hell of a time celebrating Christmas up there with Pops."

Clinking our glasses together, no one says anything else as we all silently swallow. Words won't cover it. Lola was far beyond them. In fact, words haven't been enough since she left us.

"Mummy?" Arianna whispers.

Sniffling, Willow wipes underneath her eyes. "I'm fine, baby girl. Eat up."

Zach waves a Christmas cracker in my face. "Come on then, Mi. Pull one."

"What are we, five years old?"

"Pull the damn cracker before I hit you with it."

I do as told just to appease him and snort when he loses. Pulling the miniature dice set and paper hat free from the ruined remains, I read out the joke.

"What do you call a boomerang that doesn't come back?"

Zach shrugs. "No idea."

"A stick."

Bursting into hysterical laughter, Arianna doubles over as she giggles maniacally. "A stick! That's so funny."

"That was terrible." Zach wrinkles his nose in disgust. "Alright, let me try one."

Ripping open another cracker, he pulls his own paper hat on before reading the joke inside. His present was a crappy nail file.

"Okay. Who hides in a bakery at Christmas?"

"Who?" Arianna asks excitedly.

"A mince spy."

She stares without understanding. "I don't get it."

"A mince pie." Willow nudges her in the ribs. "Like the dessert?"

Her eyebrows crease in confusion. I guess she didn't have them in Mexico. Part of me wonders what they were both doing this time last year while still living under that bastard's roof.

"Lola made the best homemade mince pies," Killian muses, his eyes filled with sadness. "Even made the pastry herself too."

"With the little stars on top," Ryder chimes in.

"She spiked the cream on the side with whiskey as well." Zach laughs to himself. "That stuff was seriously dangerous."

"I always wanted to see what one of Lola's famous Christmas dinners would be like," Willow adds to their reminiscing. "Now I never will."

"You'll always have a place at this table," Killian says gruffly. "Regardless of where life takes us."

"Thank you, Kill."

Placing her hand on top of his, the pair share a loaded look. Hope sparks deep in my mind. Since agreeing to stick around, Willow's been different.

Part of me wants it to be true, but I'm struggling to believe she'll stay. She's made promises before, yet that didn't stop her from leaving us at the earliest opportunity.

When Ryder's phone chirps, he mutters something about a video call with Ethan and dips outside to answer. Willow's demeanour immediately changes, locking back up and becoming defensive.

"I'm finished!" Arianna licks her plate clean. "Can I go and play with Demon now please?"

"Sure, baby," Willow murmurs.

Arianna vanishes to roll around in the living room with her new best friend, leaving us to finish up in peace. Killian follows Willow's gaze out of the window to where Ryder's taking his call.

"When does Ethan want you to travel down to London?" he asks abruptly.

"Couple of weeks," she sighs.

When I heard about the plan, I was sceptical. Rehashing the past isn't fun for anyone. It's going to be hard on Willow, and she'll be re-traumatised by dragging it all back up.

"What's he gonna do, then?" Zach jumps in.

"I guess I'll testify on record, and they'll use my story as part of their investigation. Mr Sanchez is just one of several big players being looked into by Sabre Security."

"So there's a real chance to bring this motherfucker down?" he asks.

"Not in the way I want to," Killian grumbles back. "He needs a bullet between his eyes, not a prison cell."

"I'm not visiting you in a prison cell," Willow snaps at him. "That's final."

"How are they going to take him down?" I interrupt. "He's in Mexico, right?"

Willow shrugs. "Extradition, I suppose. It's an international investigation, so they have a lot of resources."

The whole thing sounds precarious. I have a lot of respect for Ethan and his work, but from what we know, Dimitri Sanchez is the real deal.

It's going to take a lot to bring that son of a bitch to justice. Perhaps more than Ethan's company can manage. More than any of us can.

"We're going to be here every single step of the way." Zach grasps her hand.

I can feel his trepidation from here. Our twin bond has always been a two-way street, but in recent years, I've struggled to connect with Zach. That changed when Willow came on the scene.

"So what happens now?" I drag them back.

Her eyes flick up to mine. "I'm staying, if that's what you mean."

"For how long?"

"Forever, Mi," Killian drawls.

"I don't believe it."

Pain flares in her eyes. "You don't believe me?"

Scraping my chair back, I stand up. "You made a promise before. I can't fall for that again."

All of their stunned faces watch me leave the cabin, slamming the door behind me. Anxiety is pushing a hot burst of vomit up my throat, aided by last night's vodka binge, but I hold it back.

"Mi!" Ryder shouts.

I don't stop running until I'm safely back in the confines of my studio, away from the pressure of socialising and plastering on a fake smile like the rest of them. As much as I want to trust Willow, I can't do that.

I won't survive her breaking my heart again.

This is for my own self-preservation.

# CHAPTER 10
# WILLOW
## NEED IT – HALF MOON RUN

IT TAKES until New Year's Eve for me to work up the emotional strength to return to our cabin. We've been living out of the guys' spare room since arriving home before Christmas.

While Arianna plays with the other children out in the snow, I begin to move our bags across the road. The cabin door squeaks in protest as I heave it open and step inside.

Thick dust surges up my nose, and the scent of stale air greets me home. The cabin is exactly as we left it—clean dishes next to the sink, paint swatches scattered about.

It's like we never left.

Yet everything is different now.

Closing the door, I make a beeline for the open fireplace and start stacking logs and kindling to light a fire. I can see my breath fogging up the air, it's so cold. Mountain winters are no joke.

With the fire beginning to crackle, I stand up to survey the space. Everything needs a good clean, but it's still the warm, cosy slice of home that I spent months making perfect for our family.

I missed this place.

The apartment never felt like home, it was merely a temporary solution to our overnight homelessness. I dreamed about coming back to this cabin every night for months on end.

When my dreams turned into nightmares, I stopped wishing for the unthinkable, instead resorting to telling myself that letting go was safer. Easier. Less heartache. I was wrong about that too.

After depositing Arianna's suitcase in her pink bedroom, complete with the fairytale-themed mural that Micah painted what feels like a lifetime ago, I move to the master room.

The room causes my heart to twinge. It's dark-wood flooring and deep turquoise walls match the rest of the colour theme—calming and homey. This place is full of so many happy memories.

"Food for thought?" a voice rumbles.

Heart leaping into my throat, I clutch my chest and spin to face Killian behind me. "Where did you come from so quietly?"

He lifts a burly shoulder in a shrug. "Outside."

"I've never heard you move so silently."

Killian inches closer—creeping, stealthier than a coiled snake, into my personal space. The smell of freshly chopped wood and the surrounding forest clings to his green flannel shirt and mud-splattered jeans.

"What are you thinking about?"

My throat catches. "The past."

He cocks an eyebrow. "Our past?"

"All of ours."

Sliding a calloused finger beneath my chin, he ever so gently strokes along the curved length of my jawbone.

"I've been thinking about that too," he admits roughly. "We've lost a lot of time. I don't want to go into next year without knowing we're going to be okay."

Unable to resist the magnetic pull of his raw power,

crackling over me like rapidly spreading flames that sear through my bone and muscle, I surrender.

To him. To us.

To whatever the fuck he needs right now.

"New Year's Eve got you feeling all emotional, Kill?"

He scoffs. "Me? Emotional?"

"Let's skip pretending like you're not capable of it. We both know the truth. For all of your anger, I know that you still love me. I have to believe that."

His breathing halts for a long, painful second. "I do. That's true."

"Then what do you want next year to look like?"

Stroking the backs of his knuckles against my cheek, he slides a hand into my hair and kneads my head. His touch adds to the acute sense of pressure that his fire-lit gaze is causing to build inside of me.

"You, me and the kid," he answers.

"What about the twins?"

"If Micah gets his shit together and I can avoid killing Zach, then sure. But I need us first. If we're broken, I can't look after this family anymore."

"Don't say that, Kill."

"It's the truth," he admits, stroking his hand through my short hair. "I can't look after them if I don't have you here to keep me sane. I'm done living this life alone. I can't do it."

Heart squeezing, I reach onto my tiptoes to wrap my arms around his neck. Killian's hand moves to the small of my back and holds me against his huge, muscled frame.

"You never have to walk alone again," I whisper into his scruff-covered face. "Arianna and I will have protection soon. That means we can stay."

"Am I not enough protection for you, baby?"

I peck his lips, soft and coaxing. "You know that's not what this is about. We need professional security, capable of handling the threat that Mr Sanchez poses."

"My rifle and I looked after you well enough before," he reasons.

"And I know that you always will. This is me trying to look after you as well. That future won't happen for either of us if you're dead."

Killian smirks against my mouth. "That's cute. This motherfucker won't have a head left to talk bullshit with if he comes anywhere near us."

"Alright, big, scary man. That's enough decapitation talk. We should be celebrating the new year."

His smile cracks and fades. I watch the grief filter back into his eyes—infecting the iris and causing his pupil to contract as he retreats from my grasp. It feels like being punched in the chest.

"She should be here," Killian croaks.

I bury my face in his soft shirt. "I know."

"It wasn't her time, Willow. I don't fucking understand this world."

"No one does. All we can hope for is the strength to hold on to each other for as long as we can. Lola would want us to live for that."

"She would, I suppose."

"You know she would."

Tangling our fingers together, I drag his mountainous body back through the cabin and into the living room. It's warming up as the fire roars, spewing heat and the wonderful smell of crackling wood.

Killian lets me deposit him on the rug, and I grab the half-empty bottle of whiskey from the kitchen. It's still there from our last drinking session earlier in the year. We don't bother with glasses and pass it between us instead.

He stares into the flames, warm orange light dappling across his strong, rugged features and lips which are pressed tightly together. I wish I could fathom what goes on in his mind, if only for a second.

"Do you think she's watching us?" he randomly asks. "Up there?"

"In heaven?"

"If that's what you believe in."

"You don't?" I frown at him.

Killian takes a swig and shrugs. "I'm not sure what I believe. Sometimes, it hurts more to think they're watching us and can't let us know they're okay... wherever they are."

I know he's talking about his parents. Killian was barely eighteen when his parents died, and he took the twins under his care not long after, as their father had passed on years before.

"I like to think there's a heaven." I take the bottle from him and sip. "Pedro would be there too, watching over us. And my... my baby. I have to believe they're safe somewhere."

"Shit," Killian curses. "I'm sorry, Willow. I didn't think."

"No, you're fine." I bump our shoulders together. "You've lost people too. Even more than I have. We can talk about this stuff."

Clearing his throat, he stares deep into the fire. "I just... I miss them. Every goddamn day. We never got the chance to say goodbye, now Lola's gone too."

Resting my head on his shoulder, I snuggle closer to try to offer him some comfort. Even if there's nothing I can ever do to fix the cruelness of grief and sudden loss.

"They're here," I murmur through my clogged throat. "Even when we can't see them, they're here. You've never been alone."

"Even when I feel like it?"

"Especially when you feel like it, Kill."

Resting his head on top of mine, I hear him drag in a ragged breath. I don't want to move an inch or cause him to run away. Not now. His shields are down for the first time since I returned.

We sit in silence for what feels like hours, the only sound

our breathing and the crackle of flames. The bottle is empty by the time Killian finally shifts and speaks again.

"I'm so fucking glad you're home."

"Yeah," I rasp. "Me too."

"Promise me you'll never leave again?"

"You know I won't make a promise that I can't keep. I will always do what's necessary to protect my daughter. But I have no intention of leaving after I've spoken to Ethan's team."

Killian moans in displeasure. "Fuck, I'd forgotten about that. I can't believe we're going to the biggest damn city in the entire country... voluntarily."

"Stop your grumbling. It isn't a field trip."

"Feels like it," he complains.

"I can go with Zach and Ryder. You don't have to come."

"Like hell. I'm coming."

The creak of footsteps approaching ends our solitude. There's a second's warning before the door to the cabin slams open, and Arianna comes flying in. Her face is a mask of excitement.

"We're home!" she yells.

Aalia follows her in, wearing a blazing smile. "Sorry, Willow. She was missing you."

I throw my arms open. "Come here, baby."

Running towards me, Arianna leaps into my arms. I fall backwards from the weight of her growing body and end up landing across Killian's lap. He peers down at us both in amusement.

"You're getting too big, peanut."

"No, I'm not," Arianna protests. "I need to be as big as you, Giant!"

"Good luck with that," he snorts.

Untangling myself, I dump Arianna in Killian's lap then stand up to hug Aalia. She declines the offer of a drink, too busy fussing over me and pinching my still-gaunt cheeks.

"It's New Year's Eve," she declares grandly.

"So?"

"You need to come and celebrate with us."

"I don't kn—"

"I insist," she cuts me off. "You can't just sit here and drink alone. Come for dinner in a couple of hours. I'm sure Walker would like to get to know you. He and the girls are living in our spare two bedrooms."

"How's that going?"

Her smile broadens. "Very well."

Snickering behind me, Killian seems to be in on the joke. It takes me a moment to catch on to the light dusting of pink across Aalia's olive-toned skin. Oh. It's like *that*, apparently.

"You're… enjoying his company?" I laugh.

She splutters. "I never kiss and tell."

"Sure, sure. Looks like I missed all the drama while I was away."

"Something like that." Aalia winks. "Dinner! Two hours!"

Breezing out of the cabin, she leaves us laughing to ourselves. Walker seemed very nervous when we first met, so I'm glad he's come out of his shell and that Aalia has found someone.

"How long has that been going on for?" I spin around.

"Few weeks now," Killian answers while tickling Arianna's ribcage. "It wasn't overnight. Walker's still pretty mistrusting of us all after all he's been through. Widowed, I hear."

"Poor guy. Recently?"

"Couple of years."

Briar Valley has a way of collecting the lost and broken people in life. It sounds like Walker and his two daughters are no different. I hope they can find some peace here.

"You up for dinner?"

"Got no other plans," Killian replies. "Zach's helping Ryder in the garage, and Micah's in the studio. Doubt he'll come."

The mention of Micah's name causes my heart to thud

against my ribcage. He hasn't spoken to me since storming out on Christmas Day, no matter what assurances I give.

"Stop," he interjects.

"Huh?"

"You're worrying about him again. I can tell by the look on your face. Micah will come around eventually."

"How long until he forgives me?"

Placing Arianna down on the rug, Killian approaches and pulls me into a bear hug. "That I can't answer. I'm sorry."

"Not your fault."

He chuckles. "For a change."

With his bearded chin resting on my head, I let out a long sigh. He and Zach have come around, slowly but surely. I never expected Micah to be the one to hold a grudge for the longest.

But in many ways, I've hurt him even more than them. I took his trust and ground it into pathetic pieces after he dared to open himself up. That can't be forgotten overnight.

"Where's Demon?" I pull out of his hug.

"Eating dinner across the road," Arianna answers as she rolls around on the floor. "She was hungry after playing all afternoon."

"Let's go and find her, yeah?"

"Okay!"

Arianna leaps up and zips from the cabin in a blur of energy. Even after running around with the other children, she's still borderline hyperactive, and has been ever since we returned.

With her gone, Killian sneaks up behind me and bands his arms around my waist. His hand finds my wrist and tugs on the long sleeve, a single fingertip skating underneath the fabric.

"When are we gonna talk about this?"

I suppress a shudder as he gently strokes over the rigid lump of a new scar. "We don't need to discuss it."

"I disagree very fucking strongly with that."

"And I'm allowed to have some privacy," I argue. "We all coped in our own ways the last few months."

"So you're not going to do it again?"

"Just leave it alone."

"I can't do that," he retorts.

"You don't have a choice."

Pulling his arms from my body, I step out of his embrace and follow in Arianna's footsteps. I don't have an answer for him right now, and I refuse to lie anymore.

I wish I could say that I'm done with it, but the urge is still there in the background. It flows with each breath that I take, and it's only a matter of time before that overtakes everything again.

# CHAPTER 11
# WILLOW
JUST LIKE YOU – NF

SLICK SWEAT COVERS my palms as I clench and unclench them in my lap. The hum of Killian's truck cuts through the blare of horns and humming traffic all around us.

"Motherfuckers," Killian snarls.

"Take a breath, cuz." Zach laughs at him. "This is London. Traffic is pretty much guaranteed."

"It's everywhere!"

"Your point being?"

"Shut the fuck up, kid. You're not helping."

"Kill," I hum anxiously. "Please calm down. I'm struggling to keep it together as it is."

Glancing into the rearview mirror, he takes one look at my pale, clammy face and shuts up. We made the tough call to leave Arianna in Briar Valley while we left Wales and travelled into England's capital city.

I didn't want to risk anyone spotting her and raising the alarm. We've already seen that Mr Sanchez has allies in this country—the incident with Mason several months ago proved that.

"Sorry," Killian mutters. "Where is this place anyway?"

"Ethan said we'll know it when we see it," Zach replies, the window open as he lights a cigarette. "Sabre HQ is huge."

Crawling through the huge line of traffic, he's finished his cigarette by the time we arrive in an intimidating business district. Massive skyscrapers kiss the clouds all around us.

The buildings are made of sleek panels of glass and polished steel, forming monstrosities that carve the city's landscape. Killian's grip on the wheel tightens. He really hates this place.

All around us, men and women run all over the place in their smart business wear and sleek high heels. No one walks at a casual pace. We're far from the slow living of Briar Valley.

"That's the place." Zach whistles. "I recognise the logo from the news."

The biggest building of them all lies up ahead in huge, tinted proportions. It stretches up so high, I can't see the top floor, surrounded by low-hanging London clouds.

A logo is proudly displayed above the sprawling entrance steps, lined with dark-clothed security agents in black sunglasses. It's an intricate thumb print, the text below pronouncing the words *Sabre Security.*

"We're here," Killian declares.

"Fuck me," Zach exclaims. "It's even bigger than I imagined."

Following the signs into the parking garage, we're screened by security and given a thorough checking over before we're allowed through. Ethan has our names on a visitor's list in preparation.

Killian curses constantly while attempting to park the truck between two slick sports cars, both worth more money than we'll ever see in our lifetimes. It takes him three attempts.

"Bastard thing," he hisses. "Let's get this over and done with. I want to get home before the next snowstorm blows in."

Zach claps him on the shoulder. "We need to worry about one thing at a time. Ethan's booked us a hotel for the night."

Cursing again, Killian climbs out in a storm of annoyance. He really is a grumpy son of a bitch today. I wish I could blame him.

"Willow!"

Walking through a rear entrance door, Ethan waves us over. He's whispering into the comms slotted in his ear when we reach him.

"Yeah, they're here. Alright, Hud. We can handle the interview if you need to head off early to be with Brooklyn."

Finishing up his conversation, Ethan offers us a round of handshakes. Killian's silently sizing him up with a scowl on his face.

"Sorry for that," Ethan apologises. "You've caught us on a busy day. A friend of ours has gone into labour."

"Bad timing?" I laugh nervously.

"Not at all. Thank you for coming in, Willow. We're glad you're here. Let's go inside."

He waves us in and scans his security pass to let us inside. That's where my jaw drops. Led through a service corridor, the reception we step into is breathtaking.

A seemingly endless ceiling stretches into the heavens, while sleek floors and glass walls brighten the space. Much like outside, people buzz around in all corners.

Some talk on phones while others talk to one another, exchanging whispers and heated conversations. There's an intense hum of energy from everyone amidst the hustle and bustle.

"We're going to head upstairs and meet the rest of my team first," Ethan advises. "Then we'll have a chat about the investigation and your role moving forward."

Without thinking, I take both Zach's and Killian's hands. I need them to hold on to me right now so I don't run out of here screaming.

The elevator ride is full of tense silence until we arrive on a high level, the floor-to-ceiling windows offering a panoramic view of London's impressive skyline.

Holding the door open for us, we're ushered into a big, plush office, complete with a dark-wood conference table, coffee trolley and several people whose heads turn in our direction.

"Everyone, this is Willow Sanchez." Ethan gestures towards me. "And Killian." He waves again. "Along with his cousin, Zach."

We all smile tightly, feeling the tension and pressure. There are two men and one woman sitting inside, all in their mid to late thirties and wearing the same all-black clothing as everyone else.

"Warner." Ethan points at the salt and pepper haired man. "This is Hyland." He includes the huge, boulder-like man in his wave. "And this is Tara. We're the Anaconda team."

The woman offers me a wave. Her long, light-brown hair is tied up in a no-nonsense ponytail that shows off her young face and cool, professional smile.

"Sit down, guys. Help yourselves to a refreshment."

After introductions, we take our seats and a round of coffees. Ethan sets himself up at the head of the table to preside over us all.

"There are several teams at Sabre Security operating under different divisions," he explains. "We're one of the investigating teams. It's a big operation."

"Looks like it," I croak.

"Our team has been investigating this human trafficking ring for over a year now, stretching from here to the United States, Mexico and Brazil. We're looking at a massive international gang."

My throat thickens with the surge of sickness threatening to rise up. I swallow hard, washing it down with a swig of coffee. Their eyes are all on me, even subtly when they think I'm not looking.

"How many victims have you tracked down?" Killian asks in a hard, angry voice.

"Officially? Over forty-five," Warner replies. "Along with another thirty who refuse to go on record about what happened."

"We suspect the real number to be in the tens of hundreds," Tara adds with a shudder. "There are more people out there."

Sliding my hand beneath my sweater sleeve, I stroke my fingertips across the fresh cut I slashed into my wrist this morning. I had to hide my face in a towel as I sobbed so Arianna didn't hear.

Those women out there are me. We're the same person, our blueprints reproduced and reprinted across the globe, over and over, for other people's sick pleasure.

No matter what I say or do here, I can't take back the pain and bloodshed I know they've suffered. Intimately. The memories are still raw in my mind despite a year passing since I escaped.

"Willow?" Hyland prompts.

I look up at him. "Yes?"

"We understand that you've requested protection. Our team will be returning to Briar Valley with you to ensure your security."

"All of you?"

"Myself and Hyland," Tara supplies.

"I'll remain here with Ethan and the other teams to continue the investigation," Warner finishes. "We'll get the job done."

"I… feel bad," I admit in a low voice.

Killian rubs my shoulder. "Why, baby?"

"I'm taking them from their jobs and the investigation."

"Our number one priority is to keep you safe," Ethan offers. "That matters above all else, including the case."

Absently rubbing my chest, I nod and force a breath. "I'll tell you everything I remember about Mr Sanchez and his men. He had a lot of people working for him, and other business associates."

"Any information you can give us will help." Warner nods encouragingly. "We want to identify these people to ensure everyone involved is brought to justice."

All drawing out laptops and notepads, the entire room's focus is on me as they start a voice recorder. Sipping more coffee, I dive into a description of Mr Sanchez's Mexico mansion and all its staff.

I get halfway through before it becomes too much. Just describing the marble floors and dark, brocade wallpaper brings up a plethora of awful memories, dipped in blood and tears.

"We understand that Dimitri Sanchez has a personal security team." Ethan slides a file across the table to me. "Tell me, do you recognise this individual as one of them?"

Opening the file with shaking hands, I almost throw up at the photograph inside. Pedro's face is staring back at me in printed pixels, displaying every last smile line and twinkle in his eyes.

"P-P-Pedro," I gasp.

"He's been missing for over a year," Ethan says sadly. "We've also heard from Mexican authorities that his family disappeared at the same time he did."

*Buddum.*

*Buddum.*

*Buddum.*

All I can hear is my heartbeat roaring in my ears, drowning out the rest of his words. I stare down into his familiar, love-filled eyes. A gaze that soothed me in the darkest of times.

He died alone. In agony. Knowing that his actions had cost him, and his family, their lives. I walked away from that mansion, but none of them did. I have to live with that.

"I... excuse me," I blurt, my chair scraping back. "I'll be right back."

Zach tries to snag my sleeve as I pass, but I flash him a warning look and burst out of the room alone. I need a moment to take a breath without all of their eyes weighing me down.

Scanning the corridor, I spot the sign for a bathroom then run at full speed to escape. The stall door doesn't even shut behind me before I'm on my knees and retching into the toilet bowl.

Over and over, acid spews up from my stomach and splatters against the pristine ceramic as I sob my eyes out. I can't even stop when the bathroom door creaks open.

"Are you okay in there?" a female voice asks.

Uncaring of how gross it is, I rest my sweaty head on the toilet lid and suck in a breath. "Not really."

"Breathe in through your mouth, so you can't smell it," she advises kindly. "Want me to get you some water?"

"I'm f-fine."

"You don't look it."

The sound of a tap running precedes her reappearance at the stall doorway. A wet paper towel is pressed against my forehead as she cleans the sweat from my face.

"That's it, deep breaths."

She sucks in a loud breath then blows it out for me to copy. Following her lead, I make myself recreate her exaggerated breathing to free up my lungs. The shadows at the edges of my vision begin to fade as each intake relieves some of the pressure.

"Give me your hand, I'll help you up."

"Th-Thanks."

Putting my faith in the complete stranger, I let her drag

me to my feet and flush the toilet. Turning to face her, I realise she's a similar age to me, at least in her mid-twenties.

Her mousy brown hair is long, almost brushing her lower back, framing flawless blue eyes that compliment her porcelain skin and slightly crooked nose.

Something about her makes me pause. Maybe it's the haunted look in her crystal-clear eyes. Or maybe it's the darkness wrapped around her features that seems to call out to my soul.

"I'm so sorry you had to witness that," I choke out.

She shrugs. "I've seen worse. You looked like you needed a friend. I'm Harlow."

"Willow."

"Our names are kinda similar, huh?"

I move to the sink to wash up. "I guess so."

"That means we were meant to meet each other in here," she jokes.

"I guess so."

"You're not Willow Sanchez, are you?"

"You know me?" I look up at her.

Harlow smiles reassuringly. "Nothing bad, I swear. Ethan told me you were coming in today. I was hoping to catch you at some point."

"Do you work here or something?"

"Not really," she says mysteriously. "It's complicated. I wanted to say hi and see how you're getting on with the team, but it seems my question has been answered already."

"It's going okay, I just freaked out a bit," I admit with a short laugh. "It's intense, going on the record in front of strangers."

"I've been there." She holds my gaze. "It's the hardest thing you'll ever do, but I promise, this is the right thing for everyone."

Her voice tells me that she understands, perhaps more than anyone has ever been able to before. I can see it in her eyes, the familiar pain and heartache mixed in with that darkness.

She's been where I am. I can't fathom how or why I know, but that kind of trauma reveals itself to fellow survivors. We can see each other's pain for what it is as clear as day.

"How did you do this?" I ask honestly.

Harlow offers me a hand. "Not alone."

Even though she's a stranger who I barely know, I trust her. The shadows in her eyes are so familiar, I can almost taste them, but there's light too. It clings to every part of her—the glimmers of hope.

With a deep breath, I take her hand. "Thank you."

She winks. "Don't mention it."

Chest still tight, we exit the bathroom together and head back down the corridor. Harlow refuses to release my hand, holding on tight so I don't fall over in my dizziness.

"You do this on your terms, though." She squeezes my hand. "Don't let them push you to your breaking point. Take another break if you need it."

"You're suspiciously well-versed in how all this works."

"Personal experience," she admits.

"As part of this investigation?"

"No, not this one. My case wrapped up around six months ago."

"Then why are you still here?"

Her lips twist in a rueful smile. "The owners of the company keep me around. For now."

I have a feeling this is an inside joke that I'm not privy to. I've yet to meet Ethan's bosses, but if they're anything like this place, they must be intimidating.

Outside the door, I almost freak out again. Harlow stops in her steps before the panic attack can fully take hold and places her hands on my shoulders so she can encourage me to breathe again.

Dragging in deep gulps of air, I make myself remain calm.

It's just a room full of people. I've faced far worse and survived. Blood. Pain. Death. Torture. I can tell my story and live through it again.

"Remember, you've survived 100 percent of your worst days," she says with a knowing wink. "You sure as hell can survive this."

"Shit." I laugh shortly. "Maybe we *were* meant to meet each other today, Harlow."

Her hand squeezes my shoulder. "I don't believe in maybes anymore. Only fate."

"Is that so?"

"Doesn't everything happen for a reason?" she challenges. "We're here right now because we're supposed to be."

"I'm not sure that I believe in fate."

Harlow shrugs. "Then believe in yourself. It's the same thing. Believe in the fact that you'll get through this because you have to."

Blinking away tears, I rest my hand on top of hers. "Thank you, Harlow. I'm glad we bumped into each other."

She smiles. "Me too. Ready to do this?"

"As I'll ever be."

## CHAPTER 12
# ZACH

MAN OR A MONSTER – SAM
TINNESZ & ZAYDE WOLF

I DON'T KNOW who is more traumatised by the day's events—Willow, Killian or myself. Hearing every last horrific, blood-slick detail of her kidnapping, trafficking and abuse has left me gutted.

But not just gutted.

That word can't adequately describe how I'm feeling right now. I am incandescent with rage unlike anything I've ever felt before. Fury. Hellfire. Righteous anger that'll consume us all if I'm not careful.

That son of a bitch, Dimitri Sanchez, targeted Willow as a vulnerable teenager, trafficked her across the globe then stuck a ring on her finger to make it all seem legal to the public eye.

He locked her in a mansion and spent a decade raping, beating and emotionally and physically abusing the living daylights out of her. And he got her pregnant. Young. Before abusing his kid too.

*Son of a fucking bitch!*

"I need a drink," I grumble.

Ethan claps me on the shoulder as we walk on the hotel's plush carpet. "You've got the suite for the night. After today,

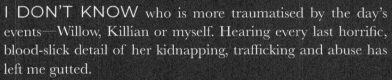

you certainly deserve to rest up, and take full advantage of the room service."

"You can bet your ass we intend to."

He chuckles under his breath. "I'll send a car tomorrow morning. We want to ask a few more questions before discussing Willow's protection moving forward."

"Sounds good. Willow needs a break."

"Make sure she gets some rest, Zach."

Both of us are studying her slumped shoulders and lowered head in front of us. Willow is exhausted after almost four hours of cross-examination and evidence documentation.

After her breakdown, she knuckled down and got through it like a motherfucking trooper. An incredible goddamn warrior princess far more capable than I've ever given her credit for.

Now Killian is carrying her in his arms back to our hotel room. I think it makes him feel better to hold her close like a child, offering the only shred of comfort and protection he can after hearing all she's endured.

"Alright, this is yours." Ethan hands me the key card outside our hotel room. "See you first thing. Thanks again for today, Willow."

She lifts her head to spare him a glance. "No problem."

"Your testimony is truly invaluable. We can't thank you enough."

"I just want to see him brought down," she says tiredly. "That's all."

"We're going to do our very best to do exactly that." Ethan offers her a reassuring smile. "Sleep. We'll talk more tomorrow."

With a final friendly wave, he disappears back down the corridor and into the elevator. We unlock the hotel room door then step inside the fanciest room I've ever seen.

*Fuck.*

*Is this how the other half live?*

Thick, silver-speckled grey carpets span the massive floorspace, split into sections that organise the suite. There's a sprawling king-sized bed covered in gold-laced sheets and a fully-stocked bar.

Several over-stuffed sofas surround a glass coffee table topped with perfect red roses, and a quick peek in the bathroom reveals a clawfoot tub big enough to fit a whole family.

"Fucking fancy shit," Killian mutters as he sets Willow down. "I miss home."

"It's been twelve hours," she points out.

"Twelve hours too long."

I roll my eyes. "Caveman here can't be without his axe for too long. The world will implode if he is."

Killian flips me the bird. "Shut up, kid."

"Love you too, cuz."

"Love isn't the word I'd use to describe how I feel about your annoying backside."

"Ever the charmer, Kill."

Shaking her head at us both, Willow mumbles about using the bathroom and vanishes. The sound of the shower flicking on follows, then her quiet sobbing in the falling water.

"Should we go in there?"

Killian shrugs. "She needs time. That was rough going."

"I hate the thought of her going through this shit alone," I grit out. "She survived that hell on her own. That doesn't mean she has to now."

"You want to go in there and figure out what the fuck to say after what we just heard?"

Defensive, I square up against him. "Maybe I do."

"Then be my guest. I don't have any words right now."

As much as I feel like a deer caught in the headlights, and words are failing me too, I won't sit out here while Willow suffers. She deserves better than that from us, regardless of the past.

Mind churning with ideas, I snap my fingers. "What about the ring? We still need to ask her."

All he does is stare at me—a thick, blonde eyebrow raised in an incredulous look. Fine. It may not be my brightest or most romantic idea, but at least I'm trying.

Killian lowers his voice. "Right now? You really want this to be her memory of that moment?"

"I'm just fishing here. I want to make her feel better."

"The thought of spending the rest of her life with a shit-for-brains twat like you isn't going to improve her day."

"Hey, I don't have shit for brains."

"Could've fooled me."

"I just have no brain at all, apparently."

He breaks out into quiet, rumbling laughter. "That I don't disagree with. Terrible idea, Zach."

"Alright, back off. It was just a thought."

When the sound of Willow's hiccupping sobs intensifies, Killian's blank façade breaks. He scrubs a hand over his beard and snarls under his breath with the same fury that's eating me up.

"She's in pain, and I can't fucking fix it. Again."

Gingerly approaching, I rest a hand on his shoulder. "This isn't on you. We always knew that testifying for Ethan was going to be messy."

"Still," he harrumphs. "I can never bloody fix it, can I? Whenever she's hurting, I can't do a goddamn thing."

"None of us can, Kill."

"That really doesn't make me feel better."

Unable to give him a single crumb of comfort, I pat his arm and decide to hell with it. He can sit here and feel sorry for himself all he likes. I'll step up and be whatever the hell Willow needs right now.

She's back in the trenches of her past, and I won't let her wallow in the darkness alone. Someone has to reach on down there and yank her up before she drowns herself.

Letting myself into the steam-filled bathroom, I can see the soft, rounded slopes of her curves through the moisture-flecked glass. She's still crying in the shower but quieter now.

"Willow?" I call out.

Her sniffling stops. "Zach?"

"I'm coming in. Make some space."

Quickly peeling off my tight blue jeans and long-sleeved tee, I step into the walk-in shower and pull her straight into my arms. She feels like a tiny, trembling wreck against my bare chest.

"I'm here," I whisper into her wet hair. "Right here, babe. You aren't alone."

Her face buries in my pectorals, hidden from sight. I hate to admit that I know the sight of her swollen eyes and devastated smile a little too well now. We've been through hell together over the last year.

And something tells me that hellish ride to the depths of Lucifer's fires is only just beginning. What Willow did today will change everything—for the better or worse, I can't yet decide.

The race is on.

We're coming for Sanchez.

Rocking Willow beneath the warm spray of water, I stroke a hand up and down the length of her spine. She's managed to put some weight on since returning, but not enough to make up for what she's lost.

Studying her small curves, my eyes catch on a bright-red slash that causes an invisible hand to squeeze my windpipe. Taking a closer look, I realise what I'm looking at.

"Uh, babe?"

Willow hums tiredly in response.

"Mind telling me what the fuck this is all about?"

I'm holding her wrist in my hand, gently rotating it to show the fresh, jagged slash across her milky skin. It's layered on top of scars—thin, silvery scars that weren't previously there.

I've seen these marks before. Only once. My brother bears the same scars on his skin. The alcohol wasn't always his worst coping mechanism, and the fear I once felt for him is rushing through me now.

"It's n-nothing," Willow protests.

"Nothing? Doesn't look like *nothing* to me," I spit back.

She tries to pull her wrist from my grip, but I tighten my hold and hold it in plain view. My eyes won't tear from those damned silver spikes of pain and self-inflicted fury that blemish her skin like lightning strikes.

"How long has this been going on for?"

Her throat bobs. "A… A few months. I wanted to tell you—"

"But you didn't," I interrupt.

"I promised Killian that I'd stop." Tears well in her eyes again. "He's going to kill me."

"Killian fucking knows?"

Anger pulsates through my veins. I'm not an angry person. My cousin holds enough hatred for the world for the both of us. But this shit… This is too much. He should've told me.

"I'll kill him!"

"Zach," Willow protests, grabbing my bicep. "Just take a breath. It's one tiny little cut. I needed something this morning, and it's nothing serious."

"Nothing serious? You're cutting yourself, babe! You've been doing it for months."

The tears are now coursing down her cheeks in shimmering rivers of shame. Making myself stop and breathe through my fury, I bring a hand up to cup her cheek.

My thumb tenderly brushes over her skin, smoothing the tears aside. "I'm sorry, gorgeous girl. I just can't deal with the thought of you doing this to yourself."

"It was only a few times, Zach."

"I can see for myself that isn't true."

"But... I had stopped." She gnaws on her bottom lip. "I wanted to. For Ari and for myself. Today just got the better of me. It was a one-off thing."

I stroke my thumb down to her lips, caressing the soft, pillowy swells. "Promise?"

She lets me probe her mouth with my finger, the tip of her tongue swiping over my thumb. With her wide, hazel eyes staring up at me like bottomless pools of freshly brewed coffee, I can't stay mad.

Even though I want to scream.

Smash. Rave. Shout.

Willow doesn't need rage right now. Killian's or mine. She needs compassion and understanding. If anyone knows how to love someone on the verge of self-destructing, it's me. I'm a self-taught expert.

"Promise," she murmurs around my thumb.

Moving my hand to her hair, I ease my fingers into the wet strands to massage her scalp. She leans into my touch, her mouth parted on a low, needy whine. My other hand moves to squeeze her hip.

Despite everything, the feel of her slick, wet body turns me on. I can't help it. I'm magnetised to her like a moth to a flame, unable to resist the tempting glow of light.

"Willow," I say throatily.

Her chest pushes into mine, the hardened points of her nipples teasing my skin. "Yes?"

"I need you right now, babe. I'm sorry, but I can't think straight."

Her leg hitches up to catch on my hip. "I need you too. Make me feel good again."

"Are you sure? After today?"

"Please."

*Dammit.* That word on her tongue has always been my downfall. Powerless against her siren's call, I bring my hand between her legs then skate upwards. Her pussy is already soaking wet.

"Fuck, babe. You're so wet already."

"I'm sorry."

My grip on her tightens. "Don't you dare fucking apologise to me for that. I'm going to make you feel good, okay?"

Nodding obediently, she lets me seize her mouth in a firm kiss. Her lips are like molten caramel against mine—sweet and velvety soft. God, she's perfect. So fucking incredible, I can hardly take it.

We continue to kiss in the steam-filled shower, our bodies slick and sliding against each other. With her leg hooked up on my hip, I have the space to explore her cunt, teasing her clit before sliding a finger deep inside of her.

Willow gasps in pleasure as I curl it slightly to stroke against her sensitive nerve endings. Her warmth beckons me in, so I add a second finger to stretch her tight cunt wider.

"That's it," I encourage, fucking her with my hand. "Let me stretch this tight little pussy nice and wide before I fuck you."

"Jesus, Zach. You have the filthiest mouth."

"You love it."

Willow's blush is evident, even in the hot shower. "I do."

Working her into a frenzy, I pull my hand away before she can finish and bring my fingers to her lips. Willow opens her mouth, willingly sucking them in to taste her own tang on my skin.

"Perfect," I praise, letting my fingers glide against her tongue. "Now a little deeper, babe."

Relaxing, she lets me slide the fingers farther into her mouth. I want to see how much she can take. She needs a distraction right now, and I'm more than willing to give it.

Pushing my fingers towards her throat, she takes them all the way in before gagging a little. When I pull them out, they're coated in strings of saliva that stretch from her gorgeous mouth.

"Such a good princess, aren't you?" I whisper, smearing her saliva across my thumb pad. "What if I pushed my cock deep into that perfect throat of yours now?"

Rather than answering, Willow sinks to her knees. She takes my cock with both hands then sucks it into her mouth, causing me to throw my head back as I'm hit by a wave of bliss.

"Shit, babe. You take it so fucking good for me."

Bobbing on my length, she hollows out her cheeks to increase the pressure. Each suck causes my balls to tighten. Her mouth is a warm, heavenly prison wrapped around my cock.

Gathering her short hair into my left hand, I hold it tight and guide her movements until I'm roughly fucking her mouth. I want to fuck the despair from her mind and leave no space for it to return.

Each thrust into her mouth feels blissful. She's an absolute pro. Her mouth tightens and loosens at the perfect moments with tiny little rotations.

Cupping the back of her head, I push deeper into her mouth, feeling the tip of my cock press against her throat. She struggles a little but doesn't make a move to push me away, continuing to suck instead.

"That's it, gorgeous girl. Keep going."

I want to bury myself in her cunt and fuck her until she cries out my name for the whole hotel to hear. This is how wild she makes me. Fucking reckless. Out of my mind with lust.

My heart beats in a rapid staccato as my balls tighten, ready to burst. She's driving me right to the edge. My legs are trembling, and I fight to control myself, overcome by tingles zipping up and down my spine.

Around her, I can never think straight, let alone when she's on her knees in front of me, those stunning hazel eyes looking up at me through thick, luscious black lashes.

Seconds before I shoot my load down her pretty throat, I still her movements and slide out. She licks her glistening lips and peers up at me with an innocent look.

"Are you going to fuck me now?"

"Yes, babe. Stand up, and bend over for me like the good little slut you are."

"Yes, Zachariah."

"There's a good girl."

Eyes flaring with desire, she follows my orders and presses her hands to the shower wall. Her pert, perfect ass is pushed out as her spine curves, giving me full access to her pussy.

Pumping my cock, I line myself up with her then slam into her. I just need to feel her clenched around me. Willow cries out, louder than the shower can possibly drown out.

I pull out and surge back into her again, over and over, letting her know that she can't expect sweet and gentle. Not after today. I'm too fucking angry to look after her right now.

But we need this.

Both of us.

The rough, painful collision of two angry people fucking out their frustrations at the world. Her brokenness is only enraging me more, and I can't do a damn thing to fix it but this.

My palm tingles as it smacks against her ass, roughly spanking her skin. She moans again, losing herself to the storm of sensations as her cunt squeezes around my cock buried inside her.

"Zach," she keens.

"Yeah? Are you okay?"

"M-More. I need more. Please... choke me like you used to."

Hesitation sets in. "You want that?"

"I can't fucking breathe, knowing that asshole is out there, hurting other people. I need you to help me breathe."

Sneaking my hand around her torso, I bring it up to the smooth slope of her neck. I can feel how fast her heart is beating as I clench her throat.

"You want to breathe, baby girl?" I whisper in her ear. "Well, you're not allowed to. Not until I say so."

Pushing backwards against me, she encourages me to resume slamming into her. I keep her throat clamped tight in my hand and resume a battering pace, worshipping her cunt into oblivion.

Water cascades around us, the entire hotel ceasing to exist. Nothing else matters. Not Sabre. Not Sanchez. Not even the investigation. It's just us—safe in each other's anger and passion.

Sensing her struggling for air, I release her throat and grant her a brief second of salvation. "Breathe, babe."

She follows my orders, gulping down air into her stuttering lungs. When my generosity expires, I resume my tightening grip and cut off her air supply again.

It goes on... clamping, releasing, squeezing and breathing. Each time she comes close to an orgasm, I still my movements and offer her a sliver of air to keep her on that painful cliff, without allowing her to fall off.

"Zach," she whimpers during a breath.

Hearing the pain in her voice, I quickly drop my hand. "What is it? Too much?"

Certain I've gone too far, dread rips through me. Her head falls, shoulders slumping and tears flowing. Quickly pulling out, I spin her around so I can tilt her chin up and see her face.

"Talk to me," I beg her.

Willow's tears are flowing. "Why me? Why did he do this to me?"

"I... don't know, babe."

The knife buried deep in my heart twists at the misery in her voice.

"Anyone in th-the whole entire fucking world, and he chose m-me. Why?"

After pressing kisses to the flushed skin on her throat, I secure my lips to hers. "There isn't an answer to that question, my love. You can't drive yourself crazy asking it."

"But I need to know. I *have* to know what I did to deserve this pain."

Wishing I could take it all away, I wipe her tears instead. "Nothing. You did absolutely nothing. You're all that's good and pure in this world."

Sniffling, she swats away her tears, her pupils dilating. When she reaches for my still-hard cock, I know we're going to finish what I started, regardless of how fucked this moment is.

I grab her ass cheeks and lift her, walking forward until her back meets the tiled shower wall. Her mouth seeks mine out, hot and heavy as I slide back into her cunt at a new angle.

With her pussy walls hugging my length, I can't hold on for long. It's too much to handle. Plunging in and out in rapid succession, I chase my release to the finish line, thrusting at a hard and fast pace.

Burying my face in her chest, I roar through a climax so intense, it blurs my vision. I can feel her falling apart too— quivering and moaning as I hold her up. The emotional storm caught in this shower with us heightens the moment, leaving us both winded.

Once her aftershocks have stopped, I let Willow slide down my body. "Are you okay?"

She nods, red-faced and breathless. "Better now, thanks."

I crook a finger under her chin then stroke a stray tear from her cheek. "I love you so fucking much, Willow. I'd do anything for you. Anything at all."

"I know, Zach. I feel the same way."

"You don't need to hide shit from me." My eyes stray down to the cut on her wrist. "Just talk to me. Please. There's nothing we can't figure out together."

She gulps hard. "I'll try."

"Good enough for me."

Before our mouths can gravitate back together, there's a loud bang on the bathroom door and Killian's voice echoes through the wood.

"You two done in there? Some of us have to pee."

Willow's forehead crashes against my sternum. "Charming."

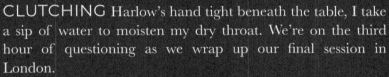

# CHAPTER 13
# WILLOW

## HEAVY IN YOUR ARMS –
## FLORENCE & THE MACHINE

CLUTCHING Harlow's hand tight beneath the table, I take a sip of water to moisten my dry throat. We're on the third hour of questioning as we wrap up our final session in London.

Having exchanged numbers the day before, Harlow offered to sit in on the session with Ethan and the Anaconda team for moral support. I didn't hesitate before accepting her kind offer.

Having the guys here makes me feel more comfortable, but it's harder to be honest in front of them. I don't feel the same pressure with Harlow—she can clearly handle herself and isn't shocked by my story.

"If I'm understanding correctly." Ethan taps a pen against his lips, "Mason Stevenson is Dimitri's supplier, yes?"

"He's a fixer," I reply with a sigh.

"How so?"

"Supplying is only half of his role. Whatever mess Mr Sanchez makes, Mason cleans up. Including the dead prostitutes."

"I see. He's more of a right-hand man, then."

"You could say that."

Keyboards tap and pens scribble. Brows are furrowed in concentration. Faces are pale. The deeper down Alice's rabbit hole we fall, the grimmer their expressions become.

Mason is the tip of the iceberg. There are suppliers, fixers, security detail, dealers and so much more that props up Mr Sanchez's legal real estate business' foundation of evil and sin.

The version of him that exists for the outside world isn't real. His slick smiles, designer finery and eloquent speeches at charity fundraisers are all part of that carefully constructed image.

Harlow's grip on my hand tightens. "You okay?"

"Yeah," I whisper back.

"We can take a break if you need to."

"I'm okay to continue."

She offers me a smile of encouragement. Refocusing on Ethan and Warner, both leading today's questioning, I blow out my held breath.

"Mason is the man who tracked us down several months ago. He later travelled to Briar Valley to threaten my daughter's life if we didn't return to Mr Sanchez."

"That won't happen again," Tara interjects. "We'll be providing you with round-the-clock security from now on."

"Mason's the real deal." I lean forward, taking the time to look intently at each team member. "Don't underestimate him. If Mr Sanchez has tasked him with bringing us back, he won't rest until that's done."

"Don't underestimate us," Hyland grumbles.

Tall, well-muscled and broad-shouldered, he's an even burlier version of Killian, something I didn't think was possible. My Viking lumberjack has some muscular competition in this guy.

Despite the heavy scarring across his knuckles and continuous lack of a smile gracing his lips, Hyland is solid. I can see the goodness behind his grumpy disposition and gruff kindness.

"Threats aside," Ethan intervenes with a frown, "Mason Stevenson could be our way in. He can lead us straight to Sanchez's black market operations."

"He also owns a successful real estate business and dabbles in investment banking, so he often travels across Europe." I take another sip of water. "It won't be hard to find him. Capturing him will be the issue."

"How so?"

"Mason travels nowhere without his personal security detail and months of preparation. He's careful. Conscientious. You won't find a single shred of evidence to pin on him."

"We'll see about that," Ethan quips. "I'm going to need a list of his known associates."

Nodding, I take the pen and notebook he offers. I was invisible to all of Mr Sanchez's men which allowed me to hide in plain sight, listening and observing their every move.

I know a damn sight more about their businesses, both legal and not, than any of those monsters would ever give me credit for. I just never had a reason to use the information until now.

Sliding the list of names back over to him, I bite my bottom lip. "There are more, but I can't remember all of it. Most probably used false identities too."

"Something is better than nothing," Warner remarks as he flips through his notes. "What about Pedro? Was he involved in the darker sides of Sanchez's business?"

A shiver runs down my spine, but I hold it together. My voice comes out raspy and forced.

"No. Only personal protection."

"You're sure about that?" he challenges.

"I have no reason to protect a dead man."

Blanching, Warner ducks his gaze. "Right you are."

The urge to snap at him again burns through me. I have to bite my tongue to hold a sarcastic retort in. I've made it clear that Pedro is off limits.

I won't have his name dragged through the dirt, regardless of what his job was. Yes, he protected the animal who made my life a living hell. That doesn't mean he's to blame for Mr Sanchez's depravity.

"I think we have everything that we need for now." Ethan clicks his laptop shut. "You'll be needed for further questioning should anything new come up, Willow."

"I understand."

"Thank you again for your cooperation. We'll keep you updated on the case's progress and ensure this information is put to good use."

"What about our protection?"

"We'll be following you back to Briar Valley," Tara supplies. "Hyland and I will take it in shifts to ensure your security until the case is through."

Killian's deep, growing voice speaks for the first time. "We'll arrange suitable accommodation for you in town."

"That would be appreciated," Hyland replies.

"I expect hourly updates," Ethan instructs his team members. "Nothing gets past you. Understood? Willow and Arianna's safety are my sole concern at this point."

Tara dips her head in submission. "We've got this."

"Alright, then. You're all free to leave."

With a deep sigh of relief, Zach shoots to his feet. He's practically itching with nervous energy and starts bouncing on the balls of his feet.

Killian's warm hand grips my shoulder. "Come on, baby. Let's get the fuck out of here."

"Yes please. I need to see Arianna."

Letting him pull me to my feet, I summon what feels like a pathetic excuse of a smile for the Anaconda team. All offer their thanks while Hyland and Tara climb to their feet to follow us.

"Mind if I walk you out?" Harlow asks.

"Not at all."

"My ride's waiting downstairs for me anyway."

Bringing up the rear, she tails us to the elevator, then we ride down in exhausted silence. Killian's still holding my shoulder, drawing tiny circles into my skin with his thumb.

On the ground floor, Harlow skips ahead to meet the three shadows leaning on the reception desk. They're talking amongst themselves, but two stop talking when Harlow approaches them.

"Hunter," she chirps happily.

Tall, dark-haired and sporting a shiny metal disk that's implanted into the side of his head above a scarred ear, the man throws his arms open to embrace her.

Hunter's classically handsome and well-dressed in what are clearly expensive jeans. He moves with an air of authority, even in the almost-empty reception area. Everyone seems to gravitate around him.

His partner in crime is an intimidating boulder of a man who causes prickles of fear to stab into my scalp. He's huge—bigger than Killian and Hyland—as though his body is literally carved from muscle.

"Where's my kiss?" he growls.

Harlow pecks Hunter's cheek. "Sorry, Enz. You're still in the doghouse for messing up my takeout order last night."

"I forgot one bloody dish!"

"The steamed broccoli is her favourite part of the meal," Hunter snarks.

"Too right." Harlow straightens and waves us over. "Willow, this is Hunter and Enzo. They used to run Sabre Security."

"Before we handed it over to this lump of meat." Enzo smacks the shoulder of the third man.

With raven-coloured hair, several shiny facial piercings and a body full of dark, intricate tattoos, he's no less intimidating than his friends, though his blue eyes are warm with recognition.

"Willow," he greets. "I'm Hudson Knight. My brother and I run the company. Heard a lot about you."

I subconsciously curl into Killian's side. "Nice to meet you all."

"How's the Anaconda team treating you?" Hunter asks.

Trying not to stare at his strange head implant, I shrug off his question. "They've been great."

"You're in good hands, Willow. They'll take care of you."

He smiles at Tara and Hyland, who both seem to blossom under Hunter's praise. Despite not running the company anymore, it's clear he's still the true source of authority around here.

Hudson's palpable authority is a little different, more entrenched in silent threat than overt power. He looks terrifying, but there's also a strange softness about him that sets me at ease.

"Where's Leighton?" Harlow pouts. "He promised me bubble tea."

"At the hospital with the others and Brooklyn," Hudson answers. "Want to head there now?"

"Yes! I am dying for baby snuggles."

Turning back to me, Harlow pulls me into a tight, fast hug. Her lips touch my ear so she can whisper.

"You've got my number. Call anytime, night or day. I'll be a non-judgemental listening ear."

"Thank you. That means a lot."

"You're not alone, Willow. Even when it feels like it."

Reluctantly releasing me, she pecks my cheek and gives me a final stern look. All four of them gift us with handshakes and goodbyes before disappearing towards the parking garage.

"Shall we get this show on the road?" Hyland suggests. "It's a long drive back to Wales."

Killian cracks his neck. "Let's get out of this damned city."

"Not a fan?" Tara laughs.

"You could say that," Zach answers for his cousin. "Killian's allergic to people and traffic. You'll see once you arrive in Briar Valley."

Both nod, seemingly prepared for what will undoubtedly be a shock to the system. Our tiny, quiet town is the polar opposite of this people-infested sweatbox, even in the dead of winter.

After loading up into Killian's truck with the other's blacked-out SUV parked nearby, we peel out of the parking garage with a squeal of tyres. Killian is clearly desperate to escape.

"You alright?" Zach asks quietly.

I snuggle closer to him in the backseat where we're both sitting. "Tired and I miss Arianna. But I feel good about doing that."

"You were amazing, babe."

"I hardly think so. All I did was tell the truth."

"Zach's right," Killian chimes in. "You did so well. That questioning was rough to listen to, let alone face."

Chest warm with appreciation, I lean between the seats to kiss Killian's beard-covered cheek before cuddling close to Zach again.

"Thanks, guys. I'm glad you were both here. I know it can't have been easy."

Neither answers me. The truth is heavy in the air between us. They both knew what happened to me in Mexico, but hearing about the abuse first-hand has confirmed their suspicions.

I'm broken.

Perhaps irreparably so.

But around them, I want to be whole again. I'm desperate to stitch my shattered pieces together and live the life I always dreamed of while stuck in that soulless mansion.

I deserve that chance at happiness. We all do—especially Arianna. Now's the time to put the past aside and fight like hell for it, even if it's the hardest thing I've ever done in my life.

Winding through the afternoon traffic, Killian curses and swerves his way out to the motorway heading west. Hyland and Tara follow behind in their SUV.

"How do we feel about those two?" Killian asks.

"They're helping us," I point out.

"I know, just don't love the idea of inviting two strangers into Briar Valley. How do we know they're trustworthy?"

"Because Ethan trusts them," Zach answers. "We have to respect his judgement. He assigned them to this job for a reason."

"I still don't like it. Strangers don't belong in Briar Valley."

"If you want me and Arianna there, then you'll accept them too," I snap at him. "That's final."

Jaw setting in a tight line, Killian nods once. "Fine."

He swerves past a slow-moving lorry, and my stomach lurches. I've been nauseous, awash with anxiety, the entire time we've been in London. His sour mood isn't helping.

An hour into our journey, Killian lays down on the accelerator. I watch our speed creep up, frowning at the back of his head. We're on a quiet country road, heading through rural England.

"Kill?"

He doesn't acknowledge me.

Tara and Hyland are a couple of cars behind us, maintaining a safe distance since our last stop for coffee and fuel. Between us, the other two cars are nondescript and unassuming.

"Killian? You okay?"

Still nothing.

When he abruptly brakes before speeding up again, Zach seems to catch on to something. He glances over his shoulder to look through the rear window, his brows furrowed together.

"Take the left here," he orders.

At the last second, Killian indicates and quickly turns with a squeal. The blacked-out SUV follows along with one other car—a dark-red, new model with tinted windows.

"They're following us," Killian clips out.

"How do you know?" I glance between them.

"They've been tailing us since we left London," he responds grimly. "Watch this."

Laying down on the accelerator once more, he takes another turn then speeds ahead, leaving the other two to catch up. The red car follows, battling to regain the distance between us.

Right on cue, Zach's phone rings. He answers with a barked grunt.

"Yeah?"

On the other end, I can hear Hyland's raspy growl.

"We thought so too. What should we do?"

As he speaks, an invisible demon wraps its claws around my windpipe and begins to twist. Wrenching. Strangling. Clenching. Air ceases to fill my lungs as panic sets in.

"Who is it?" I squeeze out.

"Could be nothing." Zach takes my hand into his. "Breathe, babe. We have security with us."

"What if it's him?"

"There's a gun in the glove compartment," Killian reveals, sending a swarm of hornets through my belly. "Just not a legal one. Zach, grab it."

"You have an illegal gun?" he barks. "Jesus, Kill!"

"I'm not fucking apologising. I got it for exactly this reason. Now take the damn thing, and be ready."

Swearing under his breath, Zach ducks between the seats to take the gun out. It's a small, compact model, different from Killian's usual hunting rifle. I feel the colour drain from my face.

This is real.

It's happening.

Cutting in front of a slow car, our tail quickly approaches. Also undercutting the dawdling driver, Tara and Hyland are hot on their heels, sandwiching the suspicious vehicle between us.

When it drops back slightly, the vice around my lungs eases enough for me to drag in a stuttered breath. My relief is short-lived, though. The red car quickly surges forward. I scream as it rams into us from behind.

We lurch to the side, and Killian fights to keep his truck on the road. The car doesn't hesitate before slamming into us again—harder this time, causing metal to groan in protest.

"Fuck!" he roars.

With another ram, he loses control of the steering wheel, and we careen off the road. We fly over a grassy slope, heading straight for a wooden fence.

"Killian!" I scream.

But it's too late.

There's no time to move out of the path of danger. At the last second, Zach throws himself on top of me to shield my body, an almighty bang of airbags exploding as we make impact.

Crunch.

Smash.

Shatter.

Pain explodes through my body as we're jerked forwards, the truck falling onto its side and beginning to tumble. The warmth of blood seeps across my head, and I can hear Killian's yelling, but it sounds far away.

*Please*, I whisper internally.

I can't die like this.

When the truck eventually crashes to a stop, I'm somehow still conscious. The weight of Zach's body is crushing me, still slumped over my curled-up form. Killian has fallen silent.

The stench of smoke invades the vehicle. All I can hear is

my own roaring heartbeat which slams against my ribcage in a painful beat. Agony is pulsating through my extremities.

"Willow!" I hear someone shout.

My eyes feel heavy, almost too heavy to hold open. With the last wisps of my strength, I heave Zach's weight aside and manage to lift my head. The awaiting sight cuts off my hammering heartbeat.

*Zach.*

*No.*

Bright-red blood pours from a huge gash in his forehead, slashed wide open by a jagged shard of glass. He's unconscious. Slumped over. Rapidly paling and bleeding profusely.

I scream. Beg. Plead and wail. His eyes don't lift. Killian remains silent. Voices and shouts surround me before the blast of a gunshot pierces the ringing in my ears. Then silence.

The last thing I see before I black out is Zach's slack face.

Empty and lifeless.

## CHAPTER 14
# MICAH

STAY WITH ME – YOU ME AT SIX

I HATE HOSPITALS.

The noise is overwhelming after so many months of silence in the quiet bliss of my studio. If I close my eyes, I can almost imagine the wet clay sliding between my fingers as I find my happy place.

The wail of a baby crying interrupts my daydream. After waiting for hours on end in the rural, countryside hospital near the crash site, my mind can't help but wander.

"Mi?" Ryder waves a hand in front of my face.

My eyes snap up to meet his. "Yeah?"

"Need a coffee or something?"

"Have you got anything stronger?"

"I wish," he snorts.

We're sitting in the clinical, white-washed waiting area of the emergency care unit. Opposite me, Killian has his elbows braced on his knees and his head in his hands.

By some miracle, he escaped the accident with only superficial cuts and a sprained shoulder, despite being in the driver's seat. The truck hit the fence and rolled, according to authorities.

"You guys doing okay?" Ethan strolls into the waiting area.

Standing up, Ryder walks into his arms so the pair can exchange kisses. He arrived by helicopter not long after Willow, Zach and Killian were all rushed in for urgent care.

We got the call a few hours ago. Some asshole ran them off the road—paid for by Mr Sanchez, no doubt. The son of a bitches were on a suicide mission to end Willow's life no matter what.

"Peachy," Killian speaks for the first time.

Ethan gives him a sympathetic look. "If it's any consolation, our two perps are dead. Tara and Hyland shot them on sight."

"Jesus," I mutter.

"We'll identify them as soon as possible, but if this is Sanchez, he would've been careful to use people who can't be traced back to him."

"So we're screwed?" Killian deadpans.

Ethan shrugs. "We're doing what we can."

This shit is a far cry from the peaceful life we're supposed to be living. Guns and violence don't belong in our story, but here we are. Living out the plot of a damn action movie.

Taking their seats, Ryder and Ethan's hands remain tightly entwined. Killian finds the energy to lift his head and looks at me beneath the gauze covering his sliced-up face.

"We should be in there," he croaks.

"We will be," I assure him.

"When?"

We're really in shit if Killian's deferring to me for some kind of plan here. With a sigh, I leave my seat and take the creaky plastic chair next to him so our shoulders brush together.

"As soon as the doctors will let us see them, we'll be in there."

"She needs us."

"And we're here, aren't we?"

Here—but that doesn't make up for the weeks I've spent treating Willow like crap and avoiding her. I thought that by keeping my distance, it wouldn't hurt when she left.

But she didn't leave. Not by her own choice. Those assholes almost took my girl from me, and I've wasted all this time keeping her at arm's length, all for nothing.

We could've lost her. Fuck, we still may. Nothing in this life is guaranteed, just the promise that more pain will always come. It's up to me whether I want to face that pain alone or with her by my side.

Killian's hand reaches out and clasps mine tight. "This has to stop, Mi. She needs you."

It's like he can read my mind. Sighing again, I silently wish I had a very strong drink in hand and force myself to nod.

"I know, Kill. It will."

"You swear it?"

"I'll make this right, I promise. Willow deserves that much."

"She never wanted to leave us," he tries to explain. "I know it's hard to accept. Believe me, I do. But she did what she felt that she had to for her daughter's life."

And deep down, beneath the anger and sadness, I know that. Better than anyone. Arianna is her whole life, and being a Mum is what kept Willow alive all the years she spent fighting to survive.

But that didn't stop it from hurting like hell when she took my heart in her hand, ripped it clean out from behind my ribcage and tossed it aside in a blood-slick lump. That pain was unbearable.

"She's my everything," I admit. "I just... I didn't know how to handle her coming back. It hasn't felt real."

"And it's up to us to keep her here, no matter how much she wants to run and hide," he urges. "This is going to be the fight of our lives, Mi. We need each other."

"More than ever," Ryder interjects. "You guys aren't doing this alone. The whole town wants to keep Willow and Arianna safe."

Between them both staring at me, I feel my cheeks flame red. The realisation of exactly how fucking stupid I've been washes over me. That ends today.

If Willow needs me, I'll be there. Regardless of the past. She came back to us, and it's high time I grew up. That blessing can't be ignored any longer in favour of my depression and grief.

The door to a clinical room clicks open, and Willow's two doctors emerge, both dressed in white and carrying clipboards. We all immediately stand, though Killian is stiff and grunts in pain.

"How are they?" Ryder asks.

"Zach has a moderate concussion and has required several stitches," Doctor Putland answer him. "He's doing well and has regained consciousness. We'll be discharging him in the morning."

"And Melody?" Killian demands, being careful to use Willow's false identity.

The second man, Doctor Vale, glances between us all. "Might I ask if any of you are Melody's significant other?"

"I am," we blurt at the same time.

Both doctors stare at us for a moment before quickly hiding their surprise. Doctor Putland waves us over to follow them into the room.

Leaving Ryder and Ethan behind, we're led into a brightly-lit clinical space down the corridor. Behind a blue curtain, Willow is resting upright in a hospital bed.

She's banged up, her arm bandaged from being sliced by glass and face bruised in mottled shades of green and purple down one side. My throat tightens. Shit. They've done this to my girl.

But she's awake and still looking so fucking stunning, it

hurts my heart to see her coal-black hair and shining eyes. She bursts into tears when she spots us entering the room.

Shoving me forwards, Killian hangs back so I can approach first. I move without an ounce of hesitation. Willow lets me bury my face in her neck as my own tears well up.

"You're okay." My words sound strangled.

Her hand buries in my overgrown hair. "I'm alright, Mi."

I repeat it again, needing to convince myself. While I locked myself away at home like a petulant fucking child, she was out there, getting hurt. I'll never forgive myself for leaving her again.

"I'm so sorry I wasn't there—"

"Stop," she interrupts, lifting my head so our eyes can meet. "This isn't on you."

"But you needed me."

Willow hesitates. "I did."

"Then this is on me. I swear to you, angel, I won't ever do that to you again. Please forgive me."

Her expression softens. "There's nothing to forgive."

We embrace again, sharing a soft, gentle kiss despite our audience. When one of the doctors clears their throat, I reluctantly release her and take a small step backwards.

"Miss Tanner," Doctor Putland begins.

Willow startles at the false name but quickly smooths a blank expression into place. "Yes?"

"Your injuries are all mild; you've been incredibly lucky to escape unscathed."

"Then why are you still holding her?" Killian asks suspiciously.

Doctor Vale steps forward. "We sent Miss Tanner for a routine scan and some blood tests when she arrived. As you didn't mention it, I think this will come as a surprise to you."

He looks at our girl meaningfully.

"What is it?" Willow breathes.

"Melody, you are pregnant. Congratulations."

You could hear a pin drop in the hospital room. No one says a fucking word. All I can do is stare at the look of complete and utter shock on Willow's face as her mouth opens and shuts several times.

Silence.

Long, suffocating silence.

"P-Pregnant?" she finally speaks.

The doctor nods. "Approximately five weeks. The baby is healthy, no signs of injury following the accident."

My mind rushes to connect the dots. She's been back with us for a while now, since before Christmas. Unless she's seeing someone else, the baby is ours. One of us is having a kid.

Or… all of us.

I really don't know.

"Are you sure?" Willow squeaks.

They both nod back.

"A baby," Killian repeats, dumbfounded.

"But I thought…" Willow trails off. "They told us that I'd never be able to conceive again when I had a miscarriage last year. I have too much scarring."

"Miracles do happen, Miss Tanner. You're going to have a rainbow baby after all."

Oh my God.

An actual child.

*Our* baby.

Bursting into loud, back-breaking sobs, Willow crumbles between us as we surround her. Killian buries his face in her hair as I hold her against my chest, stroking her back.

It seems neither of us know what to say.

We don't need to ask whose it is.

That doesn't matter right now. Willow's having a kid, and we're going to be fathers. Everyone and everything else pales into insignificance—even the differences that have kept us apart.

"A baby," she hiccups. "We're having a baby."

The doctors file out to give us some privacy, but we don't move. Willow remains trapped between us until her sobs fade into tiny whimpers of what sounds a lot like fear.

I tilt her chin up with a crooked finger, forcing her tear-logged eyes to lock on me. "Talk to us, angel."

"I never th-thought I'd get another chance," she whispers.

Killian smooths her hair. "You heard them. It's a miracle."

"But… there's so much going on." She shakes her head. "How can I possibly bring a baby into this mess? We're not safe yet. I can't have another child."

I grip her chin tight. "Whatever you want to do, we'll support you. But don't throw away this chance because of that bastard. He's taken enough from you."

"Micah's right," Killian agrees. "Do you want this baby?"

Willow bites her lip and nods. "More than anything."

"Then I guess we're having a kid."

Hearing him say it out loud feels like an electric shock to the system. For the first time in months, I can feel my body. It's humming. Trembling. Shaking with anticipation.

I'm alive.

The numbness leaves me.

I don't have time to waste, wallowing in the pits of my loneliness when Willow's here, pregnant and hurt. Pregnant with *our* child.

She shakes her head. "We haven't used protection. Jesus Christ."

Killian strokes a single finger down the slope of her crooked nose. "Fuck. I completely forgot about that."

Both of them glance up at me.

"What?" I frown back.

I can see the worry dancing in her eyes. We all know the baby isn't mine. It sounds like Killian and Zach are both in the running.

They're waiting for me to be upset. While part of me feels like I'm intruding on their moment, I sure as hell am not walking away. Not now. I've done more than enough of that.

"Do we want to know?" I ask honestly.

Killian shrugs. "I don't think it matters whose it is. If we're doing this, then we're going to do it together as a family."

Relief floods me at his words. The assumption I made is correct. We've never discussed this, it didn't seem like it would ever be a possibility. But I'm glad we're on the same page.

There's a knock on the door before it creaks open, emitting a limping, bandaged Zach. He shrugs off the nurse's grip on his arm and steps into the room.

"Willow!"

"It's okay," she rushes out. "I'm fine."

Slowing down, Zach wobbles on his feet for a moment, and I'm forced to grab him so he doesn't fall. He steadies himself on my arm.

"Someone drove a damn car into me," he complains moodily. "Is that why I have such a bad headache? Or did I drink too much?"

I quickly pull him into a back-slapping hug. "Good to see you awake, brother."

"Jesus. Who are you, and what have you done with Micah?"

"Hilarious. Want me to hit you with another car?"

"Try it," he challenges. "I survived one hit, I can take another."

"No!" Willow shrieks. "Christ, guys."

Rolling my eyes, I release him. That's when he spots our faces, all misty-eyed and flushed, realising that something is going on.

"What's wrong?" Zach quickly asks.

Willow wipes her tear-stained face. "We... uh, have some news."

"News," he repeats. "Are you okay? Did the doctors say

something? I tried to shield you as best as I could from the crash."

"I really am okay, Zach." She flashes him a wobbly smile. "Better than okay."

Looking between us all, grinning like fucking idiots who don't have clue what rollercoaster lies ahead, Zach doesn't catch on.

"Mind filling me in, babe?"

Willow's tears begin to flow again. "You're going to be a dad."

Frozen on the spot, his mouth falls open. "Come again?"

I squeeze his shoulder. "She's pregnant."

Still, Zach doesn't unfreeze. "With…?"

"Our baby," Killian finishes.

Hearing those words, the most magnificent, over-enthusiastic smile blooms on his lips. Zach crosses the room in a limping blur to gather Willow into his arms, bruised skin and all.

"Holy motherfuck!" he yells so loud, I'm sure the whole hospital can hear us.

"Zach," she scolds him, mortified. "Language!"

We all burst into laughter. Despite the pain and turmoil of the past few hours, it feels good to hear that tinkling, excited sound fall from Willow's lips. Shit. We're really doing this.

Zach's eyebrows raise. "Ah, hell. Last month?"

Flushed pink, Willow shrugs. "I guess so."

"I totally forgot."

"We both did." Killian laughs.

All huddling together, we hug in a breathless tangle. None of us have the right words. Maybe there aren't any. Just happiness and pure fucking bliss for a single, solitary moment of our lives.

This is it.

Our forever.

It's on the horizon.

Once Willow's tears have dried up, she shoos us out of the room to speak to the doctors in private. We catch the words *high-risk pregnancy* before the door to her room clicks shut.

We look at one another, silently communicating before we slip outside to talk in private, away from Ethan and his team. The moment the cool, winter air slaps my face outside, reality settles in.

Willow isn't safe.

That sick piece of shit tried to have her killed. There's no doubt that the two idiots in the car were paid for by his dime, even if we don't have evidence to prove it yet. That wasn't an accident.

"What now?" I ask, urgency surging like a shot of adrenaline through my veins.

Killian faces the overcast clouds as his shoulders slump. "Shit, we're in so much trouble. We can't risk anything making this even harder for Willow than it already will be."

"What do you mean?" Zach questions.

"You heard them in there. The chances of her losing this baby are already higher than average. Do you want her to go through another miscarriage?"

I feel myself blanch. "Fuck no."

Zach shakes his head. "Not a chance."

"There's a possibility it will happen. We need a game plan and fast. I won't let that asshole get another chance to hurt our girl."

"So what do we do?"

His expression hardens. "We go on the attack. I want him taken down in every single way possible."

Zach leans against the wall, clearly exhausted. "How do we do that?"

"Hiding isn't working anymore."

"So what do we do?" I frown.

"Whatever it takes. We need him to stop spreading lies

about Willow and her disappearance. Then Sabre Security can find that motherfucker and bury him."

We both nod in agreement. The day that wanker is behind bars—or even better, dead in the ground—will be the day we finally rest. This is a war that we have to win now.

"What about Willow?" Zach glances at me. "And the... you know?"

Killian's jaw tightens. "Yeah. I know."

"Know what?" I look between them.

Neither looks willing to tell me what's going on. Frustrated, I raise my hands in exasperation.

"What are you both talking about?"

"Willow's been cutting," Zach reveals.

For the second time today, I'm caught off guard and speechless. Killian avoids looking at me while Zach won't look away, ensuring I know exactly what's been going on while I've been fucking around with paint and clay.

"She's self-harming?" I ask in an unfamiliar voice. "Again?"

He nods. "For a while now."

Memories of the last time this happened threaten to overwhelm me. Finding Willow in that bathtub, crying and blood-stained, was harrowing. I was the only one equipped to deal with her in that situation.

"How long?"

"Mi—"

"How fucking long?"

"Months," Killian answers, sadness etched into his features.

Bracing my hands on my knees, I let my head fall in shame. "Shit. How bad?"

"Pretty superficial," Zach replies weakly. "She hasn't been doing it much since coming home. Looks like the worst of it was done during her time away."

Right around the time I hated her for leaving and spent

every waking moment cursing her existence. Meanwhile, she was out there, hurting herself and unable to cope with her own personal hell.

I'm an asshole.

The world's biggest.

"Fuck!" I shout, kicking the hard brick wall. "I can't believe I didn't realise."

"Mi—" Zach begins.

"No, don't even say it."

"How could you have known she was doing that?"

"I get it," Killian interrupts us, laying a hand on my shoulder. "I felt the same way when I found out. But we know now, and we have to help her."

"You said she'd stopped?"

They exchange a long, hard look.

"Mostly," Zach replies, his lower lip trapped between his teeth.

Fucking *fuck!*

Feeling like the absolute worst person on the planet, I walk away from them to gather myself before I do something stupid like punch the wall and break my hand.

I could've helped her. Hell, I could've stopped her. I did before. Instead, she lived with this alone for months. Just like I did at one time. She swore she'd come to me, but I pushed her away too far.

No more.

That ends today. She's my girl, and I won't rest until I make this right again. For her, for Arianna… and for our baby. Willow will never be alone in this world again for as long as I draw breath.

That's a vow.

# CHAPTER 15
## WILLOW

SPOTLESS – ZACH BRYAN & THE
LUMINEERS

THE SMELL of toast and frying bacon meets my nostrils. Peeling my eyes open, I catch sight of Killian walking in, dressed in a pink, flowery apron. *Huh*. I'm definitely still asleep.

"Morning sunshine," he coos.

Blinking hard, I wait for the dream to fade and reveal the real world. Instead of that happening, he places the tray of breakfast down in front of me, a blazing smile on his usually grumpy face.

"Kill?" I moan groggily.

"Wake up. It's time to eat."

"Are you… real?"

Cursing, he unties the apron and swiftly chucks it on the floor. "Do you believe I'm real now?"

For extra measure, he moodily stomps on the floral fabric to convince me. From the sour look on his face, tinted with a hint of humour, I realise this isn't actually a dream.

"Why are you cooking for me?"

"You're knocked up with my kid," he replies happily. "Therefore, I am going to stuff you full of food at every opportunity for the next nine months. Get used to it."

Letting my head hit the pillows, I huff in annoyance. "Great."

Day one of this bullshit and I am already over it. I knew from the moment I saw their faces that this would send their overprotective instincts into overdrive.

Around me, the pale walls of my cabin are lit by winter sunshine as Killian opens the curtains. I pull myself up and take a bite of toast.

We arrived home late yesterday afternoon from the hospital. Zach and I were discharged after being kept overnight for observation, both roughed-up and heavily bruised.

"Where's Ari?"

"Eating eggs with Micah." Killian sits down on the bed next to me. "I convinced her not to come screaming in here for attention."

"Thanks. My head is pounding."

"Need some more pain relief?"

Nodding, I wait for him to grab the pills I was discharged with, then I wash the tablets down with coffee. Peering over the rim of the mug, I pin him with a look.

"This is decaf, isn't it?"

Killian plasters on his best innocent expression. "No idea."

"You're such a controlling son of a bitch."

"You're pregnant!"

"Shh." He playfully nips at my fingers when I attempt to cover his mouth. "Don't go yelling about it. I'm not ready for Ari to know just yet."

"When can we tell people?"

Lord, I never thought I'd see the day Killian acts like an excited puppy who's got the bone. All it took was getting knocked up after a protection-less sandwich.

"Not yet! It's way too early. I need to get to at least twelve weeks, when things are more stable."

His face softens. "It's going to be okay, baby."

"You can't promise that."

"But I can promise that we'll do everything in our power to make it okay, no matter what it takes."

Reaching up, I stroke his blonde beard until I'm cupping his cheek. Killian leans into my touch, his fire-lit eyes piercing mine and filled with determination.

"You promise?" I ask huskily.

Passion burns in his gaze. "Swear on my life."

"It isn't just our lives we're gambling with anymore, Kill. This baby is at risk now too."

"Don't say that," he murmurs, his big hand reaching around the tray to cover my belly. "You and our baby are going to be just fine. Arianna too. We're going to fix everything."

"Lola used to say the same thing to me." I put down the toast, which turns to ash in my mouth.

Pain flickers in Killian's eyes. Even he can't believe that we're safe. Not here. Not now. We've fired the first shot, and that convenient little car accident was Mr Sanchez responding.

"She'd be so fucking thrilled right now," he says.

"Yeah... She would."

"Having Arianna around was the highlight of her life... but seeing us have a baby together? Damn, princess. That would've been everything to her."

"If we live long enough to have this baby."

He leans forward, his eyes narrowing. "Don't say that."

"Why not?" I challenge. "It's true. You think he'll stop at a car crash? Mr Sanchez obviously knows we're on to him."

"Tara and Hyland are outside," he reminds me. "Armed to the teeth and looking scary as fuck, I might add."

"That doesn't make me feel better."

"This was your plan!"

"And maybe I was wrong." I shrug. "We can't beat him. Not like this. I won't risk our lives again."

Incensed, he looms over me on the bed, pausing a beat before capturing my lips in a breath-stealing kiss. I let his mouth devour mine for as long as he needs. The crash has shaken us all badly.

Seeing Zach unconscious and covered in blood is something I never intend to repeat. But I won't hide away—that isn't going to stop Mr Sanchez from threatening our lives all over again.

No.

I'm going to flush him out.

Expose every last drop of his depravity and force him to show his true colours to every single person he's poisoned against me with his false narratives. Only then will I let Sabre drag his ass to prison.

We're taking our lives back.

"I need to pee," I mumble against Killian's lips. "Don't get any ideas."

"Damn," he grunts. "This kid is being a cockblock already, huh?"

Pushing his shoulder, I quickly relieve myself and find him gone when I return. His shadow looms in the kitchen where another technicoloured, heavily bruised face greets me.

"Morning," Zach offers.

I have to swallow the bubble of shame that looking at his painful face brings. "Hey. How are you feeling?"

"Like someone rammed a car into me." He laughs it off. "What about you?"

"Pretty much the same."

"What about…?"

Trailing off, he casts a side look at Arianna who is happily stabbing the pile of scrambled eggs on her plate. When his eyes duck down to my midsection, I catch on.

"Fine. Just a little nauseous."

"Sit down." Killian guides me over to the table. "I'll bring your breakfast in."

Before taking the empty seat, I pause to drop a kiss on Arianna's head. She's eagerly shovelling her breakfast down in preparation to return to school with the other children this morning.

"Does your face hurt, Mummy?"

I ghost a finger over the bandage covering a stitched cut on my forehead. "It's fine, baby."

She freaked out and had a meltdown when we arrived home yesterday, all bruised and battered from the crash. It took hours for her to stop crying out of fear.

"Who are those funny people outside?" Arianna wrinkles her nose.

Just outside the window of our cabin, two figures stand at the front door, one on either side. Tara and Hyland are wearing their usual all-black clothing with thick jackets on top to protect against the wind chill.

"They're friends of mine," I quickly lie.

"Friends?"

"To keep us safe, Ari."

"You mean like knights?" she asks excitedly.

"Yes, like knights protecting their princess. That's you, baby."

"Wow! I've never seen real knights before. Can I go and say hello?"

I ruffle her perfect braids, no doubt courtesy of Zach. "Of course. Maybe ask if they want a cup of coffee?"

With a huge smile, she skips off to introduce herself. We all stifle laughter as Hyland crouches down on one knee to reach her height, folding his massive body in half to do so.

"What's your name, sweet pea?"

"Arianna," she replies matter-of-factly.

"My name's Hyland." He sticks out a paw-like hand for

her to shake. "You're gonna come to me if anything makes you feel scared around here, alright, kid?"

"Alright. My mummy wanted to know if you'd like coffee."

He chuckles. "I think we're okay, kiddo."

Tara makes a pout at me then mouths, "So cute."

When both of them stiffen, pushing Arianna behind them and reaching for concealed weapons, my heart leaps into my mouth. But the tinkle of Aalia's voice settles me again.

"Morning!" she calls cheerfully.

"Aalia and Johan are here!" Arianna cheers.

She rushes back inside to grab her backpack and coat. I help her pull the pink, sparkly pack on and fuss over her for a few more seconds before eventually dropping a kiss to her cheek.

"Have a good first day back at school, Ari. Be good for Rachel and Miranda."

"I'm always good," she sasses, hands on her hips.

"Yeah, yeah. I mean it."

Arianna rolls her eyes. "I will, Mummy! I promise."

"Good girl." I smooth her plaits.

Stepping outside, Hyland secures himself to her side. I move to the door to watch Aalia size up Arianna's new protection with a visible gulp. He looks even bigger next to my tiny little girl.

"Morning, Willow!"

I wave back at her. "Hi."

"You new here?" Aalia jokes as she peers up at Hyland's monstrous height.

The smile that graces his lips is weirdly gentle and patient.

"Something like that. Shall we go?"

"Lead the way."

"I'll let you do the honours," Hyland jokes.

"What a gentleman."

He laughs and falls to the back of the group, remaining an invisible but ever-looming presence to protect Arianna from harm. They vanish, leaving the three of us in peace, with Tara remaining on guard outside.

We return to breakfast and eat in silence until the front door clicks open again, emitting a shocking sight. Zach's fork clatters loudly against his plate.

Micah is dressed, showered and walking steadily as he enters my kitchen to make his own coffee. There's almost a bounce to his movements after weeks of being hunched-over and downbeat.

"What?" He frowns at us all.

"You feeling okay?" Zach chuckles.

"Fine. Just got some work to do this morning."

"Did you sleep in the studio last night?" I ask.

He shakes his head. "My bed."

When he vanished after we came home from the hospital, we assumed he was too overwhelmed by what happened and would lock himself away again.

"We should talk about sleeping arrangements," Micah declares. "We can't be split across two cabins when the baby gets here. It won't work."

Reaching over to Zach, I gently click his mouth shut from where it's hanging open. "Um, sure. We can talk about that. Bit early, though, isn't it?"

"Never too early to be prepared," Micah quips.

Stuffing a banana into his pocket, he takes his coffee and vanishes back out into the early winter morning to head for his studio. We're left in stunned silence, watching his perky footsteps.

"Did everyone else see that as well?" Zach asks urgently. "Or am I just losing my shit after that head injury?"

"How many fingers am I holding up?" Killian lifts a hand.

"Uh, four."

"Seven." He shakes his head. "You're definitely losing your shit, kid."

"No!" Zach protests. "That was totally four."

"Clinically insane, in my professional opinion. That head injury knocked whatever brains you had left out of you."

Eyes narrowed, Zach grabs an unbuttered slice of toast and launches it at Killian's head. "Fuck you, Kill!"

"The truth hurts!" he chortles.

Needing to escape their antics and loud voices, I take my coffee back to the bedroom and softly shut the door. Stronger waves of nausea crash over me with each footstep I take.

When they subside, a prickle of anxiety remains. This is really happening. I couldn't believe my ears when the doctors revealed that I was pregnant again, after being told it was virtually impossible.

Standing in front of the floor-length mirror in the corner of my bedroom, I rest two hands above my slightly rounded belly. It hasn't been truly flat after having Arianna, and I'm naturally curvy anyway.

"Hey there, little bean," I whisper to myself.

Inside me, there's a new life growing. Expanding. Developing senses, neurons, nerve connections. Thoughts and feelings. Hopes. Dreams. So many endless possibilities lie within my belly.

"I'm going to keep you safe. I promise."

Even to my own ears, the promise doesn't ring true. I can't keep my unborn child safe without throwing myself into the cage to fight to the death. Mr Sanchez can't be beaten from the shadows.

I have to take this into the real world.

I have to speak up for all the victims.

Still cradling my belly, I gently stroke the rounded slope, envisaging the person who will one day stand beside me. Another Arianna, or a younger brother for her to endlessly annoy.

I can picture Micah's tiny, sweet smile on them, or Zach's deep, empathetic green eyes. Killian's strong angles and his gruff, gentle kindness. All the best parts of them.

We're going to have a baby.

A life. A future. A chance.

I can't waste that—not for Mr Sanchez.

"Okay, kiddo." I let my hands drop from my belly. "Let's do this."

# CHAPTER 16
# WILLOW

## WHERE IT STAYS – CHARLOTTE
## OC

"WOW," Ethan's voice crackles through the speaker.

"Yes. I know it's a bit radical."

"You could say that." He chuckles. "Where'd this idea come from?"

Sitting at the table in Lola's kitchen, I nurse my green tea, almost losing the mug in the stacks of paperwork and bound files. This place is an absolute mess.

On the opposite end of the table, Albie is combing through a box full of receipts for Lola's monthly expenses. He hasn't spoken a word since we got to work a few hours ago.

"Me," I answer honestly.

"Making a public statement against Dimitri Sanchez is a very bold move," Ethan points out. "You'll be making even more of a target of yourself."

"I prefer to look at it as defending myself. He's been speaking about me to the world through the press for months. I deserve the right to offer some kind of defence."

"I'm not disagreeing with you," Ethan replies. "Just concerned for your welfare. This won't be an easy thing to do, but we can help you to do it if that's your wish."

Looking up, I meet Albie's eyes. He's staring at me now,

his focus no longer on the receipts. Holding his gaze, we share a silent conversation. I can see his fear and concern. It's all there on his face.

But there's something else.

Something *more*.

It's a look of respect... and pride. Mouth gently curving upwards in a small, encouraging smile, he nods and returns to his task. I blow out the breath I didn't realise I was holding.

"It is," I confirm.

"Alright, then." Ethan clears his throat. "Our PR representative, Lucas, will be in touch to discuss the details. Start to think about what message you want Sanchez to receive with this."

"That he's a sick son of a bitch, and we're coming for him?"

"Maybe not that." He laughs back. "We want to play our cards close to our chest until we're ready to make a move. Clear your name without setting off his suspicions even more."

"Got it. Do we have an update on the car accident?"

"We've been investigating the two perps. Both are ex-inmates who have long rap sheets for paid illegal activities, least of all murder-for-hire."

My blood freezes. "Seriously?"

"He paid them, Willow. Of that we're certain. We may not be able to prove it right now, but we will in time. Someone must've spotted you in London and reported back to him."

"Who on earth would be able to do that?"

Ethan hesitates. "I... don't know."

There's pain in his voice at admitting that. I wish I could give him a hug. He's got the shitty job of steering this crazy train to its final destination.

"That's okay, Ethan. We'll figure it out."

"I really hope so, love. Give Ryder a kiss for me?"

"I will. Be safe."

He ends the call, and I lock my phone, dropping it in between the stacks of files.

"Damn, Willow." Albie smirks. "Hell of a move."

"I have to do something." I knead the back of my neck. "We can't go on like this forever."

"I think you're doing the right thing."

"You do?"

"Hiding from this shit isn't going to make it go away. The last year has proved that much already. It's time to get up and fight the bastard."

My chest warms with appreciation. "Thanks, Al."

"You got it, kid."

Standing up to refill our drinks, I peek outside the kitchen window at the garden and vegetable patch. Hyland is standing outside while Tara takes her break, nursing his coffee and watching the perimeter.

It's been weird, getting used to being followed around everyday. Arianna quickly adjusted to having an escort to school after the first few days, but I'm still finding the whole thing a bit odd.

"Isn't he cold?" I wonder.

"That man's made of fucking steel," Albie answers in a gruff voice. "Never seen such a lump of meat in my life. Doubt he even feels the cold."

"He must."

Tara and Hyland have been welcomed by the town, taking one of the smaller, older cabins at the edge of the property. They don't spend much time in it anyway.

Ethan calls to check in with them every day, along with regular contact from the rest of the team. Having them here does give me a sense of reassurance as we heal from the accident.

"What else is there to do?" I change the subject.

"Most of the necessary arrangements are done." Albie

flicks through his papers. "The lawyer will deal with Lola's will, and we'll have to take it from there."

"Okay, good."

Diving back into organising the papers I've got strewn around us, we don't come up for air until the guys arrive with lunch. Killian has made it his mission to feed me at any available opportunity.

He slaps down a thick-crusted ham sandwich in front of me and growls in his low, gravelly voice, sounding more like a wolf feeding its cub than a grown human.

"Eat."

"Yes, sir," I snark back.

"Good girl."

Zach suppresses a laugh as he boosts himself up on the kitchen counter and dives into his sandwich. He and Killian are covered in sawdust after working on a new cabin on the east side of the town.

Micah pauses to kiss my cheek. "Afternoon, angel. How are you feeling?"

"Okay." I beam up at him. "What are you painting?" I swipe a lick of wet paint from his cheek.

"That's a secret."

He winks, causing prickles of desire to sweep through me.

"Even from me?"

"Even from you," Micah replies.

Plopping himself down on the counter next to Zach, Micah's eyes are filled with humour. He's been working on some secret project for the past week, since the accident.

The change in him has been huge in the last few days. He's been coming out of the studio for meals and sleeping in his bed again. Even showering everyday, without my assistance.

He's coming back to us.

Slowly but surely.

"What's with you guys?" Albie watches us suspiciously.

"What do you mean?"

"Something's up." He studies each of our faces, his gaze pinging between us.

"No, it isn't," I lie.

"That's some steaming bullshit right there."

Zach looks like he's ready to burst. When his face begins to turn pink from the force of holding it in, I finally crack.

"Fine." I sigh dramatically. "You can tell him."

"Really?" Zach grins.

"Just no one else."

"If we tell Albie, then we have to tell Ryder too," Killian reasons. "That's only fair."

"Guys! We said we weren't doing this until twelve weeks!"

Connecting the dots, Albie's face lights up. "Oh God."

It's been a long time since I saw him with a genuine smile on his face. Albie abandons his work and scoops me into a huge hug.

"Willow! Are you…?"

"Yes," I breathe into his flannel shirt. "Around six weeks."

"Heck!" he bellows.

Stomach fluttering with excited butterflies, I hug him until he puts me back down in my chair. Albie's smile hasn't faded. It's plastered on and oh-so-bright.

But I spot the moment it hits—the grief. Filtering in like the inevitability of night swallowing day, his features fall as his eyes fill with pain.

"Your Grams… she'd be over the moon."

I grasp his hand tight. "I know, Al."

"I wish she were here to see this day."

"She is. Somewhere."

His throat bobs. "Somewhere."

Releasing my hand, Albie slips out of the room to take a moment to himself. The guys are all wincing and looking a little contrite for setting him off again.

"That went well," Killian rasps.

I scrub my face. "We should've known it would upset him."

"We can't tiptoe around Albie and the others forever," Zach says. "This is our good news to share. We deserve the chance to celebrate it."

"He's right," Micah chimes in.

Sitting back down before the nausea sets in again, I take a big bite of my sandwich, which tastes like dust in my mouth. All of this is so bittersweet.

With lunch finished, the guys hang around, waiting for the lawyer to arrive. Albie makes a reappearance, and we all stand up when the growl of an engine approaches Lola's cabin.

Hyland moves to the front of the house to greet our guest. Stepping outside onto the front porch, I watch the tall, willowy woman from Highbridge get a pat-down search for weaponry.

"Apologies," Hyland tells her.

She appears flustered. "Why is this necessary?"

"That's our business, ma'am. Thanks for your cooperation."

Checking her briefcase for good measure, he declares her clean before she's allowed to approach the cabin. Her slick brown hair is slightly rumpled from the thorough search over.

"Good afternoon. Are you Killian Clearwater?"

Killian steps forward. "That's me."

"Pauline Arkwright."

"Good to meet you. Come inside."

Ushering our guest into the cabin, we return to the kitchen and quickly clear some space on the table. Micah sets to work making Pauline a hot drink as I take the seat opposite her.

"Mrs Sanchez," she begins, eyeing me. "I understand you have some concerns about our discretion regarding your identity."

I swallow the lump in my throat. "That's correct."

"Allow me to assure you that any information discussed here is protected by client privilege. I am not at liberty to disclose your identity to anybody. You can be honest with me."

Reassured, I nod back. "Thank you."

"So to confirm, your full name is Willow Sanchez?"

"That's correct."

Her eyes sparkle with recognition. "Very well."

After we questioned the identification procedure, I had no doubt that her office would investigate me. My name is splashed all over the news, courtesy of Mr Sanchez's PR campaign.

"I was Lola's lawyer for twelve years," she continues, seeming to soften. "I'm sorry for your loss. She was an incredible woman."

My throat tightens. "That she was."

"Lola has a significant number of assets that we need to discuss, most of all being Briar Valley."

Snapping open her briefcase, Pauline pulls out a glossy manilla folder then slides it over to me. I gingerly accept it, my heart slamming against my ribcage.

Inside, the lines of text and complicated legal jargon blur across the page. I'm too overwhelmed to understand any of it. This is the final confirmation I didn't want.

Lola's gone.

Dead.

Never to return.

I thought it had hit me at the funeral, but sitting here, confronted by the monumental task of settling her affairs, the realisation deepens.

She isn't going to walk through those doors at any moment. This is it now, all we're left with is paperwork and happy memories. It feels wrong for such a huge presence in our lives to amount to so little.

"Lola recently changed her will," Pauline reveals. "A little under twelve months ago. She has made you the sole beneficiary of her entire estate."

"M-Me?" I gasp.

She nods. "You will be inheriting the deeds for Briar Valley, her cabin, and a significant lump sum of assets and cash amounting to two hundred thousand pounds."

"Fuck me," Zach mutters.

Wiping off my sweaty palms, I fight to keep my voice even. "I… d-don't understand. Why so much?"

"Lola has been resettling families for the government for decades and reaping the rewards of that arrangement. She invested in a wide portfolio of stocks during that time."

*Holy. Freaking. Shit.*

"This is too much!" I protest. "I don't want the town. I don't even want her money."

"It's yours now," she explains kindly. "Lola has gifted her estate to you. She must have loved you very much and wanted you to have it."

Feeling dizzy, I take a moment to breathe. Briar Valley. It's mine. She wanted me to take the town in the event of her death and continue the work she started here.

The town that saved my life.

The town I love, more than anything.

"Oh my God," I say to myself. "I c-can't do this alone."

The warmth of a hand circles between my shoulder blades, offering silent support. I can smell Killian's musky, pine tree scent behind me as he ducks low to whisper in my ear.

"You're not alone, baby. We can help you figure this out."

"I'm here to help too," Albie speaks up.

I glance at him. "You knew about this, didn't you?"

He shrugs. "Might've."

Zach and Micah crowd me so I have the warmth of three bodies pressing into me. Their touch grounds me before I lose my mind over what's happening right now.

"I need you to sign some paperwork for me." Pauline taps the folder. "Property deeds will be transferred into your name by the end of the week."

This can't be happening. I've barely come to terms with last week's surprise... Now this? It's all too much. Abruptly standing up, I make my apologies and bolt outside.

"Willow?" Hyland calls as I rush past him.

Halting, I clutch my tight chest. "I'm fine. Just need a moment."

He moves to stand next to me. "Take a deep breath. In through your nose, out through your mouth. Let's do it together."

Clasping my shoulders, he mimics the breathing pattern and encourages me to follow. I take several deep breaths, forcing air into my panicking lungs.

"That's it," he whispers reassuringly. "You're doing good."

We stand like that for several long moments. I can practically feel the pressure of the guys' gazes through the kitchen window, giving me a moment of privacy.

When the rush of fear has begun to abate, I breathe clearly and murmur my thanks. Hyland releases my shoulders after a final squeeze.

"My kid brother has OCD," he informs me without me asking. "He's suffered with panic attacks for years. Used to scare the hell out of me when we were younger."

"You're good at calming people down."

Hyland offers me a toothy grin that doesn't match his rough exterior. "It's my job to look after you."

"Thanks." I force a wobbly smile.

"Go back inside. Those men of yours are about to lose their shit, if their faces are anything to go by."

Snorting to myself, I slip back inside. Everyone's where I left them—drinking and chatting. Thankfully, no one says anything about my outburst and lets me quietly sit down again.

Retaking my seat, I pick up the pen that Pauline left and flip to the last page. It's a legal contract, allowing me to officially accept the contents of Lola's will. This is it.

"Where am I signing?" I ask, itching to escape again.

Pauline points towards a dotted line. "Right here."

Hand shaking, I manage to scrawl my signature across the line before placing the pen back down. Seeing it there, spelled out in ink, ignites a sudden rush of determination that overtakes everything.

I can do this.

For Lola. For us.

I have to continue her legacy.

# CHAPTER 17
# KILLIAN
THE OTHER SIDE OF LOVE – JACK
SAVORETTI

HURTLING the axe into the woodblock, I split it into two perfect halves. My shoulders ache from several hours of aggressive chopping to release my anxiety.

Willow's inside puking her guts up. I hate seeing her suffering, even if it is for a good reason. Hell, a fucking amazing reason. We're having a kid. Us. Together.

I've been a wreck on the inside ever since finding out. This pregnancy isn't going to be easy, none of us are under any illusions about that. But we've been given something so precious.

We can't ignore that.

This could be our last shot.

Lining up the next log, I falter at the last second and almost hack into the ground next to the cabin instead. Ryder's truck is careening up the steep slope at full speed.

"Killian!" he yells out the window.

I drop the axe. "What is it?"

"You need to see this."

Slamming on the brakes, he comes to a halt with a spray of mud. I quickly wipe my hands off on my ratty blue jeans and climb into his truck. He's panting hard, like he ran to his truck then drove straight here.

"Did someone get hurt?"

All he can do is wordlessly shake his head.

"Show me, then."

Instructing Hyland to stay back and watch Willow while we're gone, I climb into the truck, and Ryder takes off with a hissed curse.

Driving back into town quickly, we bump over rocks and uneven bends in the makeshift road. It's a quiet Friday, and everyone's preparing for the weekend ahead.

As we make it back into the town centre, I can immediately tell that something is off. I spot the swarm of black vehicles haphazardly parked around the town square from far off.

All are marked with a logo.

*SANCHEZ REAL ESTATE.*

My entire body freezes up with an icy stab of rage. There are at least a dozen vehicles—cars, trucks and vans—parked near workers in matching uniforms.

At the head of the group, two men wearing hardhats are deep in discussion over a clipboard and measuring tape.

"What the fuck is this?" I growl.

Ryder quickly parks up. "No idea. We should go back for Tara and Hyland."

"Hyland's covering Willow, and Tara's off duty. Come on, we can handle this."

Climbing out of the truck, I approach the two developers who appear to be surveying the land around them, exchanging ideas under their breaths. Both watch me coming towards them with matching, smug smiles.

"What are you doing on our land? This is private property."

"Mr Clearwater, I assume," the first greets. "We've been instructed to begin prepping for the upcoming development."

"What fucking development? Briar Valley is not for sale!"

He flashes a shark-like smile. "Everything is for sale for the right price. We can make you a very significant offer."

"Even if this was my land to sell, I'd rather see Briar Valley burn to ash than end up in your fucking hands."

The second developer laughs. "That can be arranged. We'll be needing a fresh start for our modern apartment blocks to be built."

I'll die before seeing Lola's legacy be demolished to make way for some shitty apartments sold at half a million pounds apiece. That isn't happening while I'm alive.

"Get out of here!" I snarl, shaking all over.

"It isn't illegal to look around. We're simply sizing up the land and having a little exploration of your delightful town."

Ryder hisses from beside me. "Trespassing is illegal!"

"Go before I put a goddamn bullet between your eyes," I add menacingly. "This is my town. You're not fucking welcome."

After smirking to one other, they pack up their belongings and instruct their workers to load up. At the last moment, the first developer presses an envelope into my hands.

I don't open it until their taillights are heading out of town and climbing back up the unforgiving slopes of Mount Helena. My insides are searing with anger at the intrusion.

*That motherfucking animal!*

If Dimitri Sanchez thinks he can intimidate us with these psychological games, he's got another thing coming. We're not so easily scared off, and this is our property to defend.

"What does it say?" Ryder asks, panic clear in his tone.

Taking his arm, we walk over to Lola's porch and sit down on the wide steps. I tear into the letter then scan over the neat, pretentious writing that turns my stomach.

*If you think that my wife belongs to you, then*

*you're sincerely mistaken. Willow Sanchez will always be mine.*

*I'll burn down this pathetic town of yours unless you return my property. It will be my sincere pleasure to see it destroyed.*

*Don't test me.*

*Dimitri Sanchez*

"Son of a bitch."

Ryder reads over my shoulder. "He's a twisted fuck, isn't he?"

"This bastard is really starting to piss me off. Someone needs to end him."

"Just say the word. I'll do it with pleasure."

Scanning around the town square, my scalp prickles with alarm. If those dickheads can just drive in here like they own the place, then we're not secure enough to keep Willow safe.

"We need to step things up around here." I scrunch the letter up into a ball. "I want people on the town's perimeter."

"To do what?" Ryder scoffs.

"We at least need to know if some asshole is gonna turn up in town and start making threats. We have the right to defend our land."

Looking thoughtful, he nods. "We could have some of our best hunters out there keeping an eye. Not our fault if someone accidentally gets shot while crossing our land."

After sharing a laugh, we fall back into silence. I'm fucking shaken up. Nothing much used to faze me, but worry and fear are quickly becoming new constants.

We have so much to lose. Willow. Arianna. Our future. The stakes are higher than ever, and so much of this is out of my control. I can't just sit here and split logs all day. I have to do something.

"She needs to make that public statement," I decide. "Sooner rather than later. This bastard needs putting in his place."

"Did she tell you what she's gonna say?"

"Not yet."

Ryder bites his lip. "I think she's planning to announce that she's filing for divorce. Willow wants to kick him where it hurts."

"Fucking good."

The amount of pleasure that gives me almost makes me dizzy. I hate the fact that that man can still call her his wife. We're the only ones who deserve the right to one day call her that. Not him.

"I hope she kicks him in the teeth, and he looks like a wanker in front of the whole world," I spit. "He deserves nothing more."

Ryder stands up and offers me a hand. "Let's go speak to Harold. He can arrange a team of people to maintain the perimeter."

I take his hand and let him heave me up. Never thought I'd see the day we'd have to turn the quiet bliss of Briar Valley into a damn battleground, but nothing in our lives makes sense anymore.

This madness won't last forever.

We'll find a way to beat him.

———

With evening shadows cloaking the cabin in darkness, I leave Micah and Zach to entertain the little terror in the living room.

Willow's in bed nursing a headache after spending the afternoon on the phone to Lucas, Sabre's PR rep. She doesn't protest as I begin to run her a steaming hot bath.

"Come on, princess." I scoop her up into my arms. "Let's get you relaxed and comfortable."

"My head hurts," she whimpers.

"I know. The painkillers will start working soon."

Sitting her down on the edge of the huge clawfoot bathtub, I tip in an extra large scoop of jasmine bubble bath then check the temperature. I don't want it too hot for her.

Willow's head lolls, resting on my shoulder as we wait for the tub to fill up. She's wrung-out and exhausted. Morning sickness has well and truly arrived in the past few days.

"When are we releasing the statement?"

"At the end of the week," she replies sleepily.

"And you're happy with that?"

"It's just a written statement, I don't have to show my face or anything. Pauline has draw up divorce papers."

Relief pierces my chest. Despite the emotional turmoil, I'm still glad that she's taking this step. It's another inch in the right direction after a year of letting that man continue to oppress her.

"I'm proud of you, baby."

"You are?" she hums.

"Hell yeah, I am. This is you fighting back against Sanchez. I'm so fucking proud of how strong you're being right now."

Turning her head, she kisses my shoulder. "Thanks, Kill."

"Always."

Easing myself from her embrace, I flick off the taps then beckon for her to stand. Willow lets me undress her, peeling off comfortable sweats and one of my t-shirts that's swamping her body.

I duck low then brush my lips down—over her ribcage, hips, pubic bone—until I can press a tender kiss to her belly. My voice chokes up as I picture the little baby growing inside.

"We've got you, sweetheart," I whisper into her warm

skin. "Just keep cooking in there, and let us take care of the mess out here."

Willow's hands slip into my hair, releasing it from the hair tie keeping it in a loose bun so it slips over my shoulders. When I stand up, she tugs on the hem of my flannel shirt and tee.

"Come in with me?"

I raise an eyebrow.

"Not like that," she quickly adds. "I just need you to hold me tonight. I don't want to be alone with my thoughts."

"I'm here, Willow. You're never alone when it's us. I made you a promise before, and I'll never break it."

"They were here," she whispers brokenly. "His men were in our town. I still can't believe it."

"I shouldn't have told all of you."

"How can you keep your promise when the devil is already knocking on our front door?"

After lifting her into the steaming hot water, I kick off my jeans and boxers to follow her into the bath. We settle together in the water, her small body cradled against my chest, between my legs.

"He's playing games with us." I stroke her hair, soaking the short black strands. "We're not going to rise to it."

"Rise to it?" she laughs. "He's threatening to bury the whole damn town unless I return to him."

"And that isn't going to happen."

Willow remains silent.

"Is it?" I demand, grabbing her chin and twisting so she looks up at me. "Your place is right here. This is your land now."

"What if I don't want it? What if all I want is to live a quiet, peaceful life, away from all of this madness?"

Pressing our foreheads together, I softly kiss her parted lips. "It's coming, baby. You just need to hold on a little longer."

Moving my hand around her body beneath the water, I bring it to the slope of her belly and rest it there. Her eyes fill with tears as she peers up at me beneath thick lashes.

"This is our future," I murmur.

"Yeah?"

"The baby, Arianna and the twins. We're a family, and I won't let anything take that away from us. Not even you."

"I don't want to take it away," she sniffles.

"Then trust me. Trust us. Trust that we will see this through… together. As a fucking family."

When the tears spill over, I slowly kiss them away, tasting the salty tang of her sadness. My hand strokes over her stomach before moving lower to dip between her thighs.

"Let me make you feel good, baby girl."

"Mmm." She pushes her ass against my cock.

Teasing her inner thighs with gentle strokes, I move lower, easing my hand down to her core. She's slick in the bath water, her legs parting to grant me access to her wet folds.

Rubbing my thumb over her clit, I love the little moans that slip from her mouth. Her back arches against my chest, pushing her legs farther open so I have more access to her cunt.

"Is my girl's perfect pussy wet for me?"

"Yes," she whines.

"Tell me what you want."

"P-Please… touch me."

"Where?" I bite down on her ear lobe.

Willow sighs, her thighs clenching around my hand. "I need to feel your fingers inside of me."

"You're such a good girl, aren't you?"

Rewarding her, I dip a digit into her molten core. She's wet—receptive and sensitive to even the slightest of touches from me. Easing my finger out, I push it back in deeper.

"Kill," she moans.

"Yes, princess?"

"More."

Chuckling, I kiss around her ear and down to her neck, letting my teeth nip the soft expanse of skin there. I want her to be covered in my marks and touch. She's mine. Every goddamn inch of her.

Pushing a second finger into her slit, I stretch her wider. Willow's moans grow in pitch with each thrust, her body writhing in the steam and scented bubbles.

I begin to move faster, picking up the pace and teasing each moan past her lips with a feeling of total satisfaction. Only we can take every ounce of control from her in such an intimate way.

"Are you going to come all over my hand?"

"Yes," she mewls.

"Show me. I want to feel your juices running all over me."

Flicking her bud again, I slam my two fingers deeper into her cunt and watch as her mouth parts in a perfect, pink O. She cries out in pleasure, her walls clenching tight around me.

"Killian!"

"That's it, baby. Say my fucking name."

With a final cry of ecstasy, she falls apart. Her sexy body quivers with each wave of bliss, and her warmth coats my fingers in stickiness.

Slumping against my chest, her eyes slide shut. I slip my fingers from between her legs and wash them off in the water before banding my arms around her from behind.

"Perfect." I kiss the side of her head. "You okay?"

"Yeah," she breathes out.

"Can I wash your hair for you?"

"Okay."

Lifting her head so I can access the short strands, she allows me to soak her hair in water. I grab a bottle of shampoo then begin to lather, working in methodical silence.

"Kill?"

I pause while massaging her scalp. "Yeah?"

"I need you to know that no matter what happens, I love you so much. I want to have this baby and future with all of you. I want our family."

Rinsing off the shampoo, I grab the conditioner next. "I know. Me too. We're going to be okay."

"Swear on it?"

"I swear, Willow."

Her eyes flutter shut as I massage conditioner into her scalp, swallowing a bubble of shame. I just hope that what I'm saying is true and not just a fantasy.

## CHAPTER 18
# WILLOW

I FEEL LIKE I'M DROWNING –
TWO FEET

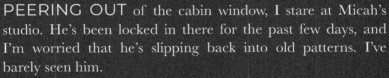

PEERING OUT of the cabin window, I stare at Micah's studio. He's been locked in there for the past few days, and I'm worried that he's slipping back into old patterns. I've barely seen him.

Zach and Killian are out doing road maintenance after the recent snowstorms washed out some of the tracks. With Arianna at school and Tara posted outside, I hate being alone.

It reminds me of the endless days spent locked in the apartment in Southampton. When I'm alone, the dark thoughts begin to swirl and expand like curling cigarette smoke in the crevices of my brain.

*This is ridiculous.*

*Just go over there, Willow.*

With a sigh, I step outside into the February air. Tara immediately perks up when she spots me, looking up from the phone clasped in her hands.

"Willow? Everything okay?"

"All good, I'm just heading over to see Micah."

Her eyes twinkle. "He's an interesting one, isn't he?"

"You could say that."

"I'll give you two some privacy. Shout if you need me."

Leaving her posted outside the cabin, I crunch over frost-bitten grass as I approach the cabin. The weather is still frigid, even with March quickly approaching.

It's as cold as the day we arrived in Briar Valley this time last year. It's almost like nothing has changed, when in reality, our lives are completely different now.

"Micah?"

Knocking on the studio door, there's no answer at first.

"Mi? It's me. Can I come in?"

When I knock again, Micah's panicked voice calls back.

"Go away!"

Gut twisting, I open the door and step inside without permission. "That's not happening. What's going on?"

The scene I was expecting to find is nowhere to be found. There's no rubbish strewn across the floors or empty liquor bottles. No scent of vodka or cigarettes. Instead, Micah's old chaos awaits.

Paint is covering every surface along with a fine dusting of sawdust and wood chippings. At the centre of the room lies a massive baby cot, under which Micah is laying with a paintbrush in hand.

"Mi?" I squeak.

He moves to sit up so fast, he smacks his head on the cot. "Shit, Willow. I told you not to come in. It was supposed to be a surprise."

"I thought you were drinking in here!"

Rubbing his head, he sits up properly. "Just working. You don't need to worry."

Inching closer, I take in the breathtakingly beautiful cot. It's been carved with painstaking detail, from tiny wooden roses cut into the glossy mahogany to intricate brocade designs in the walls.

"Wow, Mi. It's so freaking incredible."

A blush tinges his cheeks. "It's not done. You weren't supposed to see it yet."

I trail my fingers over the exquisitely carved handlebars, loving the smooth wooden surface. "It's perfect."

"Consider it an apology for being such a dick to you when you returned."

"You had every right to be angry with me, Mi."

He shakes his head. "Avoiding you and drowning my sorrows wasn't the answer, though."

Taking a seat on the floor next to him, I grab a paintbrush and dip it in the pot. We work together, painting the slopes of the cot and each joint in the frame individually.

"I'm sorry," he adds.

"You can stop apologising."

"Not yet."

Sighing, I dab paint on one of the carved roses. "I'm sorry too. We haven't treated each other right. I'd like to fix that."

"Me too, angel."

"So… where do we go from here?"

Micah gnaws on his bottom lip. "Do you still want to be with me?"

"Of course, I do."

"I really wouldn't blame you if you didn't want to."

Annoyed, I dab him with the paintbrush, smearing his arm with the light cream colour. "We're not discussing this."

"Yes, we are. We're adults."

"I don't want to be an adult today. I'm over it."

Smirking to himself, Micah lifts his brush and taps the tip of my nose with it. I can feel the thick paint on my skin, dripping down until it's smeared across my chin.

"Got you back," he teases.

I hit him again—on the cheek this time, covering him in paint.

"If you want a war, I can bring it."

Micah lifts an eyebrow. "Is that a threat?"

"You bet your ass it is."

Dabbing me again with another smear of paint, he takes

my wrist and yanks me closer so our mouths smack together. The moment his lips are on mine, everything changes.

The gentle playfulness melts into something else, something hotter. A roaring bonfire ignites between my thighs as his tongue slips into my mouth to tangle with mine.

Mouths duelling and hands exploring each other, the pace quickly picks up. Months of nothing but building tension erupts to an explosion between us. I want to crawl inside the shell of his skin.

"Fuck," he gasps into my mouth.

"I need you, Mi."

"I need you too, angel." He grabs a handful of my ass and squeezes. "But should we... you know, in your state?"

"State?" I repeat with a laugh. "I'm pregnant. Not out of action. Stop being cute, and fuck me already."

Grinning so wide it reveals the soft dimples that mark his cheeks, he uses the tip of his finger to gather the paint on my face, wiping it onto his other hand. Micah slowly massages his way down my shoulder and arm.

Once the paint is smeared over the marks on my arms, covering them from sight, he hesitantly clicks his mouth open to speak again.

"You should've told me."

My eyes laser in on his sad face. "You should've too."

"With what?"

"The drinking, Mi."

"You weren't here."

"Neither were you."

Sighing, his lips ghost over mine. "I guess that's fair."

Grabbing his chin, I kiss him more firmly, staking my claim across his mouth with a lash of teeth and tongue. We've treated each other like shit, but that doesn't matter now. Nothing else does.

It's just us.

As it should be.

With the slickness of fresh paint still between us, Micah pulls the short-sleeved t-shirt from my body and quickly unclasps my bra to free my breasts.

He palms them, spreading paint over my stiff nipples with his fingertips. The sensation of the cool liquid causes me to gasp into his mouth, loving the strange feeling.

"I missed these gorgeous tits," he marvels. "Did they get bigger?"

"Everything's going to get bigger."

"Damn. That's awesome."

"You're so adorable."

Cocking an eyebrow, he leans in again to bite down on my bottom lip so hard, pain zips down my spine.

"Adorable?" His palm smacks against my ass. "I'll show you adorable."

The quiet, shy virgin I met a year ago vanishes as lust blazes in his eyes. It's been too long. Too hard. Too much distance.

With a hand against my sternum, he pushes me backwards so I'm laying down on the paint-splattered sheet covering his studio floor. Micah unfastens my jeans then begins to pull them off.

The sides of his hands brush against my thighs and hips, adding to the tantalising sense of pressure that's blurring my vision. I want him. Us. Everything and anything in between.

"I want to bury my face between your thighs, angel," he purrs, peeling off my white panties. "And I want to make you come all over my tongue."

"Jesus, Mi."

Pushing my legs open, he kneels before settling between them to gain full access to my core. The moment his mouth meets my pussy, I arch off the sheet and cry out.

"Fuck!"

He's hesitant for a moment, but he soon forgets his nervousness and buries his tongue in my cunt. Adding his thumb to my clit and swirling it, I'm soon seeing stars behind my eyes.

"That's it, baby girl," he coos.

Gripping handfuls of the sheet, I buck and writhe, melting under his increasingly confident attention. Once he sees my reaction, Micah goes to town as he dives into his meal with enthusiasm.

Sliding his finger through my folds, he spreads come and saliva to moisten it before pushing inside my entrance. I slam a hand over my mouth to swallow my scream of pleasure.

"No," he scolds, prising my hand away. "I want to hear you. I've thought about this moment for months."

Working his finger in and out of my tight hole, he begins to thrust, his eyes locked on me. I can't run away from his gaze. I'm pinned and at the mercy of his tongue lavishing me.

"Come for me," Micah orders, flicking my bundle of nerves. "Let me taste those sweet juices in my mouth."

His filthy words leave me with no choice but to give in. The waves are approaching—building, expanding, growing more intense. I'm swallowed whole and shoved off into the deep end.

When Micah looks up from between my thighs, his mouth is scored with shiny moisture. He takes his time licking his lips, slowly but surely showing me how much he enjoys the taste of my release.

"You're so perfect, angel. That was incredible to watch."

Sitting up on my elbows, I grab the scruff of his stained t-shirt. "We're not done yet. Come here and finish what you've started."

Eyes on fire with need, he strips off his paint-covered clothing, leaving him standing in his tight black boxer shorts. My throat tightens as every sculpted inch of lean, compact muscle in his short frame is unveiled.

The bulge in his boxers offers a silent promise. He's as

gorgeous as the day we first slept together on the mountaintop amidst wildflowers and evening mist.

"Like what you see?" Micah asks, sounding far too much like his cocky brother.

"Maybe."

"I missed you so fucking much, angel."

I crook a finger, beckoning him closer. "Come and show me how much you really missed me."

He approaches then covers his body with mine. We're still on the floor, disregarding the paint pots and mess of brushes causing chaos around us.

Micah retakes his place between my legs then secures his mouth to my nipple, gently biting down. I wriggle beneath him, desperate to feel his touch. His throbbing cock is so close to my centre.

"Do we need protection?" he murmurs.

"I can't get more pregnant, can I?"

Micah chuckles. "I have no idea. But if you're fine going without…"

I'm unprepared for him to pin my left leg to the floor and slam inside me in one slick pump. The sudden impact causes me to scream out so loud, I worry that Tara will come running at any moment.

He buries himself to the hilt inside me, his eyes rolling back in his head. Shifting my hips, I encourage him to move and slam back into me. I'm practically shaking with need.

"We should slow down," Micah worries, his movements stilling. "I don't want to hurt you while you're like this."

"I'm fine, Mi. Stop worrying so much."

"Are you sure? It doesn't hurt, does it?"

"No," I answer, cupping his dimpled cheek. "Please. I want you so bad. Make me forget all the months we've wasted."

With a wicked gleam entering his eyes, he kisses me fully on the mouth. The lines between him and his twin are blurring so much. If I didn't know better, I'd struggle to tell the difference.

He's changed.

I've changed.

We're in the unknown now.

Pulling out, Micah repositions himself then pumps back into my pussy. The thrust is punishing, slamming his length deep inside me and igniting my core. I rake my nails over his paint-slick skin.

"Oh God," I groan.

Each jerk of his hips sends me spiralling, deeper and deeper into a bottomless pit of desire. I'm falling. Tumbling. Losing myself and all the anxiety that's plagued me for months.

All that exists is us—our bodies, breath, minds—entwined and moving together in a tantalising dance. Nothing else matters when we're together.

"Willow," Micah moans, pumping into me in fast, frenzied strokes. "You feel so good, angel. So good."

Before I can come again, he abruptly pulls out and halts his movements. I scream at the loss of pressure, feeling suddenly empty.

"Come and ride me," he gasps, sitting back on his haunches. "I don't want to come yet. You're so tight and wet."

Letting him pull me up, I clamber onto his lap then position my legs on either side of his waist. Micah hisses when I take his length and push it against my entrance.

Sinking down on him, we both moan loudly, locked in a breathless, sweaty tangle. At this angle, he reaches an even deeper place, brushing that illusive spot that drives me wild.

I lift myself on his lap then push back down, feeding his length back into me at a steady pace. Each pump drives me back to the edge of falling apart.

"You're so fucking gorgeous," he praises, cupping my bouncing tits. "Like a damn goddess, riding my cock."

Fuck, has this dirty-mouthed devil been inside of Micah all along? He's forgotten how to be shy, and his compliments feel so good.

Grabbing a nearby paint pot, he winks at me with that damn wicked gleam in his eyes again. I watch him lather his hands in paint and move them back to the swell of my breasts.

"I want to paint you, Willow. Every luscious inch of you. Will you let me do that one day?"

"Yes," I mewl.

"Naked?"

Working myself on his shaft, I can't protest. "Yes."

"That's my perfect, little angel. Let me see these incredible tits covered in paint now."

Smearing the paint over my chest, the bite of cold liquid heightens my pleasure. He massages it into my skin, holding the heaviness of my breasts in each of his palms.

"Does it feel good, baby?"

"God, yes," I bite out.

"Imagine this body laid out on my canvas in paint and ink," he muses, mostly to himself. "It'll be a masterpiece."

Thumbs swirling and fingers spreading, he covers me in paint then tweaks my rock-hard nipples again. As the paint warms up, my skin flushes with sweat, and I'm overtaken by trembles.

"I'm close," I cry out.

Micah begins to thrust upwards, lifting his hips to meet me halfway. "Me too."

We're both moving and grinding, chasing our own highs with nothing but mess and madness around us. If anyone else were to walk in, there'd be no explaining this scenario.

Just before I can fall apart, Micah captures my lips in a final kiss that swallows my moans. I gasp into his mouth, feeling the swipe of his tongue against mine as our orgasms hit.

We come at the same time, and Micah growls through his release, our lips remaining locked together.

I can feel his hot come pouring into me and slipping between us. The warmth causes fireworks to explode beneath my skin—popping, bursting, crackling with flames and almighty bursts of ecstasy. I slump against his chest, my arms wound around his neck.

"Christ." Micah holds me close, our skin practically glued together. "I love you so much, angel. It scares me to death."

"You won't lose me again."

"Now we have even more to lose. I want this family with you so badly, but I'm terrified of what it means for us."

Lifting my head, I look into his dark, forest green eyes. So much uncertainty stares back at me. Fear. Grief. Anxiety. Excitement. There are too many emotions for me to begin to untangle.

"I promise you, Micah, that we will make this work. Our family will survive. We always do."

He nods with a scared, slightly crooked smile. "We always do."

"No matter what."

After holding me against his chest for a few moments, he heaves me up and spoons me in his arms like a small child. Micah grabs a clean sheet from his shelf then throws it around us to cover our naked bodies.

"Let's clean up," he decides. "I want to take care of you."

"Okay." I smile at him, brushing a sweaty tendril of hair off his forehead.

We leave the studio and make a beeline for the guys' cabin. Across the street, Tara is still standing in place outside of my cabin, taking a phone call. She blanches when she sees us.

Grimacing in shame, all I can do is give her a little wave. She tries really hard not to laugh while she waves back and continues her phone call.

"New friend of yours?" Micah asks quietly.

"She's nice actually."

"I still don't love having strangers here."

"They're keeping us safe," I remind him. "That's the condition of us staying. We have to be safe from any threats."

"I know, angel."

Carrying me into the cabin, Micah heads for his bedroom and into the bathroom. He places me down on the floor and flicks the shower on before spinning to face me.

"Can I... No, never mind," he trails off.

"What is it?"

Rubbing the back of his neck, he peeks up at me shyly. "I just wondered if I could touch the baby for a second."

My heart melts. "You don't have to ask, Mi."

"Yeah, I do. I'm not just going to touch you without your permission. That's totally weird."

"It's your baby too!"

"Whatever, I still want consent."

Laughing hard, I drop the sheet and stand naked in front of him. "Okay, then you have my consent."

Smiling to himself, Micah kneels down in front of me. I have the tiniest, almost imperceptible baby bump, accentuated by my already round belly and wide hips.

"What do I do?" he wonders anxiously.

Rolling my eyes, I take his hands and lift them to my belly. With his palms cupping me, I hold his wrists to keep them there. His thumbs stroke over my skin in wonderment.

"Hey," he whispers in a tiny, amazed voice. "Hi, little one."

Tears well up in my eyes. The paint smeared all over me is drying and flaking off, but it doesn't conceal the life that's blossoming between us.

Our life. Our future.

It's right there for the taking.

"I'm going to look after your mama, alright? We love you so much already. So much."

I have to blink tears aside before they roll down my cheeks.

"Be good," Micah instructs, placing a gentle kiss right above my belly button. "We'll see each other soon, little one."

With his lips on my belly, I feel content for the first time since returning. I'm whole again in this moment. Nothing else matters, and the miles still to climb fall into insignificance.

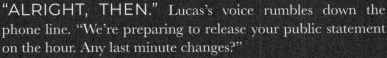

# CHAPTER 19
# WILLOW

## FALLING APART – MICHAEL SCHULTE

"ALRIGHT, THEN." Lucas's voice rumbles down the phone line. "We're preparing to release your public statement on the hour. Any last minute changes?"

I clear my dry throat. "I don't think so."

"Good. We can expect a barrage of media attention. Probably nothing national, but the sleazy gossip mags and celebrity news pages will be all over this shit as Sanchez is involved."

Scratching Demon's ears, I focus on the feeling of her coarse black fur. "I understand."

We're sitting in Lola's living room, surrounded by half-filled boxes and packing tape. Killian and Zach are working on boxing up her possessions while Albie continues to sort paperwork in the kitchen.

"You're doing a brave thing, Willow," Lucas offers. "We'll do our best to manage any fallout and Dimitri Sanchez's response if any."

"Thank you, Lucas. You've been a huge help."

"Well, that's my job. It's been a pleasure. Take care of yourself."

"You too."

Tossing Zach's phone aside, I rub my aching temples. This isn't a day I thought I'd ever see—I'm getting a divorce. Officially.

Lola's lawyer has arranged the paperwork. It's been delivered to Mr Sanchez's real estate offices by courier, and now the real war will begin.

"Babe? You good?"

Zach stands behind the sofa, leaning over to massage my shoulders. Releasing my temples, I blow out a tense breath. That phone call was tougher than I'd anticipated.

"The statement will be released on the hour," I answer shakily. "Lucas and his team will monitor the response and keep us posted."

"And what's in the final statement?" Killian asks, his head in a box. "Did you make any changes?"

"That Mr Sanchez was abusive throughout our marriage and engaged in illegal activity. I've fled from his violence, filed for a divorce and will be taking full custody of our child."

Nodding to himself, Killian seals the box in his hands. "Good. Short and simple."

"I don't like it," Zach gripes.

"Why not?"

"Abusive?" He stops massaging, his lips wrinkled with disgust. "That doesn't even begin to cover what he did to you and others. The world needs to know what a piece of shit he is."

"And it will when the time is right. Ethan instructed me to protect the ongoing investigation."

He huffs in frustration. "This is bullshit. He's out there strutting around and running his mouth. I want to fucking end him."

Reaching up from my seated position, I clasp his firm bicep. "We will, Zach. Be patient. His time will come."

"We don't have time to be patient."

"We have plenty!"

"Nine months." He throws his hands in the air, his eyes darkening. "Two of which have already gone. I want him behind bars by the time our baby is here."

"Who's talking bullshit now?" Killian glowers at him. "He should've been behind bars years ago. Willow and Arianna matter just as much as our baby does."

Slumping, Zach looks contrite. "Yeah, of course. It's just—"

"No, kid. Just nothing. That's final."

Falling silent, Zach looks like a kicked puppy. I hate that look on his face.

"I really didn't mean it like that," he mutters.

"I know. It's okay, we're all stressed."

"No excuse to be an asshole," Killian comments.

"Hey," Zach snaps at him. "Is this coming from you, oh mighty one? King of the assholes on his throne?"

"If I'm king of the assholes, you're my lackey. And I say get back to work, packing bitch. We have shit to do."

"Not your packing bitch," Zach murmurs under his breath in a derisive tone as he resumes bubble wrapping delicate trinkets.

We're finally beginning the mountainous task of clearing up Lola's stuff. It won't be thrown away but put into storage, safe and sound. Having it around is just a constant reminder of her absence.

Returning to the stacks of TV magazines next to the sofa, I laugh to myself at the folded down corners and circled programs that she wanted to watch. She loved her gardening shows.

"Nice," Zach snorts as he glances over my shoulder. "If it involved a rake or soil, you can bet Grams would watch it."

"I don't know how she found the time alongside running the town. There's so much to do around here."

"We're doing alright," Killian chimes in. "The place hasn't burned down yet, so that's something."

Lifting my notepad from next to me on the sofa, I flash it at him. "Have you seen my to-do list?"

"You're making an actual list?"

"Summer will be here soon! There's so much to do!"

Zach snatches the notepad from my hands and begins reading before I can steal it back. He dances away from me in the process.

"Plant summer crops, weed vegetable patches, organise hunting schedule, clear out cold storage, catch up on taxes…"

His huge, dramatic yawn causes me to glower at him.

"Boring," he singsongs.

I manage to snatch the notepad back. "She left me in charge. I have to take that responsibility seriously, or this won't work."

The easy smile falls from his lips. "I know, babe. I'm just kidding around with you."

"Well, don't. Not about this. Lola trusted me to do her job. I can't let her down."

Standing up, I stack the magazines in the overflowing rubbish bag then leave the living room to find Albie. My eyes catch on the ticking grandfather clock in the hallway as I pass.

It's time.

The statement just dropped.

The panic and fear I was expecting to rush over me doesn't come. Instead, determination filters into my bones. I'm taking control of my life and finally standing up to that monster.

Now we wait. He will fire back, there's no doubt about that. Letting me or Arianna go without a fight isn't in his nature. But we're in the limelight now, and the public will protect us. At least, I hope so.

He can't hurt us if the entire world is watching, or he'll

risk tearing apart his only defence against the oncoming storm —his picture-perfect public image. That gives us an advantage.

"Albie?" I step into the kitchen.

He looks up from his perch at the kitchen table, and the moment our eyes lock, I feel a rush of stickiness between my legs. It takes a moment for the penny to drop and terror to set in.

Warmth.

Blood.

Bracing my hand against the doorframe, I bring my hand to my stomach and breathe through my gritted teeth.

"No," I whine. "Please, no."

"Willow?" Albie immediately shoots to his feet. "What is it? Are you okay?"

"Not again. Please!"

He rushes over, gripping my shoulders and taking my weight against his body. The warm sensation has settled, but I can feel it soaking through my panties and plain black leggings.

"Is it the baby?" he asks urgently.

All I can do is nod.

"Guys!" Albie shouts. "Kitchen, now!"

The thud of a box being dropped echoes through the house followed by thumping feet. When Killian appears next to me, he takes one look at my face and goes white.

"What is it?"

"I'm b-bleeding," I choke out.

He looks down between my legs. "A lot?"

Nodding, I let Albie transfer me into his arms. Zach is fisting his hair and freaking out behind Killian.

"Call Doc," Killian snaps at him before turning to Albie. "Go and find Micah."

Both step aside to follow his orders as Killian tows me

towards the downstairs bathroom. Once inside, he squats down in front of me and grabs the waistband of my leggings.

"Can I?"

"Y-Yes."

Pulling them down, he takes a look at the sodden fabric and somehow manages to turn an even paler shade of white.

"Fuck, Willow."

"Kill," I begin to sob. "What if…?"

"No, don't say it. Let Doc come and take a look at you, okay?"

Shaking my head, I'm hardly able to see him through my falling tears. I brace my hands on his shoulders and let him pull me onto his lap, not caring about the blood smeared over my thighs.

We cling to each other, terrified and desperate, until Zach returns with Doc in tow. He stands back to let him into the room.

"Willow?" Doc asks in a gentle voice. "Can I come in and have a look at you please?"

"Yes, D-Doc."

"Zach's filled me in on the situation. You should've told me about the baby. I need to know so I can look after you properly."

"We're sorry," Killian cuts in. "We wanted to wait until after the first trimester before telling anyone, given it's high-risk."

"That shouldn't include her physician."

"No," he admits shamefully. "I guess not."

Crouching down next to us, Doc takes a look at the wet leggings and blood smeared across my legs. It's not much compared to the tsunami that poured out of me last time.

"We need to bring her over to ours," Doc decides. "I have sonogram equipment in my home office. It'll be quicker than travelling to Highbridge."

"Am I having a m-miscarriage?" I hiccup through my tears.

"I don't think so, Willow. Some bleeding can be expected, especially as you're having a high-risk pregnancy. But let's make sure, okay?"

His words are a tiny pinprick to the balloon of fear sitting on my chest. I draw in an unsteady breath and nod. Killian wraps a towel around my lower half as I'm boosted into his arms.

I bury my face in his flannel shirt to hide from anyone milling around outside. It's the middle of the day, so most people are busy working on allotments or housework while the kids are at school.

Racing across the town square with Hyland following hot on our heels, we get to Doc's cabin. He leads us down a dark, wood-lined corridor to his home office, leaving my bodyguard outside to stand sentry.

It's a huge room, filled with bookshelves and medical equipment. After rolling a piece of blue protective paper over the examination table, he gestures for Killian to set me down.

"Just here please."

Removing the towel, I'm laid down in my panties and shirt. When Killian tries to move away, I cry out, snatching his hand into mine.

"Please d-don't leave me!"

He ducks his head to kiss my knuckles. "Never, princess."

Killian perches himself on the end of the table to let Doc wheel the sonogram machine closer. I lift my shirt so he can squirt gel across my raised belly and bring the wand to my skin.

"Let's take a look, then," he hums, his eyes on the black and white screen. "How many weeks are you?"

"Nine," Killian answers for me.

Before Doc can respond, the door to his office slams open. Zach, Micah and Albie arrive, all puffing from running fast.

Micah's face is a picture of terror as he looks between me and the machine.

"What happened?"

"Just a little blood." Doc frowns at the screen as he moves the wand around. "We're doing some tests to assess the baby."

"Blood?" Micah repeats.

Pulling his twin into a side-hug, Zach holds him close. "Didn't the doctors say this could happen? Like spotting or something?"

"It can happen," Doc replies. "Willow has a scarred womb and significant internal trauma from Arianna's birth, so some blood would not be entirely surprising."

Breathing evenly through my nose, I fight to remain calm by latching on to his words. Just the sight of red between my legs caused me to spiral into a pit of panic after what happened.

"Okay, here we go." Doc turns the screen so we can all see as he points to a speck of grey. "There's your little one."

It feels like everyone is holding their breath—terrified and silent.

"And there's the heartbeat. A very strong one too, for this stage of the pregnancy. Would you like to hear?"

"Yes," Micah rushes out.

Fiddling with the machine, he flicks a few switches and moves the wand again. The sound of a rapidly fluttering heartbeat fills the room. My tears intensify, and I'm quickly sobbing again.

"It's okay," I weep, still clutching Killian's hand. "I didn't lose it again."

Head lowered, he kisses my hand. "You're okay."

The twins crowd around us, both misty-eyed and sagging with relief. We all cling together in a tangle, their hands rubbing my back and smoothing hair from my tear-soaked face.

"I'll give you guys a moment." Doc retreats, smiling to himself as Albie follows him out.

"Thank you, Doc."

"It's a pleasure, Willow."

Once we're alone, Micah lifts my chin and presses a kiss to my forehead. "Breathe, angel. Our little one is okay. You're okay."

"I w-was so scared, Mi."

Standing next to his brother, Zach kisses the top of my head and smooths my hair. "Everything is going to be alright now."

"Zach," Killian warns.

I know what he's thinking. That's a promise Zach can't keep. We may be here again another week's time, having the same conversation but with a different ending.

The sound of a phone ringing breaks the moment, and Zach fishes it from his pocket. He takes one look at the caller ID and frowns.

"It's Lucas."

"Don't answer it," Killian snarls.

Before he can hit the red button, I shout. "No, we need to know what's been going on since the statement was released."

"After what just happened?" Killian pins me with a glare. "You need to rest. No more stress."

"Back off, Kill. I've been working towards this day for weeks. Give me the damn phone."

Caught between us, Zach relents and passes the phone over. I accept the call and hold it to my ear, pulling the towel back over me to hide my bloodstained legs.

"Lucas?"

"Willow. I'm just calling with an update for you. The statement dropped half an hour ago, and we're getting a positive reaction so far."

"Positive?"

"The media is taking your claims very seriously." Despite

the good news, his voice sounds strained. "But that's not the reason why I'm calling."

I look around the room, meeting the eyes of each guy surrounding me. My family. My loves. I can face anything with them at my sides, holding me steady in the comfort of their love.

"It's Dimitri Sanchez," he continues grimly. "He's responded."

## CHAPTER 20
# ZACH

### WHERE THE WILD THINGS ARE –
### LABRINTH

SPREAD ACROSS OUR KITCHEN TABLE, the newspapers are all open to yesterday's leading story in the trashy gossip section. Ryder brought them back from a trip into town for supplies.

A photograph of Dimitri Sanchez at his most recent charity ball is splashed for the world to see.

**Sanchez: I'm not an abuser.**

**Real estate tycoon at centre of divorce battle.**

**Missing mother speaks up.**

Nursing her morning coffee, Willow stares at the newspaper with a blank look on her face. I close the nearest one, hiding Sanchez's ugly mug from sight. I really hate that motherfucker.

He's released his own statement, disputing all of Willow's claims and labelling her as a psychotic, unhinged mother on the run with his precious angel. It's a steaming pile of crap, obviously.

But that didn't stop it from triggering Willow and sending her spiralling over the news last night. She went to bed a sobbing wreck, needing all three of us to hold her until she eventually dropped off.

"Enough," I scold her. "Stop reading them."

"I need to know what's going on, Zach."

"You've been staring at them all morning. Let's get out and do something to take your mind off it."

"Like what?"

I snap my fingers. "We could carry on clearing Lola's cabin. I'm not moving in there if it's full of those creepy stuffed animals and fine china——"

"We're not moving into her cabin, period," she cuts me off. "We've discussed this already."

"No, we suggested it last week, and you shot us down. That isn't a discussion in my books."

Sighing, Willow swallows another mouthful of coffee. "Why would we want to live in her cabin? We have two perfect homes."

"You've answered your own question. Two homes. That isn't going to work once the baby arrives."

She tugs at her bottom lip, seeming to consider my words, before moving to the sink to wash her empty cup. "Maybe you're right."

I almost fall over. "Wait, what?"

"I said maybe you're right."

"Just like that?"

"What is with you?" she laughs. "I hadn't thought of it like that. I just didn't like the idea of washing the memory of Lola away."

"Jesus, we're in trouble if you're gonna start agreeing with me all the time. I'm a bit freaked out right now."

Willow flips me the bird. "Screw you, Zach."

"Love you too, babe."

"Yeah, whatever."

"So what are we doing today?" I flip all of the newspapers shut. "Not reading these, that's for sure."

Willow creases her brows, deep in thought. "What about shopping? Arianna needs some lighter stuff for the spring."

Her eyes stray back to the newspapers, full of that asshole's vicious lies. Willow is the most dedicated, incredible mother to Arianna, making all of this even more difficult to swallow.

"Let's go shopping."

"Not a chance." Killian speaks from his perch on the sofa, nursing a headache. "My head is killing me."

"You weren't invited, oaf." I narrow my eyes on him. "It's just me and Willow. We'll take the cheerful twins for protection."

"Cheerful?" she chuckles.

"He's talking about Tara and Hyland." Killian snorts to himself. "They hate Zach so fucking much."

"I don't know why." I sigh dramatically. "All I tried to do was tell some jokes to break the ice."

"What kind of jokes?"

"Dad jokes," Killian replies for me.

"There's nothing wrong with my dad jokes!" I defend. "They're the best kind. The cheerful twins just have no sense of humour."

"Or your sense of humour sucks."

I lay a hand over my heart. "You wound me!"

Killian rolls his eyes. "And you give me a headache. Shut your big mouth, and go shopping already."

Willow moves outside to let Tara and Hyland know about our plan. The moment she's gone, I get hit with a typical Killian lecture about safety. Like I'm not capable of looking after our girl.

By the time she returns, he's chewed my ear off, and I'm ready to run at full speed out of Briar Valley for some peace and quiet. We grab our jackets and Willow kisses Killian goodbye.

"Be safe," he commands sternly.

She pecks his cheek. "Yes, boss."

"I mean it, princess. Don't make me regret letting the pair

of you out. Stick with the security, and watch each other's backs."

"We'll be fine, Kill."

All piling into Hyland's huge, blacked-out SUV, I rattle off the instructions to Highbridge. The pair are as stony-faced as usual and on high alert after the public statement was released.

"I don't like this," Hyland complains.

"I still need some freedom," Willow combats, refusing to be intimidated. "I can't hide away up here forever."

Harrumphing, he tightens his grip on the steering wheel and focuses straight ahead. Tara gifts us both a tight smile in the rearview mirror. She's a little friendlier than her counterpart.

The drive into Highbridge is tense, but we make it in good time. Now that it's almost spring and the snow has thawed, the drive down Mount Helena is smoother.

People mill about the quiet town, the day in full swing. Shops are open, letting in the first whispers of almost-warm air while customers drink hot beverages outside cafes.

Hyland parks up in a tight space and lets us climb out before locking the SUV. Both he and Tara look out of place in their smart black clothing and concealed holsters that only we can spot.

"Go and get a coffee." Willow points towards a shop across the road. "We'll be in there."

"Not a chance," Tara snips.

Hyland crosses his arms. "Seconded."

With a sigh, Willow takes my hand. "Come on. Let's just pretend we're alone."

After fighting so hard for protection, it seems she's as exasperated as the rest of us are by the constant shadows following us. It's been exhausting since the novelty wore off.

Inside the small clothing store, I'm hit by a wave of déjà

vu. It's the same store that we shopped in when they first arrived in Briar Valley, over one tumultuous year ago.

"Let's do this." I pick up a sparkly pink dress and hold it to my body. "How does this look? Reckon I can pull it off?"

Willow giggles. "You look handsome."

"Pink is definitely my colour, right?"

"Sure, princess."

I blow her a kiss. "Thanks, babe."

Placing the dress back on the rack, I opt for a knitted, flower-spotted cardigan next, eliciting another laugh when I struggle to fit my wrist inside. Even Tara manages a small smile.

Willow shakes her head at my antics. "You're insane."

"The best kind of insane." I drop a kiss on her cheek. "Insanely in love."

"Christ. How long have you been working on that line?"

"Only the past three hours. Did I do good?"

"Terrible."

"Ouch, babe. That hurts."

Bypassing my grabby hands, Willow stops to select some short-sleeved t-shirts and lighter dresses. Once spring hits, the heat in the mountains will quickly follow.

It's my favourite time of year, when the snow thaws and everything comes back to life. Wildflowers bloom throughout the valley in every shade imaginable.

"Arianna's been a lot better since we came home." Willow adds the clothes to the basket in my hands. "I think she really missed Briar Valley and her routine."

"She's a good kid. Living in that apartment for twenty-four hours a day must've been hard on her."

"Temper tantrums had never been an issue before then," Willow admits. "But she hasn't had one in a while. I think Demon helps her keep her calm and manage her anxiety."

"Don't tell Killian. He's already gunning for the boyfriend

of the year award, and we don't want to give him anymore ammo."

Grabbing some striped white and pink tights, Willow rolls her eyes. "You guys are the worst."

"I'm taking that as a compliment."

"You really shouldn't."

Moving to the back of the store with our silent guards in tow, Willow searches through a pile of glitter-covered sandals as I survey the store. The hair on the back of my neck is standing on end.

It's just being out in public again. We've been keeping ourselves even more secluded than usual since the accident. It scared the shit out of us all. Apparently, even I wasn't ready for the outside world so soon.

But maybe the threat is always there. Hidden. Ticking away in the background. I have no way of mitigating something I can't even see. That's Sanchez's real power over us.

"Zach?" Willow holds up a pair of shoes. "What do you think?"

"Not really my style, babe."

"Jackass," she mutters. "For Arianna, obviously."

"Doesn't she have enough shoes? And clothes, for that matter?"

Willow shrugs. "I like spoiling my little girl."

"Lord. We're gonna have the world's most pampered kid, aren't we?"

Glancing around, she checks that neither Hyland nor Tara can hear us and gives me a sweet smile.

"You bet we are. This baby's going to have everything they'll ever need, living in Briar Valley."

"The whole town is going to freak out and spoil our kid when they find out you're pregnant. Rachel and Miranda will lose their shit."

"Aalia too," Willow chimes in.

Metal hangers clang against the railing as she roots through the clothing, searching for her next find. Tara and Hyland chat in low murmurs nearby.

"When are we going to tell them?"

"Soon," she says vaguely.

"We agreed twelve weeks. That isn't far away now."

"Maybe we should have a party or something. That'll be a good excuse. But we need to tell Arianna first."

"Yeah, of course. Do you think she'll be happy?"

Willow hesitates over a pair of denim dungarees. "I don't know. I thought so, but I'm worried she'll feel threatened by the idea of another child around."

"It's normal for kids to feel that way. She'll be fine once the baby is here, though."

"You think?"

Wrapping my arm around her shoulders, I peck her cheek. "Definitely. Don't worry about Ari, we'll make sure she's okay with everything."

"Do you know how much I appreciate you guys treating her like she's your own?" Willow beams up at me. "I just realised that I never told you that."

Ignoring the store around us, we share a tender kiss. I stroke her lips with mine, needing her to know that the pleasure is all mine. Arianna has brightened all of our lives.

Willow finishes the kiss with a final peck. "I love you, Zachariah."

"Ditto, babe."

Stealing the dungarees from her hands, I chuck them in the basket. There's plenty in there, but we keep shopping for another hour, buying too much and goofing around.

"God, this feels good." Willow sighs happily as we check out. "I didn't realise how stir-crazy I was starting to feel in town."

"We needed to get out for sure."

"I just wish we could do it without looking over our shoulders the whole time."

Before she can pay, I snatch the purse from her hands and tuck it under my arm where she can't steal it back. The cashier takes my bank card instead.

"Hey!" Willow protests, adorable with her scrunched nose and pout.

"No arguments. This is my treat."

"Zach, you can't just do that."

"Why the hell not? You're mine. I can treat you and Arianna any damn time I please, and I will."

Clutching my arm, she manages to wrestle the purse back. "You don't need to pay for us all the time."

"I want to. End of discussion."

Willow snorts in derision. "Who isn't open to discussion now, huh?"

Tucking loose black hair behind her ear, I bop her nose for good measure. "Touché, baby girl."

With the clothes paid for, I chuck them at Hyland to carry. He looks less than impressed but doesn't complain as he takes the bags.

"Asshole," he whispers just loud enough for me to hear.

"Careful," I warn with a sweet smile. "Your boss is fucking my best friend. I'd hate to put in a bad word against you."

That immediately causes his back to stiffen as he plasters on a false smile. "Shall we head out?"

Trying hard not to laugh, Willow and Tara take the lead as we exit the shop. We've just stepped onto the pavement outside when our peaceful morning trip shatters spectacularly.

The flash of cameras almost blinds me from the small team of reporters clustered outside the store. They swarm us until we're surrounded on all sides with no way of escaping.

"Willow Sanchez! Over here!"

"Zach," she gasps in horror.

Stepping in front of Willow, I attempt to shield her from

the hum of reporters with their cameras. Tara is yelling at Hyland to bring the car around as she takes Willow's other side for protection.

"Is it true that you kidnapped your daughter?"

"Why would you lie about Dimitri Sanchez and the abuse?"

"Did he rape you?"

"Enough," I scream at them. "Back the fuck up before we have a problem. I have zero qualms about breaking your goddamn faces."

One asshole snaps a photo up close of me. I grab the camera from his hands and smash it so hard against the pavement, shards of glass go flying into the air.

"Hey!" he barks. "I'll sue you for that."

"Go ahead. I ain't worth shit, mate."

"Asshole!"

Grinding the remaining pieces beneath my shoe to piss him off even more, I let Willow curl into my side to hide from them. She's trembling all over, a hand pressed protectively over her belly.

"Babe," I grind out in warning. "Careful."

It takes her a moment to realise what she's doing. The last thing we want is for her piece of shit ex to realise she's pregnant with our baby.

Quickly dropping her hand, Willow squares her shoulders and faces the cameras. "I'm telling the truth. Dimitri Sanchez is an abuser."

The camera flashes intensify.

"Is that why you fled?" a female reporter asks, somewhat more kindly. "To escape the violence and abuse?"

"I left Mexico to protect my daughter. I didn't want to see her get hurt anymore."

"Are you saying he abused his daughter too?"

"I'm saying he isn't the person the world thinks he is. You should be asking him these questions, not me."

With a roaring engine, Hyland jumps the curb and brings the car to a halt. Tara yells at the top of her lungs for the reporters to move aside as she bundles us through the madness unscathed.

We fall into the back of the car, and I quickly buckle Willow in before Hyland can floor it and send her flying. At the last moment, she rolls her window down to shout out a final comment.

"Watch yourself, Dimitri," she warns in a cold, hard voice. "The past is going to catch up to you, sooner rather than later."

Closing her window, Willow instructs Hyland to get us out of here. We take off with another throaty purr and merge back into traffic, leaving the chaos behind us.

"How the hell did they find us?" Tara asks.

"They must've traced me back to Briar Valley, and they've been camping out here in case we showed up," Willow answers grimly.

Grabbing Willow's hand, I tune Tara's cursing out. "Babe... do you realise what you just did?"

She blinks up at me in confusion. "What?"

"Jesus, Willow. You named him. Publicly. I've never heard you call him Dimitri before."

Pink rushes to Willow's cheeks as she realises the incredible feat she's just achieved. Naming her monster, in front of the country's cameras, no less. It was spectacular to watch.

"I did." She seems shocked, her mouth opening and closing.

"You said his fucking name, baby. I am so proud of you right now. He needed to hear that warning."

My heart feels like it's going to burst. The son of a bitch can watch that footage and panic his sick little heart out at the thought of all the dirt Willow has on him.

"I meant it," Willow adds, steeling her spine. "He's going

to pay. I'm done hiding. His days as a free man are numbered."

"Promise?"

Willow's forehead presses against mine as she breathes me in. "Promise."

## CHAPTER 21
# WILLOW
### HOME – EDITH WHISKERS

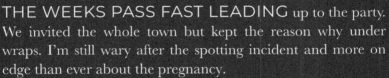

THE WEEKS PASS FAST LEADING up to the party. We invited the whole town but kept the reason why under wraps. I'm still wary after the spotting incident and more on edge than ever about the pregnancy.

We stopped buying newspapers after the first couple of days, instead opting to block out Mr Sanchez's lies. His crusade against me has gone rather quiet, almost suspiciously so.

He's still out there.

Plotting.

Biding his time.

Choosing a loose linen dress that covers my slightly raised midsection, I leave my short hair loose and curly, opting for no makeup. I'm too worn out to make much of an effort.

"Hey," Micah murmurs as he enters the bedroom and stops behind me. "You doing okay?"

"Just tired."

"We don't have to do this if you don't want to."

"I know, but I don't want to let everyone down. Besides, we can't keep this a secret for much longer."

He skates his knuckles against my cheek then drops a kiss

on my lips. "Then let's face the music, blow it off early and curl up with a movie. Sound good?"

I lean into his warmth. "So bloody good."

"Problem solved. If it gets to be too much, just tell us, and we'll send everyone home. You know people are going to be freaking out."

My eyes flutter shut. "Oh God. I'm not ready for this."

"Yes, gorgeous. You are."

He runs his hands over my hair to smooth the curls, peppering my jawline with kisses before dropping a final one right between my eyebrows. I'd rather lock us both in here for the day.

"Mi," I whine.

"We can't right now, angel."

"Then don't tease me!"

He raises an eyebrow, trying hard not to laugh at me. "Is this a pregnancy thing? One kiss and you're good to go?"

I squirm uncomfortably on the spot. "Pretty much."

"Let's see what we can do about that then, shall we?" He hums to himself as he fondles my overly sensitive breasts. "You gotta be quick, though."

Heat floods my core. "I can do quick."

Walking me backwards, my legs hit the bed, making me slump on the mattress. Micah kisses his way down to my collarbones as he raises the hem of my dress, pushing it up over my thighs.

"Be quiet," he orders, kissing his way up my inner-leg. "I don't want the others to interrupt us."

Pulling my panties off, his mouth secures itself to my mound, and I swallow a moan. Micah's lips are so sweet and attentive, he knows how to apply just the right amount of pressure.

With his tongue gliding through my folds, his thumb circles over my clit, sending sparks flying. I moan again, unable to hold it in. That's when the footsteps begin to approach.

"Dammit," Micah grumbles. "That didn't take long."

Without bothering to knock, Zach prowls in with a smirk on his face. He has a knack for appearing at the worst possible moments.

But as I note the tent at the front of his plain black jeans, evidence of his arousal at overhearing a single moan, I reconsider. Perhaps this is exactly the right moment to appear.

"I thought I heard something." He grins at us both. "Maybe I was mistaken. Did I hear anything?"

Leaving the decision up to us, I spread my legs wider, giving him a flash of my bareness. "You did."

Micah shakes his head with a grin. "I can never escape this asshole, can I?"

"Nope," Zach answers for me.

Inching closer, he settles on the bed behind me, leaving Micah to resume his task. "You're in charge, little brother. Don't mind me watching over here."

My lips are claimed by Zach in a hard, fast kiss as Micah's wet tongue returns to my pussy. With Zach's tongue in my mouth while his twin lavishes my core, I'm set alight with both of them pleasuring me at once.

Caught between them both, all I can feel is the steadily increasing embers of desire crisping my insides. I need a release, an end to the constant onslaught of fear and worry.

Their touch leaves no space for the bad thoughts to sneak in. Rather than Zach bossing Micah around, this time, the shyer twin is taking charge and torturing me instead.

"Are you going to come all over my twin's face?" Zach whispers in my ear before biting down on the lobe.

"Zach," I gasp.

"Yes, babe?"

His hand has snuck down my body to cup my breast through my dress. I need more. Want more. My nipples have stiffened into peaks and are begging to feel his lips wrapped around them.

"What is it, babe?" he teases. "Do you want more?"

"Yes."

"Too bad we have guests arriving in ten minutes then, isn't it?"

Plunging a finger deep into my entrance, Micah pauses to look up. "She's going to come at least twice before then. That's a promise."

"He sounds confident, doesn't he?" Zach laughs.

"I am," Micah snips back.

Curling his finger deep inside of me, I fall apart within seconds. Having both of them watching me is so damn hot, the feel of their skin on mine pushing me over the edge.

"Mi," I moan, my eyes squeezing shut.

"That's it, angel. Let go."

He doesn't stop fucking me with his hand, the heel of his palm grinding up against my sensitive clit. It milks every last drop of my release from me until I'm spent and trembling all over.

"Pretty good," Zach critiques. "But I think I can do better."

Micah narrows his eyes. "You're welcome to try."

"Turn around, babe. Show me that gorgeous ass of yours."

Taking the hand that Micah offers, I eagerly spin around on the bed so that my rear is facing Zach in a doggy position. I feel so naked and exposed like this, every inch of me on display to him from behind.

"Look at that glistening cunt," he preens happily. "So fucking perfect. Reckon we have time for you to take my cock?"

My insides quiver at the thought. "Please."

"Please what, Willow?"

Micah watches his twin tease me, a hand snaking into his own jeans.

"Please give me your cock," I whisper through my embarrassment.

"That's my perfect girl," Zach praises. "You only had to ask."

Pain crackles down my spine as his hand connects with my ass cheek in a playful spank. The spikes of heat cause wetness to flood my core all over again as I prepare to be filled by him.

These endless seconds of anticipation are torturous. I'm staring up into Micah's interested eyes, a hand fisting his shaft as Zach unzips his jeans to free his length behind me.

Knowing his twin is watching every moment is gasoline on the inferno between my legs. I feel the tip of his dick press up against my slit, the pressure intense. I'm so oversensitive these days, the slightest touches are mind-blowing.

"Fuck," Zach hisses as he slowly slides in. "This gorgeous little cunt is so fucking tight, babe."

Gripping the bed sheets, my eyes don't drop from Micah's as he begins to pump his dick in long, measured strokes. At the exact same time, his twin moves and thrusts into me from behind.

"So hot," Micah whispers in awe.

A hand gripping my hip, Zach spanks me again. "Isn't she just?"

I want to scream and shatter into a thousand spectacular pieces. Their attention is too much. Too acute. There's nowhere to hide beneath the weight of their combined eyes locked on me as I'm thoroughly fucked.

Each slam of Zach's hips adds to the strength of the second orgasm that's rising up inside of me. The time pressure only makes this hotter. At any moment, guests could arrive and interrupt us.

When Micah kneels on the bed and kisses my lips, I lose

myself to the soft, gentle sweetness of his mouth. I can still taste the salty tang of my come on his tongue.

"I want to fuck this pretty mouth of yours," he murmurs. "Is that okay, angel?"

The fact that he still asks melts me inside. Nodding, I open my mouth and greedily accept his length. His cock is long and hard as it slides against my tongue like velvet.

He takes a handful of my hair and grips it tight as he begins fucking my mouth. The twins must have some kind of psychic ability because they move in perfect synchronicity without uttering a single word to each other.

With both holes filled by them, my orgasm is inches away from falling into my lap. So close. I'm a moaning, writhing mess between them as my core tightens and heart explodes.

"Come all over my cock." Zach pushes into me. "Show me how good we make you feel, babe."

"We want to see you fall apart," Micah adds.

Fisting the sheets even tighter, I let the rush of heat consume me. Blistering. Overwhelming. I'm on fire and falling in a tight, dizzying spiral into the deepest depths of pleasure.

With another hard spank, I let myself implode. Zach shudders behind me and roars through his own release, triggered by my pussy clenching tight around his length. We climax together in a breathless tangle.

Still rutting into my mouth, Micah watches us both in fascination, chasing his own orgasm until the very end. I'm relishing the delicious pang of aftershocks when his hot, salty come fills my mouth.

Pouring himself into me, he cups my jaw and strokes a thumb over my cheek, silently praising me. I blink in recognition, sucking on his length to steal every last drop before I obediently swallow his seed.

"Fuck me, angel," he whispers with wonderment in his eyes. "How are you so bloody perfect for us?"

Wiping off my mouth, I collapse on the bed. "I'm really not perfect."

Zach carefully rolls me over so the pressure is off my belly. "You damn well are."

Climbing off the bed, Micah disappears into my ensuite then reappears with a wet washcloth. He passes it off to his brother who brings it between my legs to clean the mess from my inner thighs.

They're so thoughtful and attentive—even more so now than ever. But they still aren't afraid to touch me and give me the pleasure I need to survive each day without losing my mind. I love that about them.

"You... uh, may need to fix your hair." Micah points at my head, looking sheepish.

I glance up at the full-length mirror in the corner of the room, finding a bird's nest of black curls. "Awesome. Good job, guys."

Zach soothes my sore, spanked ass with a gentle stroke as he pulls my dress back down. "You're totally welcome."

With a sigh, I sit back up. "I suppose we should go out there and face the music."

"Together." Micah takes my hand.

"Together," Zach echoes, taking the other.

With both of them by my side, I blow out a breath and prepare to tell the world our secret. I can do this. With them to keep me safe, there's nothing we can't face... together.

––––––

The party is in full swing in my back garden. Dozens of tables are dotted about with glasses and dishes. Everyone is in attendance—the whole town turning up for hog roast and red wine in the cool sunshine.

After scarfing down food and a few too many drinks, the

mood is relaxed. Killian's cleaning up the food as he shoots me a knowing wink from across the grass. It's almost time.

"Shit." I shake out my sweaty hands. "I don't think I can do this."

Standing on the wraparound porch, Aalia's arm slips around my waist. "Of course, you can. This is your family. They're all going to be so happy for you."

She was ecstatic when we told her a few days ago. I needed a woman to talk to, someone I could trust. Aalia was thrilled to be one of the very first to know.

But the one person who should be here today, the one person I actually *want* to tell, is nowhere to be found. I hope that somewhere, Lola's watching down on us and smiling at the madness.

Leaving her fiancé to continue chatting with Albie and Ryder, Katie walks over to us and bundles me into a hug. She smells like floral perfume, and red wine clings to her lips, but I hug her back.

"You okay, sweetheart?"

"I'm good, Katie."

"Are you going to get this mysterious announcement over and done with so we can finally talk about this?"

Blinking, I stare up at her grin. "I'm sorry?"

She rubs my arms. "I'm your mother, Willow. A mother always knows."

Mouth opening and closing, I can't even deny it. Her smile is too wide. With tears pricking my eyes, all I can do is nod in confirmation.

"You are?" She's practically bouncing on her toes.

"Twelve weeks."

"Holy shit, sweetheart! What did Arianna say?"

"She was so excited." I smile at the memory of her squealing and grinning when we told her last night. "She wants a little sister to play with."

"I bet she does."

We embrace again, Aalia watching on with tears in her eyes. It feels better than I expected to tell them, like we don't have to be alone in this wild, crazy journey anymore.

With both of them boxing me in, all three guys meet me at the bottom of the porch steps, and we call everyone to attention. Everyone's eyes are on us at the head of the garden.

"What's the big stink?" Ryder jokes, knowing full well what's going on since the guys told him.

I wave him off, feeling nervous. "We wanted to get the whole town together for a party. This is the first time we've been together since Lola passed."

The mood sobers. Everyone knows that Lola left me Briar Valley in her will—news travels fast around here. Yet no one has raised the issue. We're all still mourning the loss of our leader.

"I know she's here in spirit today with us all because we have some exciting news to share."

Clinging tight to Micah's hand for courage, I drop a palm to my belly. My eyes are locked on the pine trees at the back of the garden so I don't run away from the sudden roar of applause.

"Oh my God!"

"Congratulations!"

The first people to reach us are Harold and Marilyn, offering their personal congratulations. One by one, we're bombarded by people, all hugging and squeezing each one of us.

Killian saves Arianna from the crowd by boosting her onto his shoulders, so she doesn't get squished. She's beaming, obviously enjoying all the extra fuss over her as everyone asks if she's excited.

"I'm going to be a big sister," she tells everyone animatedly. "How cool is that?"

Killian bounces her on his shoulders. "Very cool, peanut."

"Higher, Giant. Higher!" she yells.

I'm bundled into another lung-squeezing, tight hug from Ryder. He pecks my cheek too then steps aside to shake each of the guys' hands.

"Willow." Ethan nods, his expression grim. "I'm really sorry to do this right now, but can we talk? Something has come up."

"What is it?"

"Not here."

Waving the guys off before they can follow us, I take Katie's arm instead. She looks surprised by my decision but lets me drag her back into the cabin with Ethan in tow behind us.

Closing the door against the party that's kicking up a notch, I turn to face Ethan. "Do you want a drink or something?"

"No, I'm fine. I have to drive back to London tonight."

"Has something happened?"

He gestures for me to sit down. "You could say that."

Taking a seat at the dining table, I clutch Katie's hand tight. She looks as anxious as I feel.

"What is it?"

Ethan begins to pace the kitchen. "We've been monitoring Sanchez's official residence since your divorce announcement. Now that we have more evidence, we're preparing to make a move on him."

My heart leaps into my mouth. "You are?"

"We've been gathering witnesses and evidence for months to get to this point. Monitoring his location was part of our information gathering phase."

"I don't understand," Katie interjects. "You've known where he is this entire time? Why not just go in there and arrest him?"

Ethan shakes his head. "Not that simple. This is a very complex investigation, and we needed to wait for the perfect moment to make our move. We've been preparing for that to come."

"So… it's time?" I ask hopefully.

He looks crestfallen. "He's gone, Willow."

The floor falls out from beneath my feet, my stomach dropping with it. "What do you mean, gone?"

"Our surveillance team performed their daily check-in and found the place deserted. Nothing left. Not even a single piece of furniture or speck of dust."

Gobsmacked, I have no words. Not a single one. That mansion was an impenetrable fortress, the pinnacle of Sanchez's empire, but a trace on his location at least.

Gone.

Gone.

Gone.

The word echoes on a loop in my mind, taunting me over and over again. I should've known his silence was too good to be true.

"Where could he have gone?" Katie asks urgently.

"Anywhere in the world. He has the money and resources to run faraway from anywhere we can find him. We think he may have been spooked."

"By me," I finish.

Ethan says nothing. I don't need him to. The day I threatened Mr Sanchez to those cameras, I sealed this moment's inevitability.

"We'll find him," Ethan reassures. "His assets and wealth are still traceable. He can't hide from us for long."

*But he hid his true self all this time*, my inner-voice whispers. Long enough to take me and keep his illegal operations under wraps while presenting a lie to the outside world. A whole decade, if not longer.

Fingers itching with the urge to find my switchblade and a quiet corner to cut in, I make myself take a deep breath. I can't do that anymore. I don't want to. No matter what my demons say.

"What happens now?" I gulp down the lump in my throat.

"We work on picking up his trail. My team is already on it. Tara and Hyland will remain here for your protection."

"Do you think Mr Sanchez will come for us now?"

Ethan wrings his hands together. "There's a possibility."

With terror spiking through my veins, I let Katie pull me into a side-hug. It's as much for her comfort as it is for mine.

While I'm grateful for our miracle, this is seriously bad timing.

I can't let him find us.

Not now.

Not ever.

"Should she run?"

"Running won't help anyone," Ethan replies with a head shake. "He can find you anywhere, Willow. Stay here where my team and your family can keep you safe. The limelight will protect you."

"There's enough of that on me at the moment." I squeeze the bridge of my nose.

"Exactly. Sanchez can't try anything while the world is watching. He wouldn't take that risk. Use that to your advantage."

"I'm not going anywhere. This is my home. I have to protect it, as much as it protects me. Lola would want that."

Smiling, Ethan nods. "I think she would."

"I don't think it's safe," Katie worries, clenching my hand tight. "You should come back with me. The apartment is still there."

"No. I'm not leaving."

"Willow—"

"My decision is final."

Hearing the conviction in my voice, she doesn't press the issue. "If that's your decision, then I'll respect it."

"There's something else." Ethan glances at me, uncertain. "We've found another victim, but she's refusing to go on the record."

"Of Mr Sanchez?"

He nods grimly. "We're trying to convince her to aid the investigation, but we've been unsuccessful so far."

"So what does this have to do with me?"

"We want your help to convince her to go on record and help us nail this motherfucker."

Stumped, I gnaw on my bottom lip. I have no desire to look in the eyes of another woman who was in my position. Facing my own darkness is hard enough without being confronted by others.

But the more evidence and testimony we have against him, the safer my children will be from that monster. He needs to be put away, and for a long time. This will help to achieve that.

"What do you say?" he asks hopefully.

Looking up at Katie for confirmation, I force myself to nod.

"I'll do it."

## CHAPTER 22
# WILLOW

### THE STAGES OF GRIEF – AWAKEN
### I AM

FLICKING THROUGH THE CASE FILES, I fight to stave off an impending headache. There are hundreds of pages of witness testimony in here along with other case evidence and logs of information.

Ethan left the file with me when he returned to London a few days ago, asking me to read over the other women's evidence to prepare myself to speak to the new victim that has been found.

It's hard reading.

One woman, named only as Caroline, describes meeting Mr Sanchez in a bar in Norwich almost fourteen years ago. He offered to buy her a drink, but it must have been drugged.

Next thing she knew, England was a distant memory, and she'd been shipped across the world under a false identity, drugged up and compliant. Just reading it triggered a memory that I'd long since buried.

*There's a noxious, bitter taste in my mouth. Head spinning, I stumble and almost trip up the aeroplane steps until a man with an earpiece catches me. He's tall and dark-haired with cruel, terrifying eyes.*

*"Careful, bitch," he growls.*

*"Bring her," another voice commands.*

*I'm lifted over the man's shoulder, and the world flips on its head. Pain radiates through my jaw from the swift punch he delivered when I tried to run away earlier.*

*Blood is thick on my tongue, mixing with the taste of whatever they've forced into me. It's been nothing but pain and blood since we left the club under the cover of night.*

*"Get on the fucking plane." He takes a handful of my hair and yanks hard. "You've got a long flight ahead of you, whore."*

*Flight?*

*Plane?*

*I want to scream. I want to beg for my life, run and leave these scary people far behind. What happened in the club… I can't even think about it. The blood. The pleading. Mr Sanchez didn't stop violating me even as I begged for my life.*

Snapping out of the horrid memory, I feel a shudder wrack my body. I try not to think about those early days. What I can remember of that journey was hard enough to tell Ethan's team.

It's the same story.

Vulnerable women, targeted and drugged, taken from their homes to be exploited and abused at the hands of a monster. All different ages and circumstances but bound by their suffering.

There are countless other stories just like Caroline's in this file. Heidi. Paula. Erika. I have no doubt these aren't their real names, needing protection from someone like Mr Sanchez and his associates.

There's a whole ring of them—powerful businessmen, hiding behind their confident smirks and blazing personalities to conceal the real source of their wealth and power.

"Shit," I curse to myself.

Flipping to the section on the identified players in the human trafficking ring, I recognise several of the men who have been photographed with long-range lenses.

They're his friends. Associates.

*Bastards.*

Mason's in there, grinning widely as he drinks champagne with his wife, Georgina, outside a fancy cocktail bar. I recognise the dusty streets of the Mexican capital. I have no idea when this was taken.

When a hand lands on my shoulder, I startle from fear. Killian spreads his hands in surrender, a worried smile on his face.

"Only me. What's all this?"

"Information." I blow out a breath. "I'm preparing to speak to that woman Ethan told me about."

"Sure you're up for that?"

"No, not in the slightest. But I have to try."

Nodding, he drains the last of his coffee then fills the kettle to boil another. He and Zach have been working all morning on the new cabin while Micah is back in the studio, finishing up his latest project.

Life has been normal. Too normal, almost. I can't relax or feel safe while knowing that Mr Sanchez could be anywhere in the world right now, even England. He's prowling ever closer.

"He needs to find the fucking bastard before worrying about more damn evidence," Killian grumbles. "I'm sick of watching you torture yourself over this man."

"Ethan will find Mr Sanchez. I trust him."

"It's Sanchez I don't trust, not Ethan."

"Are you still running patrols on the perimeter?"

Killian smooths his long hair, tied back in a messy ponytail. "Every night. The hunters are having a hell of a time catching deer while out there all night."

"I bet Harold's loving it."

"To his bones."

After kissing the top of my head, he brews a fresh coffee. I resume looking at the case files, nausea twisting in my stomach. Their faces are still staring back at me, those smiles burned onto my brain.

"You eaten today?"

I hum noncommittally.

"You have to eat, Willow. And rest. I don't like you sitting there for hours, reading this shit over and over again."

"Kill," I warn.

"It's true. At least go and sit on the sofa where it's comfier. You need to rest after what happened with the bleeding."

"I am resting. Right here. Go back to work."

"Fine." With a curse, Killian heads back outside.

He's been even more overbearing than usual recently, and I'm over it. While I appreciate everyone's concern, it isn't needed. I know how to take care of myself, and I have work to do.

Another lengthy case file later, Demon nips at my feet, demanding attention. I scratch her ears to satisfy her.

"You're such a little attention hog when Arianna isn't here."

The cute as hell dog licks my hand in response then begins to bark. She's getting antsy after being inside all morning.

"Come on, then. Let's go for a walk."

Closing the files up, I stick my head outside to look for the guys, finding them nowhere in sight. Only Tara is standing guard on the porch steps with her phone in hand, no sign of Hyland.

"Everything okay?" she asks.

"Good. Just getting ready for a walk."

"Sure thing."

Snatching my phone from the kitchen counter, I write a quick note for the guys on the pad stuck to the fridge then lace up my walking boots. I need to clear my head after reading those files.

Demon follows me outside when I whistle, letting me attach her lead so we can go for a walk in the dreary afternoon drizzle. I don't mind the rain. It's soothing to me.

Tara straightens as I step outside, her eyes flicking over me.

"Where are we off to?"

"Walking this troublemaker." I waggle the dog lead.

She smiles brightly. "Let's go."

We leave the cabin and head into the woods together, enjoying the plush greenery and moss-covered trees. Everything smells wet and earthy. Wildflowers are beginning to bloom as spring arrives.

"I'd forgotten how lovely the town is in the spring."

Tara nods, walking slightly ahead of me. "It's definitely a lot different than London."

"I bet. I'm sorry you're stuck here with me."

"You don't have to apologise. It's my job."

"I just feel bad for pulling you both off the investigation."

"I've been working for Sabre for a long time. Investigations come and go." She hesitates, sparing me a glance over her shoulder. "It's the people who matter most."

"Even when they drive you insane?" I laugh. "Zach has a tendency to fill silence with humour."

"Doesn't he just," she jokes before sobering. "This place has been a welcome break. Working for Sabre isn't exactly easy or allows for much time in the quiet countryside."

"Well, you're welcome anytime. I mean it."

"Thank you, Willow."

Deeper into the woodland, we pass Harold and Theodore out hunting. Both stop for a quick chat and to rub Demon's belly. She loves all the fuss and attention that people give her.

Leaving them to continue hunting, I decide to push on, loving the fresh air and sense of freedom. The guys wouldn't like me walking so far, but their over-protectiveness is stifling at times.

"There's an outcrop up here." I point ahead into the trees. "You can see the whole t—"

A sudden, fiery burst of pain explodes through the back of

my head. My hands and knees hit the earth, agony blurring my vision until the forest is a green blur around me.

Slumped over, I can just make out the bloodstained rock that's clasped in Tara's left hand. It hits the ground with a thud. My pain-filled mind is spinning at the sight of her looming over me.

"I'm so sorry, Willow," she keens. "I have no choice."

"Ch-Choice?" I slur.

"The threats he made… Look, I have a family too. I need to protect them. This is life or death."

*He.*

Mr Sanchez.

Trying to push myself upright, I crumple when her boot connects with my lower back, shoving me back down. I'm too weak to fight back as warm blood trickles down my neck.

"Shit," Tara curses in a panic. "Shit, shit, shit."

"Please. You d-don't have to do this."

"He's going to kill everyone I love," she sobs. "Unless I deliver you to him. That's what he said when he tracked me down."

"How long h-have you been working for him?"

Rather than answering me, she just looks sick. At herself. The world. Everything. The Tara I thought I knew was a lie all along. That's when the missing puzzle piece clicks into place in my foggy brain.

"The accident… They followed us," the words stumble out. "That was you, wasn't it? You told them where to f-find us."

"I'm sorry," she repeats, reaching for her gun. "Now you're going to come with me. We need to get out of here without being seen."

"This will never work!"

"Get up and walk."

Unable to stand up alone, she's forced to drag me to my feet. More pain bursts behind my eyes as the blood continues to flow from my head. I'm woozy and dizzy, so much that I can only stagger.

"I'm sorry, Willow. I didn't want any of this to happen."

"Then s-stop this."

"I can't do that."

"What h-happened to this job being about the p-people?"

I can feel the gun pressing into my back. One shot and that'll be it. Over. She'll send me and the baby hurtling into the arms of death with a single, split-second decision.

I can't let that happen.

Not now. Not like this.

Focusing on the sound of Demon chasing after us and barking like crazy, I ignore Tara's cursing and try to formulate a plan. She's clearly acting impulsively after seeing an opening to snatch me.

That's my advantage. Her panic. If I can find the right opening, I have to make a run for it. I'll die on my feet fighting to be alive before letting her shoot me in the middle of a forest.

"There's a mountain road out of Briar Valley up ahead," Tara instructs, the gun still painfully pressing into me. "Take a right, and keep walking."

"What's your plan from there?"

"God knows," she mutters. "Staying alive."

"When did he contact you? How?"

"Enough talking! Just walk."

Ducking beneath a fruit tree, I spot several cabins in the distance, through the underbrush. Briar Valley is far below us. As far as anyone is concerned, I'm safe with Tara. No one is coming for me.

I have to do this myself.

Alone.

With a breath, I deliberately trip over a rock and fall to my knees again with a dramatic cry. Pain slices through my legs, but it's overshadowed by the violent hammering of my heart.

"Get up," Tara hisses.

"I can't."

"I don't have time for this!"

Ducking down to slide her hands beneath my arms, she's momentarily distracted. This is my opening. Murmuring a silent prayer, I dig my heel in and prepare to strike.

Rising above her as fast as my unsteady body will allow, I move quickly and snap out my balled-up hand. It collides with her left cheek harder than I was expecting, and she falls backwards.

Something in my brain clicks. I shift into a strange, focused state where all I can see is the bead of blood on her cheek from my punch. Keeping up the momentum, I hit her again.

*THWACK.*

Tara falls flat on her ass, grunting in pain. I take the chance to bolt away from her into the nearby trees. The forest passes in a terrifying blur around me as Demon chases, hot on my heels.

"Willow!" Tara shouts.

Screaming as loud as my lungs will allow, I race back in the direction we came, hoping to come across somebody. The woods are unrecognisable in my state of complete and utter panic.

"Willow! Stop!"

"Leave me alone!" I scream back.

Dodging through fir trees and wild berry bushes, I don't notice the tree root until it's too late. Hurtling through thin air, I fall again, scraping my hands on a thorny bush in the process.

Face-planting in a muddy puddle, I scramble and try to find my feet again, but it's too late. Demon whines as Tara approaches, a trail of blood staining her face.

"There you are." She grimaces. "You have a hell of a right hook."

"Get away from me!"

"I can't do that, Willow. Come quietly, or this will get messy for both of you."

Tara nods at the swell of my small bump. I protectively cover it, feeling a surge of fury. She'll have to go through me to touch my baby. I'll rip her fucking face off with my bare hands.

"Touch me again, and you'll live to regret it," I spit at her.

Lifting the gun, she trains it on my midsection. My heart stops dead in my chest, and the tears almost threaten to fall, but I hold them back, refusing to show her even the smallest shred of weakness.

"Move," she snarls.

"Please, Tara. Don't do this."

"I have no choice."

Before I can stand up again, there's a distinct, metallic click. Footsteps crunch over fallen twigs, and a figure emerges through the thick tree line with a hunting rifle raised high.

"Hands up," Harold barks, holding the gun steady.

Tara switches her aim to him. "Back off, old man. This doesn't concern you."

"Well, you're pointing a fuckin' gun at my girl here, so I think that it does."

Shuffling backwards, I grab Demon and hold her close to keep her safe. She's snarling her head off and far too ready to throw herself into the fight despite still only being a tiny puppy.

"Final warning." Tara cocks the gun threateningly. "I'm leaving with Willow, one way or another."

Harold refuses to back down, inching closer to the gun instead. I want to grab him and scream at him to run away. She's unhinged and more than ready to shoot him.

Everything happens so fast, it's a petrifying blur. Tara lunges at the same time Harold moves to squeeze the trigger on his rifle. The pair smash into each other, then there's an almighty bang.

Ears buzzing, I desperately crawl through the mud to reach Harold. He's fallen backwards, winded and pale-faced. I search his body for injuries, but find nothing.

Opposite him, Tara is gasping in pain. She's curled up tight and clutching her stomach where blood gushes out, encircling her in a crimson puddle that soaks into the moss.

"Gotcha," Harold wheezes. "Are you okay, Willow?"

"N-No."

"It's alright, kid. I'm here. You're safe now."

After struggling to lift himself, he pulls me into a side-hug. I peel his hands away to crawl closer to Tara. She's still conscious and trying to cover the gushing wound in her midsection.

"We can't let her die!"

"She deserves it," Harold spits. "Self-defence."

"Help me!"

Muttering to himself, he pushes Tara's hands away and uses his own to apply pressure to the wound. I just watch. I'm barely able to hold myself upright, let alone tend to her. Blood is still trickling from the back of my head.

Reaching for my phone, I blink through my dizziness to find Zach's number. He always has his phone on him. The ringing sounds far away as I sway, battling to remain kneeling upright.

"Hello, hot stuff," he answers. "To what do I owe the pleasure of hearing your heavenly voice?"

"Zach," I sob.

His tone immediately changes.

"Willow? What is it?"

"T-Tara… she… H-Harold shot… Help. Need help."

"Woah, slow down. Take a breath, babe. Where are you?"

"N-Near St David's Pointe, below the outcrop you sh-showed me."

"Hold on, babe. We'll be there soon."

Clutching the phone in my bloody hand, sobs begin to rattle my frame. Over and over. Violent, chest-aching sobs that I can't control. We came so close to losing everything.

"Willow," Tara chokes out. "I'm s-s-sorry. He didn't g-give me a choice."

Blood is trickling from the corners of her mouth as Harold struggles to keep her conscious. She's ghostly white and staring at me with so much pain in her widened eyes.

"You always have a choice," I reply shakily. "Always."

Another wave of dizziness taking over, I lay down on the moss-covered ground, and my eyes slide shut. I can hear Harold repeating my name, but it's easier to curl inwards to protect my belly and let the darkness take over.

It feels like hours have passed before approaching voices and shouting startles me back to reality. Tara's unconscious a few metres away while Harold shakes her, over and over again to no avail.

"Willow!" Killian's voice echoes through the woods.

Harold shouts back, directing them over to our blood-slick tangle amidst the trees. When the first pair of hands reach for me, I yelp and battle against them, terrified of being touched.

"Baby," Killian pleads, his voice low and broken. "It's me. You're safe."

"K-Killian!"

I'm lifted onto his lap, and Zach leans over us both to cup my cheeks. He searches my face and eyes, wearing a look of total panic that sends my own anxiety spiralling again.

"What happened?" he asks urgently.

All I can do is point at Tara, unconscious and bloodied.

"Who shot her? Is Sanchez here?"

"Tara t-tried to take me," I weep, still cuddling my bump. "She's w-working for him."

Zach swears colourfully, glancing over the scene as he tries to process the madness around us. Killian is also cursing beneath me as his hands find the source of the blood covering my mud-stained clothing.

"Fuck," he says to himself.

"She... hit me with... a r-rock."

Gently probing my head with soft fingers, I hiss when he hits a sore spot. Killian kisses my hair and apologises, holding me so tight in his arms, I almost can't breathe properly.

"She was supposed to be protecting you!" he growls in a deadly tone. "I'm going to fucking kill her myself. She doesn't deserve our help."

"No," I gasp.

"Willow—"

"Get D-Doc. Help her."

Curling my arms around his neck, I snuggle into his flannel shirt, needing the comfort of familiarity. The pain in my head reaches its peak, and my vision darkens again, swallowing me whole.

Fading.

Fading.

Gone.

## CHAPTER 23
# MICAH

DAWNS – ZACH BRYAN & MAGGIE ROGERS

"I DO NOT GIVE A FLYING fuck about your excuses, Ethan!"

Killian screams down the phone as he paces the length of the living room. His hair is standing up in all directions as he tugs at it, on the verge of pulling the whole damn lot out.

"No, it's not good enough. She was supposed to be protecting Willow, not trying to fucking kidnap her! She has a bloody concussion and five stitches because of that woman!"

"We should intervene," I suggest.

Sitting next to me at the dining table with a beer, Zach shakes his head. "It won't help. He's been like this since finding Willow yesterday, no matter what we say to him."

"Can you blame him?"

His expression hardens as rage filters back in. "Not in the slightest."

I can taste his anger on the tip of my tongue. I'm feeling it too. Seeing Willow, trembling and bloodstained in Killian's arms, was a fucking harrowing sight. Doc had to stitch up the nasty gash in her head.

After another scan, he confirmed that the baby is fine. No

damage from what happened. Despite that, I can't help but feel like our luck is bound to run out eventually.

"I want the other one gone too," Killian hisses into the phone. "I don't trust the lot of you. My family will take care of what's ours. Focus on finding that motherfucker so we can move on with our lives."

"Shit. We need Hyland." I rub my throbbing temples.

"Do we?" Zach combats, staring at the beer clasped in his hands. "The guy could be on Sanchez's payroll too for all we know."

"I highly doubt it. He's as angry as Killian, if not more."

His expression turns sour. "I don't need your fucking doubt, Mi. I want our girl to be safe from assholes looking to hurt her. Is that too much to ask?"

Apparently, it is.

The very people we were supposed to trust with Willow's safety are now in doubt and everything has been turned upside down. Willow's traumatised by what happened, and frankly, so are we.

"Sort your shit out," Killian snaps. "Then we'll talk."

Ending the call, he tosses the phone aside and fists his hair again. His pacing doesn't stop—back and forth, up and down, beating the floor into submission. He'll wear footprints into it at this rate.

"Kill, enough," I try to placate.

"No. This is bullshit. Ethan has nothing but excuses for why one of his own was blackmailed by that sicko. Apparently, Tara featured in a press conference and her name was given."

"That's all he needed?" Zach scoffs. "A name?"

"He has the resources to track people down if he wants to."

"Son of a bitch." I rub my eyes.

Killian nods, his face a mask of fear and anger. "No one is safe. We can't trust anyone."

All of our eyes sweep over to the front door where Hyland

is stationed outside and beating the hell out of himself too. Deep down, I know he had no idea. But that doesn't mean the mistrust isn't there.

"What do we do?"

Shrugging at my question, Killian resumes marching up and down. "Ethan's hauling the whole team in for questioning. The entire investigation is up in the air until they find out if any information has been compromised."

"What about Tara?" Zach asks.

"Still in the hospital, under arrest."

Digesting that, we all fall silent. This is a huge mess. Not only has it derailed our one shot at peace—Sabre's investigation into Sanchez—it's shaken us all to our very cores. Someone got to Willow. On our land.

If Briar Valley isn't safe, then nowhere is. We can't protect her, no matter where she runs or hides. There will always be that threat in the background, regardless of what we do otherwise.

"Is she still asleep?" Killian glances towards the back of the cabin. "Arianna left for school hours ago."

"I'll go and check," I offer.

Leaving them to continue fretting, I head through the partition door that leads into the back of the cabin. Willow didn't want to go home after what happened and being checked over by Doc.

She opted to sleep in Killian's bed and we all piled in together, needing our own reassurance that she was still with us.

Softly knocking on his bedroom door, I peer inside. The bed is empty, sheets rumpled and unmade. Checking the bathroom next, I follow the quiet sound of crying that's becoming louder.

"Willow?" I knock on the door.

The sound suddenly stops.

"It's Micah. Can I come in?"

"Mi," she cries. "I… think I need to be alone."

"I understand, angel, but I don't think I can give you that right now. Please let me in."

It's several long, painful seconds before the door clicks open. Willow stands on the other side in her comfortable clothes for a day of bedrest—stretchy yoga pants and one of Zach's oversized tees.

"You doing okay in here?"

Her face is red from crying. "Not really."

"Want to talk about it? No pressure, I promise. Just me and you."

Eyes darting from side to side, Willow swallows hard. "Come in."

I enter the bathroom and look around, finding everything in place. She was clearly hiding in here for a reason, though. She's shaking all over and refusing to even make eye contact with me.

"How are you feeling?" I stroke a hand over her arm.

"Bit dizzy still, but okay," she hiccups, wiping moisture from her face. "I'm just a bit overwhelmed with everything. I heard Killian on the phone and freaked out."

"He's just upset, angel. Ethan's team was supposed to be trustworthy."

"It isn't Ethan's fault."

"Killian needs someone to blame right now. He's angry."

"Being angry won't help anyone." Her tear-logged eyes finally flick up to me. "When will it all end, Mi? I don't think I can do this anymore."

Cupping her cheeks, I stroke her tears aside. "Soon, baby. It'll all be over soon."

"You can't promise that."

The pain emanating from her is a knife to my heart.

"But I can promise that we're here, no matter what happens. You can always trust us."

"Just no one else," she finishes.

Moving down to her mouth, I run my finger over her bottom lip. "Well, no. Not right now. We can't risk trusting anyone else with your safety after what happened."

"It just makes no sense. I thought Tara was a good person."

"Good people can still make mistakes. Sanchez found her pressure point and threatened it. Fear must've taken over."

Willow nods. "That's what he does."

"She's been placed under arrest in the hospital. Sabre's investigating the entire team to weed out anyone else who's been compromised."

"Shit, Mi. This is such a huge mess. How did we get here?"

Pulling her into my arms, I hold her close. "I don't know. But we're here, and you're not alone right now. You don't have to hide away in here from us."

"I wasn't hiding, I.…"

Mouth snapping shut, she shakes her head. I dip a finger beneath her chin to raise her eyes back up to mine.

"Then what?"

Tears fill her eyes again. "I wasn't going to do it, I promise."

"Do what, Willow?" I press.

With a sigh, she reaches into her bra and pulls out a small, metal switchblade. My stomach flips. I stare at her in disbelief, trying hard not to appear judgemental.

"What were you doing with it?"

She bites her lip. "I was just trying to figure out how to get rid of it. I don't need the temptation just laying around. Not when I feel like this."

Taking a deep breath, I hold out a hand, and she drops the blade into it. I turn the cool metal weight over, hating the mental image it conjures. All I can imagine is her making those scars on her skin.

"You want to use it?"

Hesitant, she nods. "I'm scared. It's triggering me."

"You don't need to be ashamed of that, angel. I said before that you can tell me anything. I won't ever judge you for feeling triggered."

Tucking the switchblade into my jeans pocket, I take her hand. She lets me guide her from the bathroom, and I pull her into my side so we can slip past the other two.

"Where are we going?" Willow whispers.

"To a safe space. You need to feel that again."

In the living room, Killian halts his pacing. "Where are you two off to?"

"We'll be in the studio if you need us."

Before he can protest, I steer Willow outside and wave off Hyland. The last thing we need is that lump of meat following us around. That'll only trigger Willow even more.

At the bottom of the garden, we enter my quiet, dimly lit studio where comfortable silence and the smell of oil paint envelopes us.

When I feel overwhelmed, I come to my safe place to escape. Perhaps she can do the same. Firmly closing the door behind her, I gesture around the warm space.

"Make yourself at home. We can hide out in here for as long as you need. I promise, it's safe."

Willow manages a small, sad smile. "Thank you, Mi."

"Don't mention it."

Walking over to the shelf housing canvases and supplies, I use the step to reach the very top shelf where a small, carved box is hidden at the back. Fetching it down, I twist the padlock to open it.

"What's that?" Willow looks over my shoulder.

"This is a fail-safe, for when I don't think I can control myself. I lock everything away and put it out of reach."

Opening the box, inside is stashed my own blade—a black-handled knife, antibacterial wipes and bandages. The self-harmers holy grail. I can hear how loud she gulps from just behind me.

"But you can still reach it," she points out. "And you know the code to unlock the padlock."

"That's the whole point."

"I don't understand."

"The power not to cut will always be mine. This is just a way of proving that to myself. Plus, out of sight, out of mind."

Putting her switchblade inside, I lock the box and put it back up on the shelf before moving the step away so it's unreachable. Immediately, Willow seems to deflate a little, her shoulders slumping.

"Does that feel a bit better?"

Surprisingly, she nods. "Actually, it does."

"Tricking the mind sometimes works."

"Sometimes?" She laughs weakly.

"I'm not perfect. Nobody is. I just take it a day at a time."

Turning to face her, she snuggles into my chest, her lips brushing against my pulse point. We stand and cuddle for several silent seconds, just feeling each other's breath. We're here. Alive. Safe.

Those blades won't win—not while we have each other. I'll pull her out of the depths of hell for as long as this stunning, perfect angel needs me to, whether she'll admit it to herself or not.

And in return, the breath entering and leaving her lungs will keep me alive. She doesn't even have to do anything. Her existence in this world is enough to keep blood pumping through my veins.

"What should we do now?" Her breath catches. "I don't want to go back in there and face this mess yet."

"Then we don't have to."

"Are we just going to hide in here?"

"What if we did some painting instead?" I hesitate, my eyes trailing over her. "Or... I could paint you, if you wanted."

"Right now?"

"Just sit for me, that's all. It could be relaxing. Shit… don't worry, it's a stupid idea."

"No, Mi. It's not." She smiles shyly. "I'd like to sit for you. Can I keep my clothes on, though?"

"Yes, of course."

"Cool. Let's do it."

Grabbing one of the bean bags on the floor, I fluff it up then add a couple of cushions to make a comfortable place for her. Willow smooths her t-shirt and hair, appearing self-conscious.

"Is what I'm wearing alright?"

"You could be wearing a bin bag, and you'd still be the most gorgeous woman on the entire fucking planet."

She bites the inside of her cheek, her eyes ducked. "You always say the sweetest things."

"Just the truth, that's all."

Taking a seat on the bean bag, she gets comfortable in the nest of cushions. I set up my easel and stool a few metres away before turning my attention to the paints. I have to get this just right.

Oil paints are too harsh to capture her beauty, so I opt for watercolours instead. I want it to be subtle and striking at the same time, built with layers of shadow and perfectly blended hues.

With the colours set up, I light a couple of candles and fiddle with the lighting in the room until it reflects off her perfect features at just the right intensity. Willow watches me the whole time—her gaze curious as she nervously wrings her hands.

"I like how you move around your space." She laughs ruefully. "Is that a weird thing to say?"

"This is my safe place. It's where I feel most at home, and I can be myself."

"I can tell. You're different in here."

"Different in a bad way?" I take my seat.

Willow shakes her head. "No, it's a good thing."

"You can relax. No one will bother us in here."

Releasing a sigh, Willow relaxes further into the bean bag and stares off into space. I begin sketching the outline of her rounded features, slightly crooked nose and full, plump lips.

Every inch of her is incredible. She's so beautiful, but in an effortless way. It's completely natural, from her makeup-free skin to every blemish and freckle on her face.

We sit in comfortable, relaxed silence, the only sound my pencil scratching against the canvas as I complete the outline. Candlelight flickers against her features, softening each curved line.

"When did you start painting?"

Wetting my paintbrush, I dip it into the palette. "A few years after my dad died. It was Pops's idea, actually. He bought my first easel."

"Really?" she asks.

"I was a bit of a wild child as a teenager. I'd get into trouble for drinking and causing trouble. Pops thought I needed an outlet to deal with stuff."

"But why art? What about it allows you to cope?"

Focusing on the shape of her hips, I lean closer to paint the edges of her body. "The world feels safer when it's being painted by my hand. I can make reality whatever I want it to be."

Her expression is wistful. "That sounds peaceful."

"It can be, until the thoughts creep back in. I couldn't find much solace in my art while you were gone. It didn't work anymore."

She continues twisting her hands together, mouth opening and closing with hesitation. "I understand that. It's how I felt when I started... you know... while I was away."

"How did it happen?"

"By accident at first." Willow shrugs.

"Tell me about it."

"I was feeling so overwhelmed and like I couldn't cope. I wasn't able to look after myself, let alone be a mother to Arianna. It happened in a desperate moment."

"And you never regretted it?"

"Every single time."

I continue painting, slowly pulling her secrets free with each stroke of the brush. "Why?"

"I felt like I was letting Arianna down by doing it, but cutting was the only thing that gave me clarity during all those months. I had no other choice but to take that risk."

"I get it. Whatever lets you cope, right?"

"Right." She smiles weakly. "But things are different now. I'm home, and I have you guys again. I don't need to listen to that voice anymore."

"That doesn't mean it isn't still there," I point out. "That's why you need to keep your promise and come to me when it gets too loud. We'll figure it out together."

"Thanks, Mi. I'm lucky to have you in my life."

"Meeting you was the best thing that ever happened to me." I spare her a quick glance. "You've changed everything. For all of us. We're not whole without you, angel."

"Me neither. Let's hope we never have to separate again."

Gloom slips over her, the shadows entering her eyes again. "Let's hope."

Because that's all we have left now.

Hope.

Pointless, flimsy fucking hope.

# CHAPTER 24
# WILLOW

FORGED IN THE FIRE – CAYLEE
HAMMACK

A KNOCK on the cabin door startles me from brushing Arianna's hair. We both freeze, and my hands quake a little, even though I know I'm being ridiculous.

If someone were here to kidnap me, they wouldn't knock. But after everything that happened with Tara, I'm feeling more on-edge than ever and unable to relax.

"Mummy?" Arianna whimpers.

"It's okay, baby. Carry on brushing your hair for me."

Handing her the brush, I peck her cheek then move to answer the door. I've been on bedrest since the incident, letting my concussion heal and the events settle in my mind.

But this morning, I was determined to get up and return to our cabin. The guys are stiflingly protective enough without me laying in their bed all day, being waited on hand and foot.

Swinging the door open, I find Ryder waiting on the other side. "Since when did you start knocking?"

With a sheepish expression, he steps aside to reveal Ethan standing behind him. I immediately go on high alert, taking a step back and preparing to slam the door shut.

"Wait," Ryder rushes out. "Just let him speak."

"Why? I want nothing else to do with his team."

"Willow," Ethan attempts. "Please, hear me out. I know you're shaken. We all are. This isn't us, and I want to make it up to you."

"Make it up to me? Your employee tried to kill me!" I lower my voice before Arianna follows me out here. "She pointed a fucking gun at my unborn child, Ethan. How can you fix that?"

"We've arrested Mario Luciano."

Feeling like the floor has been swept out from beneath my feet, I almost stumble. Both men wait on the other side of the door, silently pleading for me to let them in.

Mario.

The man who sold me to Sanchez.

It's been years since I thought of him. The slimy bastard was my first employer for the few shifts I worked at his seedy nightclub, giving lap dances and wearing ridiculously skimpy clothing.

"Fine," I say stiffly. "Come in."

Before they pass me, I stop Ryder in his tracks. He instructs Ethan to go ahead and sit in the living room with Arianna.

"I know you love this man, Ry. But do you trust him?"

"With my life." He nods solemnly. "This isn't Ethan's fault. He's trying his best to fix things and see this case through."

"You better be right. We can't handle anything else."

"I know, sweetheart. If you can't trust Ethan, then trust me."

I let him wrap his arm around my shoulders. "I do trust you."

"Then hear him out."

Ryder takes me into the living room where Arianna is telling Ethan all about her homework assignment for Miranda's class. Micah has been helping her sculpt a miniature model of Briar Valley.

"Ari," I call out. "Time to get going, missus."

Hopping down from the sofa, she rushes to grab her schoolbag and lace up her boots. I can see Aalia and Johan walking up the snaking path to the cabins through the window, ready to pick her up.

"Bye, Demon." She scratches her dog's ears lovingly. "Look after my mummy today."

My heart squeezes. "Come on, baby. Say goodbye to Uncle Ryder."

"Bye, Ryder!"

With her passed off to Aalia, I return inside to find Ethan and Ryder sitting on the sofa together. Both decline the offer of coffee, so I sit down in the armchair next to the fireplace.

"Willow," Ethan begins. "Look, I know that nothing I can say will ever make what happened better. We're all in shock, as much as you are. I've worked with Tara for the last eight years."

"Yet she still managed to pull the wool over your eyes?" I snap at him.

"Truthfully, yes. We've been blindsided by this. No one anticipated Sanchez to target the team in an attempt to get to you."

"The team? There are others?"

He winces a little. "Two of our support staff were also threatened. That's how he knew that she was placed on your personal security detail."

Hands balling into fists, I fight the urge to toss him out of the cabin. Anger is far from my default setting, but my baby's life was threatened. I have to protect the life growing inside of me at all costs.

"How can I trust any of you again?"

He raises his hands in a placating way. "Because we're the good guys here. This was a huge slip-up, but it won't happen again. Please give us a chance to prove that to you."

I lean forward in the armchair. "Tell me about Mario."

Ethan sighs. "After hearing your testimony, we worked on

tracking him down. The nightclub you worked in was shut down several years ago by the police, so tracing him was a little difficult."

"But you found him?"

"We did—running in a club in Soho under a new identity. Thought he'd slipped off the radar. He was arrested late last night and brought in to custody."

Despite everything, I feel a surge of victory. It feels good to know that he didn't slip through our fingers after what he did to me as a child. If it wasn't for Mario, Mr Sanchez never would've found me.

"What happens now?" I ask in anticipation.

"He's being questioned by Hudson and Kade as we speak. Mario is facing charges of human trafficking and more. We've got our first player behind bars, Willow."

My heart is trying to break through my rib cage, but for the first time in what feels like forever, it's for a good reason.

"Oh my God."

I wish the guys were listening to this instead of working. Even though his team is responsible for the recent mess, I could kiss Ethan right now. Mario is facing the rest of his life in prison, and it feels incredible.

"He will be formally charged and face trial for his crimes," Ethan continues. "But we're also going to use him to gain more information on the ring as a whole."

"You're not offering him a plea deal, are you?"

"No. He may negotiate for a reduced sentence if he provides helpful intel, but his crimes are too severe to be dismissed. You're not the first woman he's sold into sexual slavery."

Flinching at those words, I wrap my hands around my belly as if I can protect the life inside me from all this evil. I don't want my child to ever know the pain and suffering that I have.

"This leads us back to why I'm here." Ethan leans

forward, his eyes pinned on me. "We still need your help with the other victim. I want you to meet her and convince her to testify for the case."

"Seriously?" I scoff. "You want me to involve another innocent person in this after what happened to me? You can't keep her safe. Hell, you can't keep any of us safe."

"The sooner we end this, the safer you will all be," he contends. "Her information may give us a new lead. Sanchez is gone, and we need to find him as fast as possible."

"Please, Willow," Ryder begs. "We're all here to support you. This is the right thing to do."

"Don't lecture me on what the right thing to do is," I bark at them. "Where were you when I was bleeding on the ground and inches from death, huh?"

Pain lances across his features. "That isn't fair. We had no idea."

"Exactly my point! You had no idea. Nowhere is safe anymore, and I can't risk my life or my baby's life again. Please… just go."

When Ethan opens his mouth to speak again, I raise a hand to halt him. His shoulders sink as disappointment visibly slips over him.

"I'm sorry," he offers sincerely.

"I know you are. But it isn't enough. I just want my life back."

"You won't get it on your own." He stares at me, hardened determination in his gaze. "You have to fight for it."

Standing up, Ethan casts me a final look and shows himself out. Ryder pauses on the threshold, looking back over his shoulder at me with furrowed brows.

"He's right, sweetheart."

"Just go, Ry."

He shakes his head. "You have to fight for it."

Leaving me in silence, I stare down at my trembling

hands. Their words still echo in my head, even as the front door slams shut so I'm alone again.

All I've ever done is fight. I'm tired. No, I'm exhausted. The constant fighting to survive has taken everything from me, and now that I finally have another chance to live, I'm being pulled in two different directions.

Demon jumps up on my lap and burrows into my body, seeking attention. I stroke her coarse black fur and fight back a wave of tears.

"What do I do?"

Too bad she can't answer me.

"I'm so fucking scared of losing this chance... of losing my family," I admit, my cheeks wet. "But if I don't do this, he won't ever stop. My family will never, ever be safe. I have no choice."

Licking the back of my hand, Demon blinks at me with wide puppy eyes. I can see my own reflection in her glossy black irises—tear-stained and rumpled. I look beyond done with the world.

But the world isn't done with me. Not yet. I still have one more fight left to win, and it's the biggest fight of them all. I said it myself... There's no choice but to keep going and bring Mr Sanchez down.

The door creaks, and Killian sticks his head full of tousled, dark-blonde hair in. He sees me curled up with Demon, and his expression softens.

"You alright?"

"I'm okay."

"I just passed Ethan and Ryder outside." He steps into the room, his usual jeans mud-stained and messy. "Can't believe that guy had the nerve to show his face around here."

"He's still Ryder's boyfriend, Kill."

"But that's not what he came for, is it?"

I shake my head. "He still wants me to speak to the victim

they've found. I told him to get lost, but now I'm not so sure it was the right thing to do."

Moving closer, Killian crouches down in front of me, his huge hands landing on my legs. Conflict burns in his bonfire eyes, twisting and writhing, reflecting back my own inner turmoil.

"Part of me wants to tell Sabre to fuck off to kingdom come," he admits roughly. "But I don't know how else we're going to fix the mess we're in without them."

"Yeah," I say flatly. "I feel the same."

"As much as I want to make this decision for you… baby, I can't do that. This is your call to make."

Staring at him incredulously, I realise he's serious. Protective, overbearing Killian who forces me to eat meals and makes sure I get eight hours sleep every single night is letting me make this decision.

"Since when?" I laugh.

He shrugs. "Some battles I can't fight for you, as much as I want to. I've realised that hiding you away and pretending this isn't happening is not going to keep you safe from harm."

"Jesus. Who are you, and what have you done with Killian?"

"People change, princess."

"Clearly."

"After all the shit we've been through, I trust you more than anyone else in this fiasco. You'll make the right decision for everyone. We need to end this."

Too stunned to speak, I let Killian drop a kiss on my forehead and stand back up to return outside. I'm left staring after him, gobsmacked at the person who's just given me free rein to make this call.

*Shit.*

This is exactly what Mr Sanchez wants.

He wants to break my spirit and force me to give up. He

wants me to be alone, afraid and too weak to continue. Then I'll give in. He'll get what he wants—my submission.

No matter how hard things get, I cannot give that to him. He spent a decade breaking me down into the weak, damaged person he needed me to be, and I refuse to be his broken toy any longer.

"No more," I whisper to myself.

Quickly chasing after Killian, I stop him on the porch steps and grab his shirt sleeve. He's wearing this weird, knowing smile, like he knew all along that all I needed was a push.

"Go and get them to come back. Please."

Killian's smile broadens.

"That's my girl."

## CHAPTER 25
# WILLOW
### ANGEL ON FIRE – HALSEY

I NEVER THOUGHT I'd be back in London.

Sitting in the backseat of Killian's truck, we park up outside a small, closed café on the outskirts of Hammersmith. It's empty aside from the three men who wait outside wearing hardened expressions, surrounded by their armed guards.

I recognise Hudson and Ethan, both in matching all-black clothing and gun holsters. The third man has slicked-back, pearly-blonde hair and wears a blue suit that sets him apart.

Releasing the steering wheel, Killian shuts off the engine. "Looks like this is the place. Who's the new guy?"

"Not a clue," Zach replies from the seat next to me. "Some welcoming committee. They look like fucking stormtroopers or something."

"This isn't Star Wars, Zachariah," Micah chuffs.

"As Grams would say, they've got a face like a slapped ass."

I choke on a laugh. "She'd say that?"

"It was one of her favourite lines."

"Classic Lola," Killian concurs.

Heart twinging in my chest, I rub a hand over the phantom pain. Her absence shows itself in the strangest of moments. I wish she was here now to hug me and tell me that everything's going to be okay.

No one dares to walk near the three men, seeming to sense the threat that radiates off their packed shoulders and muscular frames.

They've shut the café for this meeting and set up surveillance. Every precaution under the sun has been taken to keep us safe now that we're exposed in the capital city again. Mr Sanchez would have to be a miracle worker to make it through their layers of security.

I blow out a breath. "Let's get this over and done with."

"Wait." Killian pins me with a fearsome look. "Just say the word, and we'll get you out of there. No questions asked."

"I'll be okay, Kill."

"He's right." Micah grabs my hand. "If it gets too much, you need to tell us. This isn't worth risking your health for."

"I'll let you guys know, okay?"

Zach gives me a charming smile. "Okay, babe."

"Come on. We shouldn't keep them waiting."

Micah climbs out of the car, then moves to open my door for me, wearing one of his usual reassuring smiles. It immediately sets me more at ease. I'm glad to have all three of them here this time around.

With the guys trapping me between them, we approach the others. Ethan smiles tightly, wearing a mask of tension, while Hudson offers me a hand to shake before introducing the third man.

"This is my brother, Kade."

A welcoming smile tilts Kade's lips. "It's a pleasure, Willow."

"Nice to meet you."

His hazel eyes are friendly as they search my face, giving the impression that he can see past all my layers of defences. But I don't feel threatened—he has a warm, reassuring presence.

"We're expecting Elaine to arrive shortly," Hudson informs us. "Let's all move inside."

Guiding us into the café, we all take seats around a small table. The atmosphere is heavy with anticipation, and the guys glower at everyone but me, all on high-alert.

"So," Kade breaks the silence. "We need to put a wire on you to record the meeting."

"You're not fucking touching her," Killian thunders. "Hands off or lose them."

Kade laughs. "Willow can attach it herself."

Lips sealed in a tight line, Killian still doesn't look happy as Ethan hands me the wire and voice recorder. I feed it beneath my t-shirt then tape the wire onto my breastbone.

The small black box is tucked into the waistband of my jeans to pick up the conversation with Elaine. I've memorised the brief and questions Ethan sent me beforehand.

"When is she arriving?" Killian fires off, obviously still grumpy. "We have places to be."

"Any moment. We're only here for security, given recent events," Hudson answers. "We'll move to guard the entrances and exits while you talk to Elaine."

Ethan shifts forward to look at me. "Willow, it's really important that we get her testimony. We need a lead on Sanchez, and she may know someone or something that could help track him down."

"After all this time?" I frown at him.

"We've checked all of his registered properties and everywhere mentioned by other victims." Hudson's words are clipped, sounding frustrated. "This victim is older, from before your time. She may have new intel."

"He's holed up somewhere," Zach surmises.

"Exactly. Someone is helping him."

"Who?" I ask.

"Well, we've got Mason and his other associates in Mexico and the States under surveillance too. They aren't involved."

*Crap.* Mr Sanchez could be anywhere, plotting anything, and we have no idea. If this woman can help us, then I have to try.

"What about Mario? Did he give you anything?"

"Not a damn thing." Kade scowls. "He's clammed up and is refusing to speak."

"Yet," Hudson adds ominously.

Cracking his knuckles, the sense of danger is so palpable, I have to force myself not to flinch away from him. I mentally remind myself he's one of the good ones. Even if my brain can't see past his intimidating exterior.

"How did you find this woman in the first place?"

"Her name was given up by another victim," Ethan answers. "But she's unwilling to speak to us directly. It took weeks to convince her to meet with you."

"What is she so afraid of?"

"The same thing you are." His eyes duck low. "Dimitri Sanchez and the power he wields. She has too much to lose."

A lump forms in my throat.

Here I am, risking it all.

Am I doing the right thing?

The sound of voices from outside interrupts our murmurings. The layer of armed guards maintaining the perimeter have stopped a short, thin woman with greying-brown hair from entering the café.

"That's her." Hudson stands up. "We'll be right outside, Willow."

"Okay, thanks."

The others follow suit, waiting for my guys to copy them and stand up. Zach and Micah both stop to kiss my hands.

"Be careful," Zach whispers.

"I will."

"Shout if you need us," Micah adds.

Letting them both pass him, Killian hesitates, staring at

me for several seconds as if attempting to burrow deep into my brain.

"I'll be fine," I whisper to him. "Go."

"Are you sure about this?"

"What happened to trusting me, Kill?"

"I trust you," he insists. "It's this fucking world that I don't trust. It seems determined to take you away from me."

I hold his gaze, reaching up to smooth the wrinkle between his brows. "I won't let it."

He nods once then kisses me firmly on the lips. I watch the three of them leave, passing Elaine in the doorway as she timidly enters the café.

Standing up, I wait for her to approach. Her narrow hips are cloaked in an ill-fitting pair of jeans with a cream sweater.

"Willow?" she croaks.

"Hi. Elaine, I'm guessing?"

Nodding, Elaine takes the seat opposite me. "Hello."

"Is that your real name, can I ask?"

"What do you think?" she snaps back.

"Fair enough."

"I'm not staying for long." She sighs wearily. "I just wanted to tell these people to leave me alone. I don't want to speak to anyone about the past. That's final."

"I understand. I thought we could just talk——"

"No," she interrupts.

"Please, Elaine."

"There's nothing else to discuss. Instruct your associates to leave me alone. I have a life and a family. I don't want them knowing about this."

"Look, you're scared. I get it. I'm terrified too, all of the time. But that's no way to live, and it won't end unless we bring Mr Sanchez down."

Elaine flinches. "He made you call him that too?"

"Yes. We're not so different."

"I hardly think so."

"We went through something similar at the hands of that monster. You can talk to me about what happened to you. All we want is the truth so we can bring him to justice for what he's done."

Air hisses out of her nostrils. "I just want peace."

"So do I. Help me to get it for all of us."

Visibly wilting, Elaine looks down at her entwined fingers, twisting together. I can tell that I'm getting through to her. She just needs a push.

"He hurt me every day," I reveal, my chest tight with pain. "It was relentless. My daughter suffered too."

"You have a daughter? With him?" she asks in shock.

"Yes, Arianna is his. He beat her as well."

She looks stunned to learn this, her features twisting with anger at the thought of Mr Sanchez hurting an innocent child. I decide to keep going.

"Some nights I just laid there and let him do it. That was easier than fighting back. But other times, I would kick and scream until he beat me into submission."

She hesitates, paling further. "I never fought back."

"That isn't something to be ashamed of."

"Isn't it?"

"No," I insist fiercely. "What he did to us was evil. It's his fault, not yours. That's why he has to be punished."

Elaine looks contemplative as she chews her lip. "He deserves to rot in prison for everything he's done to you. To all of us."

"Then help me put him there. Please."

Softening, she moves to the edge of her seat. "I'm so scared."

"That's why we do this together. Not alone."

"And if I do this, will I be left alone?"

"Yes. All we need is your testimony."

She nods tersely. "What do you want to know, then?"

"When did you last see him?" I quickly ask before she changes her mind.

Her eyes go faraway, misted-over by the past. "Twelve years ago. I managed to run during a business trip in London."

"You were married?"

"No," she says quietly. "Nothing so formal. When we met, Dimitri was very charming. I was enamoured immediately. I had no idea who he really was until it was too late."

"So you were in a relationship?" I poke further.

"Yes, a very passionate one at that."

I want to delve into what she means, but I force myself to stick to the list of questions that Ethan drilled into me.

"And how did he take you?"

"I agreed to go on holiday with him to Florida. That was the last time I saw England until we returned to London, almost a year later."

"Did you ever think about going to the police?"

"I was too scared to speak up after I escaped him. You know how powerful he is."

I've never heard of Mr Sanchez having a relationship like this. There were women involved in our life together—women he'd rape, beat and abuse, provided by Mason's supply lines.

But the way Elaine describes her time with him is different. He didn't traffic her using violence and threats like the rest of us. This version of him took his time to groom her before making his move.

"What happened then?"

"It felt like a honeymoon. We were so in love with each other, I thought I was the luckiest girl in the world." Her eyes well up. "I still remember when everything changed and the first time he hit me."

Her words take me back. I remember it too. Strapped into a seat in the aeroplane, groggy and drugged up to my eyeballs, Mr Sanchez struck me for sobbing and ruining his peace.

Elaine wipes underneath her eyes. "It got bad fast. He'd become so angry, furious even, and take it all out on me. The beatings worsened, and I was so terrified, all I wanted was to go home. But he wouldn't let me."

"He kept you there?"

"Not in America. After the holiday, we returned to Mexico. He was living in Tijuana at the time. The trip there was so awful... He wouldn't stop hurting me, even when I begged for relief from the constant pain."

Reaching across the table, I take her hand into mine. Instead of pulling away as I was expecting, Elaine squeezes my fingers and gives me a wobbly smile. We've both been through the same living hell.

"These locations in Florida and Tijuana... do you have any addresses?"

Her eyes scurry around the café. "One, maybe."

"What about a description for the other? Rough location?"

"I may... Maybe I can write a description or something. It's been a long time, and a lot of the memories are a blur."

Excitement pulsates through me. "Anything can help."

"I don't want my new name attached to any of this information," she hurries to say. "I have a new life now, and my husband knows nothing about what happened to me. That's why I didn't want to come forward."

"We can keep the information anonymous."

Nodding, she pulls a pen from her handbag then scribbles down some information on a napkin. I eagerly take it, feeling like I'm holding the Holy Grail. This could be something we can use to track him down.

"When are you due?" She nods towards the hand rubbing my small bump.

"I'm about sixteen weeks along, so another five months or so."

"An autumn baby. How wonderful."

I rub a hand over my belly. "We haven't found out the gender, we want it to be a surprise."

"We did the same with my first two." Elaine smiles wistfully. "It makes things even more exciting."

"You have kids?"

"Four altogether."

"Wow, busy house."

"You don't know the half of it." She laughs a little before sobering again. "I have to keep them safe, Willow. They can never know about any of this. It would kill them."

Unable to stop myself, I lean closer, softening towards her. "You never wanted to tell your husband?"

"Of course, but he wouldn't understand. I don't want anyone to look at me differently. They would if they knew what Dimitri Sanchez did to me all those years ago."

"I thought the same thing for a long time." My chest burns at the thought of the guys. "But people will always surprise you, and I should've given the men I love more credit than that."

"Men?" she repeats.

"Uh, it's a little complicated."

Her eyes twinkle as she becomes more comfortable. "As long as they make you happy, it doesn't matter how complicated things get. You hold on to those men, and never let them go."

"I have no intention of ever doing that."

"Then you're one of the lucky ones."

Releasing her hand, I swallow to clear the lump growing in my throat. Old Willow never would've believed I'd be here now, facing my fears and doing it regardless of how terrified I am.

She didn't have the strength to run headfirst into the war we're currently facing. I'm not entirely sure I have that strength now, but it isn't going to stop me from proving Mr Sanchez wrong in his quest to break me.

"I think your husband may surprise you too," I offer honestly.

She snorts. "I really don't think so."

"He deserves to know, Elaine. If he loves you as much as it sounds like he does, he'll stand by you regardless of your past. That's what love is, right? Accepting each other unconditionally."

She looks down at the scarred Formica table, seeming to think about that. I glance outside where the others are standing guard, surely trying hard not to watch the meeting unfold behind them.

If I'd trusted the guys long before I did and told them the truth, things may have ended differently. They begged for it so many times, but I couldn't give it to them until I had no other choice.

But they loved me anyway.

I'm so lucky to have that.

"That's why I'm going to fight this until the end," I continue, feeling my determination harden. "For that unconditional love and the people who gave it to me. They deserve my fight."

Elaine watches me, the corners of her mouth curling upwards a little. "Not all of us are as strong as you, Willow. But I suppose…" She waves her hand as if to wipe away the rest of her unspoken thought. "I'm glad we have someone to fight for all of us."

"I'm not strong." I shrug her off. "A few days ago, I kicked the team out of my house and swore I'd never meet you. I was afraid of putting myself back in the firing line again."

She nods in understanding.

"But here I am." I gesture around the empty café. "Because no matter how afraid or tired of this world I am, I want to be a good person, not the broken little girl Mr Sanchez made me into."

This time, she reaches across the table to initiate, taking my hand into hers again and gripping tightly.

"Thank you. From all of us."

I squeeze her hand back. "You don't have to thank me."

"I do. I'm just praying this will be enough to bring that monster down… for all of our sakes."

"Me too."

Letting me go, she stands up and grabs her handbag. I panic, desperately trying to remember the list of questions. My mind has gone blank, filled with emotion instead.

"It was nice to meet you," she offers sincerely. "And I hope you find whatever it is you're looking for in life. I hope… you can find peace. That we can all find peace."

I stand up too, following in her footsteps. "Let me give you my phone number. Please call me if you need to talk to someone."

Quickly scribbling it down on a napkin, I hand the number over to her. She hesitantly takes it then nods in thanks.

"See you around, Willow."

Watching her go, I feel a twinge of pity for the small, frightened woman. I can see strength in her, beneath the battle scars and pain. She survived Sanchez. That takes a strength most could never dream of.

Elaine walks out with her head held high, straight past Ethan, Hudson and Kade. She doesn't stop to speak to them, even as they call her name. This trip wasn't for them. It was for her… And me.

Striding back in, Killian rushes to my side first, pulling me into a hug like we've been separated for years rather than minutes. The other two aren't far behind with the team.

"Are you okay?" Killian fusses over me. "Did she upset you? I'll go drag her back here by her hair if need be."

"Cool it, Kill." I chuckle. "We're good."

"Sure?" he worries, his gaze and hands roaming over me.

"Alright, caveman." Zach claps him on the shoulder. "Let's turn the testosterone down a notch, shall we? You're gonna drown poor Willow in it."

"Fuck off, kid," he growls.

Wading through them, I step into Micah's arms, needing his quiet assurance. "She was fine. We talked for a bit, and I got the information we needed."

Picking up the napkin from the table, Ethan scans over it. "She gave these to you?"

"Yes. Two properties from her time with Mr Sanchez twelve years ago. One in Florida and another in Tijuana. She didn't remember much else."

"What else did she say?" Hudson presses.

"That he didn't traffic her initially. They had a consensual relationship that turned bad before he forced her back to Mexico and held her there for a year. He was abusive—physically and sexually."

"Shit," Kade mutters.

"Precisely," Ethan echoes. "This just got a hell of a lot more complicated."

"Did I do something wrong?"

"No, sweetheart." Ethan smiles appreciatively. "You did good. This is information we can use. I just wasn't expecting to hear another side to the story. That may not work in our favour in Elaine's case."

"We have to protect her. She wants to remain anonymous."

"And she will. This is just information to give us a new lead on Sanchez's location."

Moving into Zach's arms last, I stifle a laugh when he blows a raspberry on my cheek. His grin widens as he spots the smile on my face. Only he can make me feel better in tense situations like this.

"Well done, Willow," Kade compliments.

"Thanks. I don't know how you guys do this for a living."

Hudson shrugs. "You get used to it."

Pulling the wire from my chest, I hand it and the voice recorder to Ethan. "Got everything you need?"

"We'll see if it's enough to give us a lead. Thank you for coming back. We're going to try and end this now, I promise you."

"Better keep your word."

"He will." Killian wears his best hunter's smile. "Else he won't have any fucking legs while running around after criminals."

"That a threat?" Ethan chuckles.

"Consider it a promise. Ryder can always find a new boyfriend."

"Alright." I grab Killian's arm to steer him away. "That's our cue to leave. I want to go home."

"Amen to that," Zach hums.

# CHAPTER 26
# KILLIAN

DEAD MAN'S ARMS – BISHOP
BRIGGS

"FUCKING TRAFFIC," I snarl.

Staring at the line of vehicles blocking the motorway leading back into Wales, I lay my hand down on the horn, blaring the queue of red lights. Fucking assholes. I knew this trip was a shitty idea.

"We're going to be late." Zach stares ahead at the queue.

"Call Aalia, and let her know. Arianna will be waiting up for us."

"Phone's dead."

"Mine's at home," Willow adds from the backseat.

Her head is resting in Micah's lap. She spent much of the trip back from London napping after her eventful morning. He leans down to nuzzle her hair and kiss her forehead.

"We'll be home soon. I'm sure they're all fine."

"I hope so." Willow sounds worried.

"Arianna's safe with Aalia and the others," Zach chimes in. "We'll be home in a couple of hours. Go back to sleep."

I watch Willow curl her hands into her chest in the rearview mirror. She falls back asleep as we crawl through the traffic. The miles pass by at a snail's pace, stretching the journey on for twice as long as it usually takes.

"What did you think about that woman?" Zach asks quietly.

I focus on the traffic ahead. "She struck me as pretty shady, but Willow seemed to trust her. We'll see if her intel pans out."

"I don't love that we're putting all our bets on some random woman's information from twelve years ago."

"And you think that I do?" I cut past a dawdling motorist to move ahead. "She's our last resort."

"I hope you're right. I'm not sure how much more of this Willow can take."

"She's stronger than you think," Micah counters from behind me. "Look at what she did today. Sabre would have nothing if Willow hadn't gone in and spoken to Elaine for them. She did amazing."

"Micah's right," I agree. "Willow did that, not them."

"I know she's strong," Zach claps back. "I just wish she didn't have to be quite so strong. Isn't that supposed to be our jobs? Being strong for her?"

"No," I correct. "It's not anymore."

"Huh?"

"Coddling Willow has never done us any good. She's a strong, independent woman, and that's why we love her. We have to let her do this how she sees fit. Today proved that much."

"Jesus, Kill. Did you have a fucking personality transplant?"

"Shut it, kid. I'm just telling it how it is."

"Well, you're freaking me out with all this mature, non-egotistical talk. Anyone would think you'd been hit around the head."

"Feel free to walk back to Briar Valley," I growl at him.

"That's more like it."

Lapsing back into silence, we crawl through the traffic inch by painful inch. Willow doesn't stir again, lightly snoring from her balled-up position in the backseat with Micah.

By the time we arrive in the rural, rugged mountains that house Briar Valley, hours have passed, and we're all desperately tired. Zach and Willow's eyes fling open when I slam on the breaks at the sight ahead of us.

"What in the living fuck is that?"

All of us strain to look out of the window as awful, shocked silence reigns throughout the truck. Rising high above the forest of fir and pine trees is a billowing, black cloud of smoke.

"A campfire?" Micah says hopefully.

"That's no campfire." I rev the engine and take off. "It's an actual fire."

Racing up the mountain road at breakneck speed, I guide us over bumps and rocks, moving far faster than safety would usually allow for. Willow goes white as a sheet when she spots the smoke.

"What is that?" she asks in a rush of panic.

Micah holds her to his chest. "We're not sure."

"Shit! Arianna's up there!"

"Everyone is," I state grimly. "If that smoke's coming from town, we're in serious trouble."

Turning onto the mountain pass, we begin the descent into Briar Valley. Immediately, the air becomes thick with black smoke so dense, it's like tar is seeping through the car's vents. Soon we're all coughing.

The woods are hazy and speckled with black ash, choking all remaining wisps of light from the early evening shadows. We're still moving fast but having to navigate the poor visibility and woodland.

"Motherfuck," I blurt out as we hit a rock.

It scrapes along the bottom of the truck, eliciting an awful, metallic screeching sound. Bouncing to the next bump, we move from obstacle to obstacle, dodging trees and smoke in all directions.

By some miracle, we reach Briar Valley relatively unscathed. The visibility reaches an all-time low as billowing black smoke infiltrates the air, choking everything in its path. No leaf or petal escapes untouched.

I manage to guide us through the smoke, and as the trees thin out, the source of the chaos becomes clear. Wild, rampant flames stretch so high into the sky, they must kiss the heavens.

Fire is burning bright ahead of us, as if the devil himself has deigned to visit us and reign down hellfire. Wood, furniture and carpet are being consumed in a greedy roar of pure evil.

Lola's cabin.

Up in flames.

"No," I utter in horror.

Everyone stares ahead—gobsmacked and horrified. Her cabin is unrecognisable through the destruction, the structure being eaten alive by fire. I can just make out the shadows of people in the clearing around us.

Slamming my door open, I immediately double over at the rush of heat and ash that greets me. It sears my lungs— crisping, infecting and metastasising into a red-hot cancer.

"Stay inside," I yell at the others.

Zach completely ignores me and hops out. "Not a chance!"

"Kid!"

"Move," he shouts.

We run around the truck together, trying to fumble our way through hazy, smoke-filled air that wraps around our throats like burning-hot barbed wire.

"Killian!" someone yells.

At the edge of the property, Ryder and Albie are attempting to fight the flames. We're too remote for fire trucks to get up here, so we have some equipment for ourselves.

Fire extinguishers and powdered foam are no match for the hellish beast that's invaded Lola's home, set up shop and decided to burn the entire damn thing to nothing but ash. We're powerless.

Willow appears from the car, a hand clenched over her mouth. "Where's Ari?"

Ryder points towards Rachel and Miranda's cabin. "The schoolhouse with the other kids."

Taking off, she runs at full speed to find her daughter. I'm glad to see her away from the flames, and I wave for Micah to follow after her to keep her safe. Willow shouldn't have to see this.

Picking up a fire extinguisher, I can't even get close enough to use it. The heat is sweltering, a tidal wave of fire and ash sweeping over us all, spitting and writhing in all its God-like fury.

"What the fuck happened?" I scream.

Albie wipes his sweaty forehead. "Doc raised the alarm a couple of hours ago. Place has been burning ever since."

"How did it get so out of control?"

"By the time we got here, it was too late," he shouts back. "It was already out of control. Someone must've laid the place with gasoline."

"Someone?" Zach bellows.

With a grim expression, Albie points towards the corner of the property where a wooden sign has been hammered into the ground. It's a real estate sign, embossed with a company name.

*SANCHEZ REAL ESTATE.*

That wasn't there this morning when we left. I have to fight the urge to smash someone's fucking face, and right now, I couldn't care less whose it is. That motherfucking bastard did this.

Sanchez.

We all watch the flames crawl closer, consuming the sign until it crumbles like the rest of Lola's cabin. Sanchez's name curls up and vanishes in a puff of smoke.

"How? We have patrols!" I bark at them.

Ryder jumps back when flames spit out at him. "Whoever did this was in and out fast. They must've left their vehicle in the woods and come in on foot to dodge the patrols."

Vision hazing over with red, I stare up at Lola's legacy… burning. Nothing left to show for the woman but handfuls of hot ash and treasured possessions turned to a fine powder.

She's truly gone now.

"He knew this cabin belonged to Willow's grandmother," I spit out. "He fucking *knew* this was all she had left. And he burned it anyway. I'm going to peel the fucking skin from his face!"

That damned letter.

He warned me to stay away. Fuck, he warned us that Briar Valley would burn. But that didn't stop us from poking the devil regardless and stupidly expecting there to be no consequences.

This is it.

The consequences of our actions.

————

Morning light reveals the extent of the damage, unfiltered and unapologetic. While birds chirp and the sun rises, Briar Valley mourns the loss of its heart, cruelly torn out at the root.

Lola's cabin is gone.

I suppose we should be thanking some God or another that Mr fucking Psycho didn't decide to go on a burning spree all over town or manage to get to Arianna.

He went for the jugular. The heart of all our lives, the soul of our memories. This place represents the entire family, and he's shredded us all down to our cores, leaving everyone behind to pick up the pieces.

It's gone.

Kicking a pile of ash that I think used to be a dining chair, I continue picking through the rubble that's still burning in places. Rainfall came early, knocking out the last of the flames before they spread.

A smouldering wreckage is left now. Unrecognisable as the building it once was, Lola's ghost no longer has a home to haunt but a disaster zone instead.

"Jesus fucking Christ," Albie swears as he stares across the smoking wreck. "It's like something off the TV."

"Doesn't feel real, does it?"

Shaking his head, he continues picking through the rubble. "I can't believe it's gone. This cabin was the first thing to be built in this town."

"And the first to go."

"Don't say shit like that, Kill." He cuts me a glare. "We ain't losing anything else around here."

I gesture towards the smoky remains. "Didn't think we'd lose Lola's cabin either, did we? But here we are. Fuck, Al. Open your goddamn eyes."

"My eyes are open well enough, son. And I'm telling you that we ain't losing anything else."

Scoffing at him, I turn away only to find Willow standing in the town square, her hands over her mouth. She stares at the place where Lola's cabin once stood.

Pulling off my gloves, I slowly approach her, trying hard not to set her off. She looks dead on her feet, and her eyes are puffy from crying the night away as we watched the cabin continue to burn.

There was nothing any of us could do but let the fire burn out once the rain began. Saving the remains was impossible without heavy machinery which simply can't handle the drive into town.

"Baby." I pull her into my arms. "Go home. You don't need to see this."

"It's gone. Everything. All of it."

"Please, Willow."

"All those memories." She hugs her midsection. "Just gone."

Sighing, I kiss the side of her head. "I know, princess. There's nothing any of us could have done. It was already too late."

Rather than sobbing her eyes out for another second, her expression hardens into cold, righteous fury. "He did this. After everything… all the threats… he actually did this."

"He's a sick bastard, Willow. We knew that."

"But to send his men to do this? To burn our home?" Willow grits her teeth. "That fucking *reptile*. I'm going to see that he rots behind bars until he begs for death to come and relieve him."

Stomping away in a cloud of anger, she catches up to Micah outside of the schoolhouse. People are gathered inside for breakfast and coffee, needing the moral support of the whole community.

Ryder exits and trails over, his phone in hand. "Ethan and his team are on their way up to investigate. I told him there isn't much evidence left."

"That fucking sign," I snap, my hands tightening into fists. "I know what I saw. His men were here, and they did this."

"We know, Kill. This has Sanchez written all over it."

"Fuck! That asshole was here!"

"We don't know that," Ryder tries to placate. "He most likely sent his lackeys to do it. They were here before, pissing on our land and throwing their weight around. I doubt he's even in the country."

Despite knowing he's probably right, I can't help imagining Sanchez waltzing onto our property and setting the cabin alight with a big ass fucking smile on his face.

He would've taken so much pleasure in doing it, but I know there's no chance he would've left without taking Arianna with him. That's why he can't have possibly done this himself.

Peeling his face off won't be enough retribution. I want to nail his fucking hide to my wall like a hunting trophy and spit roast the rest of him. That son of a bitch won't get away with this.

Ryder drops a hand on my shoulder. "We should go inside and wait."

"No, Ry. I need to clean this shit up."

"There's nothing else to be done right now. You're mourning. Come and join your family."

"I don't need my fucking family!"

"Yes, you do," he shouts back. "Because that is what they're here for, you hard-headed asshole! Now march yourself inside, and be with the town. We need you right now. Willow needs you."

Taken aback, I stare into his pain-filled eyes. He stares right back, letting me see just how deep this cut has wounded us all. We've lost the last remains of our leader, and nothing will ever bring them back.

"Fine," I grumble.

Letting him guide me away from the ruins, I take one last look over my shoulder at what remains of Lola's legacy. Albie refuses to budge, still staring at the ash, his tears silently falling.

Mark my words...

This will be the last thing Sanchez ever does. I'm done letting him hurt my family and get away with it. Fuck Sabre. Fuck the investigation. Fuck all of it.

I'll kill him with my bare hands.

He'll never hurt my family again.

## CHAPTER 27
# WILLOW
### ALWAYS COME BACK (ACOUSTIC)
### – MARTIN KERR

STARING AT THE WRECKAGE, my tears don't fall. I have none left. The depression I experienced after the fire has been set alight and transformed into an anger that burns so hot, I hardly know how to contain it.

They were here.

His men.

Because of me, the entire town has been threatened, and Lola's cabin is gone. I've brought danger back to their door. Again. Like I didn't learn my lesson the last time we ended up in this situation.

Ethan and Warner pick over the rubble and sift through the ashes, searching for any evidence. They arrived several hours ago after hearing the news and rushing up from London.

"Willow?" Aalia stops at my side.

"There's nothing left."

"I know." She pats my arm with a sympathetic smile. "Stop blaming yourself, this isn't your fault."

"Yeah, it is."

Turning me to face her, she holds me tight. "This is on

him. Mr Sanchez and his men did this, not you. Remember that."

We embrace tightly, but still the tears don't come. I'm not capable of them right now. All that's left after sobbing my heart out all night long is rage. Lonely, bitter rage.

"I'm supposed to be the one protecting this town," I grind out. "Instead, it's burning because of me."

"Willow, he did this to you. He hurt you. He trafficked you. He threatened you." Aalia loses her temper. "He burned the cabin down! Stop blaming yourself for Mr Sanchez's... his..."

"His?" I find the strength to laugh.

"Asshole... behaviour," she finishes, breaking down into inappropriate laughter. "You've done nothing wrong. We need you as our leader more than ever right now."

Finally, the tears well up. "Thank you, Aalia. I'm glad that I have you in my life."

She squeezes my waist. "I've got your back."

"And I've got yours."

"Let's go inside and rejoin the others."

Taking my hand, she tows me back towards the schoolhouse. Rachel and Miranda have called off classes for the day, letting everyone gather to eat, drink and be together while Ethan's team conducts their investigation.

Being together is how Briar Valley copes with trauma. The town looks after its own, and dealing with grief isn't something that's done alone. Seeing the cabin burn has brought it all back up after Lola's death.

Inside the schoolhouse, several long tables have been set up. Rachel is buzzing around with one of her kids helping, doling out sandwiches and steaming cups of tea to the masses of people crowded inside.

Miranda sits at another table with Doc. They're talking to Harold, Marilyn, Andrea and Theodore in low murmurs. It feels like walking into another funeral, everyone's attention turning to me as I head inside.

"What's the latest?" Theodore speaks up.

"The investigation is still ongoing," I address the room. "But it's looking like arson. They've found evidence of fuel canisters near the burn site."

Whispers sweep over the other residents, gathered to listen for updates. We all knew this was deliberate, especially given the sign that Killian saw last night. But hearing the proof is another thing.

"What happens now?" Walker asks.

He's sitting with his two kids at a table with Johan and Amie. His eyes are darting around the room nervously, like he expects it to burst into flames at any moment.

"Sabre will continue their investigation for now."

"But are we safe?" he presses.

Feeling the burden of responsibility, I glance around the room, feeling the collective weight of their gazes on me.

"No," I admit. "Briar Valley isn't safe right now, but nowhere in the world is. I'm sorry that I've brought this trouble into your lives, and you're welcome to leave if that would make you feel safer."

Standing up, Harold's expression is severe. "We're not going anywhere, Willow. This is our home and yours. We won't be forced out by some punk with an attitude problem."

Marilyn takes his hand and nods. "We will stand by you."

Theodore and his wife, Andrea, both nod in agreement. Slowly but surely, everyone around the room joins in— nodding, muttering their agreement, smiling up at me in an attempt at comfort.

My chest tightens with emotion. "You'd all do that? For me?"

"You're our family," Miranda says simply.

Doc kisses the side of his wife's head. "And we protect our family in Briar Valley."

Rachel takes Doc's other hand and gifts me a small smile. "We'll stand by you until the end of the line, Willow. This fight isn't just yours now. It belongs to all of us."

Everyone hums in agreement, still filtering through the stages of shock and grief at the violence we've all witnessed. Their land burned last night too. It doesn't just belong to me.

I have to wipe my cheeks and plaster my strong, Lola-like expression of unflappable leadership back into place.

"Thank you all for being our family. For looking after me and my children. I never expected to find this when I came to Briar Valley, but I have no regrets. It was the best decision I ever made."

They all smile back—accepting and full of love.

"So thank you," I repeat, my voice thick.

Walking to the back of the room, the three pieces of my heart seal the moment. Killian beams up at me while the twins both watch on with matching looks of adoration.

I turn back to Walker. "As for what happens now... we do what we've always done in our lives. We rebuild."

Hugging his children tight, he nods back. "We rebuild."

Harold kisses his wife's cheek. "It wouldn't be the first time."

She chuckles. "Or even the second."

Stepping from the front of the room, everyone turns back to their food or begins to disperse. I find a quiet corner to move to, and the guys meet me there so we can press together.

"Good job, princess." Killian firmly kisses me on the lips. "They needed to hear that."

"I just told the truth."

"And not everyone would have the strength to do that," Micah says, sliding his fingers into mine. "But you do."

"Lying to them won't help."

Walking into the schoolhouse with his shoulders hunched, Ethan is followed closely by Hyland and Warner. The remaining members of the Anaconda team are all here to respond to last night's events.

Ryder flashes across the room to fuss over him, but Ethan brushes him aside, his eyes laser focused on us. We gather in the quietest corner of the room, away from listening ears.

"Willow," he greets.

"What's the latest?"

He hesitates, a hand raking through his hair. "Perhaps we should discuss this alone."

Before Killian can snarl at him in his usual animal-like way, I hold up a hand to stop him. "They're as involved as I am now. Whatever you have to say, we all need to hear it."

Ethan nods. "We're going to make a move on Sanchez."

"Wait, what?"

"We think that we've located the properties in Florida and Tijuana using Elaine's intel. If he's hiding out there, we will arrest him and take him into custody."

Anticipation floods my system. I knew they were searching for the houses, but it seemed like such a long shot.

"Do you really think he'll be there?"

"I can't make any promises, Willow. But we're going to try."

"When?"

"We're splitting up and flying out tonight," Warner answers solemnly. "I'll be taking Florida."

"And I'm heading to Mexico," Ethan says. "If he's there, he'll be arrested for his crimes and extradited back to England. We'll get him, Willow."

"What about Hyland?"

Ethan's eyes stray over to his man, stationed by the door with a gun strapped to his hip. He watches everyone like a hawk.

"He's clean," he confirms.

"How can you be sure?"

"We were thorough."

Tentatively, I nod. "I'm trusting you, Ethan."

"I know. We'll be leaving him here for your protection. You can trust him, despite everything that's happened. He's a good man."

I swallow the need to point out that we thought the same about Tara. Any protection is better than none. Last night's events have proven how exposed we are.

"We're going to make this right," Ethan vows. "I promise to earn your trust in us, Willow. We're not all like Tara."

"I appreciate that."

Killian looks less than impressed with the offer of protection, glowering at him so fiercely, I'm surprised the skin doesn't melt from his bones.

"We have to go back to London to prepare." Ethan briefly touches my arm. "We're going to send some extra muscle to help man the perimeter for you too. Will you be okay?"

"We don't need your help." Killian doesn't let me respond.

Ethan gestures outside at the smoking wreckage. "Clearly, you do. These men and women are highly trained. Put them to use."

With a final squeeze, Ethan backs away to speak to Ryder, who looks like he's freaking out about the Mexico trip. I watch the pair begin to argue for a moment before looking away.

"I hate that guy," Killian rumbles.

Zach rolls his eyes. "You hate everyone."

"Not true."

"Isn't it? You've been telling me that you hate me since we were eight years old. Ethan's a good guy, Kill. He's trying to help."

"We have to let him do his job," Micah chimes in.

"I don't have to fucking like it, though." Killian harrumphs. "Like, at all."

Stomping off, he leaves me with the twins. Zach moves to my back and bands his arms around me from behind, his chin resting on top of my head as he strokes my belly.

"You know… it's our birthday next weekend."

"Wait, it is?" I gasp.

"Yep." He pops the P dramatically.

"Why didn't I know that? We didn't celebrate last year."

"We don't tend to celebrate." Micah shrugs, toying with my fingers. "Birthdays just remind us of Dad."

Zach nods, his eyes filled with sadness. I hate seeing their pain. This day should be a happy occasion for them both, not filled with grief.

"We should celebrate!" I declare.

Neither looks convinced. Pinning them both with my best stern glare, I put my hands on my hips.

"We're celebrating."

"What kind of celebration?" Micah wrinkles his nose.

"There's nothing I want more than to be here with you," Zach protests.

"Like every other day? Not a chance. How old are you guys going to be?"

"Twenty-seven years young." Micah pulls me into his chest. "If we're going to celebrate, I don't want to do it here. This place is full of bad memories."

"Then where?"

"We could get a hotel in Highbridge," he suggests.

Zach frowns. "Is it safe?"

"We can take the last remaining cheerful twin with us."

Bursting into laughter, we all look out the window at Hyland, currently getting his ear chewed off by Killian outside. He looks far from cheerful, being yelled at again.

"I don't know if this is such a good idea." Zach worries his lip.

I stroke a hand over his bicep. "Leave Killian to me, I'll win him over. A break will be good for us."

"Even after what happened last night?"

"Because of what happened last night," Micah intervenes.

"We've lost so much already. I just want one normal night for once."

I rub where there's a pang in my chest. "I don't want to leave Arianna again, though. Not after everything."

"Bring her, then. I'm sure Aalia would be happy to babysit for a night in a fancy hotel." Zach winks at me, getting on board with the plan. "We don't want her to overhear anything."

Feeling myself flush, I turn to hide in Micah's chest. "Tell your twin he's making a hell of an assumption that there will be anything to hear, especially in my current state."

Micah's chest vibrates with a chuckle. "You're not getting lucky, Zach. Sorry, man."

"Dammit." He snaps his fingers. "So close. Shouldn't have knocked her up."

"Zachariah!" I splutter.

His eyes twinkle with mirth. "Only joking."

"Don't make me set Hyland on you."

Zach bursts into laughter. "I'm so scared."

"He's clearly very eager to get back in my good books. I'm sure he'd happily dole out a beating."

"Sounds kinky."

"It really won't be."

Kissing the tip of my nose, he playfully ruffles my hair. "That's what you think."

## CHAPTER 28
# WILLOW

### A LITTLE BIT HAPPY – TALK

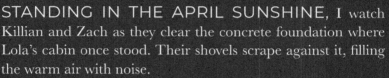

STANDING IN THE APRIL SUNSHINE, I watch Killian and Zach as they clear the concrete foundation where Lola's cabin once stood. Their shovels scrape against it, filling the warm air with noise.

They've almost cleared the whole site after working for the past several days to dig through the rubble. Anything salvageable has been set aside on the edge of the property.

We need to clear the property so plans can be made to rebuild. I'm not going to sit and mourn like the rest of the town. Lola would want me to move on and build anew.

So that's what we're going to do.

In her memory.

"You just gonna stand and gawp?" Zach yells.

Propping a hand over my eyes to shield the sun, I smile back. "Basically, yeah."

Both of them are working with their shirts off and jeans slung low, displaying rippling muscles that carve their chests and abdominals like beams of delicious steel.

Their tans are already glowing, despite it only being Spring, and a layer of sweat covers their gorgeous bodies. My core floods with heat just watching them working.

*Down, girl.*

*Not the time.*

Ignoring the ache between my thighs that seems ever-present since I got pregnant, I refocus on the clipboard in my hand. I have a list of tasks and urgent sign-offs needed for the town today.

The town is hard at work preparing for the season's transition. Summer crops are being planted while the winter vegetables are being harvested and prepared for cold storage.

Materials need to be ordered for the new cabin build, and plans have to be authorised before construction can begin. Albie is working on the paperwork and permits.

"Willow!" Aalia walks over to me from the town square. "There's a leak in the schoolhouse. Water everywhere."

"Great," I groan. "Kill!"

Placing his shovel down, he jogs to us, his fuzz-covered pectorals bouncing with each step and making my throat tighten again. Aalia watches my reaction with a low chuckle.

"Stop drooling," she whispers.

"I am not."

"You could have fooled me."

"Just checking out what's mine."

"So you should," she jokes.

"Yeah?" Killian stops in front of us.

I quickly wipe the grin from my face. "There's a leak in the schoolhouse. Can you get someone to take a look?"

Nodding, he yells over his shoulder for Zach. "Kid, go take a look at this leak."

Zach pouts. "Why is that my job?"

"Because I fucking said so, alright?"

"Dickhead," he cusses.

Complaining under his breath, Zach ditches his shovel and throws his t-shirt back on. Now it's my turn to pout. He disappears with Aalia to head over to the schoolhouse.

Killian slings an arm around my waist. "How are you feeling?"

I stretch onto my tiptoes to kiss him. "Fine."

"Tired? Sore? You should go and rest."

"I'm okay, Kill. You need to start taking my word for it."

"Never." He kisses me again, lingering for a moment. "Shall we talk about what you want this new cabin to look like?"

"Are we planning to live in it?"

He shrugs. "We need more space. This would be a good opportunity to build it exactly how we want it."

Holding my hand tight, he leads me onto the concrete. We walk through the ash piles together, trying to imagine the invisible walls and floors where Lola's home once was.

"I'd like an open plan kitchen and living room this time." I point towards the back where it used to be. "We could have a big, open space. Nice and airy."

Killian nods thoughtfully. "Should be easy enough to do. We'll need room for people to come over too."

"What about the sleeping arrangements?"

He hesitates. "Do you mean whether we should have separate rooms or not?"

"Yes. What's the plan there?"

Walking around the space, he looks up, his eyes moving as he imagines the beams of wood and steel that will build the new, modern cabin.

"I think separate bedrooms is a good idea. We still need our own personal space sometimes. But we could build one big room for nights when we all want to be together."

Glancing around, I envision the layout and nod. "That could work."

"The baby's room will go here." Killian's hand waves through the air. "And another here."

Shock floods my system.

"What? Another?" I splutter.

He shoots me a smirk. "You think I won't stick another one in your belly at the first opportunity? You're lucky I'm not trying to do it right now."

Stunned, I can't formulate a response beyond semi-hysterical laughter. "Kill! I haven't even had this baby yet!"

Sauntering over to me, he holds my hips and traps me against his bare barrel chest. Sweat clings to his muscles.

"But you look so fucking sexy like this. I can't help but feel sad, knowing it's going to be over in a few months. I love knowing that my baby is growing inside of you."

Delicious warmth pulses through me again, hot and heady. His caveman-like behaviour is both ridiculous and a huge turn on.

"Okay, then. Another baby room… apparently."

"Don't sound so surprised," he snickers. "The others are totally on board."

"Wait, you guys have *talked* about this? Since when?"

Tapping his nose with a quirked eyebrow, he releases me and resumes striding around the space. I have to take a moment to cool off before I actually jump his bones in public.

"I want a bigger garden this time." He waves towards the green space around us. "The little ones will need room to play and run around."

"We could extend in that direction, where the vegetable patch used to be."

Killian studies the strip of scorched earth, blackened and dead. He nods to himself.

"That should be big enough."

We spend another half an hour walking around, discussing and brainstorming ideas. By the time Albie interrupts us with some more papers for me to sign, we've mapped out the whole house.

"Got things figured out?" he asks.

"I think so."

"Your Grams would be happy to know you guys will live

here and make some new memories." He nods towards the blackened concrete. "Especially after what happened."

"We need some new, good memories to move on from all this."

"Exactly." He smiles for what feels like the first time in weeks.

After taking back the signed paperwork, Albie climbs in his truck to return home. I don't know what I would've done without him in recent weeks, taking care of business and showing me the ropes.

Inheriting the town has been a huge learning curve, but the responsibility feels weirdly good. This is my home, and knowing that everyone stands behind me gives me strength to run it right.

"Why haven't we heard from Ethan yet?" Killian wonders.

"I don't know, Kill."

"What's taking them so long?"

"Ethan arrived in Mexico and Warner in the States yesterday, so we should hear anytime. I think Ethan was preparing to make a move today."

"He better fucking call."

"And he will. We're trusting him, remember?"

"Right," Killian echoes in an unhappy bark.

Circling his wrist, I pull him back into my embrace. He almost has to fold himself in half so that I can hug him as I run a hand over his messy ponytail, smoothing the flyaways.

"This is the closest we've gotten in months, Kill. I'm trying really hard to have a little faith here. I need you to do the same."

"Faith?" he laughs bitterly.

I smack his chest. "What else do we have?"

Expression growing serious, he sighs. "You're right. I'm just sick and tired of constantly worrying."

"You're going to be a father soon. Better get used to constantly worrying."

He chuckles again, this time with a real smile. "I still can't believe I'm lucky enough to be having this kid with you."

Kissing him in an attempt to communicate all the words I can't get into his thick skull, I let my lips part, our tongues dancing together. It doesn't matter who sees us. I need him to taste my certainty.

"We will always have each other."

"Come hell or high water," he murmurs into my mouth.

"Exactly. I love you, Kill."

"Fuck, baby." He rests his forehead against mine. "I love you so much it hurts. I never thought I was capable of it until you came bursting into our lives, and it all went to hell."

"Hell in a good way?" I giggle.

He pecks my nose. "The best kind of hell."

"Good."

Separating before someone wolf-whistles at us, we hold hands among ashes and lost memories, both determined to create something new. Something wonderful. Our future... together.

"I should check on that leak." He groans in annoyance. "Zach will only fuck up the repair job if I'm not there to supervise."

"Lost faith already?"

"Fuck faith," he answers drily.

Stifling a laugh, I let him lead me over to the schoolhouse. Arianna is playing outside with the others on her lunch break, giving me a wave as we pass.

Inside, Zach is on his hands and knees beneath a table, inspecting a giant puddle. His head lifts and smacks into the table when he hears us approaching.

"Shit." He rubs his head.

Killian barks a laugh. "Any luck, kid?"

"I don't have a bloody clue. Something's leaking."

"Thanks for the evaluation, Einstein."

"You're so welcome. I put a lot of thought into that."

Killian rolls his eyes. "Clearly. Move out of the way."

Joining him on the floor, Killian sets to work, and I trail off to join Rachel at the front of the room. She's sorting through dried artwork and munching on her sandwich at the same time.

"Do that pair have half a brain between them?" she asks with a short laugh.

"I wouldn't hold out much hope. They're staring at a puddle of water right now."

Giggling to ourselves, she pulls out a giant sheet of paper and hands it to me. On it is a painting of a butterfly, perfectly matching the sculpture that Micah carved for Arianna last year.

"This is Ari's painting," Rachel announces happily. "She's got a real knack for it."

"Wow. This is good. Micah's been doing lots of art with her recently. She finds it calming, and it's helped with her temper tantrums a lot. She hasn't had one for weeks."

"Well, keep it up." Rachel smiles at me.

"Mind if I take this?"

"Go ahead."

Tucking the painting under my arm, panic flares in my chest when I feel my phone ringing. I make my excuses and back out of the room to answer, leaving before the guys can catch up.

"Hello?"

"Willow," Ethan greets.

*Fuck.* My heart hammers erratically as I step outside.

"What is it? Are you okay?"

"We're all fine," he assures me. "The raid went down a couple of hours ago. I'm sorry, but it was unsuccessful."

Disappointment punches me in the face.

"Nothing?"

"The properties were completely empty. Not even a single

piece of furniture. Sanchez wasn't there. I'm sorry, sweetheart."

Gulping hard, I force a breath. "It's okay. It was a long shot."

"That isn't all. We've decided that we have enough evidence, and it's time to make a move on Mason Stevenson. We got intel saying he's currently in Miami. Warner is joining the FBI to arrest him."

"Oh my God."

The net is closing in on Mr Sanchez and his associates. Just the thought of Mason being trapped behind bars gives me an exciting thrill. He's a disgusting snake who deserves to be there.

"He'll be extradited and put on trial in England. You'll be given the opportunity to testify against him and Mario Luciano."

"T-Testify?"

Ethan's breath rattles down the line. "It's important that we don't lose these convictions."

"How would we lose them?"

"We're dealing with very powerful men who've spent decades warping the law to suit them. I want everyone to take the stand so they are locked up for the maximum sentence."

Imagining myself facing either of them makes me feel sick to my stomach. I don't want to stand in front of the world and reveal anything about my past. I'll only be judged.

"I don't know, Ethan."

"Think about it. We're asking everyone who's been interviewed by Sabre to testify. He'll be in custody by tonight."

"Okay… I'll think it over."

"Good. I have to go, but I'll call when it's done. Be safe."

The line clicks as the call ends, leaving me standing here with my heart hammering. Everything has tilted on its axis at the thought of publicly testifying against these monsters.

Elaine was right about one thing... Not everyone

understands. We can't count on the world not to judge us, the victims, for our actions too. Humans always see the worst in each other.

"Willow?"

With his loose jeans and black t-shirt covered in flecks of dried paint, Micah approaches from the winding path that leads into town, carrying Killian's toolbox.

"Mi."

"You alright? What happened?"

"He wasn't there. The raid was a bust."

"Shit. I'm so sorry."

Chewing my lip, I twist my fingers together anxiously. "That isn't all. Warner and the FBI are arresting Mason tonight. He's being brought back here to be put on trial."

"Tonight?" Micah repeats, sounding as shocked as I am.

"I guess they can't risk anyone getting wind of the investigation and running now that we've raided Mr Sanchez's properties. Ethan's going to call me when it's done."

Placing the toolbox down, he pulls me into a tight hug. "Fuck, angel. That's great news."

"He's going to get what he deserves... at last."

Gripping my jawline with his hand, Micah softly kisses my lips. "It's better than nothing."

"Ethan wants me to testify against Mason and Mario during the trial."

His excitement fades. "He said that?"

"Apparently, we'll all be asked to take the stand. All the women."

Nodding, Micah runs his hands up and down my arms. I suddenly feel chilled, despite the warm weather. Talking to Sabre was terrifying enough, but getting up in front of a courtroom...

"What are you going to do?" he asks.

"I don't know. I'm scared."

"You won't be alone."

"You guys can't exactly do it for me."

"No, but all the other women will be there to support you… And us too." He sticks out his pinkie finger. "Swear on it."

Somehow managing a laugh, I take his little finger and squeeze. "You better be."

"This is your chance to confront them after all these years. You can see to it that justice is served for all the fucked up shit they've done to you all."

"I know, Mi. It's just intimidating, the thought of facing them."

"It will be, but you're a fucking badass. I know you can do it."

"A badass?" I snicker.

"You know it."

Snuggling into him, I breathe in his familiar oil-paint and sawdust scent. He smells like the studio. Our safe place. Our silence. It settles me and allows my heart rate to slow down.

"Do you realise what this means?"

"What?" I burrow into him.

"It's only a matter of time before Sanchez is caught. All of his associates are being hauled in. He's bound to be panicking, and he'll get sloppy. This is it."

Micah releases me so our eyes can meet. The certainty there astounds me. He's usually the most nervous, uncertain one of us all. But right now, he looks powerful and sure.

"This is the end of the road," he declares confidently. "We're almost there."

"And if it's not? If we can't find him?"

"Then we keep looking. None of us are going anywhere. Our future is right here in Briar Valley, regardless of Sanchez and his threats. Nothing will ever change that. We're forever."

"Forever?"

His nose nudges mine as we share a kiss.

"Forever, angel."

# CHAPTER 29
# WILLOW
I FOUND – AMBER RUN

## "I'M NOT SURE ABOUT THIS."

Aalia clicks her tongue, standing behind me in the luxurious hotel room. She scans over my outfit with admiration in her almond eyes.

"You look perfect!"

Arianna stands on my other side, smiling widely. "You look so pretty, Mummy."

Running my hands over the loose, black material, I move to cup my swollen belly. Nothing fits anymore, and I felt underdressed in the two maternity dresses that I brought to wear.

"Why do I need to get all glammed up? It's just dinner."

Aalia laughs like she's privy to some joke that I don't get. "Sure."

"What's that supposed to mean?"

"Nothing, nothing."

We're camped out in one of Highbridge's two hotels—the nicer, more expensive one. It's the twins' birthday, and Aalia agreed to look after Arianna while we get dinner in town to celebrate.

Hyland is stationed outside with three extra men, ensuring

we're as safe as can be. Despite that, I'm still nervous to go out, and the debate over my outfit hasn't helped my anxiety.

"Hair up or down?"

"Definitely down," Aalia decides. "It goes with the dress."

We settled on a black number, the light, chiffon fabric accentuating my curves. It has capped sleeves and lace detailing, matching the low pair of heels I borrowed from Miranda for the occasion.

Fluffing my loose curls, I add a swipe of pale pink lipstick and call it quits. I've gotten far too used to wearing oversized tees stolen from the guys and stretchy yoga pants.

"Okay, I think I'm ready."

Arianna pouts, flopping on the giant hotel bed in her pyjamas. "It's not fair. I want to come."

"I'm sorry, Ari. Not this time. Mummy's going out to celebrate the twins' birthday."

"But I want to celebrate as well!"

"I know, kiddo."

Pulling her into a cuddle, I smooth her hair. Leaving her behind after the fire wasn't an option. Two of Hyland's men are staying behind to guard the hotel room.

"Be good, baby." I kiss the top of her head. "You can order whatever you want to eat with Aalia, okay?"

That causes her to finally smile.

"Anything?"

I pass her the room service menu. "Go for it."

"Even ice cream?"

"Especially ice cream!"

She dives into the menu with an excited cry, flipping straight to the dessert section. Aalia smothers a laugh.

"She'll be no trouble, Willow. Stop worrying."

After pulling Aalia into a hug, I blow them both kisses and grab my handbag. There's a knock at the door, signalling the guys' arrival. Aalia opens it to reveal the three most gorgeous humans on the whole planet.

"Damn," I comment breathlessly.

Micah's hand lowers from the door. "Hi."

He's cleaned up, slicking his hair back to reveal his defined cheekbones and nose ring. His usual paint-splattered clothes are gone, replaced with plain black jeans and a polo shirt.

Next to him, Zach looks almost identical, aside from his sky-blue dress shirt hanging untucked from his jeans and lack of nose ring. He's also cleaned up, shaving and trimming his hair a little from hanging over his vibrant green eyes.

But Killian is the biggest difference. I'm used to seeing him in hole-filled clothing that's streaked in dirt, but with his hair down, dressed in a fresh pair of blue jeans and a tight black t-shirt that reveals his biceps, he looks good enough to eat.

"Drooling again." Zach smirks.

I click my mouth shut. "Sorry. Little hard not to."

"Like what you see?" Killian chuckles.

"You guys clean up well."

Micah holds out a hand for me. "You look so incredible, Willow."

"Thanks, Mi."

Giving him a little twirl to show off the flowing fabric, I take his hand, a shiver rolling down my spine as he kisses my knuckles. Zach and Killian kiss a cheek each, and it feels like I'm on fire beneath all their touches.

"Ready to go?" Killian rumbles in a low voice.

"Can't we blow off dinner and go to your room instead?"

He runs a finger over my bottom lip. "As tempting as that sounds, we have a reservation. Let's go."

"Buzzkill," I mutter.

Leaving the hotel with Hyland's men following in a tight, armed formation, we walk across the street. The evening air is pleasantly warm, and I'm toasty tucked between the twins' walls of muscle.

Stopping outside a small bistro lit by candlelight that leaks through the framed windows, Killian gestures for me to go ahead. I keep hold of the twins and head inside the quiet space.

It's the most perfect restaurant. The place only has a few tables, and it's completely empty apart from us. We're led to a circular table in the middle surrounded by candles and fresh flowers.

"This is so romantic."

Zach pulls out my chair for me. "Only the best for you, babe."

"It's your birthday we're celebrating. Not mine."

Killian takes his seat. "We haven't exactly had much opportunity to take you on dates before, so we're making the most of it."

Stomach alight with butterflies, I sit down between the twins and directly opposite Killian. The waitress comes to bring us a bottle of water and menus before leaving us alone again.

"Did you guys book the entire restaurant?"

Micah jerks a finger outside. "They insisted."

Hyland and his men are stationed at the restaurant's entrance, giving us some privacy.

"So what's with the fancy spread?" I gesture around.

"What? We can't spoil our girl?" Killian laughs.

"Something's going on. You're acting strange and… happy."

"Being happy is strange now?"

Now it's my turn to laugh.

"What do we have to be happy about right now?"

Zach takes my hand on top of the table. "Everything."

Micah nods in agreement. "We're making the most of the good and ignoring the bad tonight. That's the deal."

When the waitress returns to offer us a wine list, the guys all refuse.

"You can drink if you want. I don't mind."

"Not without you," Killian declines.

After pouring us all water instead, he braces his elbows on the table then stares intently at me. I shiver beneath his attention. There's something in his eyes tonight—an excited, burning passion.

"So," I begin. "Shall we toast?"

All lifting our water glasses, we clink them together.

"Happy Birthday." Killian lifts his glass toward the twins.

Both shrug him off.

"Happy Birthday," I echo.

Obviously, neither are comfortable with celebrating the day. Knowing the absence they must feel at their father's loss, I can empathise. Celebrating without Lola here feels hollow now.

Anticipation fills the air as we order food. Something's up. The twins are both jittery and seem on-edge, while Killian's got the smouldering stare nailed tonight.

"So what do you guys want for your birthday? I haven't gotten you anything."

"I know what I want." Zach winks at me.

"Me too," Micah adds.

"And what's that?"

Reaching across the table to take my folded hands into his, Killian brushes my knuckles with his thumbs. "Willow, there's a reason we asked you here tonight."

"I figured as much. What's going on?"

"It's nothing bad," Zach rushes to assure me, reading my trepidation. "But first, we should tell you the whole story."

"The whole story?"

Micah rests a hand on my leg beneath the table. "Before you left Briar Valley, we made a decision."

"A big one." Zach fiddles with his napkin. "We decided that we wanted our family, regardless of whatever life throws at us. Regardless of whether it meant we had to share you."

My chest constricts. "Guys, you're kinda freaking me out right now."

"No!" Killian intervenes. "Look, before you left we talked and realised that we all wanted forever with you, and we were willing to do whatever to make that happen."

My heart stops dead in my chest. I glance between them all, too terrified to ask if they're going where I think they are with this.

"We know that we're not perfect." Zach laughs nervously. "And things haven't been easy for us, but this right here is all that matters. Us. Together."

"And we don't want anything to jeopardise that ever again," Micah says with a small, shy smile. "We need to know that it will always be us at the end of every single day."

"And it will be."

"We know." Killian waggles his eyebrows. "We're going to make sure of it."

All standing up, Zach pulls my chair out so they can crowd around me. I forget how to breathe as one by one, they drop down on one knee, the candlelight flickering off their matching excited expressions.

"Oh my God," I squeak.

"Babe, I've loved you since the moment we met," Zach confesses. "You were all bruised and terrified, but I still thought you were the most beautiful, incredible woman I'd ever seen in my life."

"And I was too scared to even speak to you." Micah laughs at himself. "You thought I was Zach, but I didn't care. I wanted to see you again from that very first time. I was fascinated."

"And when you lied to me about your name, I was secretly impressed." Killian reaches into the pocket of his jeans. "You had the brains and courage to protect yourself, no matter what I said."

Pulling out a small, red, velvet ring box, he holds it in his huge hands and pops the lid. Inside is the most stunning diamond ring with an oval stone, surrounded by sparkling circles of jade on a white gold band.

Everything narrows to a snapshot. The restaurant falls away. The staff watching. Our security posted outside. Danger and violence following us at every turn. None of it matters as I stare at the ring.

"This belonged to my mother," Killian explains. "I took it out of the safe the day you left. We made a pact to propose to you, but then you were gone. I get it now, though. I know why it had to happen."

"We needed to see life without you in it." Micah looks sad for a brief moment. "That pain was necessary to make us see the truth, because we wouldn't have had the strength then to survive this."

"We had to lose you," Zach finishes. "To fight for our fucking lives to get you back, over and over, every time the world takes you away from us. And we'll spend the rest of our lives doing that."

My cheeks are soaked with hot, salty tears that stream over my skin. I have no idea what to say. That festering wound is still there—the guilt for what I did to them.

Hearing their confessions has brought it all back. I hurt them. Us. Our family and all that I hold dear in this life. We lost so much time because of my own fear.

But somehow, despite all the odds, we've managed to hold it together. Throughout fires, threats, violence and pain, it's still us. And it always will be. No matter what happens, nothing will ever tear us apart again.

"So, Willow..." Killian pinches the ring between his thick fingers. "Will you marry us?"

Mouth flopping open, I cover it with my hands to hold back a choked sob. All I can do is nod my head and look between all three of them in utter disbelief.

"You're sure?"

Zach scoffs. "You really think we'd do this if we weren't sure?"

"But… my divorce isn't even final yet…"

"We don't care about that." Micah grips my knee. "All we care about is you. Nothing else matters right now."

With a balloon of hope exploding behind my ribcage, I fight back a squeal. "Then… yes!"

Killian slides the ring onto my left hand, and I stare at the huge, twinkling diamond in shock. It's the most stunning thing I've ever seen, completely unique and delicate.

I'm crushed into Killian's chest first as he seals his mouth on mine, hot and demanding. We kiss like there's no audience, both dancing with the other in a self-destructive battle of passion.

When someone clears their throat, the twins manage to peel him away from me and launch their own attack. Mouths meet and fingers entwine as I'm trapped between them, their lips trailing over my throat and lips.

"How long have you been sitting on that ring?" I choke out.

Killian shrugs. "Since you left. We just needed to find the right time to tell you how we felt."

"I'm so sorry," I rush out. "I can't imagine how much it hurt to find me gone after you'd decided to do this."

"No apologies." Zach kisses me again. "We don't need them anymore. All we need is you."

"You've got me, Zachariah."

"Good." He nips at my chin.

"And you've got us," Micah says assuredly.

With all three of them sandwiching me in, I believe it. I've got them forever, no matter what Mr Sanchez does to us. It doesn't matter. Let him burn our whole lives down if that's what it takes.

We'll still have each other.

He can't take that away.

Zach slams my back into the hotel door, his mouth devouring mine. I can barely breathe through the intense attack as his lips consume mine in a frenzy.

Watching us both with matching lust-filled expressions, Killian and Micah patiently wait their turn. I'm at their collective mercy tonight after blowing off dinner early to return to the hotel.

"Fuck, babe," Zach growls into my lips. "I want you so bad."

"Open the door," I command.

"Yes, ma'am."

Scanning the key card, he walks me backwards into the low-lit room. There are two huge king-sized beds in the room, sat amidst opulence and thick, dark blue carpets that warm the space.

Still steering me with his hands on my hips, Zach's mouth lands back on mine, hot and heavy. His tongue pushes past my lips to meet mine in an unapologetic tangle.

The backs of my thighs hit the mattress, and I fall back onto the closest bed. Zach covers my body with his, twisting to the side to avoid squishing my midsection in the process.

With his hard muscles pressing up against me, rivulets of desire coil through me, leaving me wet and breathless. Even the slightest of touches is a huge turn on.

"I want to fuck you until you beg me to stop because you can't possibly come anymore," he says into my lips. "How does that sound?"

"Like an empty promise until you prove it."

"Oh, I'll prove it, babe."

"You better."

Lips moving to skate along my jawline, he kisses the slope of my throat, his teeth nipping my over-sensitised skin. Each nibble causes my heart to explode behind my rib cage as lust takes over.

Zach's head moves lower, dipping over my sternum as he cups my breast through my dress. My nipples are already rock-hard with anticipation. I want his mouth wrapped around one.

"This is a sexy little dress you're wearing," he hums, ignoring the other two taking seats nearby. "I'm fighting the urge to rip it off."

"It's Aalia's, so I wouldn't if I were you."

"Dammit."

He tugs me up to pull the zipper at the back of my neck. When he can't undo it, Micah leans over from his perch nearby to help his twin unzip me.

"Thanks, little brother."

"Hurry up," Micah complains. "Some of us are impatiently waiting for our turn too."

"Nothing could convince me to rush this."

"Son of a bitch," Killian curses.

Ignoring him, Zach eases the dress off my shoulders, pulling the top half down to unveil my bra. He makes short work of tearing it off to reveal my bigger, heavier breasts. His eyes are wide with satisfaction.

"You're so fucking gorgeous, babe."

"Zach," I whine. "Please touch me."

Taking a mound in each hand, he secures his mouth to my nipple, biting and torturing the rosy bud. I arch my back, pushing my chest farther into his face as I seek more friction.

Feeling the bed dip with someone moving, I open my eyes to watch Micah circle the pair of us. He moves to stand at the edge of the mattress where he pulls off my heels, pushing my bare legs apart.

"I can't wait." He flashes a dirty smirk. "I want to taste this pretty little cunt of mine."

"Yours?" I gasp.

"You're going to be my wife, aren't you?"

Kneeling on the hotel carpet, he leaves Zach to his ministrations as he pushes my dress farther up my legs. I writhe on the bed as Micah slowly peels my panties off, exposing my soaked core.

With his twin still lavishing my nipple and peppering kisses across my chest, Micah's head moves between my thighs. The moment his mouth meets my pussy, I cry out in pleasure.

"That's it, baby," Killian praises, standing over us to watch the show. "We're all going to fuck your sweet pussy tonight."

Micah's mouth is a teasing, hot presence against my clit as his tongue flicks through my folds. When his finger meets my bundle of nerves and circles, I can't suppress moaning loudly again.

Zach's hand moves to grip my chin tight. "Do you like that, babe? My twin eating your wet cunt while I play with your gorgeous tits?"

"Yes," I groan.

"How much?"

Pinching my nipple, he lightly twists, sending a burst of deliciously sweet pain through my nervous system.

"I like it a lot." I try to writhe to relieve the pressure, but Micah's head between my legs keeps me trapped.

"God, angel," Micah hums from beneath my bunched-up dress. "You're so sweet, gorgeous girl. Such a perfect, pretty pussy."

His hot, dirty mouth only turns me on even more. I moan as he dives back in for more, lapping at my core with long, enthusiastic licks. Killian unzips his jeans above us and frees his cock.

He watches me closely while beginning to stroke his length, a dark, dangerous fire burning in low embers in the depths of his irises. His cock strains in his hand, long and painfully hard.

"Jesus," he groans. "I cannot wait to bury myself inside of

you, princess. Even with these two knuckleheads watching us fuck."

Throwing my head back, I hold his eye contact as bliss washes over me. The beginning sparks of an orgasm are burning in my veins, intensified by his attention on me.

Micah slides a finger through my folds to moisten it then pushes it deep into my slit. The pressure is exquisite, stretching my walls and adding to the acute sense of impending implosion.

He begins to move, fucking me with his hand and only stopping to swipe his thumb over my clit. Zach's mouth lands back on mine, swallowing every moan escaping my lips.

"Make her come," Killian orders them. "She's on the verge."

"Such a bossy bastard," Zach whispers, his teeth nipping my bottom lip. "Come on, babe. Give it up for us."

Sliding a second finger deep into me, Micah follows his brother's words with several fast pumps, pushing me right over the edge. I scream out his name, my legs tightening around his head.

It hits me in long, slow peaks of burning bliss. My body is full of heat, tingling and filling my extremities. As I come down from the high, I find Micah sitting up from between my legs.

"That was so hot." He licks his lips.

Zach glances down at his twin. "Seconded."

"Alright." Killian kicks off his jeans, patience spent. "Come here, baby. I'm done watching this shit. I want you to sit on my cock."

"Hey," Zach protests.

"Shut up, kid. She was mine first. Get in line."

Moving out of the way to let his cousin step in, Micah sits down on the bed next to Zach. I let Killian pull me up, wrapping my legs around his waist as I'm lifted into his arms.

He ditches his boxers and walks me across the room to sit

down on the other bed, so I'm planted on his lap. His length is brushing right up against my slit, an inch from heaven.

"You okay on top?" he checks. "I don't want to hurt you."

"I'm good, Kill."

Pulling my dress over my head, I'm naked and trembling all over with need. Killian rests back, his hands braced on the bed, letting me take full control of the moment while the other two watch on.

I reach between us to fist his length, stroking it in the palm of my hand. His eyes roll back in his head as I line it up with my entrance and waste no time sinking down until he's filling me to the absolute brim.

"Goddammit," he hisses.

Lifting myself, I sink back down so he fills me again, loving the overwhelming pressure of his cock stretching me wide.

"Do you like it when I ride you?" I tease.

His hands grip my hips tight. "Fuck yeah, baby. You look so powerful on top of me like the queen you are."

Using the momentum his hands provide, I begin to move a little faster, his hips shifting upward to push his shaft deeper inside of me. The twins both watch with rapt attention, both breathing hard.

Killian moves us at a slow, steady pace, rutting into me while letting me control our movements. I shift and writhe on his lap, seeking the perfect angle to make my body sing.

When his cock brushes the hidden, sweet spot buried deep inside of me, I throw my head back and cry out. He props himself up then buries his face in my chest to lavish my tits with his tongue, moving from one breast to the other.

"Are you going to coat my cock in your sweet juices, baby?"

"Yes," I keen.

"Show me, gorgeous."

Steadily increasing his pace, he thrusts up into me until we're colliding in a hard, fast tangle of sweat and gasping. I can see Micah pulling his length from his jeans out of the corner of my eye as he begins to stroke himself.

Just seeing him pleasuring himself at the sight of us fucking is enough to finish me off. I cry through another climax, my vision dimming with the cloud of ecstasy that invades my extremities.

"Killian!"

He roars through his own release, the warmth of his come filling me up and spilling over. I slump down onto him, both of us fighting to catch our breath.

His chest vibrates with a chuckle. "Think you're done? I don't think so, dirty girl."

A pair of hands land on my hips and easily lift me. I fly through the air, ending up spooned in Zach's arms in a fireman's hold. He plants a kiss on my forehead while walking me back over to the other bed.

"We waited our turn," he quips. "Now you're ours."

Placing me down on the bed on my hands and knees, he settles behind me, his hand cracking against my ass in the perfect, spine-tingling spank.

Sliding off his clothes while I watch over my shoulder, he strokes his huge cock. I need it inside me. I want to be filled to the brim with his length. Zach obliges my frantic panting by sliding deep into my cunt.

"God!" I cry out.

"I'll take it," he jokes. "You want me to be your god, baby girl? It's a done deal."

Moving to stand in front of me, Micah's fisting his length at the perfect height to press it against my closed lips. I eagerly open up, taking his length deep into my mouth and bobbing on it.

With Zach fucking me from behind and Micah's dick deep in my mouth, I'm overwhelmed. My pussy quivers as yet another orgasm threatens. They've barely touched me, and I'm already done for.

Killian watches the entire thing, propped up on his elbow and studying our tangle with contentment. No matter what he says, he loves sharing me like this with his family.

"She's so wet now," Zach marvels. "I love fucking this sweet cunt after my cousin's loosened you up, pretty girl. Is that fucked up of me?"

I can't answer around a mouthful of his twin's dick. All of this is a little bit fucked up, but none of us are complaining. This is just how we work, regardless of what the outside world may think of this arrangement.

Cupping a handful of Micah's balls, I gently squeeze, sucking him deeper into my throat through hollowed-out cheeks. He groans, gripping my hair so tight it's almost painful.

Zach spanks me again, still moving at a relentless pace. From this position, there's no pressure on my belly, so we're free to play as rough as we like.

I know he loves seeing me like this—pregnant and full of his cock. They all do. Their mark of possession is growing inside of me, and nothing can ever take that away.

"Such a perfect princess," Zach praises, spanking me again.

Reaching around my waist, he finds my clit and tweaks it, sending another jolt up my spine. My teeth graze against Micah's shaft, and he grunts, fisting my hair tighter.

"Think my twin's getting close," Zach whispers into my ear from behind. "Shall we give him a turn?"

Pulling himself out of my mouth, Micah fists his length and pumps it. "Yes. You should."

Snickering to himself, Zach stills his movements before sliding out of my pussy. The sudden loss is painful, so I whine, needing to be filled again. He wastes no time flipping me over on the bed.

My feet land back on the thick hotel carpet so I'm facing Zach this time, bent over with my ass raised high.

"Mi," I whine.

"I'm here, angel."

Soothing my sore ass cheek with a stroke, I feel his warmth at my back. My hands are on Zach's thighs as he shifts down, giving me access to the glistening length of his cock.

"You going to let me ride your mouth?" He grins down at me.

"Maybe," I sass.

"Maybe?"

"You heard me."

Winking at him, I take his dick in my hand and begin to work it up and down. He lays down, dropping his head to the mattress, enjoying the pressure of my hand gripping his erection.

At the same time, Micah pushes the tip of his cock into my entrance, moving teasingly slow. I push back against him to fill myself up, unable to wait a second longer to feel him inside me.

"Shit," he hisses. "You're so tight, angel."

Kissing around Zach's length, I drag my tongue up the side of his shaft. "Your twin likes my pussy."

Zach bursts into laughter. "Obviously, babe."

"That doesn't make you jealous?"

"If you don't suck my cock in a moment like the dirty little slut I know you are, I may just get jealous."

Searing with need, I lick my way up to the tip of his dick then take it into my mouth. His growl of pleasure gives me so much satisfaction. I feel so powerful when I'm pleasuring them.

"That's it," Micah encourages as he begins to move. "You're going to be a hell of a wife if you keep this up, Willow."

*Wife.*

I never thought that word would make me feel so warm

and loved. I'm going to be a wife and a mother. I've gotten everything I ever wanted.

To be loved.

To belong.

To be someone's whole world.

Surrounded by the men I love, I lose myself to the moment, revelling in explosions of blissful agony. Micah's moving fast behind me, chasing his own climax.

With yet another orgasm about to take over again, I move faster on Zach's dick, determined to taste the salty tang of his come on my tongue. His erection jerks in my mouth before he explodes.

"Fuck, babe!"

Hot come pours down my throat in a long spurt. I obediently swallow before releasing his cock and licking my lips so he can watch.

"You're incredible." He cups my cheek in awe.

Micah's fingers dig into my hips. "I'm gonna come."

His climax hits at the same time as mine. We collide— falling apart together, both shattering into spectacular pieces with perfect synchronicity, his seed adding to the warmth filling me.

I grip the bed sheets as I'm wracked by so much pleasure, it makes my legs weak. After several orgasms, I'm suddenly too exhausted to hold myself up.

Micah catches me before I drop. "I've got you, angel."

I'm lifted up, and I curl up into Zach's side, feeling the warmth of Micah's body settling behind me. Killian joins us on the bed, adding to the dog pile, his boxers now replaced.

"That was an interesting show," he comments.

"Shut up," Zach claps back.

"I'll die a happy man if I never have to see your pasty backside again for the rest of my life, kid."

"No promises."

"I can't believe I'm marrying you idiots." I laugh to myself. "What the hell am I thinking? Two divorces?"

Killian snorts. "It's hilarious that you think we'd let you divorce us."

Micah chuckles. "Hysterical, actually."

"You're all morons." I let my eyes slide shut. "But… you're my morons. Forever."

Killian kisses the top of my head. "You damn well know it."

# CHAPTER 30
# ZACH
FOREVER – MUMFORD & SONS

"CONGRATULATIONS!"

Clinking our champagne glasses together, we all knock back the gross, bubbly liquid, aside from Willow and Micah. Rachel and Miranda are drinking with Doc, Ryder, Albie and the rest of us.

Willow's cabin is packed to the rafters with our family, all gathered to celebrate the big news. Arianna has been bouncing off the ceiling all day since we told her about the engagement.

"This is so exciting," Ryder exclaims. "I'm going to be a best man!"

"Bit of a bold assumption," I joke.

He cuts me a glare. "Like you'd ask anyone else. Unless you want me to be a bridesmaid, Willow? I look killer in a dress."

Giggling, she sips her orange juice. "I think we have that front covered, thanks, Ry. At this rate, half of Briar Valley will be arguing over who's doing what in our wedding."

"When's the big day?" Albie takes a seat on the sofa.

"Not for a while." Willow rubs a hand over her protruding

belly. "We need this one to come along first, and there's still the divorce to finalise."

"Your Grams would be so proud," Doc says wistfully. "She always loved an occasion to celebrate."

The room quietens as we feel her absence, but Willow's smile doesn't falter. She knows that Lola is still here with us, especially in these moments. All of us can feel her here, celebrating with us.

"You should set a date!" Aalia insists.

"No, no." Willow shuts her down. "Not until all of this is over."

Moving to the living room, we all take seats as Killian remains in the kitchen, cooking up a storm. He offered to cover Sunday dinner for everyone, taking over Grams's old post.

There's a knock at the door before Walker pokes his head in. "Mind if I join you? The kids are playing with Johan outside."

"I want to go!" Arianna squeals.

She races off to join the others, rushing past Walker as he slips inside to join us. He plants a kiss on Aalia's lips before accepting the beer that Albie offers him.

"Congrats, guys," he says to all of us.

Willow gives him a bright smile. "Thanks, Walker."

"Anything else you want to spring on us while you're here? Another baby? Extra puppy?"

We all share a laugh.

"I guess we're doing life a bit fast at the minute," Micah worries.

I clap him on the shoulder. "Making up for lost time."

He nods. "Exactly."

Willow watches us both with a grin. I know she loves it when we're getting along and not driving each other insane. After last night, I can't imagine ever being unhappy again.

She's ours. Forever. Part of me is still shocked that she said yes. There was still a hint of doubt, despite Killian's self-assuredness that this was the right time to take that leap, given recent events.

"I heard you're rebuilding the cabin," Walker says conversationally. "I was wondering if you needed any help?"

Killian halts with a saucepan in hand. "Yeah?"

"I've done my fair share of tiling and plastering over the years if you need an extra pair of hands. I'd like to be useful."

Aalia kisses his cheek. "He's been wanting a job to do ever since arriving in Briar Valley."

Nodding, Killian sets the saucepan under the tap and fills it with water. "You can start Monday. We need all the help we can get."

The smile that fills Walker's face is radiant. He's a good guy. None of us know him well as he keeps his cards close to his chest, but he's looked after Aalia well enough and treats her right.

"What about me?" I pout.

Killian narrows his eyes. "Didn't I fire you already?"

"Like ten million times over the years. I don't tend to pay attention. Where do you want me, boss?"

"As far away as possible," he says under his breath before ducking to look in the oven and check the roast chicken.

I flip off the back of his head. He'll only break my finger if he catches me. Pouring more champagne for everyone, Micah refills his glass with orange juice then fixes Willow's next. She gives him an appreciative kiss on the lips.

"Not drinking?" Albie asks him.

Micah shakes his head. "Not anymore. I've been dry for almost eight weeks now."

Everyone congratulates him, and Micah turns bright-pink. I elbow my twin in the ribs. I'm secretly so relieved, it barrels me over. He's been like a new man recently.

"Going back to the house," I redirect. "We only have a few

more months before the little spud arrives. Will it be done in time?"

"Little spud?" Willow repeats, her brows furrowed. "Are you comparing our baby to a potato?"

"Uh... maybe?"

It's her turn to flip me off.

"That's you out of this confusing, co-parenting quadrilateral."

Killian barks out a laugh from the kitchen. "Zach doesn't even know what a quadrilateral is. Right, kid?"

"Asshole. I know what it is."

Halting his cooking, he cocks an eyebrow. "Humour me, then."

"It's a... um, fuck," I stumble, my brows knitting together. "An equation? Or is it a fraction? Some maths bullshit, I think. No, it's a shape. Shit. That can't be right."

Everyone bursts into raucous laughter. I fight the urge to soak them all in shitty, over-priced champagne. Even if Willow would kill me.

"Hey! I have brains!"

"Of course, you do," Willow coos as she blows me a kiss. "We're only kidding, Zachariah."

"For the record, it's a four-sided shape," Micah whispers. "Or a confusing as fuck parenting square."

I snap my fingers. "Totally knew that."

"How does that actually work?" Aalia wonders. "The parenting, I mean. All of you."

We shake our heads.

"I guess we'll figure it out as we go along." Willow worries her bottom lip. "We can't screw it up that badly, surely?"

Micah squeezes her thigh from next to her on the sofa. "Of course, we won't. This kid's gonna be just fine."

"And you've got the whole town to help fuck them up even more." Ryder chortles.

"Like we need any more help," Killian rumbles.

Sliding a hand beneath her belly to manoeuvre herself up, Willow joins him in the kitchen to help with dinner. We all drink and chat until the food is ready, and Killian calls us to the table.

Gathering around the cramped space, we all manage to sit down. Willow rolls her eyes when Killian takes the heavier dishes from her and gives her a light bowl of veggies to carry instead.

"Sit," he orders gruffly.

"Yes, sir," she snarks back.

He swats her on the behind. "I mean it."

With everyone sitting down and the table full of food, we take a moment to toast the one person missing from the table before diving in. I halt, a forkful of food halfway up to my mouth.

I can remember when this table was empty. Not even Killian and I made it to sit down with each other, and Micah was incapable of leaving his studio for even a breath of fresh air.

Our lives have changed so much, and it's all down to her. Willow. Our forever. Our soon-to-be wife. Saying those words, even internally, gives me a little thrill. I love seeing our aunt's ring on her finger.

After dinner, I flip a coin with Micah over who gets the honour of washing up. Losing the bet, it falls to me and Ryder to clear the table while everyone else relaxes in the living room.

We get the table emptied before turning to the washing up. It's a mountainous pile next to the sink. I'm convinced Killian made an extra mess for his own amusement.

"You speak to Ethan?" I ask quietly.

Ryder drops his voice. "He arrived home a couple of days ago. They arrested Mason yesterday, and he's on his way back to England."

"That's what I heard when he called this morning to update us all. Willow seemed to take the news well."

"She's going to have to face him, you know." Ryder fills the sink with soapy water. "Mason is as much a part of her past as that asshole Sanchez is."

"I don't want her within a hundred miles of him, Ry."

"Keeping her locked away from this won't help. If she doesn't face her demons, they'll haunt her forever. He'll go on trial soon, and she'll be called to give evidence against him and that other wanker."

Just the mention of Mario Luciano, the motherfucker who sold my girl to Sanchez, causes me to drop a plate into the sink so hard, it clatters loudly. Ryder jumps and slops water everywhere.

"Chill out, Zach."

"Chill out?" I hiss.

"Yes!"

"You want us to put our wife in a room with the men who exploited her as a sixteen-year-old child. Excuse me if I'm not feeling too fucking calm about that."

"Not your wife yet, mate."

Grabbing the carving knife, I mime slicing his head off. "Keep going. I dare you."

He stifles a laugh. "I'm just saying."

"Well, don't." I drop the knife into the sink that's now full of bubbles.

"If Willow's on board with testifying publicly, then there isn't much you can do to stop her. Better get your head around that fact."

Turning to slide the next stack of dishes over to him, I gulp down a bubble of fear. Willow's doing good right now, despite all the odds. I'd hate anything to set her progress back.

But if this will ultimately give her the healing that she needs, who am I to deny her that? She deserves the chance of a happy, healthy future, without all this trauma weighing her down.

This may be how she gets that.

We have to let her try.

"I hate this shit so much."

"I know." Ryder bumps me with his shoulder. "If it's any consolation, Ethan's confident that Mason will squeal on Sanchez and reveal something we can use. That slimy fuck is desperate to save his own backside."

"What about the others they arrested?"

"Two other players are being brought in by the FBI as we speak. I reckon they'll all turn on him sooner rather than later. Loyalty doesn't run that deep in people like this."

I nod to myself. Ryder is right. The net has closed in on Sanchez even more, and his entire life is now in jeopardy. Bringing these assholes in was the right decision.

"What happens now?"

Ryder shrugs. "The Anaconda team will interrogate them all and get the information we need."

"And?"

"I don't fucking know, alright? I don't work for Sabre. Ethan can't tell me everything."

"He's your boyfriend."

"Is he?" He laughs bitterly. "I've seen him twice in the last four months. You guys speak to him more than I do. I feel like I'm in a relationship with a ghost."

Placing a clean dish in the cupboard, I rest a hand on his shoulder. "I'm sorry, Ry."

"It's not your fault."

"Have you spoken to Ethan about this?"

"What do you think?"

Scrubbing the roasting pan a little too enthusiastically, his jaw is clenched tight with tension. I feel like a complete asshole. We've been shitty friends to him, focused on our own chaos going on while Ryder's suffered for it.

"I'm thinking of leaving Briar Valley," Ryder blurts out.

"What? You're kidding?"

He shakes his head. "Long distance just isn't working anymore, and I don't want to lose Ethan. Perhaps if I move to London, we can make things work."

"You belong here with your family."

"You all have your own lives." He shakes his head. "I have nothing without Ethan. Can't you understand that?"

Making myself take a breath, I nod. "Yeah. I can."

"Then you understand why I have to do this. Albie's on board with it, and he's promised to support whatever decision I make. I have to do this for my relationship."

"Shit. This is really happening."

"I don't know when," he rushes out. "But yeah, it's happening soon. I haven't told Willow yet. I'm scared too."

"She will support you no matter what."

"I know… I just can't help but feel like I'm abandoning you all."

Ditching the dishes, I yank him into a hug. Ryder hugs me back, and I hold him there as his shoulders shake with the emotion rolling over him.

"We will support you no matter what," I whisper in his ear. "You're our brother, and all I want is for you to be happy. That's all."

"But—"

"No buts, Ry."

A breath whooshing out of his lungs, he releases me and nods. "When did you get so damn mature?"

"Can't be a kid forever, right?"

"I guess not… kid."

Hands clasped, we share a laugh then resume washing the dishes as footsteps approach. I feel Willow's arms wrap around my waist from behind, her sweet, floral scent betraying her presence.

"You look cute covered in soap suds," she murmurs.

"I always look cute, babe."

"Full of yourself much?"

"Always. You know me."

"A little too well, unfortunately."

Letting my waist go, she drops a kiss on Ryder's cheek before moving to the fridge to retrieve the orange juice. I pin him with a glare then pointedly move my eyes over to Willow.

"You've got this, right, man?"

Ryder panics, his eyes bugging out. "Uh."

"I'll leave you to finish up. Keep him company, babe."

Willow frowns at me, and I wink at her. She moves to lean against the counter, and before I leave the room, I hear Ryder splutter as he tries to figure out how to tell her the news.

Back in the living room, Killian has broken out a pack of cards and sits playing poker with Albie and Doc. I pause to scratch Demon's ears from her curled-up perch on the floor.

"What are we betting?"

Killian inspects his cards. "Who has to make the next supply run into Highbridge."

"Sweet. Deal me in."

Shuffling the cards, he hands me a stack and gestures for me to take a seat. I sit down, swallowing the rest of my abandoned champagne before inspecting my cards.

It's a couple of rounds before Willow and Ryder join us, both of their eyes red-rimmed. She gives me a small smile.

"Everything okay?" Killian asks worriedly.

"We're fine," she replies.

"Sure?"

"Go back to your game, Kill."

Grumbling, he resumes staring at his cards. Retaking her seat next to Micah on the sofa, Willow snuggles close to him. Ryder nods at me, indicating that everything is alright.

I'm happy for him, even if the thought of losing him hurts. His relationship has to take priority. This long-distance bullshit can't be easy, and Ethan's practically family at this point.

Before long, Willow has fallen asleep in Micah's lap. His eyes slide shut soon after, and I can practically feel the contentment oozing off him. He doesn't need to drink or hide anymore. His girl is all he needs.

She's all any of us need.

This right here is what we're fighting for. This crazy, imperfect life, surrounded by family and friends.

Willow gave us that.

She made us whole again.

# CHAPTER 31
# WILLOW

HAPPY NEVER AFTER – VIOLA

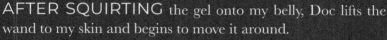

**AFTER SQUIRTING** the gel onto my belly, Doc lifts the wand to my skin and begins to move it around.

I lay back on the examination table and try not to feel nervous. It's just a six-month checkup. Nothing to worry about.

"How have the past few weeks been?" he asks.

"Good. My back's a little sore, but I'm mostly tired."

"That's to be expected at this stage."

"I felt the same with Arianna around six months pregnant."

Doc studies the sonogram equipment. "And what about your stress levels? I know that the recent arrests have been difficult for you. It's important that you're trying to rest and keep healthy."

"I'm doing okay, Doc. Really."

He summons a smile. "Good."

The past few weeks have passed in a blur with Arianna's recent eighth birthday and the case moving at a million miles an hour. We needed some time to decompress.

Almost half a dozen players in Sanchez's trafficking ring

have been arrested and charged. I've never heard Ethan sound so happy, now that he finally has results for all their hard work.

With the investigation in full swing and arrests being made, my role has been smaller, aside from regular updates and continued security protection.

It's given me some time to rest and catch up with all the changes in our lives. Things have changed so drastically, I've needed a moment just to catch my breath and exist.

"Here we are, then."

Turning my attention to the black and white screen, my eyes prickle with tears. The baby is less of an amorphous blob on the screen and now a small, miniature human, nestled in grey matter.

"Is it healthy?"

"All looking perfect," Doc confirms. "Sure you don't want to know the gender?"

"No, we still want it to be a surprise."

He grins at me. "Oh, it will be. I'll give you a moment."

Flooded with excitement, I lift a hand to stroke my fingers over the greyscale image. "Hey, baby. We're so excited to meet you soon."

After leaving me alone with the baby for a few seconds, Doc wipes the gel from my belly then gently pulls my loose t-shirt down. I wipe under my eyes to clear the few tears that escaped.

"Have you thought much about the birth?"

"Hmm?"

He gives me a pointed look. "It's only a few months away, Willow. We should discuss what arrangements you'd like to be made. I've facilitated several home births in Briar Valley before."

"Oh. I'm not so sure."

"That's understandable after Arianna's birth, but you won't be alone this time. We'll be here to support you throughout the whole thing. But if you'd prefer to go to Highbridge, we should plan in advance."

"I don't want to go to the hospital."

"You're sure?" he checks.

"Yes, I'm sure."

"Alright, then. I'll make the arrangements for a home birth."

Sitting up, I adjust my clothing. "Thank you, Doc. You've been amazing in supporting me through all of this."

"It's my job, love."

"But you've gone above and beyond. I can't thank you enough for making me feel so comfortable and at ease."

He beams at me. "It's a pleasure."

Putting my shoes back on, I give him a quick hug before leaving the clinic room. Miranda waves at me from the kitchen where she's baking as I exit their house, intent on checking on the cabin build.

The moment I've stepped outside, my phone begins to buzz in my pocket. I check the caller ID and answer when I see that it's Ethan. He's been calling almost every day with news.

"Ethan."

"Willow," he rushes to say.

"What is it? Are you okay?"

"I have news. We've been given a trial date for Mario Luciano."

My feet halt. "We have? When?"

"Given the nature of the case, the high court has moved the timeline forward. His trial will take place next month, three weeks before Mason Stevenson's will begin."

"They've both been given dates?"

"I know it's a bit of a shock."

Rubbing my chest, I battle a wave of confusing emotions. Anticipation is humming through me at the thought of getting this whole thing over and done with, along with a heavy dose of terror.

"What does this mean for me?"

"We'd like you to testify against them at both trials. You'll need to take the stand and give your version of events relating to the charges of human trafficking and sexual slavery."

"Christ, Ethan. I don't know if I can do it."

"I believe in you, sweetheart. None of this would've been possible if not for your help. You can do this."

Hesitating, I clutch the phone tight. Killian, Zach and Walker are putting up stud walls on the cabin site, loudly bickering amongst themselves in the process. I can see them from across the town square.

I have to do this for them. The guys. The town. My family. Putting these monsters behind bars is the right thing to do.

"Okay, I'll be there."

"You will?" Ethan's relief is audible.

"Of course."

"Thank you, Willow. You've been amazing. I can't thank you enough for all of your help throughout this case."

"It's the least I can do. We're family. Speaking of… When's Ryder moving? Did you set a date?"

"In a couple of weeks."

"How're you feeling about that?"

His sigh rattles through the receiver. "I'm excited to have him around more, this is a big step in our relationship. I'm just sad it means taking him from his family."

"We'll still be here for him. For both of you."

"I know, sweetheart. It's just crappy."

"When isn't life crappy? We have to live for the small moments, not the 99 percent of shit we face the rest of the time."

"Right you are," he chuckles. "Give him a kiss for me."

"I will. Be safe."

We end the call, and I begin the short walk over towards the guys. My phone rings again, and I answer with a short laugh.

"Ethan—"

"Mrs Sanchez," a deep voice booms.

Dread spikes through my veins, ice cold and sharp. Ribbons of pain slice into me, phantom sensations of a time long passed, marked by agony and misery.

"Nothing to say, darling wife?" Mr Sanchez laughs.

"Dimitri," I whisper.

"Oh, ho. Look who's getting brave. When did I give you permission to call me that, you little whore?"

"What do you want? Why are you calling me?"

"I thought we could have a chat."

Fumbling with the phone, I try to locate a setting to allow me to record the call but find nothing. Instead, I scurry over to the cabin site so there are witnesses to the phone call.

Killian raises an eyebrow as I approach, and I mouth *SANCHEZ* as clearly as possible. He immediately stiffens, his face reddening with rage as he storms over to me.

I hold a hand up and mouth *NO*.

"Willow," Mr Sanchez snarls. "Are you listening to me?"

Flicking the phone to loudspeaker, I swallow my nausea. "I'm listening."

"You've been evading me for over a year now. I think I've been patient enough, don't you?"

"Patient?" I scoff. "You burned our property, crashed our car, tried to have me killed! You think that you've been patient?"

"More than enough," he snips.

"You're delusional."

"My patience is running extremely low. It's time to come home, dearest wife. I'll forgive this divorce nonsense if you bring my daughter back to me."

"Not a damn chance in hell."

"Language, bitch!"

Zach has to restrain Killian to stop him from smashing the phone into pieces. He punches Zach in the stomach, and the pair tussle, forcing me to walk away to escape the noise.

"You don't get to call me that anymore," I snap back. "I'm not your wife. I'm not your anything. Don't contact me again."

"I'll kill her."

His words stop me on the verge of hanging up. My chest is so tight, the pain is almost too much to bear.

"W-What are you saying?"

"Arianna," he replies simply.

"You will not touch my daughter."

"When I get her back… I will slowly and painfully kill her while I make you watch for daring to fucking disobey me. How does that sound now, wife?"

Now I want to smash the phone just to bleach his disgusting voice from my brain.

"Fuck you," I spit into the phone. "She was never your daughter to begin with. You're going to get exactly what you deserve, I'll see to it."

"Ah, that brings me to the reason for my call," he singsongs, sounding even more unhinged than usual. "I've heard my friends are going to be on trial soon."

"How the hell do you know that?"

"My lawyer hears things, Willow."

*Fucking lawyer.* That must be where he got my number from too. He should stick his client privilege up his ass, and tell us where this son of a bitch is hiding.

"If you dare to testify against Mason or Mario, there will be the severest of consequences for your disobedience. Do you understand what I'm saying?"

"You can't stop me from doing the right thing."

"I'm not talking about burning a pathetic pile of wood or crashing a car," he growls threateningly. "I will end the lives of every single person you love before I take your life from you too."

"Death doesn't scare me after living with you for ten years."

"It should, darling. It really, really should."

Shaking all over, I wave off Walker as he tries to approach, the other two still wrestling with each other. Killian is bright-red and shouting his head off about killing Sanchez as Zach holds him back.

"Don't even think about doing it. I've been restrained up until now, but my patience has officially expired. You will bleed for me, wife. I've earned that penance from you, fair and square."

Rather than melting into a terrified puddle, I straighten my spine and let loose my own unhinged laughter. Mr Sanchez is silent on the other end of the phone, hopefully taken aback by my reaction.

"I've bled enough for you, *husband*," I say mockingly. "No more. Enjoy hell, you're going to rot there for an eternity by the time I'm done with you."

Ending the call, I cut off whatever response he was about to delight me with. When Zach sees the call is finished, he finally releases Killian, who shoves him away with a frustrated howl.

"You little shit! She needed me!"

"She needed no one but herself," I correct him.

Killian looks over at me. "What the hell happened?"

"More threats. Nothing I couldn't handle."

"Willow." He reaches for me.

"No, Kill. He threatened my child, and I told him exactly where to stick his bullshit. I don't need you or any man to tell me how to be a mother."

Tucking my phone away, I turn my back and storm away

from him. I'm shaking like a leaf, but deep down, I feel empowered for the first time in a long time.

Mr Sanchez has no power over me anymore.

That time has passed.

Now it's my turn to rule.

# CHAPTER 32
# WILLOW
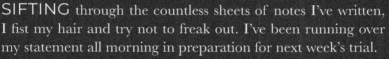
DAGGER – BRYCE SAVAGE

SIFTING through the countless sheets of notes I've written, I fist my hair and try not to freak out. I've been running over my statement all morning in preparation for next week's trial.

It has frayed my nerves, and I'm beginning to regret my decision. Burying myself in work and running the town allowed me to escape the impending trial, but now that the weeks have passed, I have to face it.

Mario's trial.

The beginning of the end.

It's been a long time since I allowed myself to think of what he did to me, but there was no avoiding sitting down and writing out what I need that courtroom to hear.

What he did to a vulnerable sixteen year old, alone and afraid in the world in the wake of her father's death. That scared little girl needed someone to look after her, and she was exploited instead.

"Bastard," I whisper to myself.

The papers crunch in my hands as my fists tighten. All of the women who worked in his club deserve to see him behind bars. He victimised us all and allowed so much violence to take place.

He's just one monster.

One of many.

Around me, the early summer breeze is warm and smells of wildflowers. I'm sitting next to the lake, relishing in the peace and quiet while the town runs through its usual Tuesday routine.

"Mummy!" Arianna shouts. "Look at what Demon can do."

She's playing with the not-so-small puppy behind me. Looking over my shoulder, I find her chasing her in a circle. The yappy thing is fighting to regain control of the chew toy.

"Don't wind her up, Ari."

"She likes it!" Arianna insists.

Sitting opposite her and sketching in his notebook, Micah looks innocent when I shoot him a glower.

"What?"

"You're supposed to be watching her, Mi."

He runs a hand through his unruly locks. "I got distracted."

"By what?"

Turning his notebook around, he shows me an amazing drawing of the lake in front of us. I'm sitting at the edge of it, sketched in smoky shades of charcoal.

"You can sketch other things than me."

"Someone's grumpy," he snickers.

"I'm not."

"Can I go for a swim?" Arianna asks excitedly. "I haven't been in the lake since last year."

"I suppose it's warm enough now."

"Yay!" she screams.

She rushes back inside the cabin to get changed, leaving us alone. I fold up the papers in my hand then tuck them inside the pocket of my discarded denim jacket.

Micah abandons his drawing and moves to sit next to me, winding his arm around my shoulders to pull me close.

"Talk to me, angel."

"I'm really not in the mood, Mi."

He taps my denim jacket. "Is it about this? The trial?"

Sighing hard, I fist a handful of grass and pull it up. "I'm just a bit nervous now that it's come around. The past month has gone too fast."

"I know, baby girl. But you're going to do just fine."

"How do you know that? What if he gets away with it? That man is a snake. He can talk his way out of anything."

Micah slides a finger beneath my chin to tilt my head up. "Mario is going down for his crimes, along with every other scumbag who dared to hurt you. I know it."

"Do you promise?"

His expression falls.

"See? You can't know that."

"I can know something," he argues. "You're going to be fine, no matter the outcome. This baby is still going to be safe. We and everyone in this town will make sure of it."

Leaning in, I rest our foreheads together, breathing in his familiar oil paint scent. "I really hope so, Mi. I'm tired of being afraid."

He moves his hand to rub my lower back which is spasming with pain. I'm becoming increasingly uncomfortable as the pregnancy goes on, and the stress is only making it worse.

"You should go in the water too," he suggests. "I read that swimming can help with aches during pregnancy."

"Since when are you reading about pregnancy?"

His eyes drop to the ground. "Since the day we found out."

Feeling my annoyance soften, I softly kiss his lips. "I love you, Micah. Thank you for always taking care of me."

"I love you too, angel. With all of my heart."

Offering me a hand, he helps me up, and I strip off my

light summer dress just in time for Arianna to return in her striped, two-piece swimsuit.

I'm wearing a bra and boy shorts which can get wet. Walking all the way inside while I'm this tired and achy doesn't sound particularly appealing.

"Let's go in, then, baby."

"I'm so excited!" she squeals.

Easing myself into the water, I watch Micah strip off before helping Arianna in. He's so stunning, carved from lean lines of muscle and tightly packed abdominals.

"Come on, squirt." Micah holds out his arms. "You can jump."

Screaming her head off, Arianna launches herself into the air and lands in his arms. Micah slowly lowers her into the water so the slight chill isn't a shock.

"It's so cold," Arianna complains.

I float around in the water, finally feeling at peace. "It's lovely and warm. You can go back inside if you don't like it."

Teeth chattering, she bobs around for a moment before squealing about how cold she is again and climbing out. Demon follows as she runs back inside to find her towel and get warm.

"So cute." Micah laughs.

"More like a little devil. It isn't that cold, and she made us get in."

"Give it up, angel. She's fine."

Swimming over to me, his body wraps around mine beneath the water. I let my legs find his waist then entwine them around him so that he's holding me in the water, taking the weight off my body.

"How does that feel?" he asks.

"So much better. My back is killing me."

"You're working too hard. Killian's warned you about getting enough rest this far into the pregnancy. He'd kill us both if he saw you going over that statement again."

"What Killian doesn't know can't hurt him, Mi."

He snorts. "That's true."

"Besides, he's working night and day on the cabin with Zach and Walker. I need something to keep me busy too."

"Yes, but not this."

"I have nothing else."

He leans close to peck my lips. "You have me. Let me be the distraction you need."

"I'll take a distraction."

Sealing our mouths together, I kiss him more passionately, letting my lips part. His tongue meets mine before sliding into my mouth to dance with it.

We sway in the water, our kiss increasing in intensity. Arianna doesn't come back to disturb us, so I tighten my legs around his waist until I feel the pressure of his cock at my heated core.

"Micah…"

"Sorry," he says sheepishly. "Can't help it."

"We can't do this here."

"No one's watching," he whispers, glancing around the empty greenery. "Arianna won't be back out until she's dried off."

My lower belly clenches with need. They've been giving me regular orgasms to help with the discomfort, relieving my tension at every available opportunity. Their touch has kept me sane.

Sliding his hand up my thigh, he moves to cup my breast through the soaked material of my bra. I moan, leaning into his touch. My nipples pebble in the water.

"What do you need, baby girl?"

"You," I plead.

"Where?"

"I need to feel you inside of me, Mi."

He cups the back of my head, his mouth pillaging mine. "You'll need to be quiet."

Humming in agreement, I let his lips devour me, our tongues battling for consumption of the other. The water sloshes around us from the nearby waterfall, silencing our quiet moans.

I undulate against him, his dick pressing up against my boy shorts. Wet fabric is the only thing keeping us apart.

"You feel so good, baby girl."

My lips touch his ear. "I'll feel even better wrapped around your cock when you bury it inside of me."

Micah groans. "You are the worst."

"I'm taking that as a compliment. Now hurry up and fuck me before my daughter comes back."

"Yes, angel."

Hands sinking beneath the water, he grips the waistband of my shorts and pushes them over my hips. The soggy fabric lands on the bank at the side of the lake.

"I'll leave your bra on in case someone comes," he says roughly. "Wrap your legs around my waist again."

Following his command, I pull our bodies flush against each other. He must kick off his boxers beneath the water because next thing I know, they're floating on the surface of the lake.

"Classy."

Micah winks. "You know me."

Tossing the wet material aside to join mine, he grabs hold of my ass to hold me against his body in the water. His length pushes into me, and I shift to guide it to my pussy.

"Oh God. Mi."

Pushing deep into my slit, he moves to pull out before sliding back in at a different angle. Open air kisses my skin, and the slosh of moving water is the only evidence of our secret tryst.

"Work yourself on my cock, baby girl," he encourages.

Wrapping my arms around his neck, I pull myself up and

push down on his length, taking him deeper inside myself with each thrust.

"Perfect," Micah compliments.

Our mouths lock again, lips crushing together and teeth clanging. His pumps beneath the water are slow and tender, stroking into me at a gentle pace that eases every last ache in my body.

Keeping an eye on our surroundings, I move with each thrust, seeking a release. I want to fall apart. Scream. Burst into pieces and relieve the pressure eating away at me.

"Mi, I can't hold on for long."

"Come for me, gorgeous."

He slips a hand inside my soaking wet bra to find my nipple. Seeking out the hard bud, Micah pinches, applying just enough pain to send me spiralling.

"Fuck!" I squeal as quietly as possible.

He holds me tight, letting me float on a cloud of happiness in the warm water. Then his hips shift, and he slams back into me—harder this time, touching that sweet spot of ecstasy.

"You look so perfect when you come, angel."

Pulling out of me, Micah swims us both over to the edge of the lake. He spins me around so that I'm pressed against the side, my hands gripping the lake's edge and ass bent out for him.

"Remember, quiet," he whispers.

Holding my waist, he pushes back into me from behind. The new position sets me off again, and I have to swallow a cry of pleasure that would certainly bring people running over.

Micah holds me tight and pushes into me, taking advantage of the position. His mouth is buried in my neck, and I can hear his ragged breathing as he roughly fucks me in the water.

"I'm close," he pants.

"Me too."

"Again?"

"Yes," I breathe.

Picking up the pace, he moves hard and fast, racing towards his own conclusion. His cock is worshipping me in all his gentle brutality, over and over again.

I feel my walls clench tight around him in the water. We climax together, setting one another off until we're both flying. Micah groans through his release as I moan loudly.

Slumping against the lake's bank, I fight to catch my breath. Micah snuggles up against my back and nuzzles my neck from behind, his lips nipping my earlobe.

"You okay?"

"I'm good," I hum. "Better than good."

"That was incredible. You're amazing."

"Mi." My lips stretch into a smile. "You're not so bad yourself."

"I love you, Willow."

My heart hammers hard. "I love you more, Mi."

"Not fucking possible."

I'm pulled into his arms, and he fetches my boy shorts for me to slide back on. I could float in the water forever, naked and satisfied.

Slowly getting dressed, we both climb out onto the bank, sheepish and satisfied. No one saw a thing.

"Hungry?" Micah holds out a hand.

"Starving."

"I could totally go for some mac and cheese right now. You know the dried stuff in the packet that you'd eat as a kid?"

Laughing, I accept his hand. "Come on. We've got some. I'll cook it for you."

"Thanks, angel."

Micah pulls me close and kisses the side of my head. I slide an arm around his narrow waist, hugging his body close to mine.

"Want me to go over your statement with you while we eat? You don't have to do this alone, you know. We're all here to help."

"That would actually be good."

He pecks the top of my head. "No problem."

With his touch keeping me warm, the last, clinging specks of anxiety melt away. I'm safe in Micah's arms. My future husband. The father of my child. My love. Nothing can hurt me here.

Not the world.

Not Mr Sanchez.

Not even myself.

## CHAPTER 33
# WILLOW
TERESA – YUNGBLUD

THE HIGH COURT IS AN IMPRESSIVE, gothic building in Central London, surrounded by bustling streets, tourists and hailing taxi cabs going about their busy lives.

Its Victorian design is made up of huge arched doorways and spiralling turrets, the slabs of smooth grey stone towering above me in an intimidating way.

Staring out through the window of the SUV, Zach's grip on my hand tightens. There are dozens of camera vans parked up outside, and reporters are swarming everywhere.

"Shit." Bile creeps up my throat.

Security officers hold them back at every opportunity, but they push and shove, desperate to catch a glimpse of the people participating in today's high-profile trial. I'm terrified to step out of the car and into the limelight.

"Babe?" Worry bleeds from Zach's tone.

"There're so many of them."

"I know, fucking vultures. We'll make this bit fast."

Ethan nods in agreement from the front seat. "In and out. No questions, no statements."

Killian sits next to him, his lips pressed together in an

unyielding line. This is his idea of hell on earth, and I don't blame him this time around.

We travelled down to London last night, bringing Rachel, Aalia and Arianna with us. Arianna is back at the hotel with Rachel, none the wiser, while Aalia opted to come with us.

"Last chance to change your mind," Killian offers.

I shake my head. "That's not going to happen. I need to do this."

"Just checking. Let's get this show on the road."

"You guys will stay with me?"

"We can't come up on the stand with you." Micah's expression is tortured. "But we will be right there listening, every step of the way. If you get overwhelmed, just look at me."

I squeeze his hand. "Thanks, Mi."

"You've got this, angel."

With a deep breath, I smooth my plain-black shift dress, the material pulled tight over my baby bump. This is the first time I will go public with my pregnancy. It's making the guys extra stabby.

I know Mr Sanchez will be watching. He'll see me and know that his control over me is well and truly done. I'm not sure what his reaction will be, but he made promises during that phone call.

I will bleed for him.

Well, that's what he thinks.

Stepping out of the SUV, a roar of noise barrels over me followed by shouts of my name, cameras flashing and even some applause. The reporters and onlookers are going wild at the sight of me.

"Willow! Willow!"

Killian grabs my shoulder. "Keep moving."

We're quickly surrounded by security and Zach has to stop his cousin from releasing my shoulder to punch a particularly overzealous reporter, determined to get a close-up shot.

"Kill," I beg.

"Fucking reporters," he snarls.

"I know. Just keep walking."

Feeling someone else's hand slip into mine, Aalia gives me a reassuring smile. We're escorted up the grand steps and into the building, far from the baying vampires determined to get a statement.

"You're okay." Aalia squeezes my hand. "We're all here."

Leaving Arianna with Rachel and Ethan's men still leaves me feeling exposed. Even if she's probably safer than where we are.

Inside the building, Killian lets go of my shoulder. We're all searched and put through security machines to scan for weapons. We're then given passes that hang around our necks on bright-yellow lanyards.

"Keep breathing," Zach advises as he kisses my tied-back hair. "You're doing great."

"This place is so huge."

"It's the real deal here, babe. Only the biggest cases are taken to the High Court to be heard."

"That doesn't help, Zach."

Rubbing a hand over my belly, he pauses to kiss my lips, despite our surroundings. I savour the brush of his mouth on mine, the warmth of his hand a balm to my frazzled nerves.

"That's my girl," he whispers in my ear.

"Always yours," I murmur back.

Killian nods in agreement, picking up on our whispered conversation despite his cold mask of concentration. He looks like a soldier at war, determined to protect me at all costs.

In contrast, Micah's anxiety is palpable. His shining nose ring twitches as he fidgets, nervously glancing around the tightly packed space. Not even our heavy security detail sets him at ease.

Ushered down a towering corridor lined with fine art and gold, gilded frames hang high above us as we're taken to our seats in the courtroom. It's another intimidatingly fine space.

The walls are made of dark wood panelling with sconces built in to light the dim space. The docks stand at the front of the room, facing a room full of red velvet chairs for the audience.

"You're up first, Willow," Ethan informs me.

"Great."

"You'll be called to the stand then asked to give an oath before giving your testimony. Mario's lawyer will have the opportunity to cross-examine you after we've asked our questions."

"That isn't fucking fair," Killian growls.

"I agree, but this is how proceedings work. There's nothing we can do."

"It's fine." I lay my palm on Killian's chest. "I don't mind."

"Willow—"

"This is how it's going to go, Kill. We've got to go along with it."

Chastised, he sits down in his seat with a loud huff. Neither of the twins look particularly happy either, but they have the sense to remain silent, unlike their grumpy cousin.

Sitting down, I cradle my bump while waiting for the room to slowly fill up. Several other women enter, dressed in formal clothing, a couple offering me tiny, shy smiles in greeting.

When one enters wearing inappropriate jeans and a blouse, my heart leaps into my mouth. She never did give a shit. Lia takes one look at me, and her eyes well up, halting several metres away from me.

"Willow?"

I slowly stand up. "Lia. You're here."

The spell breaks, and we run to each other, sobbing and hugging in a tangle. It's been over a decade since I last saw her in the club, showing me the ropes and doing her best to look after me.

"What... How?" I splutter. "I thought..."

Her smile is tight, pulling at the deep lines around her mouth and eyes. "Things changed after you left the club."

She doesn't elaborate. I don't need her to. I can see it in her eyes—the pain and horror. Mario sold her, just like he sold me. Just like he sold us all, in one disgusting way or another.

"You're here to testify?"

She nods. "I want to see that weasel get taken down, once and for all."

Squeezing her arm, I pull her back into another hug. She laughs when she can't get her arms around me properly because of my protruding bump caught in the middle of us.

"Jesus, girl. You were just a kid when I saw you last. Now you're having a baby?"

"I have an eight-year-old at the hotel."

Lia shakes her head, sending strands of bleached blonde hair flying. "Fuck, Willow."

"Things change. It's been a long time."

"That it has."

Kissing my cheek, she hugs me one last time before taking her seat next to another woman. Everyone's eyes are on me. I'm sure they've seen recent news reports or read my story online.

What am I to them?

A martyr? Someone to pity?

Or someone to look up to?

"Who was that?" Zach asks.

Ethan answers before I can, looking down at his phone. "Lia Hartley. She volunteered to testify against Mario when he was arrested. She's worked for him for the past decade, bouncing from club to club."

"I used to work with her," I admit. "She was assigned to

show me the ropes, though that meant just offering me drugs to get through the shift in most cases."

If I could, I'd smash my fist into Mario's face over and over again for what he's done. Instead, all I have are my words. I have to use them to take him down and ensure he can't get back up again.

With the room now full, we're all called to attention. The judge enters, dressed in finery and walking with his head held regally high as he takes his seat to preside over us all.

It's the defendant's turn to enter next. Taking both of the twins' hands for comfort, I hold on tight as the side door swings open, and several armed guards enter, trapping someone between them.

*This is it.*

Dressed in an expensive black suit, Mario Luciano looks the same as he did eleven long years ago, from his silvery hair to his cold, dead eyes, stone-cold and emotionless.

The moment he spots me, a grin blooms on his lips. I have to let Micah go to rest a hand on Killian's arm as Mario winks at me ever so slowly. I don't want him getting arrested too.

Mario is placed behind a thick, glass screen in a box off to the side. His lawyers gather at one of the tables adjacent to Ethan, his bosses—Kade and Hudson—along with their legal counsel.

Seeing movement out of the corner of my eye, I spot Harlow across the room, subtly waving at me. She offers me a reassuring smile that warms my chest. I nod back, thankful she's here.

Ethan's lawyer stands up. "The prosecution calls our first witness, Willow Sanchez."

Heart constricting painfully, I extricate myself from the guys, meeting each of their eyes before slipping down the aisle. My statement is clutched tight in my trembling hands.

After swearing an oath on the Bible, I take the witness stand. I'm situated to the left of the judge, overlooking the entire room and all of its occupants, their eyes all glued on me, making things even more terrifying.

"Mrs Sanchez?"

Ungluing my tongue from the roof of my mouth, I lean closer to the microphone. "Yes?"

"My name is Miss Javier, and I'm going to be asking you some questions today."

"Okay."

"Please, take your time. I appreciate this must be difficult for you." Miss Javier gestures towards Mario in his pod. "Do you recognise the defendant?"

"Yes, I do. That's Mario Luciano."

"And how did you come to know the defendant?"

Smoothing out my statement, I suck in a stuttered breath. "At sixteen years old, I went to work in a strip club in Dagenham. The club was owned by Mario."

"Sixteen is very young to be engaged in such work. Illegal, in fact."

"My father had just passed away, and I was left with significant debt to be paid off. I had no other family that I was aware of and no choice but to work."

Sweat beading on my forehead, I avoid looking at the guys. They know about my past, but it still stings to admit out loud how desperate I was back then. I hate for them to think of me like that.

"And how many shifts did you work for Mr Luciano?"

"Approximately three."

"What did this role involve, exactly?"

I wring my hands together. "I was serving drinks, dancing, speaking to customers and giving lap dances. Other girls did more, though."

"More?" she prompts.

"Sexually. I was still new and wasn't asked to perform any sexual acts at the time, but I saw them going on. Women were sold to customers in exchange for money that went to Mario."

"Interesting." She steeples her fingers in front of her. "You witnessed these acts of prostitution firsthand?"

"Yes, many times."

I try hard not to look at the jury, but I already saw the looks on their faces. My insides burn hot with shame. Their judgement hurts, even years later. Not many of us were there by choice.

"Tell me about the reason why you left the club."

I glance down at my papers. "During my third shift, Mario introduced me to a man called Dimitri Sanchez. He referred to him as a dear friend and asked me to show him a good time."

"And what did that entail?"

"Mr Sanchez took me to a back room that was reserved for sexual acts and locked the door. I was unable to escape."

Miss Javier's stare is sympathetic. "Tell me what happened next."

"Mario had told Mr Sanchez that I was a virgin. Mr Sanchez wanted to check for himself."

"I see. He wanted to check your virginity?"

Feeling sick to my stomach, I nod. "Mario had arranged for me to be sold to Mr Sanchez and assured him of the quality of his product. They had already discussed a pre-agreed price for me."

"Tell me, did he... check?"

I swallow hard. "Thoroughly."

Killian's head is lowered, a muscle twitching in his cheek. Zach is staring at a spot on the wall, his Adam's apple bobbing tellingly.

Only Micah holds my eye contact—strong and unwavering, ensuring I feel his support even from across the room.

"Mr Sanchez beat me and raped me that night. I was later drugged and transported to an aeroplane where he took me overseas, back to his home in Mexico."

Lia's cheeks are soaked with tears as she watches me from across the room. I can see her guilt, but she couldn't protect me from those monsters. No one could.

"I was purchased by Mr Sanchez from Mario for the purpose of becoming his wife. I did not consent to this, nor was I given a choice. Because of Mario, I endured a decade of abuse and sexual violence."

One woman on the jury has the strength to look at me, her face wet with tears. When our eyes meet, she quickly looks away, wiping off her cheeks. I look down at my papers.

"Mario Luciano is a cold-blooded monster, responsible for the sale and enslavement of countless women, underage and not. He doesn't feel emotion, nor does he care about what he's done."

"Is there anything else you want the jury to know, Mrs Sanchez?"

I look over at the jury members, meeting each of their gazes, one by one. "He's guilty as hell."

Miss Javier nods. "Thank you."

Taking her seat next to Ethan, my attention is drawn over to him. Ethan gives me a tiny thumbs up of approval, a poor excuse for a smile tugging at his lips and looking a little sick.

Moving my gaze to the back of the room, I look at Harlow next. She doesn't look sick. Hell, she doesn't even look fazed. Her reassuring smile hasn't faded at all, and I'm glad.

Standing up from their table, Mario's lawyer takes her place in front of the microphone. "Mrs Sanchez, my name is Mrs Teller. I'm going to be cross-examining you today."

"Hello," I say tightly.

Her smile is smug. "Let's begin by asking this—did you or did you not willingly enter Mr Luciano's employment?"

"Well, yes…"

"And did you or did you not willingly enter the room with Mr Sanchez? Were you dragged? Forced?"

"No, but I was scared—"

"Scared?" she laughs. "Or ready to make some money, hmm?"

"That isn't fair!"

"You've already told this jury that you worked for Mario to pay off your father's debts. In that sense, was he not helping you? A scared, young girl in need of a father figure?"

"Father figure?" I scoff bitterly. "He fucking sold me!"

"Language, Mrs Sanchez," the judge scolds.

Settling back in my seat, I take a second to cool off. The lawyer looks far too satisfied with the reaction she got out of me.

"Mr Luciano employed many troubled women in need of support." She looks at the jury, wearing a plastered-on, fake smile. "He performed this vital community service out of the goodness of his heart."

Killian looks ready to explode. When he finally meets my eyes, I stare at him, silently pleading for him to calm down. If he causes a scene, my entire testimony will be thrown into doubt.

"I was sold." I scowl at her.

She rolls her eyes. "You went with Mr Sanchez of your own free will, didn't you... *Mrs Sanchez.* All that money must have been very tempting for someone like you."

"Mrs Teller," the judge snaps. "That is inappropriate."

"My apologies, your honour. I'm finished."

Retaking her seat, she whispers to her colleagues, still wearing that smug-ass smile that I want to wipe from her face.

"You're done, Mrs Sanchez," the judge says in a much gentler tone.

Nodding, I gather my papers and return to my seat. There are low murmurings all around me as the next woman takes the stand, a few years older than me and avoiding all eye contact possible.

Once seated, the weight of the moment crashes over me, and I feel a wave of dizziness. I'm shaking all over from a combination of humiliation and rage. All of the air seems to have left the room.

"Willow?"

Consciously, I know Zach whispered my name, but in the panic of the moment, I can't process whether he said anything else. I can no longer hear his voice. All I can hear are Mario's words as I stood in the club, terrified and trembling in a skimpy outfit in front of two total strangers.

*She'll take good care of you, Mr Sanchez. Willow is brand new, like you requested. She's yours for the price we discussed.*

"Babe, look at me."

When he tries to touch me, I violently flinch. Zach shrinks back, wearing a horrified look at the sight of me recoiling from him.

*Go with Mr Sanchez, Willow. Best behaviour. Don't let me down now.*

"Come back, angel."

Micah's hand lands on my shaking leg. I shoot up, unable to tolerate the feel of someone touching me. I'm spiralling down a hole of terror, worsened by the pair of cold, dead eyes still locked on me across the room.

Mario grins.

He fucking *grins.*

"I-I need the bathroom," I blurt.

Aalia stands up with me. "I can take her."

The guys all look crestfallen as Zach nods on behalf of the group. I can't even look at them right now. Not while that monster is staring at me and sending me flying back into the scared skin of a sixteen year old.

Bolting down the aisle, I head for the nearest exit. Aalia follows, her heels tapping against the floor. We burst out into the corridor, and I make a beeline for the nearest bathroom.

"Willow!" Aalia calls.

Slamming the stall door shut, I quickly slide the lock into

place and collapse on the closed toilet lid. My head falls into my hands, breath coming out in short, painful rasps.

"I'm here, Willow. Just outside this door. You're not alone."

Clutching my head, I fight to breathe steadily, the air slipping between my fingers. His voice still plays in my head on repeat, blurring with Mr Sanchez's deep, throaty boom of evil.

*You will address me as Mr Sanchez. Nothing else. Is that clear?*

"You can't let him win," Aalia says emphatically. "Do you hear me, Willow? You did good. He's going to go down for a long time."

Clutching my tight chest, I try to hold on to her words, but it doesn't cut through the haze of panic. Nothing does.

Not even the knowledge that I'm the one out here, enjoying freedom, while Mario will never see the free world again.

The door to the bathroom clicks shut, then I hear Aalia shift.

"Hey, what are you do—"

There's a loud bang before a shadow hits the floor outside of the bathroom stall. Long hair peeks underneath the door as it spills around the black and white tiles.

"Aalia!" I scream.

"Quiet, Willow. Get your ass out here, or she's toast."

My fear triples. Lia. I'd recognise her voice anywhere.

"Lia? What are you doing?"

"My job," she hisses. "Open this door, or the pretty girl gets it. Your choice."

Hands slick with sweat, I quickly unlock the door to unveil Lia looming over Aalia's unconscious body. She's bleeding from a small gash in the corner of her mouth, and blood is smeared over Lia's knuckles.

"What did you do to her?"

She shrugs. "What was necessary. We don't have a lot of time."

"Time for what? You're insane!"

"I fucking have to be," Lia growls. "Do you have any idea what a huge pain in the ass you've been? If you'd just come quietly instead of fucking everything up for us all..."

Awful, sickening reality snaps into sharp focus. Bloodstained and snarling, she isn't the regretful, teary-eyed person she pretended to be in front of everyone.

That was all an act. Just like Tara's façade was.

Lia works for them.

The monsters.

"What have you done?"

She shakes her head. "I'm sorry, Willow. You don't understand. The things they give us... the money..."

"Money? You're threatening me for money?"

"Threatening." She laughs to herself. "That implies there's a negotiation. We will not be negotiating. You've gone a step too far this time."

Pulling out her phone, she flips it around to show me a video on the screen. My heart leaps into my throat as I recognise a long-range shot of the hotel we left Arianna and Rachel in.

"She's in there," Lia says triumphantly.

"You d-don't know that!"

"You just confirmed it for me. So here's what is going to happen. Unless you want your precious daughter to feel a world of pain, you're going to come quietly."

"I know you won't dare touch her!"

"Won't we?"

On the screen, the camera flips down to show a gun held in the gloved-hand of someone watching over the hotel. I gulp down a bubble of nauseous fear. They're so close to my little girl.

I pull at my hair, feeling myself unravel. "Sabre's men are guarding her. You'll never get to her."

Lia laughs again. "Four assholes playing cards and drinking coffee? I hardly think they'll be a problem."

"When did you start working for Mr Sanchez?"

"Someone had to replace you." She shrugs nonchalantly. "Mario thought I'd be a good fit for the job. He keeps me supplied with all the good stuff, and I live a happy fuckin' life. Simple."

"Simple? You're taking his drugs in exchange for hurting people!"

"Like I give a fuck about who gets hurt." Wiping blood off her knuckles, she grabs my arm. "Time to go, else the little one is going to get a rude awakening. Your choice."

"They won't let you take me out of here."

"That's why you're going to walk out yourself." Her grip tightens painfully. "Better make it convincing too, or that gun will get some use. What's it going to be?"

Swaying on my feet, I stare down at Aalia. She's still out cold but breathing. It won't take her long to wake up and raise the alarm. I can't gamble with Arianna's safety.

"Alright," I say reluctantly.

"Good choice, mama bear. Move it."

Still holding my arm under the pretence of supporting me, we leave the bathroom together and exit into a long, carpeted corridor lined with security. I have to plaster on my best fake smile.

"Where's the exit?" Lia asks innocently. "We're in need of some fresh air after that testimony, if you know what I mean."

One of the officers looks sympathetic. "I'll escort you both."

With an armed guard at our backs, I feel a burst of relief. I can make it out of this. If we can just stall long enough, the guys will come looking for us and find Aalia.

The thought of those armed assholes with guns outside

Arianna's hotel soon kills my relief. She's in imminent danger. If I have to play this ridiculous game to protect her, then that's what I'll do.

"Over here." The guard points.

"Oh, thank you," Lia gushes.

He leads us off to an alarmed door leading outside. Inputting the code, he opens it to let us out, waving off the additional security officers who jump into action.

Once through, Lia guides me over to the stone wall that marks the outside of the court and props me up. Heart pounding, I feign dizziness, still hoping to buy some time.

"You okay, ma'am?" the guard asks.

I want to scream. Run. Fight and rave. I will not go back. Not now, not ever. Forcing myself to think of Arianna at the end of a gun, I keep my head lowered to hide my terrified tears.

"Just a little dizzy."

"It's intense in there." Lia rubs my arms, doing a great job of playing the concerned friend.

The guard chuckles. "For sure. Let me go get you some water."

*No!*

Whipping my head up, I'm about to launch myself at him when Lia grabs a discarded brick from a damaged wall nearby and throws her whole weight at the guard.

With a stomach-churning thud, it connects with the back of his head. He lets out a strangled cry and hits the ground, blood gushing from his head to form a crimson pool on the concrete.

Lia chucks the brick aside, breathing hard. She pulls her phone back out from her pocket and dials a number.

"It's me. We're on the east side, third emergency exit."

Hanging up the call, Lia looks over at me. I've inched away from her, hugging my midsection tight to protect myself from her. Gaze softening, she almost looks sad for a moment.

"She'll be safe," she says in a low voice. "All he wants is you, Willow. The kid will be left alone. Do this for her."

"F-Fuck you," I spit back, my words coming out shaky. "He will never leave Arianna alone."

"I'm trying to help you. It was this or watch him kill every single person in that courtroom to stop this trial. Be grateful he opted for the first scenario."

Feeling a sudden, wild burst of courage, I decide to launch myself at her with my fists raised. I get a few inches before her knuckles slam into my jaw, and I hit the ground with a burst of pain.

"Nice try," she snorts. "You're out of practice, bitch."

"Fuck!" I scream. "Someone help me!"

Eyes flaring with alarm, Lia advances towards me, her leg pulled back on a kick. When her foot connects with my side, I beg for her to leave me alone, doing my best to shield myself.

"Next kick's on that fuckin' baby's head," she warns. "Shut the hell up."

Choking on endless sobs, I curl up on the hard ground, begging for an alarm to begin blaring. The guys can't be far behind.

An engine growling, tyres crunch as a car approaches, breaking straight through the gate and past several security guards protecting the outside of the court.

That's when an alarm begins screaming. The car is huge —a massive, muscled SUV with tinted windows not unlike Ethan's giant beast. But the men who climb out of it aren't Sabre operatives.

I recognise two of them.

Sanchez's men.

He's here.

Lyon, one of Sanchez's men, crouches down next to me, his putrid breath intensifying the nausea already curdling in my stomach. "Pleasure to see you again, Mrs Sanchez. It's been a while."

"Leave m-me alone."

"No can do, I'm afraid. The boss has been waiting very patiently for this delivery. Come on, petal. We've got somewhere to be."

I want to throw up at the repulsive pet name. He took great pleasure in calling me that before, usually as I limped out of Mr Sanchez's playroom, covered in blood and bruises.

As he tries to lift me, the alarm still slicing through the air, I fight back. Kicking. Scratching. Yelling. Anything to buy some time. It's no use, though—he's too strong, pinning my arms against my sides with the help of his men.

"Sedate her," Lyon commands.

Another man approaches with a hypodermic needle in hand, pulled from his cargo trousers. He dips it into a tiny glass bottle then draws back the syringe to fill it with clear liquid.

"No!" I wail. "Let me go!"

But my cries for help are completely useless as the needle plunges into my neck regardless, filling me with fiery ice. Still, I continue screaming my head off, desperate for someone to hear me. The reverberating sound of my pleas soon grow quieter and feebler as I lose control of my extremities.

Helplessness floods my paralyzed body. I'm lifted and carried over to the car, where Lyon tosses me in the back next to Lia.

"Stubborn woman," she whispers. "There's no escaping him, Willow. Not for any of us."

That's the last thing I hear before darkness consumes me, and the world vanishes from sight.

# CHAPTER 34
# MICAH

LOVE WILL TEAR US APART –
ODINA

SABRE HQ IS IN CHAOS.

Pure, uncontrollable chaos.

Several screens play news footage from today's postponed trial while others are set on scathing news reports, ripping the company to shreds for their negligence. It isn't Sabre's fault, though.

It's ours.

We did this.

Because of our pure stupidity and weakness, Willow is gone. Vanished. She's dissolved back into the thin air from which she appeared.

In the corner of the room, Aalia sits sobbing. She's been a wreck since we found her in the bathroom, bloodied and unconscious. The doctors looked her over, and luckily, she only has minor injuries.

"I want fucking answers!" Ethan bellows.

The entire room cowers beneath his authority. Not even Hudson or Kade bat an eye as their employee whips his subordinates into shape. Everyone is working at a million miles an hour.

Zach doesn't look up, his head in his hands. "I can't believe we let this happen."

"I know, Zach."

"She was right fucking there! Right there! We let this happen."

"I know," I repeat angrily.

"Taken from right under our goddamn noses—"

"I said I know!"

Furious, I stand up and storm away from him. I don't need to listen to his running inner-commentary to feel like complete and utter shit about this. And I don't have time to feel guilty. I'm too busy being terrified.

He's got her. That sick, twisted motherfucker has got our girl, and we cannot rest until we get her back. We all know what he'll do to her now that he's gotten her... And there's still the baby to think about.

He'll kill her.

I just know it.

I move to the back of the room where Killian is pacing up and down in a storm of destructive rage. He's preoccupied by searching through printed out screenshots of the surveillance footage.

I'm sure Sanchez threatened Arianna. It's the only reason she would've had to walk out that door and make herself exposed.

"Why would she do this?" Killian hisses.

I take the papers from his hands and touch his shoulder. "They must've threatened her little girl, Kill. You know she'd do anything to protect Arianna."

"Even jeopardise her own life? The life of her unborn child?"

"You know how she is. Her daughter comes first."

"Fuck!" he growls, punching the wall hard enough to split the plaster. "We should've gone with her."

"She didn't want us touching her."

"It doesn't fucking matter! We should've gone!"

Unable to argue against his logic, I remove my hand from his shoulder and let my head slump. The self-loathing is all-consuming.

I can't take a single breath without it crashing over me in tidal waves. We failed. And this time, it may just cost us everything.

"Guys." Ethan stops next to us. "We're going to find her, I promise."

"It's been hours," Killian barks. "Where is she?"

"We've tracked the vehicle all the way out to Twickenham, but they changed into a new truck with fake plates. We're doing our best to track where it went next."

"Your best isn't good enough." Killian glares at him.

Turning on his heel, Killian storms out of the room, taking his rage with him. It feels like a bomb has gone off in his absence. We're all reeling and trying to wrap our heads around what's happened.

"How did we let this happen?" Ethan covers his face with his hands.

"You didn't."

"We had over a dozen agents posted around the court, yet he still got to her. How is that not my fault?"

Unable to offer him any comfort, all I can do is shake my head. We're all asking ourselves the same thing right now.

It feels like there is nothing we could've done to stop Sanchez from finding a way to use his wealth and power to infiltrate the securest courtroom in the country.

"Lia was working for him this whole time," Ethan hisses. "She's been in contact with us for months. How the hell didn't we see this coming?"

"How could you?" I ask tiredly. "She wanted to help prosecute Mario."

His eyes screw shut. "This is my fault."

"No, Ethan. We all did this. All of us have failed Willow."

"I have to make it right," he says determinedly.

Returning to his tables full of operatives all working at computers and pouring over maps, I glance around the packed room. Even Harlow is here, doing her best to help.

Agonising hours pass, full of frustration and dead ends. Sanchez's men were prepared and took all the necessary precautions to avoid being traced.

The trail goes cold again, and Zach snaps, forced to leave the room to take a break. My heart aches as he passes me. I can feel the breadth of his soul-punching pain. It's in me too. The self-hatred.

God, if I could take a blade to my wrist right now, slice it down to the bone and bleed myself dry just to bring her back into our lives, I'd fucking do it. Without hesitation. I'd die for that quick fix.

Leaving the room, I step out into the stairwell for a breather and find Zach smoking on the steps. Sitting down next to him, he puts a cigarette into my outstretched hand and lights it for me.

We sit together in silence, smoking and freaking out. He doesn't need to speak for me to know what he's thinking. It's the same thing that's on repeat in my mind, a silent, frantic prayer up to the heavens.

*Dear God, please let her be okay.*

*Don't let him touch her before we come.*

"I love her so much," Zach rasps in a broken tone. "I can't lose her now, Mi."

"You won't. We're going to find her. Both of them."

"What if we're already too late?"

I touch his knee. "Don't say that. We'll find her because we promised that we always would. I'm not going to break that promise any time soon."

"We made so many promises." He smokes his cigarette dejectedly. "And we've broken them one by one, over and over. We couldn't keep her safe."

"We tried our best. All of us. This guy is just too good."

"Too good?" he scoffs. "He's a fucking psychopath. Can you imagine what he's doing to her right now?"

I've been trying my best not to imagine that. We all know what he threatened to do if he ever caught Willow again. She disobeyed him by testifying. He'll be furious beyond words.

"You think he'd hurt a pregnant woman?" I ask in a tiny voice.

Zach crushes his cigarette beneath his shoe. "I think he's spent his entire life exploiting vulnerable people, and he won't hesitate to do the same all over again."

I continue smoking my cigarette, breathing in the noxious fumes. *Don't think about it. Don't think about it.* I have to chant it internally. If I don't entertain the thoughts, I can imagine she's still okay.

She has to be.

Lord, she fucking has to be.

"Guys," a voice calls down the stairwell.

We both look up, finding Ryder looking down at us from the floor above. He moved into the city last week, taking his truck full of belongings with him. It feels like a lifetime ago.

"What are you doing here?" I call back.

"Brought Arianna and Rachel in. They wanted to be here where it's safe."

We join him on the floor above. The room we exited is still a bustling nightmare inside, but now Arianna has joined in the crying chaos.

"I want my mummy," she sobs hysterically.

Aalia's doing her best to calm her down but failing miserably. Passing Zach, I approach Arianna slowly, my hands outstretched to placate her. She only screams even louder.

"I want Giant!"

"Someone go fetch Killian."

Zach vanishes to find him. Accepting a hug from Rachel,

she runs a hand over my wild, mussed-up hair and whispers in my ear.

"Willow's a tough cookie, Micah. We'll find her, and she'll be fine."

"I hope so," I croak back.

"She survived ten years with that piece of shit."

"That was before she ran away and began the process of divorcing him. Not to mention got pregnant with another man's child and engaged to us three idiots. He's going to kill her."

Rachel falls silent, her face pale. "We don't know that."

"Don't we?"

The door slams open again, admitting Zach and a red-faced Killian. He takes one look at Arianna, and his expression shatters into a devastating look of pure grief.

"Peanut," he calls.

Arianna's head snaps up. "Giant!"

"Come here."

Rushing over to him, she's swept up into his arms and spun in a small circle. Arianna clings to his neck, her hysteria dying down into quiet, hiccupping sobs that shake her tiny body.

"Where is Mummy?" she demands.

"She'll be back soon, peanut. I promise."

Arianna's tears continue to fall. "She promised to never leave me. Was I bad? Did I do something wrong?"

I run a hand down her back, her words pushing the dagger in my heart even farther in. "You did nothing wrong, Ari. This isn't your fault."

"Micah's right," Killian consoles.

Taking a seat, he pulls her onto his lap and cuddles her close. She looks even smaller compared to his massive frame towering over her, but her sobs are steadily calming down.

"Guys, we have something." Ethan approaches us. "Mind if we talk over there?"

With Arianna looking a lot calmer, Killian reluctantly hands her off to Ryder for a cuddle then joins us to approach the packed table on the other side of the room.

A newcomer has joined the masses of people, sitting without a laptop and anxiously picking her nails. I recognise her from the trial. She's still wearing her formal clothing and low heels.

"This is Meghan." Ethan gestures towards her. "She was supposed to testify today along with Willow and Lia."

Meghan grants us a tiny wave. "Hello."

"So?" Killian growls out.

She wilts even further. "I... I know Lia a little from the outside world. We used to b-be friends when we worked for Mario."

"Tell them what you've just told me," Ethan says calmly.

She blows out a breath. "Eight or nine months ago, Lia vanished. We worked together at his new club in Soho. She disappeared overnight, and I knew that she'd been sold."

"Sold?" Zach repeats.

"To someone," Meghan clarifies. "Everyone knows it happens, but none of us talk about it. We just do our jobs and get paid, hoping that it won't one day happen to us if we're good."

"Who was she sold to?" Killian demands.

Meghan's hands shake in her lap. "Dimitri Sanchez."

Cursing up a storm, Killian throws his head back to look at the ceiling and take a cleansing breath. He's on the verge of smashing this entire office to pieces.

"Wait, hold up." Everyone's attention shifts towards me. "She was sold to Sanchez?"

Ethan nods. "It appears he was in the market for a replacement after losing Willow. She isn't working for him. She *belongs* to him."

We all wear matching expressions of shock and disgust. That sleazy bastard was literally tormenting Willow for months, playing the doting husband and father, while torturing another woman.

"Today was the first time I saw Lia in months," Meghan adds. "I couldn't believe it. She was caught off guard to see me there. I don't think she expected me to testify now that the club's been shut down."

"I don't get what this has to do with finding Willow." Killian loses patience, his hands thrown into the air. "We're wasting time!"

"Kill, slow down." Ethan holds up a hand. "That isn't all. Meghan, carry on."

"Lia came from a well-off family, you see," Meghan continues after clearing her throat. "She didn't work for Mario because she had no other choice. It was all about getting the drugs her family wouldn't fund."

"Shit," I curse.

"Her family's dead now," she rambles nervously. "There was a car accident a few years back. She inherited the family home in Lancashire."

We all freeze, catching on to her words.

"A family home?" Zach repeats. "In England?"

Meghan nods. "Mr Sanchez would need a bolthole, right? Somewhere to take Willow that isn't tied to him?"

"And the scumbag wouldn't stop to consider that we'd dig into Lia," Ethan finishes. "She isn't even a human being to him. Perhaps he's using her for somewhere to stay off the radar."

"What the fuck are we waiting for?" Killian jumps to his feet, looking ready to find that address and jump in the first available vehicle he can find.

Ethan strides over to one of his operatives, sitting behind an array of open laptops. "Find me everything you can on Lia Hartley."

# CHAPTER 35
# WILLOW
## JEALOUS LOVER – ANIMAL FLAG

"HAPPY BIRTHDAY, ARI."

*Ruffling her short blonde pigtails, I cuddle her close to my chest, ignoring the pain as her body presses against my bruised torso. On the floor of her bedroom sits a single, tiny cupcake with a candle in it that Pedro brought with him.*

*"You have to make a wish, baby."*

*She's too young to have any idea what I'm talking about, but I keep up the pretence anyway, lifting the cupcake and helping her to blow it out. Standing behind me, Pedro quietly claps.*

*"Good job, Ari," he coos.*

*Laughing to herself, Arianna claps her hands together joyfully. I peel the cupcake's wrapper then pull off a bite for her to munch on, twisting to look up at Pedro.*

*He's beaming at both of us, full of happiness. This is the side of Pedro that no one else sees. The side that's reserved just for us and no one else in this Godforsaken mansion.*

*Arianna curls up in my arms, sucking her thumb into her mouth which is smeared with cupcake icing. Her eyes flutter shut, as Pedro takes a seat next to me on her bedroom floor.*

*"I wanted to get her a present," he sighs, gently tracing a knuckle down her cheek.*

*"You would've gotten in trouble."*

*"I know, but it would have been worth it."*

*"He'd kill you, then me."*

*His eyes are sad. "He's killing you regardless, Willow."*

*Coughing wetly, I try to conceal my wince of pain. "I'm fine."*

*"No, you're not. He can't keep doing this to you."*

*"It's been nearly five years, Pedro. Nothing has changed, and nothing ever will."*

*Reaching out to grasp my hand, he holds on tight. "It won't unless you get out of here. I could help you. We could leave together."*

*I smack his hand away. "We would never make it."*

*"Of course, we would. Together."*

*"Keep on dreaming. This is my life now. I've made my peace with it, and so should you."*

*A determined fire burns in his eyes.*

*"We'll get out of here, Willow. I swear on my life, I will get you out. No matter what it takes, you and Arianna will be free to live out happy, healthy lives, far from this place."*

*I feel a single tear streak down my cheek. "Don't make promises that you can't keep."*

*Pedro smiles. "I never do."*

———

I wake up to the sound of screaming. Shooting upright on a soft, pillowy mattress, I blink to clear the haze from my vision. Where am I? This isn't my cabin. I don't recognise the pale grey walls.

That's when it all comes back to me in a horrifying rush of realisation. The trial. Lia. Being drugged. Raising my hand to my neck, I feel the sore, bruised skin where the needle went in.

My other hand immediately rests on my bump as horror infiltrates my system. I'm groggy and achy, but everything else feels normal. My clothes are still intact.

"Are you okay in there?" I whisper to the baby.

I wish I could crawl in there and check that everything's alright. I've got no idea what drugs they shot me full of, but it feels like I've been out for hours. My entire body is heavy and numb.

*Where the hell are we?*

Manoeuvring myself up, I manage to get my feet on the floor and look around the plain bedroom. It feels more like a guest room, with a wide, four-poster bed covered in fresh white linens.

I almost jump out of my skin when the sound of screaming comes again—louder this time. It sounds like it's right beneath me.

Heart beating fast, I creep over to the door and press my ear against it. The sound of fists hitting flesh is instantly recognisable to me. Someone's getting the hell beaten out of them nearby.

Crap, I need to get out of here. Is Mr Sanchez watching me right now? I know he's here, wherever we are. It's only a matter of time before he comes for me, and the torture begins.

Searching around the room, I frantically look for some kind of weapon, but there's nothing. Not a single personal possession, almost like this entire room is just a façade rather than a real home.

"Shit!"

Sitting down on the end of the bed, my head falls into my hands. I was so stupid to follow Lia out of that court, but I had no other choice. It was that or risk Arianna's life, so I'd do it all over again.

Even though I know it landed me here, back at square one—trapped, alone and afraid, in an unknown house in the middle of God knows where. But this time, I know what's coming.

I won't survive it.

Neither of us will.

The tears come, hot and overwhelming. Cradling my

unborn child, I allow myself a moment of weakness and sob uncontrollably, letting the fear take over before I have to be brave again.

When the screaming stops, I abruptly look up, awash with fear. Are they dead? Whoever was being hurt has been silenced, one way or another. A shiver rolls over me. I've seen it happen enough times.

*Enough, Willow.*

*Time to face the devil.*

With a deep breath for courage, I scrub the tears from my face and smooth my dress. The door is unlocked, the handle twisting and clicking open when I walk over to try.

There's an empty hallway on the other side, long and stretching onwards, with thick carpets and framed abstract art on the walls. The house seems old, the ceilings are high and stretch above me.

"H-Hello?"

Movement on the left startles me, and I realise that Lyon is leaning against the wall, his glossy black hair flopping over his eyes. He takes one look at me and sneers.

"Look who's up."

"Lyon," I gasp.

"It's been a long time, petal. You still know how to put up a fight."

My eyes stray to the deep, bloody scratch on the left side of his face. I have a vague memory of lashing out and scratching him as he shoved me into a car. It looks swollen and painful.

"Suits you."

He bares his teeth. "It'll suit you better when I tear your fucking face off with my bare hands."

"I'd like to see you try." I hold my midsection protectively. "Let's get this over and done with. Take me to him."

"Look who's so eager for her punishment." He chuckles maniacally. "Come on then, petal. The boss man is waiting."

Grabbing me by the wrist, he pins my arms behind my back at an awkward angle. I hiss in pain, pulling in an attempt to wrench myself free of his grip, but I'm completely stuck.

"Little bitch," he hisses.

"Ever the charmer, Lyon."

"When did you get such a smart fucking mouth?"

"Since I decided to stop giving a shit about assholes like you."

"Don't worry, we'll soon beat that attitude out of you."

Escorted down the corridor, I take in as much of our surroundings as possible. It seems to be someone's home, but it's empty and bare, almost like the owners vanished, or all of their possessions were sold.

Down a grand staircase, we emerge into an entranceway marked by a circular table with a vase full of long-dead flowers on it. The door leading outside is protected by two of Sanchez's heavily armed thugs.

"What is this place?"

"Somewhere no one will ever find you," Lyon answers confidently. "Those assholes aren't coming for you here."

But he doesn't know the guys like I do. They're not just any assholes. They're *my* assholes, and I know they'll always come for me, regardless of how long it takes. I just have to hold on.

Lead over to a set of carved double doors, Lyon stops outside then knocks once. There's movement on the other side of the door before another armed guard swings it open.

*Here we go.*

Feeling strangely calm, I lift my head high, determined to face Mr Sanchez with no fear. I'm ready. He's threatened my children for the very last time.

"Bring her in," a throaty voice booms.

Shoved into the low-lit living room lined with rich carpets and spotted with the odd piece of furniture, I come face to face with the devil himself.

"Willow. How nice of you to join us."

Mr Sanchez still looks the same—from his slicked back, salt and pepper hair, perfectly trimmed beard and strong, bearded jawline to his handsome looks and spotless, expensive suit.

He's Satan in disguise.

Evil behind a pretty exterior.

I take a wobbly step into the room. "Dimitri."

His smile slips. "What have I told you about addressing me correctly, bitch?"

"I no longer take orders from you."

Doubling over with crazed laughter, he wipes imaginary tears from his eyes. "Oh, how you've changed, darling wife. I quite like this version of you. She has some backbone."

"No thanks to you."

Shoving me farther into the room, Lyon escorts me over to a plush, green velvet sofa where I'm deposited. Mr Sanchez's icy blue gaze doesn't stray from me, taking in all the little details.

He licks his lips, already salivating over my pain. When he spots the glinting engagement ring on my left hand, his carefully constructed mask begins to fray at the edges.

I keep my head held high.

"Who are they?" he demands, his spit flying. "On what universe are these worthless pieces of shit better than me?"

"They don't beat and rape me, for starters. That should've been an easy guess."

He takes a menacing step closer. "Enough of your smart mouth!"

"No." I jump up from the sofa, refusing to let him talk down to me. "It's not enough. Nothing will ever be enough for what you put me and my child through."

"My child," he snarls, his lip curling as if he smelled something rotten. "I'll get her back, Willow. They can't keep her safe forever. Not from me."

"Touch her, and they'll kill you."

"And what if I touch you?" He cocks an eyebrow mockingly. "You're my fucking property, after all. Bought and paid for like the whore you are."

"I belong to myself! I'm not yours!"

Striding over, he backhands me so hard, I feel my lip split. Pain buzzes through my head as blood dribbles down my chin.

"Silence," he shouts in my face.

"You think I can't take one little slap?"

His dark eyes stray down to the swell of my pregnant stomach. "I know you can, wife, but can that little demon spawn inside of you?"

Covering my stomach, I cower away from him, hunching over to protect myself. Triumph burns in his eyes. I can take his beatings, but I have to think about the baby.

"Speaking of..." Mr Sanchez prowls around the sofa, his eyes locked on my belly. "I was most surprised to see you on the news all knocked up."

My mouth opens, but no words come out.

"How dare you," he spits at me. "I will burn their touch from your skin before I kill them in front of you."

"Leave them alone," I whisper brokenly.

He snorts. "Like they left my property alone? Look at the fucking state of you."

When he reaches down to painfully grab my breast through my dress, I shrink farther into myself. All I want to do is fight back, but I'm powerless to do that in this condition.

"You should be full of my baby, not theirs." His hot breath meets my ear. "But that's no trouble. We'll soon get it out of you and remedy this situation."

"No!" I screech.

Unable to hold it in any longer, I throw my fist out, striking him in the face. Mr Sanchez stumbles backwards, looking stunned.

Before I can advance, Lyon grabs hold of me from behind

and pulls me down, pinning my arms to the sofa above my head. I kick out with my legs, screaming my head off.

"Let her go," Mr Sanchez orders. "I like it when she fights back."

Lyon releases me, and I surge to my feet, determined to run. Even if it's back to my room. All I need is to get away from him before he can touch me.

Banking left, I try to flee across the expensive rug, but a foot catches me at the last second. My legs are swept out from underneath me, leaving me sprawled across the floor in a breathless tangle on my back.

Mr Sanchez laughs as he looms over me, a foot on either side of my body. He moves closer to hover over my chest then places a hand low on my belly, right above the baby's swell.

"What am I going to do to you?" he hums.

"Touch my baby, and I'll kill you."

"Hilarious, darling wife." He barks out a sinister chuckle. "I'd like to see you try."

He lowers himself to settle between my legs, pushing them open with a knee. Disgust inundates my system when I see his cock straining against his trousers. No. Not again. He won't get another chance to touch me.

When he leans close to drag his tongue up the side of my face, I snap my knee upwards, slamming it into his crotch. Mr Sanchez's eyes bug out as air whooshes out from between his lips.

"I'll cut it off next time," I warn. "You wanted me to fight back, right?"

Falling onto his side, I shove him off me then hurriedly roll over to climb to my knees. Lyon's there in a flash to restrain me again, but this time, there's a gun in his hands.

"I'll blow your goddamn brain out myself, little bitch!"

I flinch when he presses the cold steel into my temple.

"No," Mr Sanchez groans. "Take her downstairs with the other slut, and ensure she learns how to behave."

Wrestled to my feet, the room sways around me. Lyon's nails dig deep into my wrists as he drags me from the room, leaving Mr Sanchez on the ground, cupping his sore crown jewels.

His sharp, burning gaze on me is the last thing I see before the door swings shut, leaving me alone with his pet psychopath. I struggle to breathe as he drags me by my wrists.

"What is it with you ignorant sluts causing so much damn trouble?" Lyon growls.

I thrash in his grip. "Get the fuck off me."

"You want me to get off? That's what you want?"

Slamming me into a wall hard enough to send stars bursting behind my eyes, he covers my body with his, grinding his hardness into me. I want to throw up on him.

"I'll get off if you say so," he whispers in my ear, his teeth grazing the lobe. "That what you want, pretty little slut?"

Tears course down my cheeks, hot and sticky. When he finally releases me before someone notices him feeling up the boss's property, a relieved breath escapes my mouth.

"Not to worry." Lyon smirks. "We'll pass around what's left of your ass once the boss is done with you."

I don't see the blow coming until it's too late. His fist smashes into the side of my face, crunching bone and sending pain exploding through me. Before I can even open my eyes, he delivers yet another agonising punch.

"Fucking whore," he lashes out.

When his knuckles connect with my nose, I feel it burst. Hot blood runs down my throat and begins to choke me as I scream at the top of my lungs. The pain is indescribable.

*Please.*

*Please let them find me.*

"That's more like it." Lyon wraps his hands around my throat and squeezes. "I like you better when you're silent."

The squeezing tightens into a vice-like grip that makes my

lungs burn. I scratch at his hands, desperately fighting for breath, but there's no oxygen flowing into my chest.

"It's a shame I can't kill you yet." He sighs dramatically. "But I'm a patient man. I'll wait until Mr Sanchez is finished to have my turn."

Releasing my throat, I double over, feeling like my chest is on fire, spluttering and coughing as air rushes to my lungs.

Grabbing a handful of my hair, he smashes my head into the wall—once, twice, three times. I can feel blood soaking into the back of my head as the wall slices my scalp open.

"Night-night, bitch."

With the final plaster-cracking blow, the world and all of its agony wink out of existence. Only this time, I go into the darkness willingly, desperate for a brief moment of peace.

# CHAPTER 36
# WILLOW
PROMISE ME – BADFLOWER

"WILLOW. WAKE UP."

Rolling over on a painfully hard surface, I can't peel my eyes open. They're too heavy. Glued shut. Pain and nausea roll over me in great, blurring tidal waves, both warring for supremacy.

"Ari," I groan.

"It's me, dummy. Your girl isn't here."

"Ari…"

"Willow!"

I manage to lift a hand and raise it to my stuffy nose, feeling the tender skin and bruising. The burst of pain at my touch allows me to peel my eyes open.

Everything hurts. My busted nose. My head. I can feel blood crusted around my neck and ears from the blows that knocked me into the arms of unconsciousness.

"Damn, girl. They did a real number on you."

Following the familiar voice across the dank, low-lit room, the floors and ceilings made of damp concrete, I find a shadow propped up against the wall on the opposite side.

Lia's shoulders are slumped as her head hangs low, obscured by the darkness of what looks like a disused basement. She's sitting with her knees pulled up to her chest protectively.

"L-Lia?"

"The one and only."

"What are you doing down here?"

She shrugs, wincing a little. "May have pissed Mr Sanchez off when you were brought in. It didn't exactly go down quietly."

As she leans forward, her face shifts into the weak beam of light leaking through the window at the top of the room. It reveals heavy bruising and swelling, warping her features into a misshapen caricature.

"Jesus," I rasp.

"Not a pretty sight? You should look in the mirror. Not looking so hot yourself there."

I can feel just how *not hot* I'm looking based on the steady hum of agony racing through my veins. Lyon delivered a brutal beating.

"The baby!" I panic and move to cup my stomach, searching for any signs of bruises.

There's nothing, but the wet stickiness between my legs sends my pulse rate skyrocketing. Lia watches with widened eyes as I drop a hand between my legs, and it comes away smeared with red.

*No.*

*Please, God, no.*

"I'm bleeding," I state numbly.

"Fuck."

Eyes slamming shut, I feel the tears spill over. "This is all your fault."

"I know." Her voice is a broken rasp, betrayed by her pain.

Grabbing hold of my terror and strangling it, I reopen my eyes to pin her with an accusatory glower.

"You did this to me! What did I ever do to you?"

"It's nothing personal." She waves a hand dismissively. "I had to do as he asked."

"So he'd continue to supply you, right? This has to be about drugs. That's why you're working for him."

"Working." She laughs bitterly. "I was bought and paid for, just like you. There's no quid pro quo situation here. If I'm good, he gives me a bump. Simple as that."

Stunned, I wrestle my aching body upright. "He bought you?"

Lia nods, silent.

"How long?"

"Months, I think. It's hard to tell."

I search for even a shred of sympathy but come up empty.

"I never would've done this to another woman when I was in your position," I hiss at her. "Never."

"But you didn't stop him from killing them, did you? The women he hurt in front of you?"

"How... How do you know about that?"

She shrugs. "He likes to talk about you."

With that disgusting realisation, I'm hit by a wave of pain and nausea. I can still feel myself bleeding down there, worsening the sense of panic that's eating me alive.

I begin to hyperventilate, feeling the pressure of Lyon's hands at my throat again. The baby has to be okay. It has to be. This is just a bit of spotting. Nothing to worry about.

My mantras ring hollow. I'm not even twenty-eight weeks. I can't have this baby right now. That only worsens the terror causing me to fall apart.

"Willow?" Lia asks worriedly.

"Can't... d-do... this..."

"Motherfucker," she huffs. "This was not part of the goddamn deal. Alright, I'm coming over."

Managing to ease herself up, she limps over to me, cursing the entire time. I distantly realise that she must've been the one screaming. She's been beaten as badly as I have, if not even worse.

Lia slumps onto the cold, hard floor next to me then wraps an arm around my shoulders. Even if I hate her guts for landing me in here, I can't help but lean into her, needing some sense of comfort.

"You're okay," she whispers. "It's just a bit of blood. Breathe."

"The b-b-baby…"

"Don't even think that, Willow. The kid's gonna be fine, alright?"

Rubbing circles onto my back, she guides me through breathing until I can suck in a clear breath again. I rest my head on her shoulder, waiting for the sobs to dissipate.

"We good here?" Lia drones.

"What the fuck is your problem?"

"You're my problem!"

"I didn't do anything."

"If you hadn't pulled this shit and ran away… I never would've ended up here. Do you know what he does to me, for fuck's sake?"

"Yeah," I answer flatly. "Trust me, I know."

We sit there, cold and shivering. Even our hatred can't keep us warm in this freezing cold lair.

"How the hell did we end up here?"

"Beats me," Lia murmurs.

"Where are we?"

Her head lowers. "This is my old family home. Mr Sanchez needed somewhere to lay low while in England, and I wanted to avoid getting my ass beat this week."

"So you gave him a place to hide?"

"I have to survive too, dammit. You know how the game works."

Lifting my head, I glance around the basement. "We have to get out of here. There must be a way out."

"There isn't."

"I cannot die down here!"

Pushing off her shoulder, I scramble to my feet, blinking the haze of dizziness away. The basement is seven steps across and nine steps wide. There's nothing in it but us and a tonne of dust.

Trying the door in the corner of the room, it doesn't budge an inch. Locked up tight. Even when I slam my shoulder into it and cause my body to scream in pain.

"Shit!" I throw my hands up.

"Found your magic escape route yet, Mystic Meg?"

"You're really not helping."

Lia curses as she probes her bruised face. "I'm being realistic."

Leaning against the wall, I stare at her and imagine burning a hole through her head. "I really hate the sight of you right now."

"Ditto, sweetie."

My back skids down the wall as I sit back down and bury my face in my hands. I can only imagine what the guys are thinking right now. They'll be losing their minds with worry.

God, I miss them. I miss them so fucking much. All those months I spent alone in that crummy apartment were just wasted time when I could've been with them, living the life of my dreams.

"I never should've left them," I scold myself. "They were right there, and I walked away. God, I'm so stupid."

Lia almost manages to look sympathetic. "He would've gotten to you one way or another. Don't beat yourself up."

"I'm here, aren't I? Why shouldn't I blame myself? If I'd just stayed with the guys instead of pushing them away…"

But in that moment, I couldn't even see them. All I saw was my trauma, staring back at me and taunting. I wasn't able to see the overwhelming love they've given me in the past year.

"Do you love them?" Lia asks.

I swipe aside tears. "With my whole heart."

"Then fight for them, Willow. He's going to try to break you now. Don't fucking let him."

Staring at her through my tears, I somehow find the energy to laugh. "Thanks for the advice."

"One captive to another." She winks.

Falling back into silence, I watch her curl into a tight ball and squeeze her eyes shut. That's when the tears hit me at full force again, too many emotions barrelling into me like a speeding freight train.

I did this.

I left them.

If only I'd screamed or fought back. Or found some way to raise the alarm without jeopardising Arianna. But deep down, I know this isn't my fault. Not really.

Mr Sanchez would've found a way to get me back, whether through violence or subterfuge. It was this or watch the people I love suffer, and I'll always do whatever it takes to avoid that.

Even sacrifice myself.

My unborn child.

My life.

I'll die living with that guilt. The shameful guilt of realising that I've chosen one child over the other, allowing Arianna to live at the expense of my unborn baby. We won't survive this place.

It feels like hours pass in a blur of tears and quiet, desperate sobbing. Lia stays silent, leaving me to fall apart in peace. My entire body shivers and shakes in the freezing cold air.

When the sound of heavy footsteps and voices breaks our solitude, Lia's head snaps up as she quickly finds her feet.

"They're coming."

I let her pull me up. "What do we do?"

"Stay quiet, and don't piss him off even more than you already have. Do you want another beating?"

"No." I recoil, still feeling the sticky mess between my thighs. "I can't take another."

Both backing up, we press ourselves into the ice-cold wall so we're as small as possible. At the last second, Lia takes my hand into hers and clenches it tight.

"We'll be okay," she whispers.

"How do you know?"

"I don't."

The door clanks open, old and groaning on abused hinges. Lyon steps into the room first, followed shortly by Mr Sanchez in a fresh blue suit, his hair slicked back to unveil his impish grin.

"Evenin' ladies. How are we feeling?"

Neither of us responds.

Prowling into the room, Mr Sanchez glances around the space with a sneer. He doesn't even spare Lia a glance, far too fixated on staring at me like he's discovered a hidden treasure.

"No more funny business." He points his index finger at me.

I stare up at him, petrified and unable to hide it any longer.

"My patience has now expired. You're going to do as I say, when I say it, or your baby will pay the price."

A shudder rolls over me. "Yes, sir."

He grins at me. "That's more like it. We're leaving this country by sunrise, but I'm not going anywhere without my daughter."

"You'll never get to her."

"Oh, I know." His grin widens. "That's why you're going to call those bastards and convince them to surrender my girl to me. We're going to be a big, happy family again."

Alarm pierces my chest. "They'll never do that."

Pulling a gun out of the holster around his waist, Lyon

points it at me. "They will if they don't want to hear us blow your fucking brains out."

Storming across the room, Mr Sanchez grabs hold of my chin and yanks hard so I'm forced to look up at him. Righteous fury burns in his blue eyes, sending stabs of fear throughout my body.

"Don't test me again, Mrs Sanchez. This is your final warning. Don't forget what you are to me." He inhales deeply. *"Replaceable."*

I gulp hard, looking between him and the gun. "What do you want me to do?"

"Good girl. You're going to call those men and lay out the terms. I want Arianna delivered, safe and sound. She will be alone." He emphasises the last word. "Else you're going to pay the price."

"Delivered where?"

"I have men waiting near Manchester airport."

My blood chills. "The… airport?"

His eyes sparkle with malice. "This piece of shit country isn't our home, wife. We're returning to Mexico as soon as we have Arianna."

Pulling out a phone, Lyon hands it to me, the gun still aimed at my chest. "Call their number."

With trembling hands, I take the phone, shakily tapping in Zach's number and putting it on speakerphone. All I can see is that gun pointed right at me, a second away from firing and ending everything.

Mr Sanchez doesn't move an inch, still invading my personal space and staring down at me as I let the phone ring. When Zach doesn't answer, he growls out a curse.

"Again."

"It's an unknown num—"

"Again!" He slaps my face, reopening my split lip.

Licking blood from my mouth, I hit redial then wait, my heartbeat roaring in my ears. I'm a second from giving up hope when the line engages, and a familiar voice causes my adrenaline to spike.

"Who is this?" Zach answers wearily.

"Zach," I rush out. "Don't hang up the phone."

"Holy fu… Willow? Is that you?"

"I'm okay, I'm okay," I trip over my words in a panic. "You have to listen to me, Zach. I don't have a lot of time."

The gun inches closer, still trained on me. Coming to an awful, gut-wrenching decision, I crush the remains of my hammering heart, knowing I have no other choice. I won't surrender Arianna.

"No matter what they do to me, do not give her to them! Don't give them Ari!"

*Whoosh.*

*Thud.*

Mr Sanchez's fist connects with my stomach, and I fall, crashing to my knees. I can't help but cry out as a hot burst of vomit spews from my throat at the sudden avalanche of pain in my belly.

"Willow!" Zach's voice screams.

I watch through my streaming tears as Mr Sanchez picks up the phone. "I want my daughter back. You're going to bring her to me, or I'll kill your child. The choice is yours."

"Listen here, asshole—"

Drawing back his foot, Mr Sanchez boots me in the rib cage. I shriek in agony, curling inwards to try to protect myself from the blows raining down. It's all I can do.

"Stop it!" Zach howls. "Stop hurting her!"

"The girl," Mr Sanchez hisses. "Manchester airport. Two hours."

Zach hesitates. "We will never surrender Arianna to you."

"Then listen to the sound of your child dying."

As Mr Sanchez lifts his foot to kick me again, Lia flashes across the room. She moves so fast, her bruised body is a blur.

I scream as she tackles Mr Sanchez with her remaining strength.

The pair hit the floor and roll, wrestling with each other. Lyon snarls a frustrated curse as he retrains the gun on their tangle of limbs, fighting for a clear shot.

All I can see is Lia. Teeth bared and brows furrowed, battling for her life. For my life. For what's right. Not even Zach's bellows of my name pierce the slow motion bubble that's encapsulated us all.

The bang of a shot being fired slices through the room, silencing everything. Mr Sanchez pushes Lia's limp body off him before rolling up onto his knees, now covered in fresh blood.

"Fucking whore!" he bellows.

"Lia!" I yell.

But it's too late. She stares up with blank, empty eyes, slumped across the floor as blood pools around her from the hole in her chest. Dead. Gone. I can't restrain the hysterical sounds coming from me.

"Wanted to do that for months." Lyon smirks.

"You killed her!" I wail.

He turns the gun back to me. "Silence, little bitch!"

"My child!" Mr Sanchez howls. "I want my fucking daughter!"

Through the chaos, a familiar voice cuts through the haze. The first voice I heard when I woke up in Briar Valley, terrified and alone. My protector. The man who had the courage to start this whole adventure.

"We're here, baby," Killian croons through the phone. "Hold on for me. I'm coming for you."

I look down at the fallen phone as an almighty crashing sound devours his voice. The small windows high above us shatter into thousands of pieces, sending shards slashing through the air.

Gunfire swallows everything. My stuttered breathing. My

hammering heartbeat. Mr Sanchez's furious shouting. Flashes break through the darkness, and bodies begin to swing into the room.

Launching himself at me, Mr Sanchez takes me down before the first black-clad agent can collide with him. We hit the ground and roll together, both warring to gain the upper-hand.

"You're mine, Willow!" he shouts at the top of his lungs. "You will always be mine!"

Wrapping my hands around his throat, I dig my nails in and squeeze with all of my strength. It isn't enough to throw him off, but I'm able to flip us over and manoeuvre myself on top.

"I was never yours!" I spit in his face. "Not for a single second of those ten years! Rot in hell!"

His fist connects with my face, throwing me off again and allowing him to climb back on top. With blow after blow raining down on me, I begin to choke on a mouthful of blood.

"They don't get to have you." He punches me in the throat. "No one else gets to have you but me!"

With my eyes falling shut, the pummelling suddenly ceases. So much pain is running through me, I can hardly feel it anymore. My brain has found its familiar numb space and switched off to it.

This is it. My end. In those dark, desperate seconds, all I can see is them. The men who saved my life, time and time again, with their unconditional love. Their acceptance. Them. I've lost that forever.

Until there's a touch.

A whisper.

The brush of softness.

Roughened fingertips stroke over my face, swiping through blood and over bruises to push sweat-stained hair aside.

"Baby," a grief-stricken voice murmurs. "Open your eyes, princess. Come back to me. Please, please come back to me."

But I still can't open my eyes. Not yet. The world is slipping through my fingers like quicksand, and I can't hold on to it.

"I love you," he whispers heart-brokenly, his voice fractured with agony. "God, I fucking love you. Open your eyes for me, baby."

"Kill," I moan groggily.

He sucks in a sharp, relieved breath.

"It's me, Willow. I'm here."

Fighting with my last vestiges of strength, I peel my eyes open and look through the blur of pain and tears up at my saviour. He's here. Real. Looking down at me through his own tears.

Killian.

It's always been Killian.

Sliding an arm underneath me, I'm lifted upright where I manage to curl into his chest. All around us, Sabre's men infiltrate the basement, carrying heavy weaponry and fearsome expressions.

"You're here."

Killian presses the gentlest of kisses to my forehead. "I made a promise, Willow. And I never break my promises."

Lingering over us, Ethan pulls off a thick facial shield and sheaths his gun. He takes one look at me and blanches.

"Jesus, Willow. What have they done to you?"

All I can do is sob, "The o-others?"

"We need medical in here right now," he says into his earpiece. "And bring the other two in. She needs them."

Holding me in his arms, Killian wipes blood from his knuckles. Mr Sanchez has been pinned to the floor by Hyland, and Warner holds a gun at his back.

"Take her for me," Killian demands.

Ethan doesn't move. "You can't kill him."

"You think I need your fucking permission, Tarkington?"

Still refusing to budge, Ethan moves to block the path to

Mr Sanchez's pinned body. I raise a shaking, blood-slick hand to grab Killian's lapel and tug.

"Kill," I whisper weakly. "Please... I need you."

His expression breaks—shattering into a look of such intense grief and regret, it physically chokes me. His pain is almost more overwhelming than mine.

"Look at what he's done to you," he says in a pained voice. "You're bleeding, Willow. The baby—"

"He'll be okay."

"He?"

Moving my hand to my belly, I manage a nod. "I think it's a he. Don't you?"

By the grace of God, a smile lights his lips. "Yeah, I do."

"Then trust me. He'll be okay. We're survivors, aren't we?"

A single tear rolls down his cheek. "That you are, Willow Sanchez."

Shouting precedes the arrival of the twins, thumping their way down into the basement at full speed. Zach skids into the room first, wild-eyed with terror and struggling to breathe.

"Willow!" he screeches.

Closely followed by Micah, the pair fall to their knees beside me. Neither knows where to look or what to touch, sitting powerless instead as I steadily bleed onto the concrete floor.

"Angel," Micah whimpers. "What did... he..."

"I'm okay." I cough wetly. "Just a bit banged up."

"Banged up?" Zach repeats.

Killian tries to move again. "That son of a b—"

"Kill!" I cry out.

Freezing still, he holds me tighter, spooned in his arms like I'm a newborn baby unable to look after itself. I suck in a painful breath and look at Micah.

"Don't let him kill Mr Sanchez, Mi."

He shakes his head. "Willow..."

"No! He needs to be punished for what he's done. I want

justice, not death. All of the women he hurt deserve more than that."

Zach smooths down my hair. "We've got you, babe. He'll go down for the rest of his life. We'll see to it, I promise you."

Above us, Ethan nods. "Swear on it."

With their promises relieving some of the pressure on my chest, I grasp Micah and Zach's hands, letting myself float on a cloud of numbness until the medical team arrives.

"Sir, please step aside."

"No!" Killian shouts. "I will not!"

"Don't l-leave me," I sob.

He cuddles my broken body close. "Never, baby."

"Never," Zach echoes.

Micah ducks down to kiss my cheek. "Never, angel."

My eyes slide shut, safe in the knowledge that my men have me, and they'll never, ever let me go again.

# CHAPTER 37
# KILLIAN

## SOLID GROUND – VANCE JOY

HOSPITALS HAVE to be my second least favourite place on the earth, right after cities. Nothing good happens in these places. Aside from the reunions. And fuck, this is about to be a big one.

Holding Arianna's tiny hand in mine, I walk her along the long, gleaming white corridor that leads to the hospital ward. Willow's been under observation since she was brought in last night.

"Giant?" Arianna looks up at me. "Will Mummy be okay?"

"She's going to be just fine, Ari."

"Do you promise?" She wrinkles her nose. "My daddy used to promise things, like he'd hurt Mummy if I was bad or naughty."

Kneeling down so I'm at her height, I take both of her hands in mine to squeeze. "This isn't that kind of promise, Ari. I swore that I'd look after you both, and I'm a man of my word."

She finds the courage to smile. "Okay."

"Okay?"

"If you promise."

I kiss her forehead. "I do."

"Then I believe you."

Standing back up, we walk down the rest of the corridor and stop outside Willow's door. There's a small group of people inside—Doc, Aalia, Rachel and Miranda—who all step out to give us some privacy.

Katie's already back at the hotel. She stayed with her daughter all night after she heard the news. The mad woman hasn't left her side for a moment, only succumbing to sleep when we demanded that she get some rest.

"How's she doing?" I ask Doc.

He pats my shoulder. "The doctors here know what they're doing, Kill. She'll be alright."

"I'm not asking them, I'm asking you."

Doc nods, sadness emanating from his eyes. "It's nothing a little time won't fix."

"The baby?"

"Count your lucky stars the baby survived that beating. It was touch and go, but there's no permanent damage. Someone must be looking out for you lot up there after all."

I send a silent prayer up to the heavens to the one person I know is looking down on us with absolute certainty.

*Thank you, Grams.*

*Thank you.*

Releasing my shoulder, he heads off down the corridor with the others to give us some privacy. The twins are still inside, sitting at Willow's bedside, keeping her company.

I look down at Arianna. "Listen, Ari. Your mum's a little bit sore right now, so I need you to be gentle. She may look different too."

"Different? How?"

"She has some marks and bruises that look a bit scary, but I promise, she's alright. Everything is going to be fine. Can you be a big, brave girl for me?"

She sucks back in her trembling bottom lip. "I can."

"Then let's go see your mummy."

"Okay, Giant."

Holding the door to the room open for her, my eyes connect with Willow's teary ones. She's connected to several IV lines, feeding her painkillers and antibiotics. A machine is monitoring the baby too.

Her face is a heart-wrenching technicolour painting, not unlike the mess she was in when she first arrived in Briar Valley. Skin blackened and face misshapen, she looks worse for wear but still fucking beautiful.

"Ari?" she whimpers.

Tentatively stepping into the room, Arianna looks her up and down. "Mummy?"

"Come here, baby. It's me."

That's all it takes. Hearing those words, nothing else matters. Arianna runs into the room, and Zach catches her before she can launch herself at Willow and hurt her.

He places Arianna down on the edge of the bed where she takes her mum's hand and lightly cuddles her, beneath the swell of her bump that's hidden underneath the white sheets.

"I was so scared," Arianna cries. "I thought I'd never see you again."

Willow holds her daughter's hand tight and strokes her neatly plaited hair. "I'll always find you, Ari. You know that."

"I know, Mummy."

"You're my little girl. Nothing will ever tear us apart." Willow swallows hard. "Not even your daddy. He isn't going to be a problem anymore."

Arianna looks up, face frozen in fear. "He's... gone?"

Willow nods patiently. "Your daddy did some very bad things, Ari. He's going to be in prison for a long time. I'm sorry, baby."

Chewing on her lip as she thinks, Arianna eventually nods back. "Good. He's where the bad men belong."

"Yes, he is."

Laying back down on her mum's legs, Arianna clings on tight, her tears saturating the hospital sheets. I move to stand at the end of the bed between the twins who are sitting in chairs on either side.

"Have the doctors been around yet?"

Zach looks up at me. "About half an hour ago. They want to keep her in for another day before thinking about a discharge."

"And the baby?"

"The consultant did another scan." Micah strokes Willow's needle-filled arm. "Everything is looking alright for now."

I breathe out a sigh of relief. "Thank God."

Listening to us, Willow looks equally as relieved. We were all fucking terrified and convinced we'd lost the baby when we found her, barely alive and covered in blood.

She'd been bleeding again as a result of all the stress, but as Doc put it, by some miracle, she didn't go into premature labour. We dodged a very badly-timed bullet thanks to the medical team here.

All holding each other, we're left alone until Rachel and Miranda come to take Arianna back to the hotel we've commandeered near the hospital.

"Mummy," Arianna whines.

"I'll be coming home soon, baby," she tries to comfort her. "Come back and see me tomorrow, okay?"

"Okay." Arianna pouts. "But who's going to tuck me in?"

"How about Uncle Ryder?" A voice offers.

Standing in the doorway, Ryder and Ethan are holding hands. Willow smiles up at them when they enter the room together.

"You came."

The skin bunches around Ryder's eyes as he glances over her bruised face. "Couldn't miss seeing my best girl, now could I?"

After exchanging a quick hug, Willow clasps his arm. "You'll take her back and tuck her in for me? She's funny about that."

"Of course." Ryder bends down to scoop Arianna up. "Come on, poppet. Let's go and raid the hotel mini fridge for snacks."

"Okay!" she agrees enthusiastically.

After pausing to drop a kiss on Willow's cheek, Ryder takes her daughter out, and the door clicks shut behind him. Ethan watches his boyfriend go before pulling up a chair at Willow's bedside.

"How are you doing, sweetheart?"

She winces a little. "Sore."

"We're just glad you're okay. You took a hell of a beating or two in that place."

"I had no other choice." She glances between us nervously. "Keeping Arianna safe was my priority. He threatened her."

"We figured as much," Zach concludes.

"I followed along with Lia, but I had no intentions of going with her from the courthouse. By the time the car with Mr Sanchez's men came, it was too late to escape."

Micah squeezes her arm. "No one blames you, angel."

Willow shakes her head. "I blame me. I put myself and my baby in danger."

"To protect your daughter," he points out.

She gives in with a nod. "Yes. It was all for her."

"That's called being a mother." I take a seat next to Ethan. "And we understand. You did what you had to do to keep her safe."

"You forgive me?" Willow's eyes bounce between us.

Zach kisses her knuckles. "There's nothing to forgive."

Blinking tears aside, Willow looks back up to Ethan. "What about Mr Sanchez? Where is he now?"

"Being held at Sabre HQ pending further investigation,"

he answers. "He'll be transferred to a high-security prison within forty-eight hours and sentenced for his crimes."

"What are we looking at?" I interject.

Ethan smiles. "Life."

Zach whistles. "You think he'll go down?"

"Without a shadow of a doubt. We have countless witnesses and victims ready to testify and all the evidence we need. He's toast."

"And the trials?" Willow croaks.

"Rescheduled, for both Mario Luciano and Mason Stevenson. All of them will see their day in court, Willow. I'm keeping my word."

Hearing that Dimitri Sanchez is locked up in a cell right now, alone and forced to confront the reality of life behind bars, gives me the tiniest sliver of satisfaction. Tiniest. I'd rather he was dead.

But that won't give Willow the closure and peace she needs right now. There's no justice in death, just punishment, and she needs that justice to heal and move on with her life. I can respect that.

"So… it's over?" Willow asks hopefully.

Ethan rests his hand over hers. "It's over. The trafficking ring has been dismantled, and everyone is going down. You did it, Willow."

"I did nothing," she insists.

"No, you did. This investigation is over because of you. We won. The case has officially been closed."

With those words, Willow bursts into tears. Ethan looks surprised for a second before he inches closer.

"Can I… hug you?"

"Please do," she cries.

The pair carefully embrace, dodging wires and tubes. Even Ethan has tears in his eyes when they separate again.

"There's something else." Ethan says hesitantly. "I wanted you to hear it from me. I'm leaving Sabre Security."

"You're doing what?" I frown at him.

"I've worked for this company for over a decade, and I'm tired. This was my last case. Now that it's over, I've decided to go as well."

"But… Ryder just moved to London for you," Micah says.

Ethan looks sheepish as he glances back at Willow. "That's the thing. I was wondering if you had a spare cabin. I figure we'll need our own space if we move back to Briar Valley together."

She breaks out in a massive grin. "I can think of a couple that'll be empty soon. You can take your pick."

"You'd have me?" Ethan asks with a coy smile.

"Any day of the week. You can help solve the mystery of the egg stealer. It's still unsolved, twelve months later."

"Sounds like a job for an expert."

I punch him in the shoulder. "You can be our official, live-in security expert. We have some strange old types around town. Could use the muscle."

"Consider it done."

We all break into laughter. Ethan quickly makes his excuses to leave and give us some privacy, promising to come back with more news soon.

"How are you really feeling?" I narrow my eyes on Willow once it's just the four of us.

Her smile fades. "Like shit."

"What can we do?" Zach asks worriedly.

"Just hold me."

He runs a hand up and down her leg. "We're here, babe. None of us are going anywhere."

We all crowd closer around her, touching whatever bits of her we can access that aren't bruised or taped up. Willow cries until she has no tears left.

"I want to go home," she hiccups.

"Soon, baby." I entwine our fingers and squeeze. "The

doctors need to keep you in to monitor the baby. We want you both to be safe and healthy."

"I'm with you." Her hazel eyes flick up to me, full of adoration. "I'm always safe when I'm with you." She looks at the twins. "All of you."

Micah kisses the back of her hand again. "You never have to be scared again, angel. You're safe now. For good."

"I don't know about that," Zach chuckles. "She lives with us three morons. That's plenty of reason to be scared."

"And she's having our kid," I add. "Who wouldn't that terrify? What if it comes out looking like you pair of ugly oafs?"

Zach sticks his tongue out playfully and Micah looks at me with indignation. Willow laughs so hard, she winces and has to take a moment to breathe through the pain.

"Don't make me laugh. It hurts."

Zach glares at me. "Your fault."

"Don't want to get picked on? Don't look like that. Simple."

"I'm the hot twin! Look at me!"

Coughing under his breath, Micah elbows his brother in the ribs to shut him up before Willow hurts herself laughing again. Zach yelps before falling silent with a smirk.

"So... hot twins and their grumpy, oversized cousin." Willow's eyes sparkle with mirth. "What's the plan now?"

We all look at each other before I answer. "Now we go home."

She pauses to squeeze all of our hands, one by one.

"I already am home."

# CHAPTER 38
# WILLOW
SPIRIT – JUDAH & THE LION

A HAND RESTING on my huge, swollen bump, I stare up at the finished cabin as Killian installs the very last window. After months of painstaking work and a labour of love, our home is finally finished.

Killian screws in the last bolt then climbs down the ladder to stare at his handiwork. He looks gorgeous as always in low-slung jeans and no shirt, despite the autumnal weather.

"Kill!"

He spins on the spot. "What the hell are you doing up?"

Waddling over to him, I walk straight into his arms and kiss him on the mouth. "I'm tired of bed rest."

"Willow, you're five days overdue. Do I have to tie you to the damn bed?"

"Mmm, sounds kinky. Let's go."

He gives me the stink-eye. "It's really not. You're a nightmare patient. Admit it."

Rolling my eyes, I kiss him again until he softens. "I'll admit no such thing. Come on, grumpy. I just wanted to watch you finish off the last bits. It looks incredible."

Arms wrapped around each other, we look up at the cabin. It's a real beauty, carved from dark-stained oak, steel and polished glass. Even bigger than Lola's previous three-story beast.

"Better late than never," Killian grumbles.

"I reckon the baby stayed in there past its due date just to give you time to finish."

He snorts. "In that case, perfect timing."

Holding each other close, it isn't long before the twins join us, both finished up for the day. Zach took Micah into Highbridge to stock up the shop.

It took some convincing to get Micah on board with the idea of selling his artwork in an actual store. His days of ad hoc, online sales and invisibility are over. We're dragging him into the limelight.

Using money from Lola's estate, I purchased the small, corner plot a couple of months ago, located in the quieter end of Highbridge's bustling town centre.

It needed some renovation, but Killian quickly took care of that. Now everything is ready for its first official opening in a few weeks. Micah's art will finally get the appreciation it deserves.

"You get everything moved over?" I ask.

Micah drops a kiss on my lips. "That was the last of the canvases. Just got to take the last few sculptures and finish setting everything up."

"I bet the studio looks empty."

He laughs. "Plenty of space to fill it up with even more art."

Shoving his twin out of the way with a grin, Zach steals me from Killian's arms and lays a dramatic kiss on my cheek.

I push his shoulder, my body protesting at the sudden movement. All my joints are aching something fierce now that I'm overdue.

"How are we doing?" Zach singsongs.

"We? You're not the one pregnant and five days overdue,

mister. I'm fucking uncomfortable and miserable. How are *you* doing?"

"Oh, excellent. Very much not pregnant, thanks."

"Micah, please punch your brother for me."

He holds up his hands. "I'm a pacifist."

"I'll do it," Killian volunteers. "Come here, kid. Take it like a man."

"Sexist!" Zach accuses.

Getting him in a headlock, Killian thumps Zach right in the stomach, forcing him to double over with a cough.

I cringe, feeling a little guilty, but then pain hits me in the belly again, and I feel a lot less bad about it.

"Here comes another one."

"Contraction?" Micah worries.

Nodding through the pain, I rest my hands on my knees, folded over as I breathe through the spasming. They've been coming on and off, but my water hasn't broken yet.

"We're close." Killian rests a hand on my lower back. "Bed, Willow. No arguments this time."

"Yes, sir. Can someone give me a ride?"

Micah takes my hand. "We've got the truck."

Climbing into the backseat, I sit down as comfortably as possible, my bump barely fitting inside the space.

I've suddenly ballooned in the last month of my pregnancy, much to the guys' delight. They can hardly keep their hands to themselves.

We arrive home to packed boxes and chaos. Killian decided we needed to move into the cabin as soon as possible, before the baby comes. But with a few delays, the timeline has gotten all messed up.

"I'll get Ryder to help me move the rest of this stuff out of here," Zach says, lifting a box labelled *kitchen*. "We need to move fast if we're going to get this done before the spud arrives."

"Zachariah, I've warned you about the *S* word."

"And how much you love the nickname? Sure."

"Jackass."

"Your jackass, babe. Forever and ever."

With a wink, he props the box on his shoulder then disappears, leaving Micah to manoeuvre me over to the sofa. I slump onto it with a sigh, taking the weight off my swollen feet and ankles.

"You need anything, angel?" he fusses, fluffing the pillow behind me.

"Just you."

Smiling, he sits next to me and begins to massage my shoulders. "You've got me."

"Distract me. How's the shop looking?"

"Chaotic, but it'll come together." He bites his bottom lip. "I can't believe it's actually happening after all this time."

"It's going to be great, Mi. You'll be amazing."

"I'm not a good people person."

"Then we'll hire some front-of-house staff or stick a name tag on Zach." I wince as more pain stabs through my lower belly. "He can chat all the customers to death while you paint."

Micah laughs. "That's actually not a bad idea."

Inhaling sharply, more cramps hit me in a bigger wave this time, taking my breath away. I lean over, moaning through gritted teeth as my lower back twinges in protest.

"Shit." Micah rubs my back. "That was a big one."

"I don't think we have long. You should get the guys."

"What about the cabin?"

"It can wait until after. I need you all here with me."

Micah grabs my phone from the kitchen table to round everyone up. "I'll ask Aalia to pick Arianna up from school and keep her occupied for a bit."

"Thanks, Mi."

Left alone, I place both hands on my tight belly and imagine the life inside. It's been another tumultuous, messy as hell pregnancy, but despite all the odds, we've made it to this moment.

"Hey there, little one." I stroke over my swollen bump. "Thanks for sticking with me, baby. I'm so excited to meet you. We made it."

I have to keep telling myself that, over and over again. We made it. That still doesn't feel real, even if the monsters who tried to break me are all safely locked up behind bars.

Mr Sanchez's trial is set for January, while Mason Stevenson and Mario Luciano, along with other members of the human trafficking ring, have both been sent down for lengthy sentences.

I know I'll have to face him again. There's no avoiding it. But now I get to sit in that courtroom, safe in the knowledge that he will never hurt me or another woman again.

Justice will be served.

That's how I sleep at night.

The contractions continue for hours, over and over, until I'm sweaty and exhausted. When another hits, even stronger than the last, I cry out Micah's name. He's back in a flash to hold my hand, rubbing my back and whispering assurances.

As we're riding the wave of another spasm, warmth gushes from between my legs. I take one look down at the wet patch spreading across the sofa and my breath stalls in my chest.

"Mi!"

"Shit." His eyes are wider than I've ever seen them. "Was that your water breaking?"

"Yes. Call Doc! He needs to come."

"I'm on it, angel."

Briar Valley moves fast in an emergency, so before long, the guys are all back where they belong. Doc arrives soon after with Rachel and Miranda to assist, loaded down by medical bags and fresh towels.

"Alright, then." He crouches down in front of me. "It's go

time, Willow. Let's have this baby."

Tears pour down my sweaty face. "I'm scared, Doc."

He places a reassuring hand on my leg. "You're going to be just fine, kid. We've had a lot of experience. Your baby is in safe hands."

With Killian's help, I strip off my drenched lower half then manoeuvre down onto the towel-covered floor. Doc ducks his head between my legs, only to come back up seconds later.

"There's no time to move her to our cabin. She's fully dilated."

"Crap," Zach curses. "This wasn't the plan."

"Plans change." Doc looks up at me. "It's time to push, Willow."

Killian grips my hand tightly. "We're here, baby. You're not alone."

Pain rips through me again—blurring my vision with agony. Sweat drips from my forehead, and my entire body trembles with tiny earthquakes as I scream and push.

The cycle repeats. Scream. Push. Scream some more. Pain. Dizziness. Sweat.

"Push again, Willow. Just keep pushing."

Their words filter into my mind as my body takes over, entering a primitive state. Rachel dabs my forehead with a wet towel while Miranda stays with her husband, monitoring the situation.

The guys take turns holding my hand until one of the others gets impatient for a turn, and they have to swap over.

"How much longer?" Killian growls. "She's hurting!"

"We're close," Doc confirms. "I can see the head."

"I love you." Micah kisses my temple. "And so will this baby, Willow. You're so close now. Keep going."

"Almost there," Zach murmurs.

Killian nudges Micah away and takes my hand. "You've got this, baby."

The pain is blinding. Over and over. Hitting me relentlessly in every last corner of my body, until I can hardly grit out a scream through my clenched teeth. Doc's head is still ducked low.

And then... bliss.

Relief.

I draw in a deep breath.

The sound of a wailing infant fills the half-packed cabin. Everyone falls silent, as if struck by the most magical, awe-inspiring bolt of lightning. Doc's head lifts as he cradles my baby in his arms.

"One healthy baby boy," he pronounces proudly.

"Oh my God," Zach manages through tears.

"Who's cutting the cord?"

Killian claps Zach's shoulder. "You're up, kid."

"Me? Shouldn't it be you?"

"I think you can handle this one."

Zach looks completely freaked out, but more at Killian trusting him with something important than the idea of cutting the cord.

Taking the scissors from Doc, he slices through the umbilical cord, his eyes red with tears and mouth hanging open in shock.

Miranda passes her husband a towel, then Doc cleans and wraps up the screaming bundle before carrying him over to me. My heart explodes in my chest as I hold my son for the very first time.

He's here.

We made it.

Body sagging, I slump into Killian's arms as our baby cries into my chest. He's so small and perfect, his eyes sealed shut and features soft. The love that rushes over me is indescribable.

"Our son," Killian says in wonderment.

I look up and find the big guy sobbing his damn eyes out.

"Oh, Kill."

"Not a word," he snarks.

"We have a son," Micah whispers.

All of them are bawling, and unable to control it, I join in. The entire roomful is crying and smiling, all looking down at the angelic bundle of perfection clasped in my arms.

"We're dads now." Zach shakes his head. "I actually have to be an adult."

"I'll believe it when I see it, kid," Killian mumbles, wiping off his face.

"What should we name him?" Micah drops the gentlest of kisses on our son's bright-red nose. "What about after your father, Willow?"

Confusing emotions wash over me, mingling with my tears, pain and joy. That man brought nothing but misery into my life. I don't need his memory when I have my family and future right here.

"No. Not that." Looking up at the twins, I smile. "What about after your dad?"

"Hayden?" Zach asks, a grin blooming. "I like it."

"Hayden," Micah repeats.

Killian smooths a giant hand over his son's head. "Hell of a name."

"Hayden it is." Doc wipes off his hands. "Congratulations."

Leaving the room to give us a moment to ourselves, we all snuggle and pass the baby around. Seeing the guys holding their son for the very first time is enough to set me off again, the tears stinging my cheeks.

"He's so small," Killian says in awe.

Zach clasps his shoulder. "You're just huge, Kill."

"You calling me fat, asshole?"

"Hey," I snap at them. "Language. Little ears are present."

Both rush to apologise while Micah rolls his eyes at their antics. When there's a soft knock on the cabin door, I hear

Doc answer before the sound of Arianna's excited voice travels into the cabin.

"Should we let her in?" Micah asks.

"Yeah, it's fine."

Covering myself with another couple of towels, I take Hayden back into my arms and snuggle him close. His eyes are still sealed tightly shut, but he's fallen silent, his lips popping adorable little spit bubbles.

"Mummy?" a little voice whispers.

Arianna sticks her head into the room, appearing tentative. I nod for her to come in.

"It's okay, Ari. Come and meet your little brother."

"I have a brother?"

"Yes, baby. You're a big sister now."

Creeping closer, she kneels next to me, her eyes blown wide. Micah makes sure she's sitting comfortably before propping a cushion up on her lap to bridge the gap.

"Want to hold him?" I ask her.

"I can?"

"You just have to be nice and gentle, baby. Like this."

Demonstrating for her, I slowly lift Hayden onto her lap and ensure she's holding him correctly. Arianna clutches the towel-wrapped bundle, her mouth hanging open for a moment before her lips stretch in a smile.

"He's so small," she coos. "And… and… ugly."

"Hey!" Zach laughs.

"He's all red and shrivelled up!"

Killian smacks his forehead. "Aren't kids the best?"

But I'm too busy staring at my little girl holding her brother to pay any attention. My entire life is right here, bottled up into two amazing human beings. My world. My love. My everything. This is our family.

That's what I ran for.

That's what I survived for.

This moment and all that's to come.

# EPILOGUE

YOU'VE GOT THE LOVE –
FLORENCE & THE MACHINE

## WILLOW

### *Two Years Later*

Staring at myself in the mirror, I bite my gloss-covered lip. "Is it too boring?"

Fussing over me, Katie adjusts my long, white veil. "No, darling. The dress is perfect for a Briar Valley wedding."

My wedding dress is a simple, silk slip with thin spaghetti straps and a low back, exposing just the right amount of skin while maintaining a little mystery.

I wanted something light and cool for our summer wedding. It's the summer solstice today, the longest day of the year, and the whole town is geared up for a hell of a show.

"You look so beautiful." She wells up as she stares at me in the mirror.

"Thanks, Mum."

Her tears only intensify at that name. I started calling her Mum not long after Hayden was born, almost two years ago, but it still makes her teary to hear it after all that we've been through together.

Lifting my hand to rest it on top of hers, we lock eyes. Despite everything that I've suffered, a small part of me can be glad. It brought me my family, my mother, my home.

Without all that pain and suffering, I'd have nothing. No life. No future. No happily ever after. That's the thing about pain—it demands an equal and offers hope in the purest of forms.

Pain gave me life.

Pain made me who I am.

But living? That's a job for the person I am now. The person I became when I saw a world without all that pain and realised that hope is the greatest possible gift this world ever gave me.

"Are you ready?" Katie asks.

"As I'll ever be."

She kisses my cheek. "I'm so proud of you, Willow. You're an incredible woman, and it's an honour to be your mother and friend."

I blink away tears before they ruin my light makeup. "I love you."

"I love you too, my sweet girl. Come on, then. Let's get you married."

Holding her hand, I glance around our huge, master bedroom. It's three times the size of a regular bedroom with two king mattresses pushed together to make a single, mega-sized bed.

Hayden has his own room now, but more often than not, he ends up back in bed with us by midnight. Arianna is far too old for that, or so she claims. She's a mouthy little spitfire at ten years old.

Lifting the hem of my dress, I walk down the stairs to find my bridesmaids—Aalia, Rachel and Miranda—all waiting at the bottom for me in pale shades of buttery yellow.

Standing in front of them, Arianna is dressed in her own yellow dress, perfectly complementing her pearly blonde hair that's neatly plaited with bows. Her mouth falls open when she sees me.

"Mum! You look so pretty!"

I duck down to kiss her cheek. "Thanks, baby."

"Oh, Willow." Aalia covers her mouth. "You look stunning."

"Thank you, Aalia."

Rachel wipes her tears aside. "Just breathtaking."

Miranda pulls her into a side-hug, fighting her own tears. "You're perfect, Willow. So perfect."

"Come on, guys. You're all determined to make me cry."

Laughing it off, they take their places ahead of me, preparing to walk out of the arched front door that Killian carved himself.

With the tinkle of music playing, I clutch my mum's hand tight and take the bouquet of Briar Valley wildflowers, wrapped in a pink ribbon. Nothing else would've done the job.

Arianna takes her place at the head of the convoy as my flower girl. She leads us all, her head held high with pride. The bridesmaids follow until it's time for me to go.

"I'm nervous," I admit quietly.

Katie squeezes my arm. "I won't let you fall over."

"Promise, Mum?"

"Always, Willow."

With her grip holding me tight, we exit the cabin together, and brilliant sunshine blinds me. The sweet, intoxicating scent of summer washes over us, full of blooms and earthy richness.

The entire town has turned out for the wedding. Everyone sits in their Sunday best on white-painted chairs, all facing a wicker archway laden with sunflowers picked from the fields.

When I see the guys for the first time, everything stops. The rest of the wedding melts away until it's just us for the very first time all over again. The years we've been together suddenly vanish.

All three of them wear matching suits in the darkest shade of green, reminiscent of the thick, impenetrable forest around us—the same forest I almost died dragging myself through to get to them.

Micah's smile captures me first. It's as sweet and innocent as the first time I saw it over the dinner table, stunning those around us.

When Killian looks up at me, he doesn't smile. His mouth is too busy hanging open in awe, his eyes stretched wide with such intense adoration, it would scare most people.

Luckily, I'm not most people.

I love his adoration.

Zach's the last to look up—his emerald-green eyes meeting mine. Grinning like the child at heart he is, he winks at me.

Immediately, I'm set at ease. Nothing else matters but the short walk back into their arms. Eating up the distance between us, I stop next to Ryder's chair to kiss my little boy, snuggled up in his arms.

"Go get 'em," Ryder whispers.

I kiss his cheek. "Thanks, Ry."

Ethan gives me a thumb's up from the seat next to him, sitting with Harlow and all four of her plus ones, recently arriving from their new home in Australia just for the day.

Meeting the guys at the front of the town square, I pass my bouquet off to Katie then face them. We have no vicar or officiant, as this isn't a legal wedding, but everyone who matters is here.

Us.

It's always been us.

And it always will be.

"Willow." Killian takes my hands first, ever the commander. "You look so incredible, baby."

"Thank you, Kill."

He holds my hands tight. "I know I'm not a perfect man. Far from it. But you make me a better person, and I want to spend the rest of my life making you smile… just like that."

A grin on my lips, I drop my voice low so no one else can hear. "I love you because you're a grumpy, over-protective bastard."

"Good," he growls in a deeper voice. "Because I am absolutely not about to change. So we're on the same page."

Cupping the back of my head, he captures my lips in a hard, fast kiss that makes the crowd wolf-whistle. When we separate, the tips of his ears are burning pink.

"Will you marry me?"

"Yes. I will."

We kiss again, barely managing to separate when Zach clears his throat and steps up next. I'm passed along, all of us laughing at the ridiculousness of it.

"Willow—" he begins.

"Before you say anything," I interrupt him. "Zachariah, you are the most childish, infuriating person I have ever met, and I love you with my whole heart regardless. Will you marry me?"

His mouth splits into a wide smile. "I do."

We share a kiss, right where Killian's lips left off, and everyone claps again. Katie watches on with tears sparkling in her eyes.

"For the record, I love you too," Zach adds. "Even when you don't get my dad jokes or let Killian call me *kid*."

"Good. You're stuck with me now."

"Forever?" he laughs.

"You're damn right, we're forever."

Kissing again, he reluctantly hands me to Micah. My sad-eyed, quiet boy. The man who took the longest to love me and the most to forgive me. Of course, he's the last to hold me close.

"Willow," he bites his lip nervously. "I had a lot planned

out that I wanted to say, but standing here… hell, I've forgotten all of it."

"Maybe we don't need words, Mi. We have each other."

"We do." He nods. "Through the darkest of times, we've always had each other. You've loved me at my absolute worst."

"As have you."

"Then I guess we can love each other at our best for the rest of our lives, right?"

I lean in to peck his lips. "Right."

"Swear on it, angel?"

Even on our wedding day, he's still insecure. Still uncertain. Shaking my head at him, I take the first of the solid gold bands from Arianna's outstretched hand and slide it on his finger.

"I swear to love you on all of your worst days, Micah. And all of your best ones too. Hell, maybe even the days in between as well."

He steals my breath with a final kiss that scatters my thoughts. Only Micah can give me the most extraordinary butterflies, reserved solely for his quiet shyness.

I move back to Zach to slide the next ring on his finger, then Killian last. As the head of the family, he takes the honour of placing the final gold band above his mother's ring.

"Are we married now?" Zach laughs.

"I think so."

Whooping loudly, he grabs my hand and lifts it into the air, entwined for the whole town to see. We're overcome by a raucous wave of applause that must echo throughout the mountains.

As we walk back down the aisle, Killian grabs Arianna and boosts her onto his shoulders. She squeals at the top of her lungs.

The one thing that hasn't changed as she's grown up? He's still her giant, and she's still his precious peanut.

Zach takes Hayden from his Uncle Ryder and holds the

little tyke in his arms, now writhing and laughing as he's tickled. That leaves Micah to take my hand and brush a thumb over my knuckles.

"Okay?" he whispers.

I squeeze his hand. "I'll be better than okay forever, Mi."

He smiles again. "Me too. We did it, angel."

"We sure as hell did."

Swooped down low to the ground, my hair brushes against the grass as he dramatically kisses me, stealing some of his twin's moves. As soon as I'm placed back on my feet, the town engulfs us.

Surrounded by my crazy, adoptive Briar Valley family, new and old, my heart is fit to burst. It's perfect. Everything. We fled the darkness to find our home, and boy, did we find it.

I spent a decade living in empty spaces—the place between existing and living. The desolation. The darkness. The unknown.

But that space I mentioned?

Well, that's where wild things grow.

**THE END**

# PLAYLIST

**Listen Here: bit.ly/briarvalley2**

If I Come Home – Suzi Quatro & KT Tunstall
Ridiculous Thoughts – The Cranberries
IT'S ALL FADING TO BLACK – XXXTENTACION & blink-182
Hell – Olivver the Kid
heavy metal – diveliner
Silent Love – James Bay
Ribs – Lorde
How Do I Say Goodbye – Dean Lewis
I STILL LOVE YOU – Bishop Briggs
GONE – NF & Julia Michaels
Need It – Half Moon Run
JUST LIKE YOU – NF
Man or a Monster – Sam Tinnesz & Zayde Wolf
Heavy In Your Arms – Florence & The Machine
Stay with Me – You Me At Six
Spotless – Zach Bryan & The Lumineers
Where It Stays – Charlotte OC
The Other Side of Love – Jack Savoretti

I Feel Like I'm Drowning – Two Feet
Falling Apart – Michael Schulte
Where The Wild Things Are – Labrinth
Home – Edith Whiskers
The Stages of Grief – Awaken I Am
Dawns – Zach Bryan & Maggie Rogers
Forged In The Fire – Caylee Hammack
Angel On Fire – Halsey
Dead Man's Arms – Bishop Briggs
Always Come Back (Acoustic) – Martin Kerr
A Little Bit Happy – TALK
I Found – Amber Run
Forever – Mumford & Sons
Happy Never After – VIOLA
Dagger – Bryce Savage
eresa – YUNGBLUD
Love Will Tear Us Apart – Odina
Jealous Lover – Animal Flag
Promise Me – Badflower
Solid Ground – Vance Joy
Spirit – Judah & The Lion
You've Got The Love – Florence & The Machine

# ACKNOWLEDGMENTS

The end of Willow's story is here. How the hell did that happen? This duet has been a whirlwind ride into the unknown, and I'm so grateful to all of you for sticking with me.

This story has challenged me in so many ways—pushing me to delve into the mind of a mother, lost and afraid, but determined to find herself again. Willow's courage has taught me so much, and I hope you've found some hope in her tale too.

As usual, I have an army of incredible people to thank for getting me here.

Thank you to my mum, first and foremost. Your strength and determination inspired so much of this story. I love you unconditionally.

To the people who keep me going every single day. Clem. Lilith. Kristen. Eddie. Julia. There are too many of you to count, but I appreciate every one of you for keeping me afloat.

Thank you to my amazing editor and proofreader, Kim, for making this book baby shine and dealing with my many emotional breakdowns. You're the best, and I'm so lucky to have you!

I also want to say a massive thanks to the team at Valentine PR for their help with this release and for being fabulous at what they do.

Finally, thank you to my street team, ARC team and loyal

readers for supporting my work and making this dream a reality. You're all the reason why I keep writing and baring my soul. Thank you for reading.

Stay wild,

J Rose xxx

# ABOUT THE AUTHOR

J Rose is an independent dark romance author from the United Kingdom. She writes challenging, plot-driven stories packed full of angst, heartbreak and broken characters fighting for their happily ever afters.

She's an introverted bookworm at heart, with a caffeine addiction, penchant for cursing and an unhealthy attachment to fictional characters.

Feel free to reach out on social media, J Rose loves talking to her readers!

For exclusive insights, updates and general mayhem, join J Rose's Bleeding Thorns on Facebook.

Business enquiries: j_roseauthor@yahoo.com

Come join the chaos. Stalk J Rose here...
    www.jroseauthor.com/socials

# WANT MORE FROM THIS SHARED UNIVERSE?

If you love gritty dark reverse harem romance, check out the Sabre Security series—a brand new, contemporary reverse harem trilogy that follows the hunt for a violent, bloodthirsty serial killer.

https://bit.ly/CorpseRoads
https://bit.ly/SkeletalHearts
https://bit.ly/HollowVeins

# NEWSLETTER

Want more madness? Sign up to J Rose's newsletter for monthly announcements, exclusive content, sneak peeks, giveaways and more!

www.jroseauthor.com.newsletter

# ALSO BY J ROSE

**Read Here:** www.jroseauthor.com/books

**Recommended reading order:**

www.jroseauthor.com/readingorder

**Blackwood Institute**

Twisted Heathens

Sacrificial Sinners

Desecrated Saints

**Sabre Security**

Corpse Roads

Skeletal Hearts

Hollow Veins

**Briar Valley**

Where Broken Wings Fly

Where Wild Things Grow

**Standalones**

Forever Ago

Drown in You

**Writing as Jessalyn Thorn**

Departed Whispers

If You Break

Made in the USA
Las Vegas, NV
02 June 2024

90636565R00282